When Pigs Fly

KRISSY LANIER

Cover Art by Christy Jaynes

Contents

ML, Yazzie, Meadow & Londyn

It's all for you <3

CHAPTER 1

Kentucky - Then

T HE WAY DAD APPEARED when he got to the bottom of the Jack
Daniel's bottle, tipping it back — red, bloodshot eyes and rage
bubbling at the surface — was the way I imagined the monsters in my
nightmares looked too. The way he appeared those days, when the bottle
was opened and emptied, warned me to shrink to nothingness, stay
quiet, hide, not get in the path of his destruction.

Dad was a drunk. I was only seven years old but that much I knew. I'd
be eleven by the time I'd realize my mom was never going to leave him,
even with all the things he would do to her, and to me.

"Summer! Where you at?" Dad screamed. I stared at the paper where
I colored pictures of cats and tried to go somewhere else in my mind.
"Summer!"

Five, four, three...

"It will be a cold day in hell the day you can hide from me!" he yelled,
his ragged footsteps coming closer. I covered my ears with my arms and

closed my eyes tightly, as if I had the power to transport myself anywhere else in the world. But even though I was only a child, I knew I would never succeed. I could never escape.

Dad picked up my coloring, crumpled it up, and threw it to the side. My tiny arm was soon in his hand, and I let myself go...

Two, one...

Here, in this magical place, my hair blows in the soft ocean breeze. I smell something new and sweet, a smell I can't describe because I have never seen the ocean. I notice the feeling of sand and stones hot from the sun under my bare feet. I hear the sound of waves crashing against the shore, a sound that drowns out everything around me — the voices of others, cars driving by, and birds flying overhead.

"You hear me? Keep out of the way, girl!"

But not the sound of Dad, I guess.

As he stumbled out of my room, probably to find Momma or pass out, I left my safe place. The breeze left my hair, the beautiful foreign sounds and smells were soon a distant memory. I was no longer there but back in my room. Then the reality of my situation set in — my face hurt, and my little arm was red, a mark where I would see blues and purples the next day. I stared at a little corner of my room until Momma came for me.

"Summer. My baby. I'm so sorry," she said as she gathered my frail body in her arms.

Sorry.

An apology.

Why was Momma saying sorry for what Dad did to me? She carried me to my bed, and we cuddled close. I presumed this was a night Momma was preparing to "accidentally" fall asleep with me for her protection, or for mine. Or most likely, for both of us. Momma's face was blotchy and red, tearstained. And there was a spot of blood under her nose that she missed while trying to hide the truth from me.

"Momma, what did Daddy mean when he said it would be a cold day in hell when I would be able to hide from him?"

Momma looked at me. Was that sorrow on her face? Dread? She took a deep, rattled breath. "It's like saying 'when pigs fly.'" I scrunched my nose, and she caught on that I didn't know what that meant either. "It's a saying. It means it won't ever happen. Pigs won't fly, right? And hell will always be fiery and hot. That's what those phrases mean."

So, I guess that meant I could never hide from him. *When pigs fly*...that's when I would be free.

My childhood years stick out to me in speckles of memories, flashing in and out of my mind so fast that sometimes it's hard for me to grasp them — my subconscious protecting me, in its own way, from reliving a life I'd much rather forget. But I do remember loving animals, coloring, and devouring every book I could get my hands on, books much higher than my assumed reading level.

When I was in third grade, my teacher gave me a copy of *The Lion, the Witch, and the Wardrobe* to borrow.

"This is my own copy, Summer," Mrs. Harper told me, as I stood at her desk. "I want you to read it. Take your time, and whenever you're ready, you can give it back to me." She smiled at me, and it was like sunshine filling my soul, smothering all the darkness inside of me with light.

The book transported me to a magical place, and I found myself addicted to the need to escape from my life. Books did that for me, and

I let them. When I returned the book to Mrs. Harper two days later, she couldn't believe I had finished it so quickly.

"What was your favorite part?" she asked, smiling at me. I smiled back and we talked for ten straight minutes about the magical book.

"Why don't you keep it?" Mrs. Harper said, looking at me with such care.

My eyes widened. I didn't believe her. She was giving it to me? To keep? I clutched the paperback book to my chest and looked at her with gratitude. Mrs. Harper was mesmerizing to me. The way she created a sense of peace in an entire classroom full of children always amazed me because my own family couldn't settle into any sort of equilibrium. Mrs. Harper didn't have any kids of her own, and sometimes I would imagine her taking me home with her. I pictured us reading together on her couch and sharing conversations about stories and magic. I would have done anything to have a reprieve from my distraught home life.

"Thank you," I whispered.

"You are so welcome, Summer," she responded, gently patting my shoulder.

That book became my outlet to another world, my escape from the reality of everyday life. I read it over and over, and eventually I moved on to other books that took me to even more magical places.

At the end of that year, I discovered The Baby-Sitter's Club. I soaked those books up and grew attached to the characters inside the pages. When Dad was having one of his episodes, I would retreat to my closet where I created a makeshift sanctuary — blankets and pillows, stuffed animals, and my stories. I would hide in there for hours and spend time with the characters in my books, dreaming of white picket fences and families who sat around the dinner table together while Momma had started forgetting to make me dinner, and I never had a bagged lunch for school.

By fourth grade, things had started to decline even more at home. I frequently had marks on my body from Dad's wrath. I was good at hiding them, but the people around me were even better at looking the other way. I was submissive at home and spent as much time as possible hidden away in my closet. But at school, I found the strength to stand up for myself when a kid on my bus started bullying me. Whenever I would get on the bus, he would taunt me.

"Summer, Summer, such a bummer!" he would yell, and everyone would chuckle. But he didn't let it go at that. He made fun of my clothes which were sometimes too small or too dirty. He made fun of my hair which was oftentimes unbrushed, and how I always had my nose stuck in a book. And one day, I'd had enough; I looked him dead in the eye and punched him right in the face. He fell to the floor of the bus aisle, and with my dirty, worn-out shoe, I stepped right on top of him as I made my way to a seat in the back.

I smirked to myself, my back to the rest of the bus, as I walked to the very last seat and sat down. I just wanted to shut him up. I didn't think about the consequences — consequences that came in the form of a suspension from the bus and a hard hit from my dad for forcing him to have to drive me to school for a week. But I learned that day on the bus that there was a fire in me, deep down. It simmered, the embers flickered and glowed. I prayed that no matter how many times someone tried to put out that fire, it would always be reignited if I tried hard enough.

CHAPTER 2

Texas - Now

MY ALARM RATTLES ME out of a restless sleep. The sun is blinding as it streams through the open curtains — beams catching motes of dust suspended in the air. I groan, shielding my eyes from the incoming sun with my forearm. It's seven a.m., and I don't have to be at work until four this afternoon. My therapist, Janie, is always telling me I need to stay on a schedule and do things I enjoy, things that keep me intentionally busy, so I rise early to keep it up. I whip my white comforter off my body and swing my legs over the side of the bed. First coffee and then a long walk around the neighborhood. I sit at my tiny kitchen table and look around my apartment. It's small but I've intentionally made it feel homey with an excessive number of plants I had to learn to love and not kill. A comfortable tan couch and matching oversized chair face the TV, and there is a plush white area rug under them. I have a few rustic coffee tables too. Everything's from Facebook Marketplace or IKEA. Nothing fancy but definitely comfortable.

I sip my coffee from the only mug I own and wonder what the day will bring. I get up and get dressed for my walk — biker shorts and a sports bra with an oversized graphic tee. I brush my teeth and glance at the Post-it stuck to my bathroom mirror.

Summer James, you are more than the sum of your past.

Last month, Janie caught on that I was sinking back into old patterns of self-deprecation. Anxiety, intrusive thoughts, self-doubt, difficulty making meaningful connections...all things I clinically struggle with. Janie told me to come up with one statement and write it down and place it somewhere I would see it daily. She recommended that I say it out loud, and believe it, every day, even if it didn't seem possible. So, there the Post-it sticks, warped from shower steam. I smirk at it while I brush my teeth. Aren't we all made up of our past experiences? Are some of us just luckier than others? I am working on rising above the cards the universe dealt me, shuffling and shuffling until I get another hand.

Before my shift at Sullivan's, the piano bar downtown, I manage to get my walk in, grab some groceries for the next few days, jot some notes in my journal, and down a third cup of coffee before heading to the bar. It's a peaceful day with minimal human interaction. I don't want to say I like it that way because connection is what I crave most in the world, but sometimes the act of engaging exhausts me.

The bell dings over the door as I walk into Sullivan's. Farrah, my coworker and possibly my best friend, is already here.

"It's going to be a good night tonight, Summer," she says, taking a glass out of the steaming dish washer. "Silas and Kash are dueling!"

"Bring on the tips!" I say with genuine enthusiasm.

Sullivan's is a huge attraction for locals and tourists alike, and nights when Silas and Kash play are always packed. They spend their whole set together either dueling or playing their favorites solo, letting each other shine. As soon as Maverick opens the doors, the whole place begins to fill up almost every night — people coming in to enjoy J.J's ever changing menu and then staying for the entertainment.

They say music is one of our biggest triggers of memories, both good and bad. Farrah always gushes over covers played at the bar, saying things like, *Oh MAN! This is so me and my cousin drinking in my basement without my mom knowing about it*, or *This is taking me RIGHT back to the summer I turned seventeen when my friends and I just drove around aimlessly listening to mixed CDs.*

I always smile or giggle, trying to make a connection with her in hopes that she thinks I'm having similar memories, but for the most part, I'm not. Still, I love hearing Farrah reminisce. It reminds me that it's possible to look back and smile at things in your past. I long for that — with all of my being, I long for fond memories.

Before long, crowds are rolling in, and the tables are filling up. Farrah and I, along with a few other bartenders, begin taking our stations and some deep breaths to prepare ourselves for a great night. I love the way Silas and Kash interact with the crowd, making everyone laugh and feel like they are in a friends' living room. But tonight, their first song triggers a memory for me.

And it's not a good one.

The words to Journey's "Don't Stop Believin'" start to echo through the bar and I drift off in my mind.

CHAPTER 3

Kentucky - Then

I TURNED THE RADIO up ever so slightly from my spot on the couch where I sat reading my Baby-Sitters Club book. I could hear Momma and Dad fighting in their bedroom. I felt a tad bit guilty for being glad that I wasn't the one at the center of Dad's anger. Of course, I didn't want Momma hurt either, but I still had bruises that refused to heal from the week prior. Momma had stopped coming into my room and trying to protect me. I don't know if it was because I was getting bigger or she was tired or if it was because she had started drinking the year prior. Whatever the reason, I was left to fend for myself. I turned to my books, my journals, drawing...anything to escape.

I heard my dad's hand make contact with Momma's face and the screaming from both of them was dialed up. The radio could not drown out the horror that was my family. I crept off the couch and walked soundlessly to their bedroom door to peek in through the crack. Momma was weeping on the floor, holding her face. Dad saw me, and when we made eye contact, I jumped back.

"Go away, Summer; no one wants you here!" he shouted. I backed away, stunned, and then turned and ran back toward the living room and into the kitchen. For a brief moment, I feared that Momma was going to die that night, and in that split second, I picked up the phone and dialed 911. For the first time in my life, I took matters into my own hands, and I called for help.

I wallowed in depression for years because of that phone call I made, a phone call that changed the trajectory of my life forever. I know now, as an adult who's working on healing my trauma, that I was not the reason for my unlucky hand. I did not cause the ripple effect that followed the phone call I made that night while Journey played on the radio. But when you're eleven, the stories you construct in your mind about what you perceive as reality feel inherently true.

———

Three minutes and eighteen seconds. That's how long it took before I saw red and blue lights, but no sirens, pulling into our beat-up driveway. Two officers, a male and a female, walked through our tattered gate and made their way up the walkway that was surrounded by weeds to our front door. I was frozen in my chair. I didn't move a single muscle when there was a heavy knock at the door and the voice that said, "Police, open up!"

I didn't open up.

"What the fuck is going on out there?" I heard my dad's muffled grunts through the wall.

Then I remembered, the front door lock was busted and didn't work. Any second the door would open, and the officers would see me standing there frozen. And that's what happened — the door opened.

"Police! Hello," said Mrs. Officer. I walked slowly toward the door, timid and unsure of what I should do, what I should say.

"Hello, there," said Mr. Officer. "Did you call 911?" I nodded slowly as my irate dad came barreling down the hallway toward us with Momma, like a sheep, shuffling behind him.

"What's this?" my dad demanded, making it completely obvious that he was inebriated — stumbling, the devil in his eyes.

"We received a call about a dispute at this location, sir. Please put your hands up," said Mr. Officer.

Mrs. Officer looked over at me sympathetically as they handcuffed Dad, which I later realized was to gather all the necessary information for what came after.

"Can you hang tight here..." Her voice trailed off.

"Summer," I answered because I could tell she was waiting for me to say my name. She smiled endearingly at me and put out her hand. I reached my hand out to hers.

"Autumn," she said, shaking mine. "Officer Autumn Sinclair."

Summer and Autumn. Was this some sort of omen? A sign? No, just a pleasant coincidence, I was sure. But it did make me feel a connection to her, safe while she was in our home, which I guess was important, even monumental, at the time. Officer Sinclair gestured for me to have a seat on our worn living room chair. Dad was led outside by Mr. Officer where he sat handcuffed on the curb.

I glanced out the window and saw him sitting there; his hands cuffed behind his back, Mr. Officer standing in front of him, one hand securing his weapon, the other arm relaxed at his side. My dad, who was also known as Clint, Clint Walter James III, sat there looking like an animal caught in a snare.

My dad was frightening and it scared me, but he wasn't always that way, or so I was told. Momma always said that Dad was once a strong and kind man, boisterous and proud, on his way to big accomplishments. These tales always sounded as if they were spun from artificial gold, but I listened intently when Momma told them, dreaming of a day when my dad would go back to being that person I had never known.

Dad came from money — a family of investment bankers and the women who coddled them. Dad was on his way to following in his father's and grandfather's footsteps until his fall from grace, which my grandparents, apparently, blamed on Momma. But if you truly look at the whole picture, my dad had his own demons that were a product of his mind.

My momma, Nina James, or Nina Johnson before she married my dad, was raised by a single mom, my grandmother who I never met. Her dad was never in the picture — she didn't even know his name. My grandmother, Lucy, died of an overdose when Momma was seventeen, leaving her alone and desperate for a miracle.

Momma got a job at a restaurant, waiting tables to pay for the tiny apartment they had been living in. She scraped by for a few years living in what sounded to me like a false sense of reality. She would tell me about how she dreamed of a prince coming and sweeping her off her feet, saving her from her lonely despair.

And then one day her prince came, in the form of Clint James. My dad went to the restaurant she worked at between classes one day when he was a senior in college. As the story goes, they were smitten with each other — my momma, the lonely, poor girl with no future to be seen, and my dad, the well-to-do scholar who came from money. I always wondered what it was that attracted my momma to him most. Was it his charm? His money? The success that she saw in his future? Did she see him as her ticket out of her misery?

They hung out a lot, somewhat casually at first, Momma molding herself to be the type of person she assumed Dad was looking for. Eventually, they were dating, much to my grandparents' dismay. From my understanding, in my grandparent's eyes, Momma didn't fit the mold of a James. Momma never had a strong sense of identity to begin with and getting herself mixed up with Dad and his family only solidified that. She tried to be someone she wasn't in order to impress them, but it never worked. She never had a chance at the life she envisioned with him, not when his own monsters were there, hidden beneath the surface.

One day Dad found pain pills stuffed in a box under Momma's bed, apparently left behind by my grandmother. He started taking them — at first to help him through his studies, then for recreation. Dad began to unravel in front of everyone's eyes, drinking that became excessive and out of control, narcotics, and other self-destructive behavior. He never finished school and eventually found himself living in my momma's tiny apartment with her, their toxic relationship spinning into a web that neither of them could escape. Momma thought she could save him, so she nurtured him and tried to help him get back up from his fall. But I know now that my momma was enabling him. She couldn't save him. She had depended on him to save her, and he had failed. I'm sure she thought that if she could tend to him, bandage up his wounds and fix his soul, he would turn back into that person she met in her restaurant, the one who shined like a knight. So, she kept it up until he eventually broke her too.

I sometimes would wonder about these fairy tales Momma would spin for me about Dad. What would have become of me if my dad had followed the path that was laid out for him? Like Hansel following the breadcrumbs. Would we have a life that looked fantastic on the outside, but he'd still be the same as he was now on the inside? Would that at least make dealing with him more manageable? I dreamed of these *what-ifs* constantly, but then I'd wake up surrounded by my rundown, shabby life. I realized that abuse was the same no matter what jewels sparkled around you.

I always watched Dad leave for his job at the junkyard, his rusted-out truck making its way down the street and out of sight, and I would pray that he would never come home. But he always did. That's the way it always went — reprieve, turmoil, and back again, my fight-or-flight senses constantly activated. It's no wonder I eventually ended up on the path I did, unsure of how to handle any sort of difficult scenario. Dad's actions while I was growing up shaped me into the person I am now — unsure and unknowing, afraid to live and unable to thrive because I can't see past the cloud of smoke I call anxiety. When I was young I developed a habit of cowering at his hands, making myself invisible. Not much has changed. I continue to hide — my desperate attempt to remain unseen.

My dad was always yelling and hitting, but every once in a while, for a sliver of a moment, he would seem soft and kind. I would shy away from his affection, though, and he would act like his feelings were hurt. It confused me. What about my feelings?

Momma always said his brain was mixed up, and back then, I didn't know what she meant by that, so I created an image in my mind that was more literal than it actually was. I pictured a brain that had pieces in the wrong spots, black wires woven throughout his mind, causing a chaotic mess. Often, the stories we create in our heads as children are much worse than reality, much more sinister. But not for me. My reality was much more horrific than any story I had created in my head. Because the reality was that Dad's mind wasn't mixed up. It was sick.

———

Momma was led into the kitchen by Officer Sinclair where they stayed for what felt like hours. I sat, unmoving, barely breathing, attempting to hear what Momma was saying to Autumn...Officer Sinclair. It was muffled but I caught some phrases:

Hurt you

Hurt Summer

Regular occurrence?

Summer witnessed

He doesn't mean it

Good man

Five, four, three, two, one...

My toes are in the water, waves tickling my feet, wrapping around my ankles. The breeze separates my hair, and I close my eyes and listen to the gulls overhead, the shushing, rushing tide, my soft and steady heartbeat. I imagine a salty, briny smell but I'm not sure exactly what it smells like because I have still never been to the ocean before. I'm at peace here in this space. I sit down on the soft sand, my hands feeling the small, sparkly grains. The sun warms me as I look up, squinting into the cloudless sky. Shrieks of birds overhead pull my attention to their flapping wings and obnoxious cries. What else do I hear? Is someone talking to me here in this magical place? I turn away from the shore, toward the brush behind me. Who is that? Who is talking?

"Summer, this is Sarah Tate. She wants to talk with you. Is that ok?" Autumn Sinclair's voice took me out of my daydream.

And just like that, I was back in my worn-down house where an unknown person had materialized. She wanted to talk to me. Why? Was it ok? I nodded slowly, mechanically, my face dirty and non-expressive. Sarah and Officer Sinclair guided me down the hall into the kitchen and motioned for me to have a seat at our dingy kitchen table. Where was Momma? Where did she go? Was I gone in my mind for a long time? I must have been. Sarah began talking, explaining to me that I had to leave my house, alone, without my momma.

I didn't say a single word, but my mind was racing. Why did I have to leave? Why didn't Dad have to go? I wasn't the one who hurt Momma. He did. But I was leaving. Where was I going? I didn't ask any of these questions out loud, but some of them were answered just by happenstance. Sarah was from Social Services. She would be taking me, not to stay with her but to stay with *a nice family.*

I know she didn't mean to, but Sarah made me self-conscious. She pitied me. I could read it on her face. Over the last year, I started to realize that I didn't have what other kids at school had: a family who cheered for me, clean clothes, shiny hair, laughs over meals, siblings to fight with...a dad who didn't hit me and a mom who didn't let him. Sarah Tate knew these things about me, or at least she had to have assumed. How could she not? She was there, in my house, ready to take me away. It wasn't for nothing. She told me that I could pack a bag with as much stuff as I wanted to take with me.

"Like a backpack?" I asked, not understanding that I would never be coming home again.

A little while later, with my trash bag of belongings. I stood by the door of our run-down house, my eleven-year-old mind not grasping what was going on, but I had a heavy uneasiness resting in my gut. I watched Momma, standing there, helpless, unable, or unwilling to protect me anymore. She had given up on coming to my room to shield me from the darkness. There was no hope in her finding the strength to fight this battle for me. She had proven that over the last year. I watched a tear slide down her face as she wrung her hands together nervously. I ran to her and wrapped my skinny arms around her waist.

"Don't let them take me," I said, panicking as I slowly came to the realization of what was happening. Momma began to sob. I pulled away from her and looked up at her pinched, red face. *Stop your tears, Momma*, I thought to myself. *Help me. Tell them you don't want me to go. Tell them that Daddy should be the one to go, not me.*

She pulled me back to her and squeezed me tight while she continued to sob, her chin resting on my head.

"I'm sorry, baby," she said, wailing. I stayed, pathetically, in her arms, mine beginning to fall limp by my side. I was becoming numb, my tears drying up. Momma wasn't going to save me from this hell, I could see that. I pulled away from her again and took two steps back, distancing myself.

"Don't take her from me!" she yelled at the top of her lungs, the volume scaring me, making me jump.

Sarah approached her, encouraging her to take a seat on the couch and take deep breaths as I stood there like a stone, unmoving.

This was so typical of my parents — dramatizing their own lives and leaving me to fend for myself. Making it all about them. I blamed my dad for that, but I couldn't blame him for this scene unfolding. He wasn't in the room. He wouldn't care if I left for one day or a million, but Momma? She loved me, didn't she? I knew she did, but life had become unbearable for her, and here I was, paying the price.

Sarah helped calm Momma down then got up from the couch, and I knew my fate was sealed — I was leaving. Momma took a breath and got up from the worn couch and approached me.

"I'm sorry, baby. I'm so sorry," she said weakly, holding my face in her shaking hands.

I closed my eyes. "It's ok," I whispered because that was so typical of me, taking it all and carrying it on my shoulders so she didn't have to. "I love you, Momma," I said through a crack in my voice. I said a silent prayer that I would see her again real soon.

I don't remember when I learned that my momma refused to press charges the day I was removed from my home. She wouldn't agree to remove Dad from our lives, which is what led to my removal. I guess Momma was afraid to be alone. But she wasn't afraid to lose me. Sarah Tate told me they would work with her, get her some therapy and other services to help her sort through the hell my dad had put her through, and then maybe she could get me back. I clung to that hope until the day she died.

———

My palms were sweating as I sat in Sarah's car, holding the giant black trash bag filled with all the things I deemed important. Sarah had dug around my house for a bag to put my belongings in, but to her surprise, not mine, she found nothing. Under the sink, though, were some bunched up bags that may have already been used, and she decided that would be appropriate for the occasion. I'd packed some clothes — a faded, ratty sweatshirt with holes, the only pair of pajamas I owned, some pants that came above my ankle, a few T-shirts, some jeans that I think I'd had since I was nine, assorted socks and underwear. I'd packed a few books too, a stuffed animal that I'd had for as long as I could remember, my journal, and the sneakers on my feet.

We drove for twenty minutes until we reached the other side of town, where we turned down a side street lined with large houses with lush yards and long driveways. We pulled up to the most beautiful house I had ever seen. I stared at it from my seat in the back of Sarah's car, unsure and too nervous to get out.

"Are you ready?" Sarah asked.

I didn't answer. I unbuckled my seatbelt and pushed open the door. As we walked up to the door of this strange house, I looked around intrinsically, checking my surroundings, a skill I'd mastered years before and one that I would use my whole life. Sometimes this skill would fail me, other times save me.

My eyes took in the scenery — a wholesome-looking street, two cars in the driveway, some flower boxes on the windows with purple and yellow blooms poking out of the soil, a red front door, a white house — all of it looked like a scene from one of my books. I felt weathered in this scene, out of place with my battered shoes, the soles peeling away. My hair was unwashed and my fingernails were uneven and dirty. I was certainly a contrast to the backdrop surrounding me. Sarah knocked on the door, and I waited silently for someone on the other side to open it, to open the door to whatever my immediate future held.

"Hi!" said a voice as the door swung open. "I'm Cassandra, but you can call me Cassie. You must be Summer," she blurted out. I wasn't sure if Cassie knew how to take a breath while she spoke, but I nodded and shyly outstretched my hand. "Come on in, dear," she said, taking the bag from my hands without a second thought.

I self-consciously wondered if she could tell my hands were sweating from the makeshift handle I had anxiously made on the drive over. If she noticed, she didn't let on. Cassie was tall and slim with bouncy blonde hair that looked like an 80s style to me. She wore some makeup, but not too much, and clothes that made her look put together. I felt out of place and a little bit embarrassed, which made me hunch over, trying to make myself small as I questioned what she thought of me.

"No one is home yet but they should be back any minute. They ran to get a few things for dinner after Jason's baseball practice," Cassie informed me as if I knew who she was talking about. It turns out we were waiting for three more members of the Brickman family — twelve-year-old Jason, ten-year-old Claire, and Cassie's husband, Greg Brickman.

I quickly learned that the Brickmans were a sitcom family, straight from the TV. The kids played sports and went to dance class. Mom ran the PTO, and Dad went to work in the office downtown. On Friday nights, they watched movies with pizza and popcorn and had dinner around the large family table every other night. It was picturesque and reminded me of my days reading Baby-Sitters Club books in my closet. But now, as the image was laid out in front of me, it didn't feel as idyllic. Maybe that was because I was there, and I knew I didn't belong. I felt like

I stuck out like a sore thumb amongst the Brickmans. Being there didn't give me the feelings I had imagined, like the scenes I read in my books. Instead of comfort, I felt tense and on edge.

During my time with their family, I would overhear countless people commenting on how lucky I was, the poor girl from the south side, to have the privilege of being in the presence of such lovely people. And all I could think was, *Lucky*? My own Momma didn't even seem to care enough to do whatever she could to keep me from this system and protect me from the future that laid before me, a future filled with abandonment and self-doubt.

CHAPTER 4

Texas - Now

SILAS AND KASH FINISH off their rendition of "Don't Stop Believin'" to roaring cheers and a standing ovation. I smile down at my hands as I grab a lime from the divided compartment, trying to focus on the task at hand instead of the lump in my throat that nags me. I smile faintly as I try not to let my memories trigger me to tears; I am determined not to let them send me into a spiral. It's hard to face these triggers head-on but Janie has been telling me that avoiding them will only delay my healing. I have to endure them, work to heal them, and remember my mantra: *Summer James, you are more than the sum of your past.*

Avoiding my triggers for years led to me basically being a recluse, shying away from meaningful connections. Forget living, I was barely surviving. But with Janie's help, I have made noticeable improvements, and it feels like I've grown by leaps and bounds. I have a highly social job, despite my past desire for no human interaction. I have a very close friend who's not only the opposite of me, but she's helped drag me out of my hole, and she is kind and accepting.

I cherish Farrah deeply. But despite my growth, and much to Farrah's dismay, I still don't have much of a love life. She understands that I have difficulty trusting men, or people in general, based on my past trauma, but she still tries her best to encourage me to get out there. To her, finding your life partner is synonymous with eternal happiness — the idealized version of life you form when you come from a stable family. My journey through life is quite different from Farrah's. Although I think sharing life with someone is something beautiful, it's out of reach for me, because of my past. To me, happiness is letting go of others' opinions of me, and it's accepting and loving myself. This is what I want with all of my being. I'm just not there yet.

With my flashback behind me and the lump in my throat soothed, I continue on, serving the customers and enjoying the music and festivities. As the night progresses, I watch the tip jar fill up to the rim rather quickly and I'm excited. It's not a monumental thing, but I let myself relish in the little victory that could mean something enjoyable for me, a new shirt or maybe even drinks with Farrah on our next night off. I try to be thankful for the little things in my life as I search for joy and happiness.

Farrah breaks me from my thoughts. "What are you going to do without me next week when I'm on vacation?" she asks dramatically. She and her fiancé, Joey, are heading to Key West.

I laugh. "I'm going to read a book and soak up all the silence I can," I tease her.

It's only half true. I do like being alone, but also, the thought of having Farrah so far away makes me nervous. I've begun to rely on her so much but at the same time I'm also self-aware enough to know that it isn't healthy to be dependent on others entirely. I am looking forward to spending the week focused on myself, to get a better gauge of where I am in my healing process.

After last call, the bar empties and we clean up, stacking chairs and tables and moving them to the side, then we divide up our tips, roughly $311 each, a great night. Not ready to go home yet, I lean against the bar, chatting with a waitress I adore, Silvia. These moments at Sullivan's have become favorites of mine — when the crowd has cleared out, but we linger late into the night, sharing camaraderie and love. I have slowly started to realize that it isn't just Farrah who has grabbed my heart here, but the whole staff. They are becoming like family to me. A family I never had the luxury of having when I was growing up.

There's Silvia who is in her early fifties but looks like she's thirty. She's loud and sweet with a guttural laugh. Patrons adore her, request her tables, and always tip her well. I am always learning something new about Silvia, each and every shift. She fills my soul up, truly. She seems like a person who grew up doing right by people, and I have always considered myself a good judge of character.

J.J., or Chef as we endearingly call him, is, of course, the chef. He is loud and eccentric, as talented as they come. His appetizers are my favorite, so unique and savory. J.J. makes me laugh whenever I'm around him. His sous-chef is a quiet girl, Whitney who recently finished culinary school. They make a good team — one boisterous, one meek — both extraordinary at their craft.

Maverick is the owner and the heart of Sullivan's. We call him Mav for short. He isn't the type of owner who only shows up once in a while. Sullivan's is his life, and he wouldn't have it any other way. There is mutual respect between him and his staff because he isn't one of those bosses who think he's better than his employees. He's willing to jump in and do whatever it takes to make this place amazing. In addition to being the owner, he also serves as the manager, assistant manager, occasional waiter, more than occasional bartender, barback, custodian, host, and busboy. In reality, Maverick is more like a friend and less like a boss. He is warm and inviting and never hesitates to help us all with life decisions. Without even trying, he's a lion, a strong leader ruling his little space in the world.

Of course, there's Farrah Pine, my closest friend. Farrah, with her auburn hair and a freckled nose, short legs and full curves, an inability to ever stop talking, and a heart made of pure gold. The sound of her laugh is the backdrop to Sullivan's. She's engaged to Joey, and they're getting married next year under twinkling stars and fairy lights, because that's *so* Farrah.

Then there's the revolving door of entertainers, it differs all the time. Mav makes the musicians audition to make sure their music fits his style and that they are up to par with the high standards he has for Sullivan's. The ones that make the cut are always entertaining, bursting at the seams with energy and engaging the crowd so they never want to leave. Silas Dade and Kash Holden are the only two regular musicians, and we consider them to be a part of the Sullivan's family. Both dark and handsome, Silas is short and Kash, extremely tall. Silas is from London; he came here for a tourist trip and never went back. He teaches piano to kids when he's not at Sullivan's. Kash, covered in tattoos that he has to hide for his day job at a huge financial firm, is a born and raised Texan. I swear he hates his day job, but he won't say it out loud. He is a musician through and through — he's on fire when he's performing, and it's a beautiful show to see. He wasn't made to sit behind a desk, that much I know.

It has been almost eighteen months since I started working at Sullivan's. I met Farrah first, and we became fast friends, grabbing coffee, then dinners and drinks. I walked into the bar with her one evening, and I could feel the energy of the space. Employees were laughing, silverware was clunking while being rolled into napkins. I could hear the slap of palms giving high fives. It was different here compared to other places where I had worked previously. The grocery store and club where I had once earned my money gave me nothing but a paycheck. I never connected with coworkers prior to Sullivan's. I could tell the first time I walked over the threshold of the bar that the people who worked here were close. I knew it was special, even back then. Farrah encouraged me to interview for the bartender position they had open. At the time, I was nervous to interview with Maverick because I was timid and unsure of myself and bartending alongside someone as outgoing as Farrah scared me half to death. But I took her advice anyway, and I'm glad I did.

Looking back, I know working at Sullivan's was the best decision I could have made because looking around this place eighteen months later, I see that it's given me hope and purpose — a ladder to one day soon climb out of the hole I have found myself buried in. I feel myself growing stronger each day because of my time spent at Sullivan's. This place is saving my life right now and helping me heal on a level I never thought possible, something I would never have thought a bar could help me do.

"Are we going to the diner for pancakes?" Farrah pleads, desperation in her voice, or maybe just hunger. It's typical Farrah, always wanting to go out after a shift for food and laughs.

"I can't tonight. I'm exhausted. I'm going to walk home." Typical me.

Kash overhears. "I gotta work in the morning, I really shouldn't stay out much later. I'll walk you home on the way to my place," he offers.

"Cool, thanks. Let me grab my stuff," I say as I slide off the bar onto the freshly mopped, dark hardwood floors.

"Ok. Meet you for brunch at Alessia's tomorrow?" Farrah makes me promise.

"Absolutely, 11:00?" I ask, smiling. She hugs me, and we all shuffle out of the bar through the side door. Farrah, Mav, Silas, J.J., and some of the waitstaff head toward the diner, while everyone else heads home. Kash and I turn left out of the dark alley toward my apartment. We walk in comfortable silence, Kash whistling happily as I take my gaze toward the sky.

"What are you looking at?" Kash asks after we have been walking a minute.

"The stars," I respond. "They help me stay grounded."

Kash looks at me openly, inviting me to share more. He knows I'm not an open book, but I do seem to share more with him than I do with most people. We have grown rather close over the last year. He's begun to push me out of my comfort zone at times, but there's still a line I never seem to be able to cross. The details of my life before moving to Texas haunt me and inviting another soul into my nightmares frightens me.

"I used to stare up at the sky, studying the stars, all the time when I was little. It's comforting." There is so much more behind my words, but it's not in my nature to offer up such personal information on a whim, so I leave it at that. But in my cavernous subconscious where I keep all my secrets, the stars are privy to the things I keep hidden because they were once my only escape, my only safe space. My mind starts to wander back in time, speeding through years, slipping through scenes and memories until I find myself sitting back on the Brickman's roof.

CHAPTER 5

Kentucky - Then

O NE HUNDRED EIGHTY-EIGHT, ONE *hundred eighty-nine - deep breath.*

One hundred eighty-nine. That's how many stars I counted before I needed to stop and take a deep, cleansing breath. I closed my eyes, put my palms down on the grainy shingles of the Brickman's roof. I bent my knees and pushed my spine into the solid surface under me, sitting up. I sat on the roof over the garage outside the window of Claire's bedroom and tried to understand my life, where I belonged in the world I found myself in. I replayed the last few days over and over and over while gazing at the sky above me. The stars had become my journal, the only beings that would listen to me without judging.

Since I had arrived at the Brickman's house thirteen days prior, I felt like my life had been tipped upside down. Shouldn't that be expected, though, when an eleven-year-old is ripped from the only home she's ever known, ripped from the momma who slept with and comforted her when things got brutal? Cassie and Greg tiptoed on eggshells around me like I was a fragile piece of china. *Poor Summer. Can you even imagine? Don't tip her,* are words I never heard, but ones I read on their faces. Jason had feigned indifference to my presence, and Claire was over the moon with the mere idea that she had a girl her age in the house.

"We can be like sisters while you're here!" she said one night, her expression riddled with too much excitement. It made me wonder how long I would be there for.

While you're here. How long would it take Momma to fix herself? Would I go back to Dad too?

Up until then, I had always thought of myself as a kind and quiet person. I was nice to other kids (except for the time I punched that one on the bus), and I was respectful to adults, quiet, never wanting to step out of line. But the more time I spent on the Brickman's roof, the more I began to feel anger and rage beginning to boil beneath the surface. I felt completely lost, like I didn't belong. The lack of control I had over my circumstances caused me, at a young age, to lose confidence and faith in any adult, let alone in myself.

I reached up toward the sky and traced the Big Dipper with my finger, closing my right eye. I took a deep breath and felt myself getting increasingly tired, so I decided to crawl back in through the window and slip into bed. I whispered goodnight to the stars, as I had done for the last ten nights and slowly pulled the window open. I held my breath while contorting my body as I slipped through the opening, trying not to wake Claire. The roof was my sanctuary, the only place that I felt was truly mine, and every night I waited until everyone was asleep before retreating there.

I got under the covers and willed myself to fall asleep. The morning would bring another day of school that I couldn't afford to be sleeping through, and I couldn't go to school looking like a poor foster kid, ragged and disheveled. That image was not making me any friends, save for Claire. I lay awake, staring at the ceiling for a long time before I slipped into a restless sleep.

The sun came screaming in the window the next morning, ripping me from my sleep. I looked over at Claire's bed, which was unsurprisingly empty. She always bounded out of bed like the world was waiting for her, which I guess it was. Cassie and Greg were always downstairs preparing breakfast with care, with sides of hugs and compliments. Who wouldn't want to race out of dreams to be greeted with that? Most people would love that. But not me. At first, they tried to give it, but it wasn't mine for the taking.

I slowly got out of bed and stretched, looking around for my black hoodie. I quickly changed into clean clothes, slipping the sweatshirt over my head. The room was spotless. White curtains hung from the windows and peacefully blew in the soft morning breeze. The walls were a pink that was so pale it almost couldn't be classified as pink. All the furniture was white, the beautiful wood floors glistened, and two girly area rugs softened up the floors near the bed and over by the reading nook.

I stared at Claire's bookshelf and dreamed of having one of my own, ignoring Claire's voice in my head, telling I could read them any time I wanted. I knew none of it was really for me, that I could never have all of it for myself. It was all just a temporary landing spot for me as I transitioned to the next phase. And being here, in this life, that wasn't attainable to me, made me feel like I was in some cruel prison, surrounded by things I wasn't really allowed to touch and things I certainly couldn't keep, no matter how many times they said I could. I felt a sore spot in throat forming, my body trying to suffocate the tears that I knew were coming. I wanted Momma.

"Good morning, Summer!" Cassie greeted me as I rounded the bottom step and walked into the kitchen area.

"Hi," I said, climbing up onto the stool at the island next to Jason. He slid over a cup of orange juice, his mouth full of cereal.

"Thanks," I muttered, barely audible. He replied with a thumbs up.

"Sarah, your case worker, will be stopping by today to see you, Summer. She'll be here a little after you all get home from school," Cassie informed me.

"Ok," I managed to spit out as visions of meeting Sarah two weeks prior came flooding back. I was old enough to know that Sarah didn't steal me away, that she was doing what everyone thought was best for me. But that didn't stop the anger from bubbling in my belly, the way it started to last night on the roof, seemingly out of nowhere. But now my anger had a direction. I thought, *Why do I have to see her? What does she want to talk to me about? Does she want to know if I'm happy in this house? If I'm good to stay here longer?* The anxiety of this visit with Sarah began to fester and I knew for sure it would continue to grow during school.

I drank my juice and had a few bites of my muffin before putting it in a napkin to carefully pack it in my backpack, saving it for later when I would be hungry. It was a skill I had learned over the last few years — sneaking food from school to take home in case no one felt like making me dinner. A hard habit to break.

I grabbed my backpack off the hook next to Claire's and Jason's and put the muffin in there. Every morning, Cassie placed our backpacks on the hooks for us after she'd filled it with lunch and snacks for the day. The three of us slipped our bags on and walked out the front door to the bus stop, after saying goodbye to Cassie and Greg; my farewell was just a meek wave and a weak smile. Another day of sixth grade at my new school laid in front of me, and I wasn't sure how I felt about it.

———

"Here, I finished this last night. Do you want to read it?" Claire handed me a book from her backpack as we rode to school, and I took it cautiously.

"Sure. Thanks a lot," I responded. She smiled back at me as if she had just accomplished something. What did she want from me? Was it my approval she was seeking? Was she desperate for a sister and wanted me to feel the same? I wasn't sure what her motive was, but it unnerved me. How simple her life must be to have no understanding of what it's like to lose your family one day and then be plopped inside another one the next, like a puzzle piece put inside the wrong box.

I began reading the book mostly to appear busy and avoid talking but also because I wanted to read it.

Before I knew it, the bus was pulling into the school, and I was grabbing the seat in front of me to pull myself up. Claire shuffled out, me behind her, and we all paraded into the building.

I survived the day by doodling sketches in my notebooks and thinking of other things. Asking myself harmless *would you rather* questions and answering them, thinking maybe I could play this game with Claire in her room later after school. That would be a nice gesture, I thought. I could look forward to that after getting through my meeting with Sarah.

No teachers called me out of my daydreams, and no kids interrupted either. It was like I was invisible. But in reality, I think no one knew what to do with me, the girl who showed up out of nowhere and became the PTO mom, Mrs. Brickman's third child. I wasn't sure how much longer I could relish under the invisibility cloak before I started to feel depressed and lonely, but for the time being, it was my savior.

"Thanks for the book, Claire," I said on the bus ride home, and meant it. "It seems good so far."

"Can we talk about it when you're done?" she questioned with little sparkles in her eyes.

"Sure," I replied with a smile. I wrung my hands together trying to wipe the sweat starting to form.

"After Ms. Tate leaves, do you want to sit on the hammock and read our books together?" she asked me nonchalantly.

"That sounds good." I was so envious of her confidence and the lack of caterpillars crawling in her stomach, while my insides ached with the unknown.

I sat on the plush couch in the living room, the room we never used in the house. I stared, wide-eyed, at Sarah as she pulled out her notebook. I could hear Cassie in the kitchen, clanking pots and pans. Jason and Claire were in their rooms, starting their homework, and Greg wouldn't be home from work for another hour or so. I envisioned following them to where they were, busying themselves. I continued to stare, unblinking, wishing I was in the kitchen with Cassie or with Claire in her room. I wanted one of them to take me away from this, but they couldn't. This was *my* life, the part so separate from them. They all scurried to their little sacred spots of the house, oblivious to the sickening feeling retching inside me as they went about their afternoon without a care in the world, as my worries continued to pile up, day after day.

"So, Summer, how are you?" Sarah asked.

How was I? How could she ask that with a straight face?

Let's see, I haven't seen my momma or dad in fourteen days. I have no idea where they are, if my momma is ok. I am an alien in this house that doesn't belong to me, going to a school where I'm invisible. I haven't breathed easily in days, and the pit in my stomach feels like a stone that will never pass.

I shrugged my shoulders. "I'm fine."

She gave me a sympathetic smile. "Do you need anything?"

Need anything? Was she serious? Where should I start? Did she really want to hear? Could she really do anything for me anyways? I couldn't take her seriously, so my response was limited.

"No, I don't think so."

"I have a scheduled visit for you to see your mom next week. Would you like that?" she asked.

I straightened my spine. "Momma. Where is she?" I asked, beginning to panic.

"She is at home."

"Then why am I not there?" I asked, on the verge of tears.

"We need to make sure you are safe, Summer. You should not be hurt in your own home."

"Where's Dad?"

Sarah hesitated for a minute. "He is also there, Summer, which is why you cannot go back there right now." She tried to explain but I didn't understand.

"Then Momma shouldn't be there either. He hurts Momma more!" My voice began to rise, and my breaths became rapid and shallow. Sarah put her hand on my knee, but I pushed it away and ran up the stairs and into the bathroom. I gasped for air and leaned over the sink, splashing cold water on my face. As I glanced in the mirror, I saw an unrecognizable girl looking back at me. I didn't know that face. Not one bit. It held the kind of tiredness that I didn't know was possible — pale with dark rings under my eyes, though not from Dad's hand, it startled me just the same.

I quietly opened the bathroom door and heard whispers downstairs; Cassie and Sarah were talking in the living room. I moved slowly, trying not to make a sound. I sat on the top step, my shaking hands in my lap, and listened. I couldn't hear all the words, but I made out some phrases.

Refuses to stay away from him

Needs him

Erratic

Sarah.

Poor Summer

Sweet girl

Anything we can do

Get to go home?

Cassie.

When pigs fly.

Sarah.

I had nothing to say to anyone that night, so I didn't open my mouth once. There was no *would you rather* with Claire, no sharing of the day's events at the dinner table by me, nothing. I lay in bed and waited for all the Brickmans to be asleep so I could slip out the window and onto the roof, where my voice would be heard and not judged. I told the stars that night that I didn't mind if Dad died. If he were gone, there would be nothing holding Momma back from me. There would be nothing to scare her into submission, which I told myself, in different words, was what she was doing. I believed with all of my being that she was frightened. Too frightened to stand up for me. Terrified of what would happen if she did. It was the same thing that kept me up at night too.

I invited the tears to come that night, as I would do many other nights after on that roof. I let myself go completely, with only the moon and stars as my witness. And by the time I crawled back through the window, I was so spent I fell into a deep, dreamless sleep.

CHAPTER 6

Texas - Now

"**I** ONCE TOLD THE stars that I wanted my dad to die, and not too long after, he did," I confess to Kash while we both sit on the steps to my apartment, looking up at the abyss. No emotion peppers my statement, and I glance over at him to gauge his expression. There's no judgment; instead, there's an inviting look in his eyes letting me know it's ok to tell him more. I don't add anything but a deep breath.

"Damn, Summer. It sounds like there's more where that came from."

I smirk. "That is correct."

"Do you want to tell me?" Kash asks, not in an intrusive way.

I shrug. "I had a fucked-up childhood. Stuff happened to me that, for a while, I let define me. But I have been working really hard not to make excuses for myself. I am trying to build real dreams and achieve them." I look over at Kash, feeling completely exposed, not used to sharing like this. He doesn't say anything. He doesn't look like he feels bad for me, just like he's waiting for me to continue, if I want to.

Do I?

"I'm in my early thirties. Some people I have encountered, maybe even you, have wondered what I'm doing with my life. When am I going to get a real job? But if you saw me before I was *this* me, then you would understand why I'm so proud to be where I am now." I glance over at him, and he gives me a little smile.

"Sullivan's is a great place to spend your working hours, man," he laughs, and I join along with him because it's true. "Many people dream of being a bartender, connecting with people from all over the world, sharing a space with people, with passion." I look at him perplexed. I had never looked at it that way.

"That's very true, but that's not my dream," I say, looking up at the stars again.

"So, what dreams are you weaving, my friend?"

"I want to be a writer," I confess, not looking at him. "Songs specifically."

"I hope I'm around to see that become a reality," he says softly, his eyes meeting mine. He says these words as if he means them, and my heart warms a bit inside.

"It must be nice to have your life already in place," I tell him jovially. "You got your day job where you get your money and your night gig where your passion ignites."

His face turns somber. "What if I told you my dreams are still spinning too?" We gaze at each other, the light from the street brightening his eyes. My eyebrows lift. Kash leans back on his forearms and stretches out his legs. "I want to own my own bar. I want to perform at it, find the talent for it. I want it to be mine."

I put my hand out to shake his. "To chasing dreams," I say.

He takes my hand firmly, beaming a smile. "To chasing dreams."

Farrah is already sitting at a table when I walk into Alessia's the next morning. She sips her Bellini and waves me over with a smile.

"Good morning," I say, sliding into the booth. Alessia's is the place you go when you want to feel like those women who go to brunch on Sundays in New York City. When you want to feel like the women with polished ponytails and pearls, but you're really just enjoying the little things in life while desperately trying to save for a wedding (Farrah) and attempting to have a social life while also trying not to live paycheck to paycheck (me). Alessia's is inexpensive in its pricing and cheap in its appearance. And maybe we don't know what's in them, but a two-dollar Bellini is a two-dollar Bellini.

"How was the diner?" I ask.

"It was good. We ordered way too much food, though," Farrah responds, stretching her arms over her head.

"Last night was so great," I say. "So many tips!"

"Yeah, yeah. So, let's get to the good stuff. How was your walk home with Kash?" she asks, bouncing her eyebrows and peering over her bellini flute. This is classic Farrah, meddling whenever a man even remotely gives me attention.

I open my mouth to guide the conversation somewhere else when Barb comes over to greet me. She's a round woman with gray hair that she keeps pinned in the back. She is as Southern as they come, her voice as saccharin as sweet tea, until you cross her, that is. Barb treats Farrah and me like daughters and her kindness is not lost on me.

"Summer, dear! A Bellini for you as well? This one couldn't hold off for ya," she says, motioning playfully at Farrah.

"Please, Barb. Thank you," I say as she walks away to get my drink.

"I know you're thinking, *saved by the bell*, but you aren't getting off that easy," Farrah says to me, and I roll my eyes at her.

"It's not the first time Kash has walked me home, Farrah. He lives close by, it's on his way," I say, meaning it and wanting her to just let it go. "I actually consider myself lucky to have Kash as a friend." Farrah rolls her eyes with a smirk. I roll my eyes back.

"So, what time is your flight on Tuesday?" I ask, changing the subject, as I take my Bellini straight from Barb's hand and lead it directly toward my mouth for a sip.

"Seven a.m.," Farrah responds. "And Joey will have us there by 4 a.m., I'm sure," she adds with a laugh. "What are your plans for next week?"

I shrug and give a small smile. "I'm not sure. Nothing really. I picked up some extra shifts. I'll probably clean my apartment. I need to get some new pots and pans." I shrug again feeling very unsocial with my boring plans, but honestly, Farrah has become my safety net, and while she's away, I envision myself drinking lots of tea and watching copious amounts of Netflix.

My phone vibrates in my bag, and I pull it out to see a text from Kash. I open it and read it.

I counted a lot of stars last night but couldn't manage to get them all. Want to grab dinner tonight and see if we can cover more sky?

A small giggle escapes me.

"Who texted you?" Farrah asks curiously.

"Just Kash asking if I had a good night...and if I want to get dinner tonight." I try to sound casual, not wanting to ignite hysteria in Farrah, but I fail.

She squeals. "I KNEW he had a thing for you!"

"It's not a *thing*," I say, rolling my eyes. "And besides, I'm not into him, so it's a moot point." I cross my arms over my chest, lean back on the booth, and give an assured expression to her, but she's not buying it. She does this with any male she thinks could potentially be a match for me. I'm used to these reactions from her, and I find them endearing. She gets excited about the possibilities for me and always cheers me on, and I just love that about her.

"You're going to get dinner with him, right?" she asks judgmentally.

"Probably not," I say, and I mean it. There isn't room in my mind, my heart, or really anywhere for me to open myself up to another soul right now. It's my goal, though. Deep down I know I deserve a great relationship, but I'm not close to being finished with my healing process, and fear still dictates a lot of my decisions. It's something I'm working on.

Farrah looks at me thoughtfully as if she's planning her next sentence and deciding how to approach it. "You know, he is our friend, our coworker...Kash, I mean."

I stare at her, my face saying, *and your point is...?*

"I just mean, you could go out with him as a friend and get to know him better. Maybe let him in just a little bit more...as a friend of course." She adds the word *friend* a few more times as if to really try and persuade me, trying to make me think it's not really that big of a deal. I narrow my eyes. I know she's right. I need to be more vulnerable. I need more connections, and this might be an easy way to open myself up a bit, with someone I already know, someone I'm already close with. I take a deep, cleansing breath.

"You're right," I say, grabbing my phone and responding.

Sure. Pick me up at eight?

I show Farrah. "Happy?" I ask, forcing an overindulgent smile.

"Very," she responds happily. "Now, want to come help me pick out a new bathing suit for my trip?"

"Sounds like fun."

We both get up from the table, leaving behind a generous tip for Barb. As we step out the door and onto the sidewalk, the breeze takes my hair for a spin. The air is hot and the sun is blinding. I pull my sunglasses down from my head as we start walking toward the main part of the street to find a store to Farrah's liking. I look up at the sky as we walk. The sun feels good, and I try to appreciate the moment, something Janie has been coaching me to do — to appreciate the small things, find joy where I once found sorrow, change the narrative. I'm trying. With all of my strength, I am trying.

"I'm going to go try all these on," Farrah informs me as she walks toward the dressing room with a heaping pile of bathing suits, cover-ups, tank tops, shorts. I chuckle and shake my head at her.

"I'll be out here, even in two hours when you're finally done trying all that shit on," I tease. She laughs and heads in the other direction.

I sift through some racks, humming to the beat of the store music playing softly through the speakers. "Torn" by Natalie Imbruglia comes on, and I drift away; my mind, much to my dismay, taking me from the present.

CHAPTER 7

Kentucky - Then

"I JUST LOVE THIS song," Claire said as she sat at her vanity and painted her nails bright pink while I stretched out across my bed, holding a book and skimming the pages. I had to reread each sentence three or four times before I was able to grasp it, a sign that I was distracted, stressed, anxious, or a little bit of all three.

"It speaks to me," she added when I did not respond. I rolled my eyes to myself. Claire didn't know a thing about heartache, heartbreak, or distress of any kind. "Torn" didn't speak to her; it was just a fun song to sing along with, and she equated that to being relative to her stupid crush on Trevor Bayview, the blonde kid in our grade who had yet to give her the time of day. As the song continued, I heard the doorbell ring. I knew who it was — Sarah, my case worker. When I got home from school, Cassie told me that she was stopping by to talk to me.

I heard Cassie's muffled voice through the walls calling me downstairs.

"I'll be back," I said to Claire as I peeled myself from the bed and made my way downstairs. As I plopped myself down on the barely used living room chair across from Sarah, I forced a smile and a small wave to her. She sat on the couch with her notebook and smiled at me without showing her teeth. It was one of those *sorry* smiles, the kind you give to someone when you feel bad for them. My defenses were up. I was ready for whatever this impromptu visit was going to entail. What could be worse than my current situation? I had been away from my home for a year, and my momma would not stay away from my dad, which reminded me daily that I didn't matter to her. I didn't belong where I was, so if I was leaving to go somewhere else, which presumably was what was about to happen, I wouldn't even flinch. I was ready for whatever bad news she was bringing me.

"Summer...I wanted to come and talk to you in person so that...."

"Just get to the point. Don't sugar coat it. I'm not a baby." My voice was cold, but it was nothing compared to the ice that ran through my heart...my veins...my whole being...ninty-nine percent of the time.

"Ok, you're right," Sarah continued. "I hate to be the one to tell you this, it breaks my heart."

No, you're just uncomfortable.

"Your father passed away yesterday." She let out a deep breath, presumably congratulating herself on making it through the task of giving me this information. I was silent for a few beats. I stared at her, wondering if she was playing a trick on me. Her voice became muffled in my head as she went on about the tragic fall that led to my dad's death. I was barely listening.

One time, I was playing in the backyard when I was about eight years old. I got so hot that I started to sweat, so I turned on the hose and sprayed myself with it, laughing as the water splashed onto my face, and I tried to catch the streams with my tongue. Dad came barreling out of the house, stumbling on his feet, and headed toward me with rage. He slapped me so hard with the back of his hand that I saw black spots. I stumbled back into a puddle that I had created and tried to regain my balance. Dad screamed at me about wasting water and his hard-earned money. While he yelled, I stood there in the puddle, weak and scared on the outside but anger burning on the inside, silently wishing he was dead. It took four years, but my wish came true.

I continued to sit in silence, staring at Sarah. She felt the need to fill the silence with things she thought were true but were really so far from it: "I know this is hard to hear. I know it must be shocking to..."

I cut her off immediately. "Good," I said. "So, when can I go back to Momma?"

Sarah stared at me, obviously uncomfortable with my lack of emotion. "Um...so..." She stumbled on her words.

"I'm fine," I said, once again cutting her off from her jumbled mess of a speech. "I just want to be with Momma."

Sarah took a deep breath. "We are working with her, Summer. She isn't clean right now, and it's our job to make sure that you go home to a safe environment." I nodded once. My head was spinning, trying to take it all in. Dad, dead. Momma, not sober. Momma, getting help. Momma will get better. I will go home to her soon. That was the hope I needed to carry me through. I smiled at Sarah, a gesture I could tell unnerved her.

"Please help Momma so I can go home," I said as I rose from the chair and made my way toward the stairs, back to my bed and my book and Claire's pitiful excuse for trauma.

"Um. Yes, Summer. We are doing..." Sarah's voice trailed off as I climbed the stairs, rounded the hallway, walked into my room, and shut the door.

I plopped on my bed with a sigh.

"What was she here for?" Claire asked, blowing on her fingernails.

"To tell me my dad died yesterday," I responded without emotion.

"Oh my GOD, Summer. I'm so sorry!" Claire wailed.

"It's fine," I said, placing my hands behind my head. "Now, he can't hurt me or my momma ever again."

My nonchalant attitude scared Claire. I could tell by the way she looked at me. She nodded once, slowly. She would never understand me, and that both frightened her and pushed her to try and bond with me, to save me. Claire fantasized about what it meant to have another girl in the house with her. With all of her might, she tried to turn her dreams of having a sister into reality. She desperately wanted it to be something it would never be.

I didn't have the heart to ruin her dreams of us being like sisters, so I patted the spot on the bed next to me, gave her a gentle smile, forced a tear, and asked her for a hug. She beamed and jumped into my arms. I hugged her back and rolled my eyes over her shoulder. She didn't know that I wasn't going to miss her when I went back to my momma and left their house. I knew she was going to miss me, though. I think that, in her head, she thought we would always be together: sharing a room until we graduated high school, sharing a dinner table, and sharing conversations, secrets, and laughs while we lived happily ever after. But my momma and I were safe now that Dad was gone, and we were going to be back together again, forever. The thought filled me with joy.

That night when I went out on the roof, I stared up at the constellations and took a deep, cleansing breath. I was holding a dark secret. The stars knew my wish had been granted, and at that moment, they were the keeper of my secret. The stars were the only ones to know I had brought this on myself. I made a wish, and it came true. For so many years, I had wished my dad was gone, and now he was. As a child, I had never imagined what his death or disappearance from my life would look like, although I'd wished for it so many times. Turns out, a drunken fall down the stairs was all it took to extinguish a monster from existence.

"Thank you," I whispered out loud, although I wasn't sure to who. The stars? The universe in general? God, if there was one? I smiled a real smile for the first time in over a year. I couldn't wait to be home.

CHAPTER 8

Texas - Now

"Summer..." I hear Farrah saying, concern evident in her voice. She's finally done in the dressing room and has her arms full of clothes. I shake myself back to the present, away from my thoughts and my triggered memory.

I force a smile. "Sorry, I was in a daze," I say, walking with her toward the check out.

"Why do I always feel the need to spend all of my money?" Farrah asks, judgment toward herself lingering in her tone.

I give her a gentle nudge. "You're going on vacation! Live a little," I offer, trying to make her feel a little less guilty.

"You're right! Let's get out of here," she says breathlessly, carrying all of her new clothing up to the register.

"I'm going to scoot out and head home to get ready, if you don't mind," I say, thinking about my desperate need to be alone for a bit before I head back out again into civilization.

"Of course! Have so much fun with Kash tonight, and text me as soon as you can to tell me all about it," Farrah insists.

"I'll just talk to you next week when you're home," I laugh.

She rolls her eyes playfully. "At least give me a little something tonight to let me know if it was good or bad."

"Deal," I respond. I do my best to lean in and give her a big squeeze, despite her arms being full of clothing. "Have the best time and don't think about Texas at all while you're soaking up the sun on the beach."

Farrah beams. "See you in six days!"

I wave and walk toward the entrance of the store and out into the sunshine. I head left toward my apartment and start mentally preparing for my evening with Kash.

Once I'm home, I unlock the door to my apartment and step inside. My home. My safety. My sanctuary. All mine. I fiddle with the leaves on my plant while I put down my bag and keys. I plop down in my oversized chair, pull the blanket over me, and take some deep breaths. I let my muscles relax as I melt deeper into the chair and grab the remote to watch something mindless. This is what I tend to do after being out in public or when I'm prepping to be out in public. Tasks outside my home exhaust me. The triggers that Janie wants me to face head-on in order to heal, the ones I'm not supposed to avoid, zap all my energy, and it feels like it's the exact opposite of healing. It feels as if I'm broken down each time I have a memory. My triggers are all around me when I go out in public or interact with other humans. It can be so overwhelming. All the more reason that I relish my alone time in this sanctuary I've created at home.

Trying to unwind, I listen to the TV in the background as my thoughts begin to spin and I repeat my mantra: *Summer James, you are more than the sum of your past.*

I remind myself that I am beginning to rise above my past, little by little. I tell myself that I am not the only one who has struggled in life. But that thought doesn't always help me unwind from my anxiety because I remember that I *am* alone. My present doesn't connect to my past. Everyone is gone. Everyone I thought loved me betrayed me. Everyone I trusted, in spite of my walls, let me down and caused me to build higher ones. I have Farrah, Kash, Janie, and the rest of the crew at Sullivan's. But there's no one left from my childhood — no one who understands what I've been through. And I still struggle to cope with my life before *this*, and the loneliness is unbearable.

I decide to take a nap before my dinner with Kash. I set my alarm for two hours and let myself fall asleep hard, hoping that when I wake up, I will feel a little less heavy and a little more prepared for a night out.

CHAPTER 9

Kentucky - Then

I T HAD BEEN A few weeks since my dad's funeral, and I had yet to see Momma since then. She was drunk at the service. Everyone assumed she was just wracked with grief, but I smelled it on her breath. It made my heart break into tiny pieces knowing what she had turned into because of him. I knew then how much she needed me home so she could feel loved and important again.

I had asked Sarah when she last came to the Brickman's house why I hadn't had a visit with Momma in a long time. Apparently, she hadn't been in contact with the department, and they didn't know where she was living, what she was doing, where she was working, or if she even still had a job. I begged Sarah to let me see her. I let my walls come down, showing my true feelings, something I regretted almost immediately. I was desperate though. I needed to go home. The Brickman's house wasn't my home. My momma was my home. I needed her, and more importantly, she needed me.

I finally had a visit with her two months after my dad's death. I got to leave school during lunch. Sarah was waiting for me in the office with her CPB badge hanging around her neck. I walked right past her and out the door toward her car, climbing into the front seat. I stared out the window for the six-mile ride and picked at my fingernails. Sarah tried to make small talk, but I only responded with grunts and sounds.

We arrived at the Social Services office, and she parked in a spot close to the entrance. I looked at the door as I unbuckled my seat belt and saw people walking through the doors in groups, some with badges, some without. There were little kids holding hands with adults and big kids sulking, much like me. I walked a few paces behind Sarah, following her through the door and down the hallway into the lobby.

I stepped over the threshold of the lobby and saw her, my momma. Except, she didn't look like my momma. She looked awful. She stood up from the chair where she sat and outstretched her arms, waiting for me to embrace her. I stared at her before I started walking in her direction. This wasn't my momma. Her skin wasn't supple like it always was; it was ashen and gaunt. Her clothes didn't fit; they were baggy and dirty. She didn't smell like coconuts, like she used to; she smelled of nicotine and something I couldn't quite name. Her hair, once shiny and long, was short, greasy, and filled with gray streaks. I slowly, almost begrudgingly, walked toward her and let her hug me. I hugged her back, feeling the bones of her spine on the palms of my hands.

"My baby," she said through wet eyes and a raspy voice.

"Hi," I said. I was shocked at my own behavior. I had missed my momma and dreamed of seeing her. Why hadn't I run up to her, put my arms around her, and hugged her as tight as I could?

But deep down I knew why. It was because this wasn't her. "When am I coming home?" I asked her point-blank.

Her shoulders sank. "Oh, baby. I'm trying to find a place. I lost my job at the Walgreens down the street. Something about budget cuts," she went on, rolling her eyes. I didn't respond. I just stared at her, waiting for her to make it right. "But they," she said, gesturing toward the CPB office, "said they would help me find a new job and a place to stay so you can come home to me." She smiled, the gesture so gargantuan that I could see all her teeth. They looked rotten and dirty, like she hadn't brushed them in years. "I miss you, Summer. I need you home with me." I offered a small smile. I couldn't categorize how I was feeling. These were the words I had been waiting to hear her say for over a year. But this isn't how I wanted it. I wanted my momma, not this shell of a person I didn't recognize.

"Say something, love," Momma said, sounding desperate.

"I don't like it there," I managed. "I don't fit in with the Brickmans." I felt completely drained of all my energy.

Momma took my face in her hands, her glossy eyes letting a tear slip down her cheek. "You will be back with me soon, baby. As soon as I get on my feet. I promise you," she said through gritted teeth. It was exactly what I wanted to hear. I thought it would be so easy for her, and I fully trusted her to make this all happen, to get us back together.

I blamed my dad for all that Momma had become, and now he was gone. My wish had come true. And now I could help my momma get back to who she was before, when she would crawl into my bed at night, rub my hair, sing me lullabies, and protect me from the evil under our very own roof. All she had to do was get a job and get a place to live, and she would have help with that. We would be together again soon.

I didn't know then, at just twelve years old, but my momma's promises would never materialize because she was too weak to fight her own demons. I believed in her, and nothing could change that. I would continue to fight for the two of us for much longer than I should have before I'd realize the truth because she was all I had. She was my only hope for belonging and acceptance, and eventually, that hope would flicker out like a flame blown out by the wind. And when hope is gone, you have nothing left.

When the visit ended, I didn't have much to hold on to. Just some questionable promises and a momma who didn't look like herself anymore. Sarah told me she'd drive me home because Cassie was caught up at Jason's baseball game which was running late, and couldn't come get me. That might have upset another young child, feeling like being a foster kid defined them in the family, but it didn't bother me much. Why get comfortable for no reason? That wouldn't have been a safe choice for me. If I'd learned anything over the last few years, it was how to distance myself in order to keep myself safe. Jason and Claire had their mom to pick them up from their games and their *things,* but me? I had social workers to do that. There was always an invisible line in the sand separating me from the Brickmans.

"It's good this way because I want to talk to you about something on the way back to the house," Sarah said nonchalantly as we walked back out to her car.

"So, you're going to have a new social worker starting in two weeks. Her name is Gina," Sarah said as we turned left out of the parking lot. She waited for me to reply, but I just turned my head and stared at her, waiting for her to tell me more, or maybe that she was kidding. She took a breath. "She's really nice. I have filled her in on your case, and she is looking forward to helping you and your mom." I refused to speak. "I'm sorry, Summer," she finally offered. "I am moving out of state for my husband's job. I don't want you to feel like I'm abandoning you."

My face transformed — my cheeks turned pale then quickly burned red. My eyes narrowed as I looked over at Sarah in the driver's seat. I couldn't pinpoint my feelings. I didn't particularly like Sarah, but I couldn't help but feel as if I was being left behind again.

"Whatever," I responded. "It's not like it matters." I was being harsh, but my words were honest. It really didn't matter to me. Sarah only brought me stress. Whenever I heard her name, whenever I saw her, my body went into some sort of trauma response. If I had been feeling particularly bold that day, I would have told her *good riddance*. But I didn't say that. I opted for less words and more angst, and I left it that.

When we pulled up to the house, I got out and slammed the car door as Sarah was blabbering. She got out and walked me to the door, but I unlocked it, walked in, and shut it before she could reach me. I ran straight to my room, needing to be alone.

Out the window, I saw Sarah get back in her car and turn it on, but she didn't leave. I assumed she was waiting for the Brickmans to get home, so she could tell them her news. I burried my face in the pillow and screamed as loud as I could. I lost my breath, my heart was racing, and a single tear slipped down my cheek. I wiped it away and swallowed the lump in my throat before any more tears came.

"Momma," I whispered with utter desperation.

CHAPTER 10

Texas - Now

MY ALARM SOUNDS FOR two straight minutes before I rustle awake from my spot on my chair under my blanket. I turn the sound off and stretch as much as I can. I look at the time.

Six p.m.

I have two hours before Kash will be here, plenty of time to get ready at a leisurely pace. I stand up, glancing out the window at a couple walking down the street hand in hand. They're laughing so hard; it seems like tears must be streaming down their faces. He pulls her into his body, and she throws her head back, continuing to laugh. I long to know what their secret is. I want to laugh like that — so hard that barely any sound comes out of your mouth and hardly any air is making it in, making you feel like you could collapse. Your stomach hurts, your cheeks ache. I can't remember a time when I last laughed like that. I smile to myself — another dream to catch. Laughing like that would mean that I was healing, at least that's how it feels right now. I have never let my guard down enough and been able to fully let go and laugh like those people on the sidewalk. I can't even imagine finding something that funny.

I turn on the shower and let it warm up as I prepare myself a cup of coffee in my Keurig. I take a few sips before moseying over to the bathroom and placing my mug on the sink. I glance at myself in the mirror, fear starting to creep in as it hits me that I'm about to put myself out there, attempting to open up more to Kash. I take a shaky breath as I give myself a tiny pep talk: *You got this. Let someone in.* The words swimming around in my head sound desperate. What I want, or more what I *need,* and what I am capable of are completely different things.

By the time 7:57 rolls around, I look like I'm ready for the night. My hair is down, dark and wavy falling almost to my butt. I skimp on the makeup, some mascara and neutral lip stain, a little tinted moisturizer. My jeans are dark and hug my curves, which are located on all parts of my body. I went with a cream-colored shirt that falls off my shoulders. My boots are combat-ish, but a little less aggressive. I hope we aren't going somewhere fancy; I'm not prepared for an outing like that. This will have to do, no matter where Kash is taking me.

Right on time, Kash knocks on my door at eight o'clock sharp. I'm not surprised by his promptness, but it does make me smile. I open the door and smile at him without showing my teeth. My guard is up, as always, but at least I know how to make it seem like I'm approachable.

"Hi, Summer!" he says with gentle enthusiasm.

"Hi," I respond as I sling my bag across my body and step out into the hallway, closing the door behind me. "Ready to go?" I ask, walking toward the staircase.

"Of course," he responds, following close behind. Once we are on the street, Kash guides us to the right where his car is parked along the curb

— a black pickup truck that looks like it could use a wash. Rugged. I like that. The inside is neat and smells like one of those hanging tree air fresheners, with a hint of orange. I climb into the passenger seat as Kash settles into the driver side. He gives me a smile, his dark eyes glistening in the streetlights. "Thanks for coming out with me," he offers, buckling his seatbelt.

"Thanks for inviting me," I say. "Where are we going?"

"Mexican ok?"

"It's my favorite," I respond, buckling my seatbelt.

"Caliente's it is!" Kash says, pulling away from the curb. "How was your day?"

"It was good. I went to brunch with Farrah and helped her pick out some things for her trip. She's so excited."

"She really is!" Kash laughs.

"Then I went home and," I pause briefly, not sure if my description of my afternoon will seem alarming, depressing — practicing my deep breathing, taking a nap, repeating my mantra, feeling lonely. "I just hung out for a bit before you came," I finish nonchalantly. "How was your day?"

"Low-key. I vacuumed my truck," he says with a wink. "And then I went and played basketball with Silas and grabbed some groceries. Riveting, I know." He laughs again.

It is riveting, I think to myself. Being able to accomplish normal, everyday things without a hint of anxiety, trauma, fear. There was a peaceful lull in our conversation for a moment as I thought of what that must be like.

"How did you sleep last night?" Kash asks me. I look at him, confused and taken aback by the question. "Sorry, you mentioned last night that looking at the stars helps you fall asleep." I stare at him blankly. I don't know what to think or how I feel about this question. I don't even remember telling him that little tidbit of information last night. I remember counting stars with him and telling him that the stars were important to me, but not much other than that. That's what triggers do to me; steal my memory and take away my joy.

"I slept well," I say.

Lie.

I never sleep well. I never have and I don't think I ever will. As I work through the stages of my own grief on a daily basis, I've spent a lot of time in the denial, anger, bargaining, and depression stages, and having trouble sleeping is a nagging symptom of all of them, so I've struggled with it all my life. I like to think that I'm inching closer and closer toward the acceptance stage, but I sometimes travel back to the other ones. I have lived in them all, over and over again. I have repeated them time and time again without ever fully getting to acceptance. It hurts to feel that I may never get there, but that is something that I *have* embraced. I've come to terms with the fact that this is who I will be for the rest of my life. No matter how much I say I'm not, it seems that I *am* the sum of my past.

"I was so tired after the bar last night," Kash laughs, turning left into the parking garage next to Caliente's.

"You guys always put on such a great performance," I offer, and I genuinely mean it.

"Thanks," he smiles. "I'm pretty sure I fell asleep as my head was hitting the pillow."

"That is something I would love to experience," I say, unbuckling my belt. "Stars may help me get to sleep, but I don't sleep well at all," I admit, sheepishly. "I lied before." A soft laugh escapes me.

Kash taps my knee and gives it a friendly squeeze. "Let's go live life and get you tired enough to fall asleep on the way home."

Walking into Caliente's is like being transported to another country. Mexican instrumental music plays loudly through the speakers, encouraging me to move my hips to the beat as we wait to be seated. Primary colors are splashed throughout the large dining areas — reds, blues, yellows, and greens brighten the place without being too much. The tables are lined with patterned tiles of deep navy and white, and pinatas of all different shapes hang from the ceiling. The atmosphere alone is enough to make me excited about being out for the evening.

Soon after we sit down, there's a large margarita in front of me, and as I swirl the straw around through the ice and tequila, completely wrapped in my thoughts, I remind myself that I am not alone. I am with Kash. I need to be present. I need to let the wall down a little. I need a connection. I need friends. I look up at him, and he's smiling at me, a genuine, soft smile.

"Are you ok?" he asks. "You're so quiet."

"I'm fine," I respond, taking a sip and puckering my lips at the extremely strong taste of alcohol. We both laugh and that lightens up the heaviness that is present between us.

"So, tell me something cool about you," Kash says, leaning back in this chair. "A cool place you have visited? A hobby?"

Um, I hitchhiked from Kentucky to Indiana when I was thirteen because my foster family left me with another family so they could go on vacation without me...so they could have a break from me. So, I grew reckless while they were gone and got myself pretty far away. I left Kentucky when I was twenty-nine and came to Texas and never looked back. But that's as far as I have gone. Ever.

Hobby? I like to talk to my plants and reassure them and myself that I can care for them.

No, that would be a buzzkill.

"Hmm. I have only really been to Kentucky and here," I say, looking at him and waiting for judgment. "I like to write...and I read a lot," I offer, trying to offset the boringness of my first answer.

"Steven King. Thumbs up or down?" Kash asks me, sounding serious.

"Thumb up," I say, 100 percent sure of my answer. "He's brilliant and I get completely lost in his books," I add, putting a chip with salsa in my mouth.

"Agreed," Kash responds, covering his mouthful of chips.

"What about you? Have you traveled anywhere fun that you loved?" I ask out of politeness, knowing it will trigger me to feel resentful that my life is controlled by trauma. But on the other hand, hearing Kash share his experiences doesn't scare me too much. Maybe it's the way he looks at me or how conversations with him are just easy. I force my shoulders down, something I need to do regularly, as I'm always in a constant state of stress. I have to consciously work to relax.

Kash shrugs, looking around the dining area. "I have been here and there," he says. "I have been out of the country once, to Spain, to meet a distant relative, a cousin. That was awesome!" He beams. "Other than that, I have been to a few states — Florida, Vermont, Oklahoma, Louisiana — and I went to college here in my home state and never left," he finishes, taking a sip of his Corona.

"Wow, Spain. That's amazing. I can't even imagine what it would be like to see another country," I say. The whimsical thought is both beautiful and depressing. "Maybe someday," I force a smile and remind my shoulders to relax again.

"Ok, on the count of three, let's name a state that we'd go to if we had the chance to leave right this second," Kash says playfully, intertwining his fingers and leaning over the table a bit, eyes locked on mine.

"Ok, let me think about it for a second," I say. "Ok. I'm ready. Are you?"

He just nods with a small smile. He begins counting slowly. "One, two, three."

"California," we say in unison. We both laugh and Kash slaps his palm on the table. "No way," he says happily.

"That was funny," I add, smiling. "Why would you pick California?"

He shrugs his shoulders and glances around the restaurant. "California has always seemed alive to me, ya know what I mean? From the north all the way to the south — you have mountains and snow and on one end, and on the other end, hot sun and beaches, with the desert in the middle. Tons of strawberry fields too." He stops and laughs, and I assume that last part was just a funny addition to his spectacular idea of a state he has never been to before. I look at him and wait for him to say more. "My dad always told me that California was for dreamers." He looks down at his hands, almost sadly, but I can't quite read the exact emotion. I open my mouth to ask him to elaborate, but he interrupts my thoughts and asks me why I chose California. I can tell that it's his way of saying he's done talking about it, so I let it be.

I think about the question for a second and decide to answer with as much honesty as I can muster, all in the name of breaking down a piece or two my wall. All in the name of letting someone in, even if it's just partially.

"When I was a child, I would dream about seeing the ocean. I lived in Kentucky, far from the sea, and I would visualize it so clearly even though I had never seen it before. I felt like I could imagine the way it smelled, the way it felt. I would escape to these daydreams when I was having a tough time...with my family. My childhood was hard. I used my mind to transfer me somewhere else, and it was always the ocean. When I got older, that visual became the Pacific Ocean, California specifically." I look at him and shrug. "I think going there would be healing for me, and I hope I make it there someday." I can't read the look on Kash's face. It's not pity. It's not indifference. He looks thoughtful, I guess. I think he wants me to go on, to tell him more, open up. But I don't. I can't. So, I just look back at him quietly.

"Do you want to share with me anything about your childhood?" he asks, not forcefully, not intrusive, just caringly. I shake my head slowly.

"You sure?" he asks. "I'm a good listener." I still don't make a sound. My face is blank, taking in his words. "How about summing it up in three sentences," he offers with a caring smile.

Sum up my childhood in three sentences? I know this gesture is one of care, letting me know that he is there for me if I want to open up, but my childhood could only be described with a 300-page book, at the very least.

"Ok," I say slowly, knowing I can't do what he has tasked me with, but wanting to try. I think of the couple walking outside my window this afternoon. I want to feel free enough to let go and laugh like they were laughing. I will never be able to do that if I'm stuck in my own way, holding myself back. Then I think about my journey. I *am* stuck, stagnant. And I am not going to get better if I don't do things that scare me. So here goes.

"I was in foster care from ages eleven to eighteen. I was beaten. I was raped." I take a sip of my margarita and then a big gulp of water to calm the lump in my throat and the tear that's clawing at the back of my eye. My heart is pounding, and I can't believe I just opened up like this. What I shared is so matter-of-fact, but the words are abrasive, alarming. They could scare anyone who hears them. This could be the last time I make a connection with Kash. Not that I'm looking to date him or anything, but I'm longing for our friendship to continue to grow, and I might have just scared him off for good.

To my surprise, he reaches over the table with both of his hands and immediately finds mine. "That's awful and unfair that you went through those things as a child," he says, assuring me. What he says, I already know. But it doesn't change the fact that it happened to me, and I have yet to climb out of the hole I've been swallowed into, even though I am trying with all my might.

I nod once. "I know," I whisper, afraid that raising my voice any more will allow a crack to escape and along with that, my tears. He gets out of his side of the booth and climbs in next to me. He puts his arm around me and guides my head to rest on his shoulder. I don't feel the need to speak. I don't feel the need to do anything. My body just relaxes. I feel my breath slowing down, going in and out in steady waves.

"You are a star, Summer," Kash starts. "I've been drawn to you since I first met you last year. But you seemed uninterested in my friendship. Now I know there are walls that you have up for a reason. But you deserve so much more — happiness, adventure, friendship. If you ever need a friend to talk to, please know you can talk to me." He says his words with confidence and a truth that I can sense.

I pull away slightly and look up into his eyes. "Thank you," I whisper.

"Of course. Any time," he responds, rubbing my back a few times in a friendly, reassuring way.

"Shall we order?" I ask, sitting up straighter, coming back to the reality that we are sitting in a restaurant having this conversation.

"Yes, of course," he responds, heading back to his side of the table.

"I'm famished," I say, looking over the menu.

By the time our food comes, I am starved. I eat all of my street-style tacos and try a bite of his chimichangas.

A delicious meal and two margaritas later, Kash and I walk out of Caliente's and head out into the warm, dark evening. I feel full for the first time in months and my eyelids feel a cozy sense of sleepiness. His plan of getting me good and tired looks like it's working. The combination of food, alcohol, and briefly opening up to Kash seems to have taken the strain and weight off my muscles. Kash takes my hand, not intertwining our fingers like lovers would but holding it palm to palm, a friendly and caring gesture that warms me from the inside out.

As we drive to my apartment, we talk about Sullivan's, J.J.'s new menu additions, and other random things. The conversation feels easy and comfortable, and I like that. I watch the city go by — the windows, streetlights, and storefronts flashing in my line of vision. My shoulders are relaxed, my breathing is steady.

When we pull up in front of my apartment, Kash gets out of his truck and walks me to the front of my building. He puts one foot on the first step and looks up at the clear sky filled with stars.

"Should we count some?" he asks, smiling at me. I smile back and sit on the step, gesturing for him to join me just like we did last night.

"Thanks for tonight," I say after some silence. "It was just what I needed. I have really been working on opening up and truly healing from my past. I feel like you unknowingly pushed me out of my comfort zone a bit tonight."

"I never want to push," Kash offers. "But I want to be your friend, so if I can help you, let me."

I nod, lean back on my elbows, and look up at the vast expanse of stars. Intrinsically, I start to count, out of habit. "Being in foster care was the hardest thing I have ever gone through. All the things that happened to me are centered around that part of my life — what led me to it, what happened while I was there, and how I ended up getting out. It was all bad. I try to look back and find the bright side, the reason for it all, the silver lining. But I can't for the life of me figure it out."

I'm surprised at my outpouring of words about my past. Kash just looks at me, waiting for me to go on but his expression shows me that I don't have to go on if I don't want to. But I do. I do want to. And tonight, is the first time I will tell someone, besides Janie, something real and tragic that happened to me. Maybe not the most tragic thing I endured, but I have to start somewhere. Baby steps.

CHAPTER 11

Kentucky - Then

I STOOD AT THE corner of Mr. Hyde's desk while he yammered on about how I needed to put in more effort in his class.

"You're very intelligent, Summer," he lectured. "Imagine if you just applied yourself?"

I nodded, completely uninterested in his guidance. How did he know I was intelligent? I barely spoke in class. I just turned in my homework, which was always done correctly, and passed my tests. Was he trying to mentor me, the poor foster child? His words fell on deaf ears. Applying myself in junior high math was not at the top of my priority list. As he droned on, I thought about Mrs. Harper, my amazing third grade teacher. Her soft voice and welcoming smile had truly saved me that year. She saw me for who I really was, not just what my circumstances were. My junior high teachers didn't hold a candle to her. They couldn't. I gave up hoping I'd ever have another teacher who would see me the way she once did. How could they, anyway? I was constantly shrinking myself to seem invisible and it was easier for everyone to just go on pretending that I was fine. Or they thought I just needed some encouraging words about how I only needed to apply myself and then everything would be better. They only did the bare minimum, just enough to make themselves feel like they were helping the youth of America. But I wasn't interested in their help.

The bell rang, and I gathered up all my belongings from my desk and slid them into my bag, as I headed to my locker to grab my food and meet Jason for lunch. Much to Claire's dismay, Jason and I had become close over the last year. Jason did not try to force a relationship with me, like Claire did. He let me feel the way I felt and didn't try to fix me, and because of that, I tended to gravitate toward him and his friends over Claire and hers. Claire was boy crazy, hyper, and spunky, and I just wasn't any of that. Jason, on the other hand, was calm, reserved, and into sports and video games —not much else — and that was more my style. Since he had moved on to high school that year, I was thankful that the Brickman's town had a combined junior high and high school so we would be in the same building and could still hang out.

"How was math?" he asked me as he approached my locker with his best friend, Dan.

"Eighth grade algebra is...fantastic," I said sarcastically, slamming my locker and heading toward the cafeteria.

The cafeteria smelled like old gravy and stale bread, but it symbolized a break in the day that I accepted regardless of the smell. I walked to the end of an empty table with Jason and Dan following behind me. We all plopped down and began opening our lunches. We were joking around, mindlessly poking fun at each other when I blurted out something that was out of character for me.

"I'm going to try out for volleyball," I said, chewing on a bite of my sandwich and looking around the crowded cafeteria. Jason and Dan stared at me.

Jason nodded and began to smile encouragingly. "Ok," he said with a mouthful of food. "That sounds good. When are tryouts?"

"Tomorrow," I responded. Dan and Jason's eyes widened.

"Have you ever played?" Dan asked me curiously.

"No," I dragged out the word a bit too long. "But I do have the urge to bop at things that resemble heads, so I think it could be good for me," I said, shrugging my shoulders. They both laughed.

"I'll wait for you after tryouts because I have weightlifting for football," Jason added in. "Then my mom can pick us up after."

Not just *mom.*

Not *our* mom.

Just *my* mom.

Your mom is a drug addict who can't get her act together enough to take care of you.

Of course, Jason didn't say any of those things that raced through my head. No one else would even pick up on those little details in conversations, but I sure did. Because it was those conversations that nicked little holes into my heart that never seemed to heal, they only got deeper each time. I shook away the sadness that overcame me, and I buried it. My reaction was the epitome of everything I didn't want to be, weak and vulnerable.

I forced a smile. "Sounds good."

———

On the bus on the way home, Claire was standoffish with me, and I didn't know why.

"You ok?" I asked her, nudging her shoulder with mine. She just shook her head and continued reading *The Giver* for her English class, one of my favorite assignments from the year before. "When you're done with that book, I can work on the assignment with you if you want. I loved that one last year," I offered, trying to break the tension. She gave me a quick, forced smile and went on reading.

If I was being honest, I didn't care if Claire was mad at me. I didn't do anything to her, except maybe spend more time with her brother than her, but I didn't want to have any awkwardness, so there I was, extending the olive branch. I sighed to myself as she continued to give me the cold shoulder, and I kept my eyes forward, looking down the bus aisle and counting down the seconds until our stop so I could get off and put some distance between us. She would get over it eventually, and then she would be back to sucking up to me every chance she could get.

That night at dinner, Jason told his mom and dad that I was going to try out for volleyball. Cassie's eyes sparkled with joy as she passed the salad bowl down the table.

"That's outstanding!" she boasted.

I gave her a half smile, taking a sip of my water while I shrugged my shoulders. "Who knows if I'll even make it," I said nonchalantly. "I'm only in eighth grade, and I don't think many eighth graders can make JV." I sounded as if it didn't matter to me when, really, it was all I wanted — something to get me out of the house, somewhere to focus my energy.

"I think you'll be great at it," Greg offered, though I wasn't sure why. He had never seen me play a sport in the two years I'd lived in his house, but I smiled at him anyway, hoping he was right.

"I'll pick you and Jason up after you're both done. Do you think around four-thirty?" Cassie asked, eyeing both of us. I nodded.

"Yeah, sounds good," Jason said.

"How's Trevor?" I asked Claire once we were in our room for the night. She was sitting at her desk typing away on instant messenger on her computer.

"He asked me to the movies," she said, lacking her usual giddiness and excitement.

What was up with her?

"That's awesome," I said, flipping through my magazine. Claire had been ogling over Trevor for so long, and I assumed he thought she was annoying like I did, but I guess he finally caved. Maybe it was because she had started to grow boobs over the summer.

"Yeah, but Mom won't let me go on a date until I'm sixteen." She whined, annoyed with her circumstance. I stared at her for a minute and softened my expression when I realized I was holding judgment.

"We can go as a group, and she won't know the difference. I'll cover for you," I said, shrugging my shoulders like it wasn't a big deal.

Claire whipped her head towards me. "I don't want to go with you," she spat, her words full of venom. "Do you know what people are saying about you behind your back?" She looked at me disgusted.

"Uh, no," I offered, not caring about what some rich kids said that could possibly make Claire that mad.

"They say that you and Jason are going out and that you like each other and stuff." She glared at me, waiting for me to respond or confess or something. "It's embarrassing," she muttered under her breath.

I laughed so loud that it made Claire jump. "You have got to be kidding me," I said. "Are you making this up because you're mad that I hang out with Jason more than you?" I questioned her, curious about how she would respond.

"No!" There was a tone in her voice that she had never used with me. It was cold and unforgiving. "Everyone is talking about it. I thought you would want to know but I guess not," she said condescendingly, turning back to her computer.

I noticed that my mouth was agape as I leaned back on the pillows and stared up at the ceiling. What the actual hell was going on? I had to talk to Jason the next day and see if he'd heard anything, but first I had to get some rest if I was going to make the volleyball team.

———

I sat against the lockers outside the weight room, waiting for Jason after my tryout. It was 4:10 p.m., and he was supposed to be done soon. I was hoping to have a few minutes to talk to him before Cassie picked us up. But I wasn't so fortunate. Soon enough, I heard the clacking of heels on the tile floor and glanced up to see Cassie swiftly making her way down the hall toward me.

"Oh, hi, Summer. I know I'm early. Can you please get in the car? I'll get Jason." She seemed annoyed and flustered. Did I do something? What was going on?

I waited in the car for five minutes before they joined me. Cassie huffed as she slammed her door shut and buckled her seat belt.

"I need to talk to the two of you," she said, looking in the rearview mirror at me and briefly glancing at Jason to her right. Neither of us had a second to respond before she continued. "Are you in a relationship together?" she asked, in a completely disgusted manner, just like her daughter did. "Are you an *item*?" she added, her southern accent crawling under my skin. Jason's head whipped back toward me. He looked shocked and appalled. Too bad I hadn't had a chance to warn him about these rumors before Cassie arrived. Claire must have been on her high horse that day and decided it was in everyone's best interest if she told her mother those horrendous rumors.

"What the fuck, Mom?" Jason belted out.

"Watch your mouth!" she sputtered. I had never heard anyone in the Brickman house swear, so, just like Cassie, I was also shocked at Jason's outburst.

"Well, why are these rumors going around then, huh?" I had never seen Cassie so unhinged.

Obviously, Jason hadn't heard these rumors either, which was really making me question Claire and her intentions.

"No, Mom! We are friends. Good friends!" Jason was losing it, and I sat in the back seat of this luxury SUV, that wasn't really mine, and held my breath. How was this happening?

"Summer?" Cassie questioned, glaring at me in the rearview mirror.

"What?" I whispered, which, in hindsight, probably didn't help my case at all, but I was frozen. Scared. What was going to happen to me?

"You are a guest in our house," Cassie continued firmly, "and if any such behavior or inappropriateness were to happen under my roof, you would have to leave." Her statement was final and that was as clear as day.

"Jason is like a brother to me," I whispered with a tear streaming down my face. I wiped it away quickly, reprimanding myself — I hadn't cried in months. But she ignored my statement anyways and continued on.

"Do I make myself clear to both of you?"

"Yup!" Jason yelled back. I just nodded and looked out my window for the rest of the drive back to the house. When we got there, I trudged through the door, careful not to draw attention to myself, after I was so rudely reminded that I was still just a guest in their house, even after two years.

I refused to look at anyone during dinner. My body felt heavy, and my mouth was set in a frown. I felt as if it would stay that way forever. Cassie's movements were quick and cold as she set all the food on the table and poured water into glasses.

"So, anyways," Greg began, trying to break the ice and ease the tension "How was weightlifting today, Jason?" he asked.

"Fine. I'm getting stronger," Jason replied without any real enthusiasm. Greg tried to keep the conversation going, ignoring the fact that everyone was at odds and Claire began going on and on about the science test she had aced.

"That's excellent, Claire," Cassie offered to the one child she was actually happy with. I barely ate a bite and just moved the food around my plate until enough time had passed where I felt comfortable enough to ask if I could be excused. I got up from the table and headed to my room.

No one even thought to ask me how my volleyball tryouts went.

My finger moved down the list of names who made the volleyball team, my eyes scanning ahead of my finger. I was desperate to see *James, Summer* somewhere on there. I didn't know then, and I still don't know now, why I wanted it so badly. Volleyball wasn't a passion of mine. I had never even played sports, much less been on a team. But I had taken a risk by trying out, and I think I wanted to prove to myself that I was worthy of something, anything. Then, there it was, eleven letters strung together, my name. I smiled a real smile, one only for myself. I did it. I made the JV volleyball team as an eighth grader, and I decided, right then and there, that I was going to be the best player on the team. I was going to put everything I had into that team. All of my energy would be devoted to that ball and that net. I was relieved to have something to guide my thoughts instead of constantly contemplating my pathetic life.

At lunch, Dan, Jason and I were joined by an acquaintance of mine from English class, Meg. Meg had also tried out and made the team. I contemplated being her friend, but I wasn't ready to jump into that commitment yet but having lunch with her was a start.

Jason and Dan stood around me and obnoxiously clapped and cheered for my news.

"Congrats to you too!" Dan said to Meg.

"We are going to be the only eighth graders on the team," I said with my mouth full of food. "We will probably just sit on the bench." I laughed.

Meg smirked. "And then we'll be the best players on the team next year," she added, giving me a high five. I was going to be the best. I didn't know how Meg would fare, but I knew where I was headed.

———

September and October went by in a blur that year. I went to practice multiple times a week with games mixed in. When I was at the Brickman's house, I focused on my schoolwork so I didn't have to interact with them too much. Claire continued to give me the cold shoulder most of the time, and I didn't care enough to work on that friendship. She was playing field hockey and spent most of her time at home chatting with Trevor on messenger. Cassie and Greg only came to a few of my games because they always went to Claire's field hockey games and Jason's football games. I understood. I wasn't their kid, so I reasoned that it wouldn't be fair for their other kids if they divided their time even more and gave me any attention. I made myself believe it. I wondered how they would manage if they had a third child of their own. They probably would divide and conquer. But lucky for them, they only had two children. I was just a guest.

Jason skipped some of Claire's games, though, and came to mine. I really appreciated that. Dan came to most of them too. I would hear them in the bleachers cheering me on, even if I was warming the bench. I was thankful for them, my only friends.

One afternoon in November, Gina was at the house for one of her monthly check-in visits.

"How's it going, Summer?" she asked me. "It seems like you have quite a lot of exciting things going on." I stared at her from the couch as she sat across from me on the love seat.

"Yup. I'm pretty busy," I deadpanned. "Volleyball. School."

"What about socializing? Do you have a core group of friends that you can depend on?" she asked, trying to sound sympathetic, but it just annoyed me. Didn't she know that having a core group of friends meant trusting people, and I didn't know how to do that?

"I hang out with Jason at school...and his friend, Dan," I added to shut her up.

She gave me a sorry smile. "I hope you can find friends in your own grade."

"Meg," I said.

"Meg? Who is that?"

"She's in my English class, and she plays volleyball with me. She's nice," I said nonchalantly.

"That's great." She must have been satisfied with my answer because she didn't ask me any more about my friends. "And how about the rest of the Brickmans?" she asked, eyeing me, wanting me to tell her my true feelings.

I shrugged. "I don't know. They're fine. I think they are sick of me, though."

Gina didn't say anything for a moment. The silence was deafening.

"They aren't sick of you, Summer. But sometimes it is hard for foster families to muddle through the waters, especially after all this time." She sounded like she had more news to share, and I didn't want to even think about what it could possibly be. She fidgeted with her pen and shifted her legs. I wondered why the social workers were always afraid to tell me stuff. Shouldn't they have been strong for me? Shouldn't they have held me up instead of constantly knocking me down?

"What is it?" I asked, annoyed.

"The Brickmans are going to Florida for Thanksgiving," Gina said

"I know," I responded. "We are all going to see Cassie's sister and niece." I had already picked out a bathing suit. I was so excited to touch the ocean for the first time.

"Actually, Summer, you aren't going to be able to go."

"What? Why?" I asked, panicking.

"Cassie and Greg think it's important that they spend time together as a family. They think Claire might be struggling a bit and that she might need some family time." Gina felt bad. I knew she did; I could tell by the way she looked at me. I nodded once, the lump in my throat growing unbearable, as I forced the tears to remain glossy around my eyes, refusing to release them.

Gina started talking about respite care. I would go to a temporary foster home for Thanksgiving break while the family I had lived with for the past two years went on a vacation to the beach without me. I would spend Thanksgiving with strangers. I couldn't fathom why these people would want to leave me there while they went on vacation. I couldn't believe that they were even allowed to do this to me. But they were, and there was nothing I could do about it. Gina kept going on and on, and I'd had enough — I got up, stormed up the stairs, and threw myself onto my bed. I put the pillow on my head, and I cried — hard. All of the emotions I had been holding in for eighteen months came pouring out, silently. I felt the tears soaking my cheeks and neck and sliding onto my pillow, soaking it through.

When I was in first grade, Lily Sanderson came to school after spring break with a stack of pictures. Her skin looked darker, and her dirty blonde hair was a few shades lighter. Our teacher let her show us all the pictures of her trip to Mexico. She showed off a tiny braid in her hair, wrapped with turquoise string and colorful beads. Lily boasted about how her parents took her and her sister to the beach, where they went swimming with dolphins and visited an animal sanctuary. I looked at the pictures being passed around with awe, like they held secrets to magical places. After that day, I longed to be Lily Sanderson. When I was in my closet, hiding from the monsters, I would imagine I was in some faraway place, seeing things for the first time.

Vacation.

It was a word I just couldn't fathom. I knew Momma and Dad would never take me to new places. I understood that I would never be able to do such wonderful things. I didn't even let myself wish for it because I knew it would never be a real possibility. But I did allow myself to picture it and pretend I was somewhere else, someplace special and beautiful, new and exciting.

I was ok with the truth that I would never leave Kentucky — that is, until I was told that I would get to take a vacation to Florida. I let myself hope and felt the excitement of getting to go on my very first vacation, something I never thought possible. And then, it was ripped right from my hands.

I must have fallen asleep because when I lifted my head, the light was off. The clock said 6:32 p.m., and Claire wasn't in the room. I could smell dinner wafting into the room through the door that was opened just a crack. I sat up and hugged my knees to my chest. I felt empty, hollow, and weak. My eyes were puffy, my nose, raw. There was a soft knock on the door. I looked up and Jason was peering in.

"Dinner's ready," he muttered, pity spreading through his words.

"I'm not hungry," I said, turning my back to him and lying down, pulling the blankets up to my chin. I heard the door shut quietly and Jason's feet walking down the stairs to join his family for dinner. I stared, unblinking, at the window.

I did not move until Claire was asleep three hours later. It was then that I quietly crawled out of my bed, hoisted the window open, and climbed out on the roof to my spot.

I lay back on the shingles, feeling the rough edges under my hand. I began to count. I counted until my eyelids were so heavy that I feared I would fall asleep and roll off the roof. I took a deep breath, and it came out shaky and uneven. I sat up. "Thank you," I whispered to the little specks of light. They relentlessly gave me the gift of sleep, albeit restless.

CHAPTER 12

Texas - Now

"T HEY JUST LEFT AND went to Florida without you? After raising you for two years?"

Kash is appalled by my story. Of course he is. It *is* appalling. Almost as appalling as the time my dad and I went to a gas station in Louisville to get cigarettes and he left me there. I had walked down the candy aisle, ever so slowly, admiring all the different options, all the different colors. I picked up a little package of Skittles and twirled them around in my hands. I walked up to Dad, already in line buying his cigarettes and scratch tickets, and asked if I could get the Skittles. He glared at me under his hooded eyelids and snatched his stash away from the cashier, grabbing my arm and pushing me toward the door. The candy fell from my hand and landed on the floor with a thud. *What do you think you're doing, girl,* he spat at me, gnashing his disgusting teeth. *You think money grows on trees?* He asked not expecting a reply. I shook my head, whispering a pitiful apology, and he laughed in my face, jumping into the front seat of his truck. *Bet you'll never do that again*, he said, pulling out of the parking spot and skidding out of the lot, leaving me standing there on the curb, my knees shaking. I ran and hid behind a dumpster and pulled my legs up to my chest, crying into them.

Hours passed before my dad's truck came back into the lot, Momma at the wheel. I watched her in disbelief from behind the dumpster, waiting with bated breath. *Summer!* she yelled, practically falling out of the car, looking around frantically for me. I pulled myself up from the ground and made my way over to her slowly, looking like a deer in the headlights. Momma burst into tears, running to me and pulling me close to her chest. She grabbed my face in her hands, her own face soaked and red, a new black mark forming around her right eye. Momma was beaten again because of me. All because I just wanted some Skittles.

And just like I blamed myself for what happened to my momma, I blamed myself for being left out by the Brickmans. They never fully welcomed me as one of them. They made me feel like I was a stranger in their house, a guest, always reminding me of the fact. For some reason, Cassie and Greg blamed me that Claire was struggling although it was not the truth. I'm not sure why they thought it was my fault, but it was just another reason to leave me out of their family vacation.

"Yeah," I say, looking down at my hands. "It was horrible. I took it really badly."

"How was the respite family you stayed with?"

"Awful. They smoked in the house and hid it from Social Services. I had to sleep on a futon in a disgusting room that was filled with junk. I ended up sneaking out and going to my friend Dan's house, but he was afraid he'd get in trouble if I was there, so he said I couldn't come in. So, I left town. I ended up hitchhiking all the way to Indiana. It was a dangerous and crazy way to leave, but nonetheless, I left. The woman who took me was a gypsy type and praised me for protecting myself. She dropped me off at a grocery store in a small town, and I used my only five dollars to buy crackers. I spent Thanksgiving on the streets by myself, but honestly, at the time, I thought it was better than the alternative — being in a dysfunctional household with strangers, left to sit and wallow in my self-pity, realizing that the family who I thought cared for me at least a little bit had done what every other adult had done before, abandoned me. Everyone said I left for attention. Can you believe that? Attention. I had no family, was abused and neglected, and was thrown away like trash so the Brickmans could enjoy family time, but apparently all I wanted was attention. Maybe it was partly true, but what I really wanted was to be loved and accepted."

I look at Kash, his brown hair falling down over his forehead. His eyes are looking into mine with the utmost care and concern.

"I'm sorry this happened to you, Summer. I want to make it better for you, but I know that isn't possible," he says sweetly, giving me the urge to hug him.

I put my hand on his. "You are helping. I've never told anyone besides my therapist about anything that has happened to me. But I know I need to move on. I have grieved my life since I was seven years old. Grieved my dad's abuse, grieved being removed from my mom, and grieved the horrible things that happened to me while I was in foster care. I go through the stages of grief over and over again, but I never come out on the other side. Opening up to someone feels like a good step in the right direction."

We both lean back on the step and continue looking up at the stars. "When will you know if you're healing? Have you given yourself, like, a benchmark or something?" Kash asks.

I think about his question. "Laughing until my stomach hurts," I say. He smiles but stays silent, letting me go on. "Having the courage to go after my dreams." Kash nods encouragingly. I sit up and look at him, and he stares back at me. "Letting someone in," I whisper, afraid to say it too loud, afraid to face it but desperate for it at the same time.

"Then I think you might be on the right track," Kash says, smiling. He stands up and extends his hand to pull me up. "I know you aren't ready to give me more of your story right now, but can you give me a little more of your time to get some ice cream with me?"

I laugh. "Of course."

He's right. I'm not ready to give him more. Not yet at least. Facing my past is the scariest thing in the world to me. And letting someone in and worrying that I'll scare them is another real fear of mine. I never felt worthy as a child. No one protected me, no one wanted me. The fear of that continuing to happen has ruined my life for too long. But I need to take small steps, baby steps. I watch my feet as we head back toward Kash's truck. One, two, three. It's slow, but I'm getting there. One step at a time.

I'm walking around my block with a to-go cup of coffee, soaking up the midday sun. It's been a week since I went to Caliente's with Kash. I can't wait to get to work tonight. Farrah is back, Kash and Silas are playing, and all the staff will be working. I smile to myself as I pick up my pace. Is this a feeling of joy? I think it is, and I'm allowing myself to relish in it.

Over the last six days, I have spent a lot of time thinking. Not that it's any different than other days, but my thoughts have been more positive, more uplifting. Kash has texted me every day with something encouraging, and when intrusive thoughts try to break through, I do what Janie tells me to do: I identify the thought, label it as 'just a thought,' and replay the truth out loud. Kash's friendship has been like a life raft, pulling me back in from where I have been drifting out at sea. He is a great man. I'm starting to believe this, and it's replacing the fear.

I have to prepare myself for the twenty questions Farrah will ask because I know she wants this thing with Kash to be something more, something it's not. Before my shift, I have to come up with a plan so I can make it perfectly clear to her that I don't want her to pry or push.

I feel it from Kash too — there is nothing beyond friendship growing between us. He's friendly with me, almost like how I imagine childhood friends are to each other. It's almost like Kash needs our growing friendship just as much as I do.

At home, I walk into my apartment and grab my mini watering can that's shaped like an elephant, the trunk acting as the spout. I take it to the sink and fill it up. I walk around my apartment and water my few plants, humming to myself. It's twelve-thirty p.m., and I need to be at work by four. Usually, I would practice some deep breathing and let myself take a nap, waking up with enough time to shower and head out the door. But today, I decide to do some yoga, enjoy some tea, and read a magazine. I'm choosing to enjoy the day, not wish it away, hiding beneath the protective layer of my comforter.

As I brush my teeth, I glance at my mantra, wilted and warped. *Summer James, you are more than the sum of your past.* I say it out loud, and for the first time, it feels like I could believe it someday. For the first time, it doesn't feel like something I *have* to say. It feels like something that just might be true.

———

"Summer!" Farrah shrieks as I walk in the back kitchen door of Sullivan's. Sitting on the counter, she's talking to J.J. as he gets ready to cook for the evening, and she hops down and walks over to give me a hug.

"Hi! How was your trip?" I ask as we embrace, squeezing each other extra tight.

"It was the best! Sun, drinks, a real tan, what could be better?" she beams, sticking out her arm for me to admire her golden skin. "I even went zip lining, if you can believe it." She laughs at herself.

Of course I can believe it. "That sounds like so much fun!"

Maverick walks in and tells us that he's anticipating our biggest night in weeks. "There is a conference in the city that brought in a shit ton of businesses, and they are all amped to try the famous piano bar on Brattle Street." Maverick high-fives the three of us. "Lots of teamwork and good tips for y'all tonight."

"I'll take it," I say and mean it. Whitney walks in and immediately puts on her apron and sous chef hat and begins pulling out some things she is preparing as we fill her in on the news.

"Oh boy. Sounds like pressure on us," she says, fist bumping J.J.

"We got this," he tells her.

Silvia arrives next, and I'm so glad to see her.

"Damn you all, showing up early and making me look late," she jokes, lightheartedly. "My damn dog ran down the street again. Can you believe that? Pain in my ass," she adds, rolling her eyes.

I look around and think about what she said about us all arriving early. This crew, our whole staff, acts like the piano bar isn't just a job but more of a place to go hang out with family. I simmer in this thought as I listen to the hustle and bustle of the staff joking with one another and beginning the evening routine.

Tonight, Farrah and I will be behind the bar, Silvia and Mav will be serving, J.J. and Whitney will, of course, be cooking the food. Our part-time employees, Jade and Erica, are hosting tables and running food. And Silas and Kash are the evening entertainment for the night.

I walk toward the bar to cut the garnishes so they are ready to go with Farrah following close behind.

"So, any updates on..." Farrah starts, but I cut her off. Her nonchalant tone doesn't work, and her face gives her away; I can clearly see that she is very eager for me to fill her in on my "date" with Kash.

"Farrah," I start, and though I practiced and prepared earlier, I feel a little lost for words at first. She looks at me slightly concerned. "For starters, yes, I hung out with Kash a few times while you were gone. Yes, we have been talking almost daily. But no, we are not dating, and we don't like each other in that way." I get out all the words and look at her.

"But..." Her voice has a hint of a whine.

I put my hand up to stop her. "I know you are excited about what you think is happening, but I have found a good friendship with Kash, and I really want to keep it that way. I want to go slow. You know me. You know how closed off I am, and Kash is allowing me to be myself, and I am so thankful for that. I love that you love me and want me to be happy, but what I need from you is to just allow me to truly enjoy Kash as my friend." I end and take a breath. I smile at her, and she smiles back.

She puts her hands up in gentle defense. "Whatever you say, Summer. You are my best friend, and I just want you to be happy." She pulls me in for a hug

"I know you do, and I want the same, and this is what is making me happy right now," I say. "Please don't put pressure on him or me or make it weird for us when he comes in tonight. Ok?"

"Deal," Farrah says, shaking my hand. She whips her long auburn braid over her shoulder, and we both get to slicing lemons and limes.

By six o'clock, the bar is packed with diners. The ambience is mesmerizing — music plays at a medium volume and blankets the space in a warm, comforting atmosphere. Twinkle lights hang from the ceiling, flickering candles adorn the tables, and dark wood accents sweep throughout the room, enveloping the whole space. It's beautiful. I take a moment to be thankful for this job and all it has given me. There are much worse places to earn my money. Hell, I have seen those places, and I never want to go back.

There's still another hour until Kash and Silas start playing, but they set up their sound machines, check the lighting, and get everything ready while the patrons enjoy their food. The vibe is positively elevated; I can feel the excitement as everyone watches the performers get ready. Since most of the guests tonight are from out of town, they've never experienced our bar, so it raises the anticipation. You can tell everyone's looking forward to relaxing and letting loose after traveling and working all week. I can just feel it's going to be a good night.

I smile to myself while I shake the cocktail mixer and pour the contents into two short glass tumblers. Two vodka and sodas with extra lime for table four. I glance over at the table — it's a four-seater high top with four men I've never seen before. They must be here for the conference. Once the drinks are ready, I slide them over for the server to pick up and turn to see Farrah dancing along to the music while she pours a glass of rosé.

"Do you need any help with the wedding planning?" I ask, wiping up the counter where ice melted and pools of water formed. Farrah looks over at me, a glimmer in her eye, a smirk on her lips.

"Speaking of that," she says, raising her eyebrows. "I have to tell you something." She quickly moves her hand up to her mouth, covering it.

What!" I shout. "Tell me!"

Farrah inhales deeply. "Joey and I decided to get married in six weeks!" she squeals.

"Are you serious?" I shriek, completely shocked. "Instead of NEXT YEAR?"

She nods aggressively, her face beaming. "While we were on vacation, soaking up the sun, and maybe a little too much tequila, we decided that we didn't want to wait and make it a big show. We just want it to be simple and beautiful." She grabs the next list of drinks we need to make. I let her continue because I know she is itching to explain their change of plans to me. "Neither of our families are a big part of our lives. We'll have a few family members from each side there...my mom, his mom, but not many others. It's going to be mostly friends — everyone from Sullivan's and some of our college friends — fifty people tops." I smile at her. "It's still going to be a blast," she adds, as if trying to convince me. "It will be a party with my favorite people and that's what I really want." Her shoulders relax when she notices I am completely supportive of this decision. Large functions and I just don't mix.

"I can't wait!" I boast, letting her squeeze me.

"Thank you, Summer. I knew you would be happy for me."

"Of course," I say. "Whatever the two of you want is really all that matters. And I really mean it that I'll help with whatever you need. Especially now that you are on a much shorter time frame!"

We mix up and pour our next orders — three mixed drinks and two glasses of white wine for table three just as Mav walks over to the bar, slaps an order slip down, and winks at me. I give him a questioning look as I pick it up and look at it. Scribed in Mav's messy handwriting, the note says:

The only blonde at table four wants your number, Summer.

My eyes go wide as I glance up at table four and see said Blonde Guy smiling at me. I quickly look away and start walking briskly toward Farrah while she mixes her next drink. I pass her the order slip with a wide-eyed expression on my face. Confused, she looks down to read it, and in the most Farrah way possible, she gasps and lights up.

"Ohh, Summer! This is so fun!"

"Fun?" I question her. "Are you serious? This is not fun. I have to work up here all night with that table gawking at me!"

Farrah rolls her eyes. "Summer, I know you're not ready for a relationship, but he's probably only in town for the weekend. What's the harm in one date?" I stare at her. "And these are grown men, not teenagers. No one is gawking," she adds, rolling her eyes again and silencing me. I know she's right. He's good looking, I am single, and I am working on putting myself out there.

I smile and shake my head. "I'll think about it," I say, grabbing a bottle of Cabernet and filling a glass. Farrah claps, and just as she does, the lights dim, and I hear Kash's voice introducing himself to the crowd. I look over at the stage, an elevated platform with two large pianos facing each other. My heart warms as I see Kash and Silas already drawing the guests into their show. It's going to be a great performance. I can feel it. Kash points at Farrah and me as he asks the audience to give the bartenders a round of applause for keeping everyone happy. He winks at me and heads over to his piano bench. Farrah nudges me with her hip.

"Snap out of it," she says, handing me two orders as she takes her two and starts working on them.

Snap out of what? What was I doing? I decide to let it go and get to work on my drinks — five mixed drinks for table nine.

Kash's and Silas's first song is "I'm Still Standing" by Elton John, and the crowd loves them. Everyone is singing, including Farrah and me as we hustle behind the bar. Their voices are amazing, soaring through the atmosphere, while the piano keys explode, giving me goosebumps all over my body. For the next song, Silas picks one from the glass jar of requests and hands it to Kash. He reads it, and smiling brightly, he throws his head back and laughs, showing Silas the request. *Oh, this is going to be good,* I think to myself.

"Ok, next up is our first request, 'I Wanna Dance with Somebody' by Whitney Houston," Silas announces as the crowd claps and yells with excitement. Farrah and I exchange a laugh. As I slip a bottle of tequila back to its spot, I glance up to see Blonde Guy from table four standing at the bar. My stomach flips, and my heart starts beating really fast. My anxiety begins to build. I do what Janie told me to do when I begin to get anxious. Take a breath. Hold it. Release it slowly. He's just a person. Yes, he's a stranger, but that doesn't mean he has bad intentions — something I tell myself but don't really believe.

"Hi, I'm Sam," Blonde Guy says, stretching out his hand to shake mine. I wipe my hands on my apron and shake his back.

"Summer," I say with a weak smile.

"Summer. I like that." He sounds genuine, like he really does like my name. I immediately start thinking of a way to end this conversation.

"Well, I'm working so…" I trail off, hoping he'll get the hint.

"Oh, right, right. Of course. I know. I was just hoping maybe we could talk after your shift." He says it like it's a question, as if he's nervous about my response.

"Uh, maybe," I say, smiling obnoxiously and turning to walk away. When I turn away, I make a face to myself, rolling my eyes, thinking — *Why are you like this?*

"Smooth," I hear Farrah whisper to me as she makes her way down the bar. I groan. *Why can't I just be normal?* I think, as I shudder, trying to shake away the embarrassment.

I decide that when the night is over, I'll head over to table four with Farrah, because I can't imagine doing that alone, and say hello to Blonde Guy — I mean *Sam*. I will say hello and see where that takes me. I push my worries about situation out of my head and bring myself back to the present, where we now have three new drink slips to work on.

I glance over at the tip jar. It's eight o'clock now, and it's already filled to where it usually is at ten some nights. Some patrons have started coming up to the bar to order instead of ordering from their servers. I start thinking of all the things I can get this week with these tips: healthy groceries, a new book, a shirt I've been eyeing on Prime. Good tip nights are such a relief these days. Caught up in my thoughts again, I shake myself back to the present and hear Kash belting out the words to "Piano

Man" while banging on his keys, sweat forming on his face, his hair pulled back into a small bun. He must really be feeling the heat up there.

As the song continues, the words echo around me, and I can't take my eyes off Kash and Silas. It is absolutely mesmerizing. They smile at each other as they duel each verse then sing the chorus together. The audience is into it too, singing along, their arms waving in the air, feeling every part of the performance.

As the song comes to an end, I wish it could go on forever. But, of course, it can't. Nothing perfect ever lasts. But at the same time, terrible things don't either. When I was young, I remember feeling like the bad things would never go away — when my dad was hurting my momma or me, it felt like it would last forever, as if it would never be over. Or when I'd lay awake at night in my borrowed bed at the Brickman's, praying for sleep that never came, I'd feel an emptiness that felt infinite. But now, here I am, enjoying the most beautiful song, surrounded by people I am growing to love deeply. Those bad things didn't last forever. I am not still in that bed, feeling all alone, or huddled in my closet, hiding from my dad. That part of my life is long gone, even though it tries its very best to weave its way back into every facet of my being.

I realize the memories, the triggers, are there, trying to push their way to the forefront of my brain, and I frown. I try to shake them off, but at first, it doesn't work. These thoughts are invasive and when they take over, it can make me forget where I am and what's going on around me. As the memories woosh through my head, they block out the sounds surrounding me...until I hear my name.

"Summer, are you ok?" I look up and see Silvia eyeing me with concern.

"Oh, yes, of course. I'm good," I say to her, moving my body so I look productive as I regroup.

"Honey, what's wrong?" Silvia asks, looking at me lovingly. She's not trying to pry. But despite her kind and loving intentions, my anxiety flares and my desire to shut out the world brings on a sense of panic.

"Nothing," I snap. "I need some air. Can you please cover for me for a sec?" I ask, with more gentleness, feeling guilty for my outburst. Silvia doesn't deserve that.

"Sure, sure, dear," Silvia says, opening up the bar door and stepping inside to take my place. I run out of the dining room and into the kitchen, out the door, and into the side alley. Once I'm finally outside, I put my hands on my knees and take some deep breaths.

I have no idea how I got to this point from just a simple memory, a thought, a reminder of what life used to be like. But thinking about my past will do that to me. I spent many years with the Brickman's, some not so terrible, others horrendous. And the worst part of my time with them still eats away at me. I've never talked about it, not even with Janie. I've bottled it up and hidden it away in the furthest part of my heart, under all the knicks and broken pieces, because there, it can't hurt me. At least that's what I've told myself all this time. But even with it locked up for no one to see, I'm still broken.

As I take calculated, deep breaths, I listen to the sounds of the city around me. Sirens, car horns, conversations that I can't quite make out. It smells like gasoline mixed with fresh air. Slowly, my breathing becomes steadier, my breaths, deeper. I can get the air all the way in now, and I can push it out with control. I've successfully calmed myself down during my anxiety attack. I rest my hands on my hips, looking out toward the main street.

"Hey," I hear coming from the direction of the door. I turn quickly and see Kash standing there. "Silvia said you were out here. We're on a set break, and I went to the bar to get a drink from my favorite bartender, but I didn't see you." He's rambling on until he sees my eyes and understands that I wasn't just taking a leisurely break. "Are you ok? Do you need anything? Or nothing at all?" he asks gently.

Oh, ya know, I just had a panic attack.

"I'm good," I say quietly, smiling at him as I walk toward the door he's holding open. "Just needed some air."

I step back into the dining room to see that the set break has, of course, caused a massive line to form at the bar. I run to get back there and help. Silvia is busting her ass to help Farrah, and when I return, she offers to stay with us until Kash and Silas return to the stage and the line dissipates. Farrah winks at me and I give her a smile. Even though she doesn't know many of the details about my past, she knows it was awful, and her willingness to not ask questions but welcome me with open arms, is something I am beyond grateful for. The impatient crowd waiting for their drinks snaps me back to reality, and I jump right into the hustle and bustle of the evening.

As Kash announces their return to the stage, the rush starts dying down. For their first song back, they begin to play "Friends in Low Places," and the crowd whistles and claps as they get going. I look up at my next customer and notice it's Sam, Blonde Guy.

"Oh, hey again. What can I get you?" I ask with a smile, a little more genuine this time around. "A few hours of showing an out-of-towner your favorite things in the city tomorrow?" Sam asks, beaming his bright teeth. I whip my head around to get Farrah's attention, but she's pretending not to be listening, even though I know she heard every word.

"Um. Sure. I guess that would be fine," I say, knowing I can't come up with a believable excuse that quickly.

"Awesome! Want to meet here, say around two?"

"Sounds good," I say, giving a nervous smile.

He orders a beer and pays, leaving a generous tip. I throw the change in the jar as he walks backwards a few steps, smiling at me before turning toward his table.

Before I even have a second to regret what I just said, Farrah is already making her way to me, ready to pop a bottle of champagne.

I shake my head at her. "I don't want to hear it," I say, laughing.

"Oh, come on. This is exciting! He won't be in town long. It will just be a fun fling. Enjoy it, Summer!"

"You're right. Live life, isn't that what you always say?"

"Right!"

Before I know it, it's one in the morning, and Kash and Silas are waving their arms in the air while the audience gives them a standing ovation. Last call has long passed, and Farrah and I are cleaning up our station — wiping things down, putting stuff away, mopping up the sticky floor. Sam and his group left about an hour ago but not before stopping by the bar to say goodnight and "see ya tomorrow." I have to admit, he seems charming and nice, and I don't have any expectations for how this has to go, because it's not like I'll see him again since he's not a local. As the place clears out, I watch Maverick and the barbacks stacking chairs and laughing. *Mav must be so proud of this place*; I think to myself.

After everything is cleaned up, we gather around the bar to split the tips, as we do at the end of every shift. Farrah and I relish in our loot — $551 each, the most I've ever made in one single night.

"Don't you think you should share that with us?" Silas says, jokingly.

"Oh, please," starts Farrah. "How much did you get in your jar with all those requests?" she asks loudly.

"A lot," Silas admits, beaming a gigantic smile and we all laugh.

"It was a great night, guys. Good work. I love you all." Maverick is such a softy, and we all love him for it — for creating a safe and fun atmosphere where we can all be together.

"It *was* a great night. Summer got a date for tomorrow," says Farrah excitedly. The group starts to whistle and hoot. My face grows red, and I feel like my stomach is going to drop out of the bottom of me. I look around to see everyone smiling in my direction. Kash is smiling, too, but there is something else in his look that I can't quite pinpoint. Is it sadness? No, it can't be. He doesn't like me like that. He can't like me like that. I need him to be my friend. I can't lose him as a friend because he's bothered about my date.

"Stop it, everyone," I blurt out. "It's one date, and it means nothing except that Farrah thinks it's the best thing for me right now...to go on a date with a random person who doesn't even live in this state." I look at her with an annoyed expression and she bats me away.

After I shut down the excitement, everyone starts side conversations — Maverick talks to Silas, Silvia to J.J. and Whitney, Farrah to Kash. I hang up my apron and make my way to Farrah, who is driving me home tonight.

"I'm heading out. Bye, ladies," Kash announces. "I'm beat from this wild night. See y'all later." He raises his voice for the last part so everyone can hear as he walks out the door, his hands in his pockets. Everyone follows his lead, and we say bye as we make our way to the door. As I watch Kash walk by the windows, I can't ignore this sinking feeling that I've just lost him. But I have no idea why I feel this way.

After Farrah drops me off and we say goodbye, I sit down on the steps in front of my apartment for a minute. I pull my knees to my chest, wrap my arms around them, and rest my chin on top. Looking upward, my eyes gaze at the velvety sky and I take it all in. It's so vast, so encompassing. I imagine myself floating up there, being weightless, where nothing can touch me, nothing can trigger me. I think back to when I told Kash that having the faith to work toward my dream of being a songwriter would be a sign that I was actually healing. I'm not even sure it's true, but tomorrow I'm going to attempt it; I plan to buy a notebook to start songwriting, or at least jotting things down.

My gaze stays locked on the stars, appreciating the specks for all that they are. I count a few for good measure, searching for the brightest one I can find. It's two in the morning, and I should be in bed, so I walk up the steps and head to my little apartment, where I feel cozy and safe.

I walk in, shut the door, and lean my back against it for a moment, feeling tired from the excitement and adrenaline of the night. But even as tired as I feel, I dread getting into bed and lying there unable to sleep. Before my thoughts can take over and stir up my anxiety, I stop them in their tracks. I don't want to anticipate failure. My inability to settle into restorative sleep has haunted me since I was a child, but I know that I need to have faith that things can change, no matter how hard it seems. My struggles seem to define me, there is no denying that, but I don't want to live with fear and dread any longer. I don't want to be scared of laying my head down at night.

I take a breath and head to my room to change into sweatpants, and I pull an oversized crew neck over my head. I take my French braids out and shake my hair loose, rubbing my scalp then put it up in a loose, messy bun. I make a cup of herbal tea and turn off the overhead light, turning on the lamp. I'm attempting to create a calm environment, preparing myself for a good night's sleep. I try not to let my mind wander to the fact that I have to meet up with Sam tomorrow.

I send Kash a text before heading to bed.

Great job tonight, Kash. You are a rockstar.

He immediately texts back.

Thanks. Glad you had fun :)

I don't want to read too much into it, so I leave it be and take myself to bed.

I only sleep for a few hours when I wake up around four-thirty, grab some water, and toss and turn for a bit, my mind racing with random thoughts and ideas, before I finally fall back asleep.

When I start to wake to the sounds of birds and the light streaming through my blinds, I stretch a little and squint to look at the clock. It's 9:02 a.m., and with a few hours before my date with Sam, my plan is to busy myself with mindless tasks to keep from overthinking about it.

An hour later, I'm pushing a grocery cart through Kroger. My pace is slow, and I'm picking up random items, inspecting them, and putting them back on the shelf. I want to buy healthy food with my tips from last night, but here I am eyeing the packages of cookies, crackers, and snacks. I'm having a hard time committing to anything. The only thing in my cart is a container of oat milk. I push air into my cheeks as I breathe out and force myself to the outer realms of the store to try and find something fresh.

After a few more minutes of wandering around the store, I settle on some ingredients to make a salad, a bottle of olive oil and vinegar, a whole chicken, some frozen turkey burgers, a dozen eggs, some yogurt, a box of herbal tea, a bag of coffee, and a frozen pizza for good measure.

As I head back toward the entrance, I see a mom pushing a cart, her little girl sitting in the front, facing her. As she's shopping, the woman is going on and on about the little girl, fawning over her as if she's the most important person on the planet. She's showering her with all of her praise and affirmation. The little girl, who's maybe four years old, giggles at her mom as her little legs swing back and forth, soaking in all that love and attention. I wonder to myself how this happens. How is it that this mother loves her child with all her heart, looking at her with those adoring eyes? And then, as I tend to do frequently, I wonder what was wrong with me that made me so unlovable to all of those people who were supposed to care for me when I was a child.

I follow them to the register, not intentionally but because we are both heading to the checkout. I get behind them in line, still mesmerized by their display of love. A memory of my own mother flashes across my mind, from a time when I was happy. It's fuzzy, like an old movie, but I can see a smile on my face and on Momma's. I can't tell where we are, but I think I'm five or six. My momma swings me around, and we dance in the grass. Then the old movie reel spins, and my dad is in the image, the memory turns dark, and I snap back into the grocery store. My brain snatched me away before I went too far down into the memory, saving me from facing that trauma, something it's done my whole life. I grab a Snickers off the rack and throw it into the cart with all my vegetables. I deserve it.

After I drop the groceries at my apartment, I head back out to grab some bobby pins at Walgreens. I pass the stationary aisle, see the journals and notebooks, and stop. It reminds me that I told myself I would start working on my songwriting, and this might motivate me to get started — something eye-catching to write in. I grab a notebook and some pens.

I promise myself that I won't let it just gather dust on my coffee table, and I pay for my things and head home again.

When I get home, I jump in the shower. Sam wants me to show him around town so I start thinking of some fun things we could do together that are uniquely local. Too bad he doesn't know that I'm practically a recluse, so I don't have much to offer him in the way of socializing. Since I'm not one for getting out and having fun, I text Farrah for help. She'll know what we could do together.

You have to help me. It's your fault I'm in this mess. Blondie wants me to take him around to some cool local places. I'm not cool and I don't do things, so what am I supposed to do? Take him to Starbucks?

She texts me back so quickly that I'm not even sure if my text fully made its way into her phone.

First of all...Sam. His name's Sam. Stop calling him Blondie. Second...take him to Alessia's! Barb will be thrilled.

I roll my eyes. Barb will make a scene and I'll feel uncomfortable, but right now, I think it's my only option. Another text from Farrah comes in.

And don't say Starbucks. You could take him to our coffee shop over on Second Street. That's local and the best one in town. Coffee and lunch at Alessia's sounds like a good date to me!

She's lying, and I love her for that. This is not her idea of a good date. If this were her, she'd be taking him to some of the best country bars in town, or to the cool outdoor bar on the river downtown, or even bull riding. Farrah would leave no stone unturned if she had a date with an out of towner. But that's the difference between her and me. She knows that, for me, this is about as good as it's going to get, it's about all I can manage. I'm only doing this to prove to myself that I can physically get out of my comfort zone and go on a date with a complete stranger.

Farrah tells me to call her after the date, and I promise I will. I head to my closet and throw on some high-waisted shorts and a flowy white shirt that I got at Marshall's a few weeks ago then slip on some flip-flops. I put my long hair in a French braid, grab my sunglasses and crossbody bag, and head out the door. Farrah would cringe if she knew I hadn't even looked in the mirror or put on makeup. But it's 1:54 p.m. I'm going to be late.

Sam is standing outside of Sullivan's when I turn the corner of Brattle Street. He sees me and waves, looking elated that I actually showed up now that it's passed the time we said we would meet.

"Sorry I'm late," I say as I approach him.

"Not a problem." He's beaming. "Thanks for agreeing to show me around," Sam says, his hands in his pocket.

I smile embarrassingly. "About that," I start. "I'm not the most exciting person. I don't go out much. But I do have a favorite coffee shop and a favorite diner that has the best French toast I have ever had...and bottomless mimosas," I add, hoping it's enough to entertain him.

"Sounds good," he says. "Which way do we go?"

I point to the side of the street that heads deeper into the city, and we start moving that way. "So, are you here on business?" I ask, moving my sunglasses up on my head as we move into the shade.

"Yeah, I'm heading out tomorrow. Back to Chicago." I nod, and he continues talking, and I'm grateful that he's taking the lead in the conversation. He doesn't know how utterly exhausting this is for me. "My team and I got here Tuesday. We didn't do much except work and then ate dinner at the hotel each night. But Friday was amazing! Sullivan's is the best dueling piano bar I have ever been to."

How many of those could you possibly have been to? I wonder, but I keep it to myself.

"The energy, the performers, the ambiance...it was all perfect," Sam adds, his face lighting up.

"I love it too. But for different reasons," I offer, shrugging my shoulders.

"What's that?" he asks, genuinely interested.

"They are my family. I don't know where I would be without the people who work there." I say it without any sort of emotion, just the facts, because I don't want him to pry and ask questions about my actual family.

"You did seem to get along really well," he says and I smile and nod because I don't have anything else to add. A girl of few words.

We walk another minute and then I point to Alessia's.

"We're here," I say.

Sam looks up at the sign and squints into the sunlight, putting his hand over his eyes to read it. "Oh, the diner first?"

"I'm hungry," I respond, shrugging and pulling the door open, not waiting for him to do it. He smiles and we head in.

Barb spots me immediately and heads over to wrap me in an embrace. "Dear! It's so good to see you! And who is this fella?" she asks, beaming at Sam.

"This is Sam. He's visiting from Chicago, and he came into Sullivan's last night," I say. They shake hands.

"It's nice to meet you." Sam greets her with a smile.

"Likewise," Barb responds, ushering us over to mine and Farrah's regular table. She hands us menus and lets us know that she'll be back momentarily to take our order.

"Barb is the best," I say, opening my menu, even though I know what I'm getting — French toast with a side of fruit, cinnamon oatmeal, and a bottomless grapefruit mimosa.

"It seems like everyone is so friendly here," Sam acknowledges, looking directly at me. He really is handsome. At least I can admit that. I shrug my shoulders as if to agree. I know Sam's right, even if I don't have the emotional capacity to notice and appreciate friendly gestures. Of the few places I have been, Texas is the friendliest.

"People aren't friendly in Chicago?" I ask curiously.

He shrugs. "No, they are, I guess," he says. "But everyone's always rushing around. Everyone wants to just get to the next thing. No one is looking up and smiling at each other like I have experienced here."

"Would you ever leave? Pick a new city to live in and find some smiling people?" I ask this jokingly and his response throws me.

"When pigs fly, I'll leave Chicago," he smirks, glancing out the window.

My body freezes as I stare at him. "Don't get me wrong..." he continues, raving about Chicago, but I'm not listening.

I'm gone.

CHAPTER 13

Kentucky - Then

"WHEN PIGS FLY," I heard Gina quietly say to Cassie from my perch on the top step. They were talking about finding a permanent home for me. Momma continued not to do what she was supposed to do to get me back, and I started to hear the word adoption being thrown around when I wasn't supposed to be listening. "It's going to be really hard to find a home for her at this age and with her history of running away," Gina added.

A scowl came over my face. *History?* That happened one time, and running away one time hardly constituted a history. Why was all of this being put on me? Why was it my fault? I didn't want to run away. But I felt like I had no choice because they had left me in a terrible situation. And there that phrase was again — *when pigs fly*. First my dad, then Sarah, and now Gina. No one ever had any faith or hope in me or my situation. Gina was basically saying: *When pigs fly, Summer will find a family who loves her.*

When I first came back to the Brickmans after running away on Thanksgiving last year, everyone was mad and disappointed, giving me cold shoulders and silent treatments. But then, things suddenly changed, and everyone was overly nice, walking on eggshells to not upset me. I had no idea what the reason was for the change, but I didn't care either way. I just kept to myself, stayed in my own lane. It seemed safer that way.

It had been seven months since the incident and it was now July. In that time, I'd seen my momma three times for supervised visitation. I wondered when I would see her again.

I decided to ask Gina myself when I could see her, so I walked loudly down the stairs, trying to make my presence known. Their heads whipped toward the staircase as they heard me coming, and they immediately stopped talking about the fact that no one would ever want to adopt me. I saw it on their faces: pity. One of the worst feelings in the world is when you can see on someone's face that they feel bad for you, that they're glad they aren't you, that they wouldn't trade places with you for a single second. I saw those looks on their faces, and never wanted to see them again.

"When can I see Momma?" I asked. Gina and Cassie looked at me sadly.

"Next week, actually," Gina said. "I'll pick you up on Tuesday at two-thirty. Does that sound good?" I nodded and headed toward the kitchen, looking for a snack, but mostly I just wanted to get out of their presence. Claire was sitting at the table, drawing on her sketch pad. I glanced over her shoulder to see her picture.

"Wow, that's cool," I offered, trying to be nice but, also, really meaning it. She had talent.

"Thanks," she replied with a smile.

Claire and I were on better terms since the incident last year and the rumor she heard (or started; I still wasn't sure) about me and her brother dating. We were back to sharing pleasantries and the books we were reading, and Claire started gushing to me about Trevor again. Over the summer, they only talked through instant messenger, but when we were at school they were always together. I would always let her talk to me about him; sometimes, I would listen, and other times my brain would wander to more important things, like where my momma was or what would happen to me if I never found a family.

Claire and I were complete opposites in every possible way. I couldn't fathom only ever worrying about when the next time I would be able to talk to a certain boy. And in all fairness, she couldn't fathom being beaten and left to the wolves by her own parents. She would never understand having her father die and feeling relieved by the news. I guess we had a mutual understanding, but, either way, things were more comfortable between us in recent months and that was good for me.

Jason and I were still close. He was the only one who stood up for me after the whole Thanksgiving debacle. When I was grounded for hitchhiking, he brought me snacks and books to pass the time. Yes, they grounded me for running away. Instead of explaining to me about trauma responses, like fight or flight, and helping me understand why I reacted the way I did, they just punished me. They kept me locked in my room to learn a lesson, and refused to ask me how I was feeling. Maybe they were afraid of my answers. No one knew what to do with me — the poor foster girl from the south side of town. My actions weren't my fault; they were just my reactions to the situation they put me in, but it took years for me to figure that out.

I grabbed a snack and some water before sitting down at the table across from Claire while she did her art. Gina and Cassie sauntered into the kitchen after a few minutes — Gina to say goodbye and Cassie to start dinner.

"I'll see you next week, Summer," Gina said, giving me a wave. I nodded but didn't look up from my cup of water. "I hope you enjoy your week," she added, heading toward the front door.

Yeah, I will. When pigs fly.

I kept those thoughts to myself.

CHAPTER 14

Texas - Now

"**E**ARTH TO SUMMER."

I snap back to reality: I'm sitting in my favorite booth at Alessia's with a stranger who's trying to get my attention.

"Oh, shit, sorry," I say, grabbing the mimosa I don't even remember Barb bringing over. I take a sip. "I zoned out there for a second." I give Sam an apologetic smile.

Suddenly, I feel like I can't manage this awkward date. My brain is not in the right space right now — my memories are fluttering about in my brain, threatening to rear their ugly heads, and to be honest, I am just not that into this date. But I stay. Because I can't run from my memories. I can't let them take me away from the present. So, I try. I try to enjoy Sam's company, if for no other reason than to prove to myself that I don't have to run to the comforts of my apartment at any sign of a trigger.

"So, tell me about your family," Sam says, leaning back in the booth. I stare at him, and he waits for me to respond. "Do you get along? Do you have siblings? A crazy uncle?" He chuckles, not a care in the world. My body goes stiff, and I feel bad that Sam doesn't know what he just did. My face remains unchanged. "Favorite vacation?" he asks, grasping for straws.

Well, I guess that's the end of my best efforts. I grab my crossbody and pull out a twenty that I earned last night and throw it on the table.

"I'm sorry. I have to go." I feel obnoxious, but I need to leave, and I don't know any other way than to just remove myself from the situation as quickly as possible. I practically trip getting to the door. I push it open and hear the bell jingling as I walk out of the diner and onto the sidewalk, swiftly heading toward my apartment.

Once I am out of sight, I slow down. Tell him about my family? What family? I remember when I was younger, people always referred to the Brickmans as my family. But in that house, I was treated like an outsider. Cassie and Greg were never my parents; they were just Claire and Jason's parents. Everyone said how lucky I was to live with them, but I didn't feel that way. I wasn't appreciative of the family I was plopped into. I was confused. I didn't feel lucky, no matter how many different people said that to me. Would those people who said this to me feel lucky if they were taken from their families and forced to assimilate into another one as if it wasn't a big deal? As if it wasn't traumatic?

Eventually I started to let my guard down in that house when things started going smoothly for a while. It was as if I was being conditioned to *believe* I was lucky for the circumstances I was in. There was a time period, however brief, where I settled into comfort with the Brickmans. Sometimes I wish I didn't do that, but my walls were not as strong, not as high, back then as they are now. Maybe if I had protected my heart more, the things that spiraled out of control after that year wouldn't have happened. I will never know if things would have been different, but it still eats away at me.

CHAPTER 15

Kentucky - Then

I STARED AT THE building where Momma was waiting for me.

"Are you ready?" Gina asked me as she unbuckled her seat belt. I nodded once and undid mine then stepped out of the car and began walking toward the door. I hadn't seen my momma in a few months so the anxious feelings that had been building all week began to twist my stomach into knots.

The lobby was abuzz with foster kids, case workers, and parents. All the adults looked tired, and the kids looked revved up.

I saw my momma immediately, sitting on a bench toward the back. She looked like a shadow of the momma who once protected me, even worse than she'd looked the last time I saw her.

She brightened slightly when she saw me, but the gesture seemed to zap all of her energy. She got up from the bench and walked toward me with her arms outstretched.

"My baby," she said, her voice raspy, hoarse from chain-smoking and whatever else she was doing these days.

"Hi," I said, barely audible.

Gina led us to a room in the back where we could sit and visit for an hour.

"How's school? Are you staying out of trouble? Getting good grades? It's important, you know." She was rambling. Did she think she even had the right to try and parent me at this point?

"Yup," I said unenthusiastically. "Are you working?" I questioned her, fiddling with a pen that was on the table. She didn't answer right away.

"Honey. No. I injured my back real bad and haven't had the ability to..." She stopped when I abruptly got up from the chair and walked toward the door.

"I'm going to the bathroom," I mumbled as I opened the door and slammed it behind me.

When I got back, my body was more relaxed, but I was unable to wipe the scowl off my face. I was only fourteen but I could smell an adult's bullshit from a mile away. "You aren't ever going to get me back, and you don't care, do you?" I said the words without emotion. They were just facts. She had gone past the point of no return, and I knew it. I was tired of getting my hopes up, just to have them dashed. How long was everyone going to continue stringing me along?

"I do care, Summer!" She wailed with the dramatics of a toddler. She began to cry and wanted me to console her, but I didn't have it in me. All the compassion I had for her was gone. I looked at her, her eyes sagging and wet, her hair matted and dirty, her clothes unwashed and worn. I felt bad, but I was so mad at her. I was the child. She was the adult. So why did it feel the other way around?

"Where are you even living?" I asked, my voice starting to rise again.

"With Mike," she said. "You know Mike." She sounded hopeful as if this tidbit of information would win me over.

"How the hell would I know Mike, Momma?" I asked through gritted teeth. "I'm out there, all alone," I said, pointing to the abyss. "And you're with MIKE, whoever the hell that is. We are in different worlds, and you refuse to fight for me."

"No, no, baby. Mike is good. He has a job. He works at the mechanic shop around the corner; you know the one?" Again, she sounded desperate.

"Does he know about me?" I asked, staring out the window, my voice sounding far off. She stared at me, defeated. I got up aggressively from my seat again. "I'm done with this shit," I mustered as a tear began forming in the back of my eye, but I was determined that I wouldn't let it out. I left the room without giving her a second glance and walked swiftly back to Gina's car.

The next day, I was sprawled on my bed writing poems and phrases in my notebook after school when Cassie gently knocked on my bedroom door and came in, taking a seat on the edge of my bed.

"Hi, sweetie," she said in a voice barely above a whisper.

"Hi," I responded, not looking up from my journal.

"Gina called today and told me that you were upset after seeing your mom yesterday." She waited for me to acknowledge but I didn't. "Do you want to talk about it?" I shook my head. "Ok, well I won't say I understand. Because I don't, and I won't pretend to, but I'm here if you need me, Summer. If you need someone to talk to. Ok?" She sounded desperate for me to give her some sort of loving response or embrace her. I had no idea what was going on. Was she extending an olive branch?

Was she feeling guilty for offering her home to a kid like me and then not being able to give me what I needed? Was she feeling bad that she grounded me for running away when they ditched me for a rumor that wasn't even true?

"Ok," I responded, looking up at her.

She patted my leg. "Dinner will be ready in thirty minutes." She got up from my bed and walked out of the room.

I allowed myself to accept Cassie's words, if for nothing else then to be able to relax around the dinner table and enjoy a meal together. It had been three years, and I still felt like I was just a friend of the Brickman children spending a few too many nights at their house. As we all heaped food onto our plates and got settled around the table, Greg spoke up.

"So, kids, we are taking an end-of-summer trip," he began. All three of us looked over at him. Claire and Jason looked with anticipation and excitement to find out where we were going. I was holding my breath, trying not to bring attention to myself and hoping maybe they would forget that I didn't belong and invite me along. I was stiff and my face began to grow red and hot.

"Where, where, where?" Claire begged her dad to tell her.

"Summersaults!" he announced. The waterpark, the place everyone had been talking about for the last two years since it was built, was constructed to look like volcanic land with steep slides and multiple pools with different functions.

Jason and Claire gave each other high fives and started to celebrate. I sat motionless, waiting for someone to address me.

"Are you excited, Summer?" Cassie asked with added enthusiasm. I suddenly realized they were bringing me, and I allowed a smile to peek through. What was this feeling I was having inside? I felt full of anticipation, and it was the most positive feeling I could recall in three years.

We still had two and a half weeks left of summer, and we were spending four whole days at Summersaults in a lodge right on the premises. My mind couldn't even fathom what it was going to be like. I just sat there while Claire and Jason commented on how they bet it was going to be like the waterpark they went to in Florida once. I couldn't relate since I'd hardly been anywhere. But this time, I was finally going to get to experience a vacation for once, and the memories of this anticipation are now some of the only positive memories I have from my childhood.

Janie once told me that anticipation is the greatest form of motivation and hope, and I agree with her because of this trip. My appreciation of the Brickman's for including me in the vacation trumped any feelings of abandonment I had toward them. And now that they had included me, I never even thought that these feelings might not last. I never even thought I'd have to hold tight to the happiness I felt because I didn't realize then just how fleeting it would be.

On the way to the waterpark, Claire and I sat in the back of the SUV while Jason sat in the middle, listening to music through his headphones. Greg drove, and Cassie was in the passenger seat bopping along to the music. I was so excited since I'd never been on a real road trip before. I watched as the trees whisked past my window until I got dizzy and had to stop. Then I grabbed my journal out of my backpack and began scribbling notes, jotting poems and lyrical phrases to pass the time. Before I knew it, we were there.

As we drove up to the resort, I could see the tips of the "mountains" poking out behind a tall gate, keeping the amusement park hidden. I watched as we passed the fence, heading toward our lodge at the other end of the massive parking lot. I rolled the window down and heard the sounds of music, people screaming in delight from the slides, waves splashing. I was mesmerized.

After we got checked in and found our rooms, we dumped our luggage in our designated spaces — kids in one room, Cassie and Greg in the other. I plopped my bag on the floor next to a bed and walked over to the window, taking my gaze out across the lot to the entrance of the waterpark. I felt my mouth curve into a smile. I couldn't believe I was there, that I was doing something so exciting. I looked back over my shoulder into the room. It was simple and clean, and smelled like carpet scrub and Pine-Sol.

My smile faded as I recalled the one other time I was in a hotel...or *motel* is a better word for what it was. I was seven, maybe eight years old and Momma had rushed me out of the house after one of Dad's benders. He was threatening her...yelling and throwing things. We had walked into the shabby room, the door squeaking shut behind us. Momma tried to make it fun, but it was anything but enjoyable; excitement ruined by Momma's swollen, tearstained face and her excessive fixation with looking out the window. The motel room smelled like it had fresh cigarettes in an ashtray because it did, on the nightstand right next to where I laid my head for the night. All night, I stared up at the ceiling, wondering what the hell was going on.

It was nothing like this room at Summersaults.

"Are you ready?" Claire's voice pulled me from my trance.

I smiled at her, giving her a nod.

We couldn't wait to hit the waterpark. Everyone changed and we met in the lobby to walk over together. Claire and I were just in our bathing suits, but we were holding our towels. I noticed Jason looked over at me and did a double take. At first, I thought I was seeing things but then I realized he had definitely given me a strange look. I gave him a questioning look back, and he quickly turned his head away from me and toward the direction we were walking. I looked down at myself and suddenly felt very self-conscious. My body had changed a lot over the last three years. I was growing up, getting more developed, looking less like a girl and more like a woman. Until that moment when my foster brother gave me a once over, I'd never really noticed or even cared that much about the changes. I wrapped my towel around my body for the remainder of the walk and decided to forget about Jason. I was his friend, a friend who happened to be a girl, who happened to live in his house and wasn't his sister. Maybe he was just surprised. I gave him the benefit of the doubt.

When we made it past the gates and into the park, the three of us posed for a picture in front of the wave pool. As Cassie adjusted the lens, we draped our arms around each other, and I thought of Lily Sanderson from the first grade. Lily and her vacation pictures that planted envy in my little heart, back when I thought I would never get to go on my own vacation. And here I was.

When those pictures were developed after we got home from our trip, my smile was enormous, my eyes were squinting in the bright sun. I looked like a carefree teenager. Even though that picture wasn't framed and hanging on the wall, it still existed and that was enough proof for me that it had actually happened. It wasn't a dream.

The experience of the trip was so surreal. I looked around at Claire and Jason and all the other kids and noticed that I was feeling just like them: elated, happy, fulfilled. The only difference between them and me was that I was spending a massive amount of time contemplating how foreign this feeling was to me. It was like I was having an out-of-body experience, and I was floating above the crowd watching myself enjoy this vacation. I truly was having the best time. Claire and I went down so many slides together and the three of us wore ourselves out in the wave pool.

After a full day at the park, we were tired, so we ordered takeout for dinner. We sat around the common room in Cassie and Greg's little suite, eating pizza but barely chewing, instead almost swallowing it whole because we were all so famished from a day in the hot Kentucky sun. My cheeks were touched by the sun, and the rest of my skin felt tight and warm. I was tired and completely relaxed. After we ate, Greg pulled out a deck of cards, and we played Crazy Eights at the little coffee table. I felt like I was part of the family. We laughed and joked until we couldn't keep our eyes open anymore.

We headed to bed, and I was sure that the exhaustion would help me fall asleep quickly, but I was wrong. I lay awake for a long time, staring at the ceiling, thinking about this perfect day and wondering if maybe the Brickmans would adopt me, to officially make me a part of their family. They say that relentless hope is a means to survival. And that glimmer of hope I concocted that night carried me through the following year.

I had given up on my momma long before I was in the ninth grade, but giving up on someone and accepting it are not the same thing. I always felt so guilty that I had given up on her; I was the last person she had in her corner cheering for her, and there I was, letting go. And if I was letting go, what was going to happen to her? I had lost all hope of her getting me back. She just didn't have it in her anymore. I was aware enough to understand that it was never going to happen. Not only was I riddled with guilt about my mom, but I was constantly anxious about what was going to become of me, and my body bore the weight of that worry and guilt.

When I started high school that year, it wasn't much different than the year before because I was still at the same school. I was still playing volleyball, and that year I'd made the varsity team. I'd prided myself on busting my ass the year before when I was on JV, on and off the bench, to earn a seat on the varsity team.

People at school still acted like they were afraid of me. They would smile and wave but then walk away quickly. To them, I was unapproachable, and that was okay with me. I didn't need any more friends. Jason and I were still close, and we started hanging out together outside of school a lot with Dan and Meg and a few more of Jason's friends. I had my crew, and I didn't let anyone else in. Claire and I didn't hang out much, but we still got along. We had different interests and different friends, and I think she finally started to accept that.

It was November before the whole family finally came to one of my varsity games for the first time. I could hear them cheering for me and I felt unimaginable pride. I was drenched in sweat from playing almost the whole game, pouring my heart and soul into every play.

It was time for the final set, and it was my serve. I set it up and sailed the ball over the net, a perfect serve. After a few minutes of play, we scored the winning point. The team jumped on one another, giving each other high fives, celebrating our victory. We shook hands with the opposing team before gathering for a quick meeting with our coach.

I grabbed my stuff and jogged toward the door where the Brickmans waited for me by the gym entrance. I couldn't wait to see what the family had to say about my performance.

"Amazing job, Summer," Greg said, putting his arm over my shoulder as we started walking out to the car.

"Yeah, you were aggressive," Claire said.

I let out a laugh. "I guess you could say that."

"You have great focus out there." Typical Cassie.

"Best on the team," Jason said, just to pump my tires.

"You better be careful," I said. "Might give me a big head." Everyone chuckled a bit.

"Let's grab dinner. I'm starved," Greg offered as we all climbed into the SUV.

It all felt surreal, like I was an actual part of the family. My heart was thawing. My armor, sliding off.

That holiday season, I didn't have any visits with my momma. The Brickman's weren't traveling for the holidays that year, and by default I knew that I was going to be included in their festivities. But it nagged me a little bit to think about what they would have done with me if they had chosen to go back to Florida again. Would they have taken me this time? Or would they have left me with a temporary family again? I pushed those thoughts to the back of my mind. I was in a place of hope. Hope was my drug.

KRISSY LANIER

That fall, I'd worked really hard to get good grades, I put my all into the team, and I was on best behavior at the Brickman's. I didn't know it at the time, but I was marketing myself, making myself lovable and trying to prove that I was worthy enough to be their poor man's daughter. Although I knew I didn't hold a candle to Claire, I had been with them for four years. That had to count for something.

During our freshman year, Meg and I became really close. Besides being on the volleyball team, we had study hall together and sat and whispered about the drama of high school. One day, we were sitting pretending to review our history homework, when she said something completely unexpected.

"I think Dan likes you," she said in a hushed tone while she put her name on her paper.

"Well, yeah. He's one of my best friends." I played dumb, but I knew that was not what she meant.

"No, *likes you* likes you. Like more than friends," she insisted. I made a look of disgust. Dan was like a brother to me.

"Why do you even think that?" I asked, genuinely curious.

Meg rolled her eyes. "Oh please!" she said while laughing a bit too loudly, which then warranted a glare from Mr. Winters, who stared at us over his glasses. "He always comes to our games. I see the way he looks at you. He's always looking out for your best interest, asking you how you are doing, if you need anything." She kept adding reasons as I continued to stare at her, unbelieving.

"Isn't that what friends do?"

"You're clueless," she said playfully, nudging my arm. I dismissed her comments almost immediately. It couldn't be true. Could it?

124

One night in March, Jason and I walked over to our friend Jake's house to hang out with everyone. Dan and Meg were already there along with some other people we were friends with. We sat in Jake's basement, watching basketball and eating popcorn. I sat next to Dan on the couch. Since Meg first brought up the idea that Dan liked me, I was curious to see what she was talking about because, honestly, I'd never really noticed anything.

"Hey, bud," he said to me, grabbing some popcorn. Bud? Bud was a friendly term. I settled back into the couch, my head dangerously close to his shoulder. He glanced down at me and smiled, and my breath hitched for a second. He hadn't ever looked at me like that. I didn't care what Meg had been saying for months. That look was new. I would have noticed something like that.

I smiled back at him, and our eyes stayed locked for a few moments, and then I broke eye contact as I sat up and took a deep breath. I was getting hot. I glanced over to see Jason on the love seat with the remote in his hand and saw that he was looking at us. I couldn't read his expression entirely, but I could tell it wasn't pleasant.

"I'll be back," I said, getting up and heading toward the mini fridge to grab a Sprite. Jason followed me and grabbed himself something too.

"Is something going on with you and Dan?" he just came out and asked.

"Uh. No," I responded, dragging out the *no*. "Don't you think you would know if something was?" He shrugged, looking annoyed. "Besides, why would you care?" I asked, not being rude; it's just that I wasn't sure where he was coming from. He looked a little taken aback, like he didn't know what to say.

"Uh. You're like a sister to me. Just protective, I guess," was his response. He was nonchalant about it, looking around the room casually.

"Protective about Dan?" I laughed. "He's your best friend."

He looked at me for a beat. "Yeah. Just forget I said anything." And with that he walked back to his spot on the love seat, and I was left to stand there and wonder what the hell that was all about.

———

If I could use one word to describe the remainder of that school year, it would be *pleasant*. It lacked chaos and turmoil, for the most part. The thoughts swimming around in my head continued to nag and torture me, but on the outside, things had improved. That year was filled with fond memories, some of the only positive moments from my adolescents.

It's like the universe was apologizing to me in one fell swoop, giving me a few solid moments to make up for all of the bad ones I'd faced. I stored those moments away in my mind — the six months where it didn't feel like my entire existence was in everyone else's hands. The memories may not seem overly grandiose to some people, but to me, they were silver linings in an otherwise dark and cloudy existence. These happy images of times gone by flash through my head once in a while — winning the state championship in volleyball, hanging out in Jake's basement, dinner around the Brickman's table every night, compliments from my teachers, a growing friendship with Meg, and a budding romance with Dan.

I rarely visited the roof and the stars that year. The walls I hid behind, the ones that protected me, had been crumbling throughout that year, and I settled into a comfortable life. I wish I could go back and warn that fourteen-year-old that a storm was brewing.

CHAPTER 16

Texas - Now

I WALK INTO MY apartment and take a deep breath, plopping down on the couch. While reminiscing about that year when I was content for a little while, I realized something. I was vulnerable then, when I was fourteen. I let myself feel joy, even if it was just for a small period of time. I let myself have faith, hope. I once viewed that as one of my faults, a product of being young and naive, and something that made me weak. I lived most of my teenage and adult life feeling like happiness, hope, and joy weren't for me because of all the things I'd been through. But what if my younger self had it right all along — I should let myself be vulnerable. Maybe happiness has always been within my reach. It's true that it hasn't always here, in my hands, but instead, maybe, it ebbs and flows. That would mean that if I was happy once, I could be happy again. Maybe I just need to seize my own happiness.

I immediately text Farrah.

Did not go well. My fault. I am a trauma-filled mess.

While I'm waiting for her to get back to me, I decide to send a text to Kash too.

Want to count some stars tonight?

A minute later, Farrah texts me back.

:(You are not a mess. I'll be there in 30 minutes. With refreshments.

Then Kash responds.

Sorry, Summer, I can't. I have plans tonight.

My shoulders sink. I'm about to ask him if he's being weird because of my "date" with Blondie but before I get the chance to hit send, he sends another message.

My moms in town and we are going out to dinner. Tomorrow?

I dodged a bullet there. I quickly respond.

Ok, have a great time. I'll talk to you tomorrow.

Pulling a blanket over my legs, I curl up and turn on the TV to watch *The Real Housewives of Beverly Hills* while I wait for Farrah to arrive. When she does, she bounds her way through the door carrying Pinot Grigio and bagged movie theater popcorn, my two favorites, and I grab some stemless wine glasses from the kitchen. We sit on the floor, our backs against the couch, our legs stretched under the coffee table. Farrah twists the cap off the bottle that's foggy from condensation.

"So, do you want to tell me about it?" Farrah asks, pouring the light liquid into our glasses while I grab a handful of popcorn straight from the bag. I shrug and she offers me a warm smile.

"He said something that triggered a memory, and before I knew it, I was back in the present with a mimosa sitting in front of me and I had no recollection of receiving it. He kept trying to get my attention and I was just zoned out," I tell her with a mouthful.

She rubs my back. "I'm proud of you for doing something hard. You are healing, Summer. It's just taking time and I'm here for you. I'm sorry I pushed you to go on this date. I feel bad now."

I shake my head. "Absolutely not your fault," I assure her. "You're such a good friend." She rests her head on my shoulder, and we sit in silence for a minute as the housewives argue in the background.

"There was a time when I thought my foster family was going to adopt me," I say, opening a door I'm not sure I want to pass through, but here goes.

Farrah looks at me softly with love in her eyes, and I know she's there for me and listening to every word. She nods her head once, encouraging me to go on, reassuring me it's safe to open up. Hesitating, I swirl the contents of my wine glass and, then gathering my courage, I decide to continue.

"At that point, I'd been living with them for three years. I overheard my case workers talking to my foster mother about adoption behind my back. This went on for quite a while and the whole time all I could think was *I hope they will adopt me.* Eventually they told me what was going on. I learned that for one reason or another, they didn't want to adopt me. It was never the plan, and they weren't going to change their minds." I pause for a second. "That type of heartbreak is unimaginable, ya know what I mean?" I ask in a whisper, tears pooling behind my eyes and a lump forming in my throat.

I shovel some popcorn in my mouth while playing with my wine glass, anything to keep myself from allowing the pain to break to the surface. "I'd had some trouble with my foster family the year before, but things had turned around, and I felt like I was finally a part of their family. I thought they'd feel sad that I might leave and go live with another family...forever." I take a deep breath. Farrah takes a handful of popcorn from the bowl but doesn't take her eyes off me. I feel safe with her as I feel some of the weight lifting off my shoulders.

"When was this?" she asks.

"My sophomore year of high school," I respond. "I had a great year in ninth grade and a great summer after that. We even went on a family vacation, my first real vacation ever, and we had a blast. We really bonded during that trip. I felt like I was being treated more like a daughter and less like a guest. I'd even started to let down some of the walls I'd built up to protect myself from being hurt." Farrah nods at me, intently listening. "But then, during my junior year, they...my caseworkers, began introducing me to potential families to adopt me. And it was like Cassie and Greg didn't care at all that I could be leaving. We never talked about it, they pretended like it wasn't even happening, like everything was normal. I would be shipped off at random times to meet with families, sometimes I'd be gone the whole day, and then I'd come back to the Brickman's just to lay my head on the pillow. When I couldn't sleep, I'd go sit on the roof and look at the stars, always wondering if Cassie and Greg were in bed, praying for a way to get me out of their life. Because of that rejection I was feeling, I hoped someone would pick me, just so it would relieve the Brickmans of having to take care of me since I was obviously such a burden to them. I wasn't excited about leaving them, but I felt like they had rejected me, so I wanted out, for their sake. That's pretty fucked up, isn't it?" I look over at Farrah, my eyes clouded from the tears hanging on. And I see that Farrah has tears in her eyes too. Her look isn't indulgent, it's kind. She loves me, and I know she wishes she could take away all the pain and hurt.

I grab another handful of popcorn and pop the kernels in my mouth, one by one, chewing slowly, concentrating, to avoid my tears spilling.

"So, what happened? Were you eventually adopted?" Farrah cringes, probably because she feels bad that she doesn't know these facts about me, though I wish she wouldn't. It's not her fault that I keep everyone at arm's length. But not anymore. I'm trying. Baby steps.

I shake my head slowly. "No one liked me because I sabotaged all my meetings with other families. I guess I was afraid of the unknown. But staying with a family that didn't want me wasn't good for me either. I chose to fight for the devil I knew rather than face the unknown. The Brickman's were overly nice to me that year. I'm not sure if it was because they didn't want me to blame them, or even hate them, when I got picked by a family. Or maybe they were hiding their guilt. Or they were just happy that their time with me was coming to an end." I shrug at the thoughts I've kept bottled up for so long.

"Things started to change with Claire and Jason too. Jason, my foster brother, and I had gotten close the year before all this started happening, but I started feeling like he was pulling away. Maybe it was because of all that mess, or maybe it was because I started dating his best friend, Dan." As I pause, I notice Farrah is listening with her whole body, completely engaged in my story. I continue to share, feeling lighter as I get some of this out in the open. "Then my foster sister, Claire, started acting like I was in her way, taking up space in HER bedroom, the room we'd shared the whole time. For years, she used to fawn all over me, acting like we were sisters and best friends, but she pulled away too. I went from finally feeling like I belonged to feeling as if the people around me were just trying to get rid of me once again. And I didn't know when they had changed their minds, when they decided they didn't want me to be a part of their family, but it wrecked me. I'd look in the mirror and see someone who was unwanted, all my flaws glaring back at me. Those walls I'd let down during my freshman year to allow myself to feel joy and belonging, I built them all back up. And I was locked behind those walls. I began ignoring my emotions all together, stuffing them down so I didn't have to deal with them. I just kept going through the motions so I could get by in all the other areas of my life." I take another breath, realizing how much I've just shared. Suddenly, I need a break. These moments in my childhood and adolescence shaped me into this shell of a person that I am today and reliving them hasn't seemed to help me before today. But talking about them with Kash and Farrah feels different than when I rehash them alone or even with Janie.

"How much longer did you stay with the Brickman family?" Farrah asks quietly. I look over at her and all my strength is gone. I begin to cry, the memory that's triggered begins to rip at my heart. The tears are coming down in streams, etching their way down my face. This sensation is crippling, and completely unsettling, but there is no stopping it. I rest my head on my arms, propped up on the coffee table, and let all of my emotions out. Farrah gently rubs my back, comforting me.

"I'm sorry I made you cry, Summer. Don't push yourself to answer the question. Whatever you need, I'm here." She assures me the best she can. I am done sharing, though. I've drained all of my energy; I'm sucked completely dry.

I lift my head, which seems to weigh as much as a bowling ball and feel the twinge of a headache forming. I know my eyes must be puffy and my nose, red. I'm sure I look like a mess, a mirror of how I feel.

"I can't share any more right now," I say, wiping my face with my shirt sleeve. "I need a break."

Farrah gives me a smile and grabs some tissues as I grip my glass and lean back against the couch again. I look up at the ceiling, as I take some deep breaths and try to regain my composure.

"You are the strongest person I know," offers Farrah. I close my eyes and contemplate what she's just said. I know she is being genuine but *strong* has never been a word I've associated with myself.

"Thanks, but can we talk about something else now?" I ask with a small laugh. "Like, can you tell me something about your life to make me feel a little less bad about mine?" I ask jokingly.

Farrah looks at me with all seriousness and begins to share. "Sure, I'll go. My dad cheated on my mom when I was eleven. She caught him and then begged him to go to counseling, but instead, he just up and left, started a new life with the other woman, had two more kids, and forgot all about me. I haven't talked to him in fifteen years."

We look at each other. My mouth drops open and I am lost for words. When Farrah reminisced about her life, it painted a picture of perfection. I had never imagined there was pain there. But I was wrong. I see that now. Then it hits me: how could I be so self-centered to think I was the only one with problems? Keeping my story to myself is a decision I made but not letting anyone else share their stories with me? I realize I haven't been a good friend. I pull Farrah into my embrace and hug her as tight as I can, my apology for not letting her open to me until now. But I also offer her a verbal one.

"I'm so sorry, Farrah. I'm sorry I haven't been a great friend. I'm sorry I made you feel like you couldn't confide in me or like your problems were nothing compared to mine because that's not true. Forgive me, please. I will be a better friend."

She laughs. "Summer! Stop. Listen, life is a journey, and we are at all different parts of that journey emotionally. I've moved on from what my dad did. I just wanted you to know that you aren't completely alone. Please don't bear the weight of all that happened to you all by yourself. Let me carry some of it." She smiles softly at me, and a small part of my heart warms.

I feel a connection that I've never felt before in my life. I must be making progress and that realization feels good. Even though it's completely draining to share, I'm finding out that it's also truly rewarding.

"Thank you so much for being there for me," I say to Farrah and mean it with every fiber of my being.

"Anytime," she says, and I know she means it too.

Not ready to call it a night yet, we hang out on the couch and watch some of *The Real Housewives*, laughing at their antics and taking turns refilling each other's wine glasses. And I realize, at this moment, I feel so content.

I look over at Farrah, my mouth full of popcorn. "What's Joey up to today?" I ask.

"He's helping his buddy move into a new apartment in North Austin. He won't be back until tomorrow. And we have tons of wedding stuff to do in the morning. Who knew how complicated it was to pack all the wedding planning into five or six weeks." She laughs.

"If you need help, just let me know."

"Thanks," she says. "Oh, make sure you save the date for Saturday, November 9 at four o'clock. The invites will hopefully be in the mail by the end of the weekend!" She squeals with delight. I smile my biggest grin; I'm so happy for her. She really deserves the best.

It's close to seven when Farrah suggests that we eat some real food. Not wanting to leave, we decide to order in and get a pizza and salads from A Slice of Heaven, the little hole in the wall down the street. It's been owned by the same family for decades and when you walk in there, they treat you like you are walking into their dining room for Sunday dinner. Because of this, the little place gets all of my take-out budget.

As we finish up our dinner, I'm feeling sad that our night is winding down. I'm having a really nice time bonding with Farrah. And then, as if she's read my mind, she offers, "Want me to stay the night?"

"Yes, please," I say, appreciative of not having to be alone for the evening.

"Ok, cool. But I gotta get up and leave first thing in the morning. I have to take advantage of a few days off of work to get some stuff done."

"I will kick you out, don't worry," I say with a laugh.

———

I wake up in the morning as soon as the sun starts peeking over the horizon, painting the sky purple and pink. I look over to see Farrah still sleeping, mouth agape, her auburn hair wildly spread all over her pillow.

Quietly, I get up and tiptoe into the kitchen to start the coffee. While it's brewing, I grab my new notebook that I just bought. Sitting down on the couch, I cover up with the blanket and open the journal. I start jotting down some phrases that have been bouncing around in my head for a while now:

The stars know my secrets
The stars are my keepers
They hold no judgment

With them I am whole.

I sketch little stars all over the page as I rest my cheek on my fist, contemplating my thoughts. Healing is a funny thing. It requires that we do the things we don't really want to: share our stories with ourselves and others, contemplate the hurt we've been through, process all our feelings.

When the coffee pot beeps, I'm stirred back into the present moment from my reflections, and I get up to fill a mug of the hot, black liquid that always wakes me up. As I sit back down, the steam reaches my face and I feel the warmth as my hands envelope the mug. I take that first sip and it's amazing, warming me from the inside. I sit there soaking this all in, and I think about this small moment as something to be grateful for — quiet, hot coffee, and time and space to heal. I make a mental note to take time each night before bed to write some things I'm grateful for, a way to keep me grounded.

It's 6:02 when Farrah shuffles out of my bedroom, her hair, usually perfectly kept, is a mess. I smile at her.

"Thanks for hanging with me all day and night," I say. "You're the best."

She bends down to where I'm sitting and gives me a hug. "Of course. Any time," she says. "But I gotta go. Wedding plans call. What are you doing today?"

"I'm not sure. I think I'll go for a walk, do some laundry. Kash and I might hang out later."

"Well, have a great day," she says, pulling her sneakers on.

"Thanks. Text me later, and let me know how today goes, and tell Joey I say hi." I walk her to the door, and close it behind her. Since it's still early, I decide to enjoy another cup of coffee, so I sit back down with my full mug.

For a little bit after Farrah leaves, I feel the dread of being alone. It was so nice to have her with me while I processed some hard things, and now that she's gone, I'm filled with loneliness. I acknowledge my feelings but also remind myself that I'm far from experiencing the loneliness I've felt in my past. I tell myself that I can be ok with being alone, and that just because I'm alone for a while doesn't mean I'm lonely. I also remind myself that I'm lucky to have a few people in my life now who I can let in. People who genuinely care about me. I feel like continuing on this path of opening up to my friends and letting people in, so I text Silvia because I know she's probably already up, doing yoga or painting or something of the like.

Morning! Want to get breakfast in a little bit?

I'm proud of myself for trying to get out of my shell a little, instead of hiding inside of it. Silvia texts back a few minutes later.

Sounds great. Kelleys Diner? I have been hankering for her ham and cheese omelet.

I smile at my phone, excited to get to spend time with her.

Sure! See you there. Want to say 9?

See you then!

After making plans with Silvia, I take myself for a long walk around my neighborhood. When it's time to meet her, I decide to take an Uber to Kelley's Diner. I could have walked but it was just a little too far, especially after already walking three miles earlier.

The city is already bustling — people carrying their to-go cups of coffee, wearing sunglasses to block the blaring Texas sun and walking with a certain pep in their steps. I find myself wondering about each person that I pass. What are their stories? Where are they headed? Are they dealing with hard things too? Are they, like me, hiding behind walls? Just trying to make it through each day? Or are they celebrating — an anniversary, the news of a new baby, the excitement of a new love? I've never really thought about this but today I'm finding it fascinating to think about people's stories and what they are going through in their own lives. So many people in this world, and we only know the stories of a handful of them. I can't decide if this is a good thing or not.

As the driver drops me off, I thank him and walk down the path along the river toward the diner. It's located right on the water and looks out over the rolling hills of the main city park where people are feeding the ducks and kids are squealing with delight as they go down the big slide at the playground. It's such a lovely day in Austin and I want to soak up all of it.

I walk into Kelley's and sit at the bar where the windows overlook the river. I order a coffee while I wait for Silvia, who arrives roughly fifteen minutes late.

"Oh, hunny, you're always making me feel bad about running a tad late. You're always waiting on me." She sits down, huffing. She must have run from her car. "*Everyone* is always waiting on me, aren't they?" she adds with a small smile, poking fun at herself.

I laugh. "Don't worry, Silvia. I was just enjoying the view."

She sits next to me and flags the waitress down and asks for some coffee. We have an easy conversation, talking about the weather, the bar, J.J.'s news about a baby on the way. We're laughing and talking, but also sharing a few moments of quiet while we watch people kayaking and canoeing on the river. It's so comfortable with Silvia, and I remind myself to enjoy this.

After a few minutes, we order our food, both getting omelets, mine with a side of fruit and hashbrowns, Silvia's with sides of toast and bacon. We continue to catch up and share some small talk.

Once our food arrives, Silvia asks, "Did you hear about Kash's plans?"

My eyebrows furrow. "No," I say, suddenly very interested in what she's about to tell me as I use a butter knife to spread some ketchup on my potatoes.

"That boy is so talented. He deserves whatever blessings come his way. Sweet boy too," she says with a mouthful of food. My eyes open a tad bit wider, letting her know I have no idea what she's talking about. She looks over at me and realizes I'm confused. "He's cutting his performances at Sullivan's. He wants to open his own place. Maverick gave him his blessing, but, of course, life won't be the same over at Sullivan's without Kash and Silas as the regular musicians," she adds.

"Wow," I say, not really sure what else to add. I'm a little surprised that Kash hasn't told me that he was actively pulling away from Sullivan's. I knew that this was his goal, but I didn't really think he was going to move on it this quickly. But then again, when did he ever really have a chance to tell me, with us always talking about my problems? I cringe. First Farrah, now Kash, people I depend on but don't ever let them depend on me. At least I'm realizing this now.

"Well, maybe it will be close by, and he can come back to Sullivan's and do some cameo appearances," I say with a shrug.

"Maybe. None of us should be surprised, though. Kash is a hard worker. He's honest and kind. They say nice guys finish last but that boy's gonna do something big. Don't ya think?" Silvia asks me. Kash is amazingly talented, and his dedication is apparent. I feel a deep pride for him. I can't wait to ask him about this news and get more information, hopefully tonight.

"What about you, dear? Do you have any plans that don't involve Sullivan's?" Silvia asks out of pure interest. There is no tone that makes me think she believes I'm not doing enough, no pressure to do or be more. She is the most fulfilled person I know. She's been at Sullivan's for a while now, and she's there for the long haul. But she's used to younger people starting there and then moving onto bigger things. She's told me that she hates it when people leave because she gets so attached to them when they are there. We are like a family, one big family, and change is hard. Though I'm dying to find out more about Kash's plan, the thought of change gives me a pang of unease, so I push it down with a big swig of coffee.

"I'm not really sure yet," I respond with a half-truth. "I enjoy writing...mostly poetry and lyrical stuff. I would like to write songs." I shrug my shoulders as if it's no big deal, like it's just a hobby and I would be perfectly happy bartending at Sullivan's for the rest of my life. I try to give off that impression, but it's not how I feel. I feel like there's something more for me out there, I just haven't been able to figure it out yet. I have been too trapped by my past and my insecurities. Silvia puts her hand on my knee and looks at me lovingly.

"Well, we'll always be there for you, even if you do fly from the nest, so to speak." Her words cause my breath to hitch. Is that what's holding me back from finding my place? Fear of losing the people who've given me new life over the last eighteen months. I give Silvia a small smile and glance at the water. *One day at a time, Summer,* I think to myself.

After enjoying our food and savoring the last of our coffee, Silvia and I settle the bill and say our goodbyes. I stop to grab a coffee to go then head out into the sunshine. As I start walking, I pull out my phone and see a text from Kash.

Still down to hang today?

I let my shoulders relax. I'm looking forward to seeing him and finding out more about his big plans.

Yup!

Ok, I'll swing by your place around six. Sound good?

See you then.

For the rest of the morning and afternoon, I take it easy. I mosey through the city, looking in windows at things I can't afford. I start to get hungry, so I head home around lunch time and make myself a salad with the groceries I bought the other day. I spend some time jotting in my notebook. I know I need to clean my living room but I don't want to, so I watch a true crime documentary on Netflix while I dust and sweep, making the cleaning at least bearable. At five, I decide to get ready — I shower and blow dry my hair, put it up in a bun, put on some light makeup, and get dressed. I choose high-waisted jeans and a thin sweater, tucked in. I put my brown boots by the door to put on when Kash arrives. Then I sit for a minute, anticipating Kash's arrival. At 5:59 p.m., he knocks on my door.

"You are the promptest person I know," I say lightheartedly as I let him inside. I pull on my boots and tie them.

Kash laughs. "Being late is my biggest pet peeve. I hate being late, and I hate it when other people are late. It's a flaw." He lets a laugh escape.

"I think it's considerate, actually," I say, swinging my small clutch on my shoulder.

He smiles. "Ready?" I nod and we head out to his truck.

"I see you got a carwash. Looking sparkly," I say, wiggling my eyebrows.

"It needed it desperately. I'm glad you're impressed." He fiddles with the dial and stops on a country station. As Luke Bryan plays through the speakers, Kash turns it down slightly and pulls away from the curb.

"Where are we heading?" I ask.

"What are you in the mood to do? Are you hungry? We could go to that Thai restaurant down the street. Or that pub over on Crescent Street. They have great nachos." He offers some suggestions.

"Yeah, the pub sounds good. Let's go there."

"Pub it is," Kash says as he starts looking through his center console. "Is my phone on the floor by you?" he asks.

I look around but don't see it. "No, it's not," I say looking behind my seat to see if it's there.

"Damn, I think it's on my kitchen table. Do you mind if we stop by my place quickly so I can grab it? My mom left to go home this afternoon, and I want to make sure she gets back safe and sound."

"Of course. Not a problem," I say. "How was your visit?"

"It was nice. We got dinner last night and did some sightseeing this morning. She lives over in Waco."

"What about your dad?" I ask, regretting it after it comes out. I hate when people ask about my family.

"He passed away when I was nine in a bad car accident," he says with feeling but not dread or heaviness.

I look over at him. "I'm so sorry," I say. "I didn't know."

He smiles at me softly and gently touches my shoulder. "Don't apologize. Do we ever really know what shit a person has gone through if we don't ask? Don't hold back from getting to know someone because you're afraid it will strike a painful chord. It's the human condition. Terrible things can happen in our lives. But there's beauty in connection." Kash's words are so moving that I find myself holding my breath, hanging on every single one.

"You're right," I whisper, but that's all I can muster.

Soon, we reach Kash's townhouse. It's a two-story brick building with modern touches. The trees along the street are glittered with white twinkle lights, making it warm and inviting. Kash parks along the curb and we both get out. We walk up the four steps onto his landing, and he unlocks the door. As we step inside and he turns the light on, I glance around. There's a staircase leading upstairs right as you walk in, the living room is neat and minimalistic, there's some art on the walls. I follow him into the kitchen, which looks new, or barely used, I can't tell which. Kash finds his phone on the counter, just where he thought he'd left it.

"She made it back, so that's good," he says with a smile, looking at his phone.

"That's great. I'm glad we stopped to check because that would be stressful not knowing, huh?"

"A little. I just like knowing she made it home safely. It's a long drive on the highway, and I worry about her."

Of course you would since your dad died in a car accident. I think this but I don't say it. I watch him as he puts his phone in his pocket. Suddenly, I think about that word he spoke about in the car. *Connection.* And I notice that I'm feeling connected to Kash right now.

"I'm just going to run to the bathroom quickly," he says, heading toward an open door off the kitchen. I walk out of the kitchen toward the front door and, again, glance around the living room. I notice an interesting brown box sitting on a shelf next to an assortment of novels. It doesn't seem to fit with the decor — it's old and worn, with faded wood and chipped paint, a little latch that has become loose. "What's this?" I ask Kash as he makes his way back from the bathroom.

He chuckles. "Oh, this old thing?" he asks, picking it up off the shelf. He opens the lid and I peer inside. What looks like junk turns out to be something more. The box is littered with movie tickets, faded Polaroids, gum wrappers, a vile of sand, and an assortment of other random trinkets. I glance up at Kash with confusion.

"It's a memory box," he says with a shrug.

"Memory box?"

"Yeah. I used to put mementos from meaningful times in my life in this box. Sometimes I like to look through and reminisce, although I haven't done that in a while," he says as I riffle through the contents of the box gently, not wanting to disturb any of the delicate pieces. I'm mesmerized. I feel goosebumps rising up all over my body. I think about my own life and what I'd put in here if I had one of these.

"This is amazing," I say so quietly that it barely comes out. I feel a lump forming in my throat, and I'm afraid to raise my voice above a whisper.

"Yeah?" he questions, placing the box back on the shelf. "You don't think it's weird?"

"No, not at all. I'm in awe of the fact that you had so many moments that meant something to you and that you had the wherewithal to save these mementos to remember them. I'm envious, really." My voice trails off. "I'm standing here trying to think of what I would put in my box of memories, and I can't think of anything." My words hold a sadness in them but saying them feels good. Kash puts his hand on my shoulder, and I lean in and let him hug me. My muscles relax, and I allow the lump in my throat to dissipate. "I think you should keep adding to it," I say, pulling away from our embrace.

He laughs. "Deal. I will start adding to it again," he says, his smile beaming. "Ready?" I nod and we head out the door to the truck. Suddenly, I'm famished, and I find myself dreaming about nachos.

As Kash turns on the car, and I buckle my seatbelt the radio plays "Strawberry Wine." The lyrics seem soft and sweet, but to me they are jarring because they bring me back to that winter when I turned sixteen, my junior year, the year Social Services gave up on finding me a home, and the year I went off the rails.

CHAPTER 17

Kentucky - Then

"H ELLO?" CASSIE ABRUPTLY TURNED down the music to answer her cell phone. "Oh, good Lord. Ok...yup. Yes. We will be home in about fifteen minutes. Sure. Yes, yes. Ok. Bye."

She hung up and stared out the windshield, gripping the wheel tightly, her knuckles turning white.

"What was that about?" Claire asked from her seat in the front. I didn't care who it was, and I continued to stare out the window, watching the town go by as we drove. Cassie didn't respond to Claire.

"Mom?" she questioned, with a tone of concern.

"Oh, it was nothing, hunny," Cassie said. She glanced in the rearview mirror at me. "Summer, um, Gina is stopping by today." She swallowed hard, discomfort evident in her voice.

"Ok," I said.

At this point in my life, I was numb, and I didn't get nervous about these visits. What could possibly be any worse than the situation I was already in?

We pulled into the garage and parked, and I slowly got out of the car. What was the rush? I didn't want to find out what Gina wanted. We made our way into the kitchen and Cassie immediately started busying herself, getting a tray of refreshments ready for Gina's visit. She was fumbling around, slamming cabinets and swearing under her breath, something she never did. I watched her, wide-eyed.

It crossed my mind that maybe they had found a family for me, and that Cassie didn't know how to manage her feelings around it. I mean, I had lived with them for five years. But this is what Cassie and Greg wanted. They'd insisted on having temporary custody until a permanent situation was found. They didn't want me. Why was she acting like her world was crumbling now?

I made my way into the living room and peered out the window to see Gina's sedan pulling up in front of the house. A police car pulled up behind her.

"What the hell?" I muttered to myself, my heart starting to race. Something was wrong. "Momma," I whispered as a tear formed in my eye. I squinted through the glass cut-out beside the door to get a better look and saw Gina and the officer walk up toward the door. It was a female officer, poised and elegant, her hair pulled back neatly in a tight, sleek, low bun. She looked so familiar to me. And then it hit me: Autumn. It was Autumn Sinclair. My knees went weak. They felt like jelly, barely holding me upright. I backed away from the door and sat on the couch, petrified of what was coming and scared from the flashbacks of the last time I'd seen Autumn.

I heard Cassie open the door and let them in. I couldn't look over at them. I stared at the opposite wall, unblinking, unmoving, until Officer Sinclair and Gina sat across from me on the love seat. Then I stared at my hands in my lap. Cassie left the room, heading back into the kitchen, removing herself from the uncomfortable situation she knew was coming.

"Hi, Summer," Gina said gently. I didn't make a sound.

"Hi, do you remember me, Summer?" Officer Sinclair asked softly. "I..." she trailed off and I cut in.

"Autumn. Yes, I remember you," I said, my voice cold and withdrawn. She gave me a warm, genuine smile. They both stared at me.

"She's dead, isn't she?" I said without emotion. Gina sucked in a breath. I looked at her and saw her eyes growing glossy. Why was she crying? I became enraged inside. My body grew hot, and my fists clenched by my sides. She wasn't allowed to cry for me. No one cared how I felt, ever. Why were they starting now? It was too late. For all of these years, no one had thought about what taking me from my momma would do to her, or to me. And here was the consequence. It had killed her.

Gina and Autumn exchanged glances with each other, hoping for some guidance on what to say next.

"Just. Say. It," I said through gritted teeth, emotion attempting to claw its way out.

"Yes, Summer. Your mom died. She's been homeless for some time. She was found this morning." Officer Sinclair was the one to break the news. I stared at them as my rage began to bubble to the surface.

"You promised you would help her!" I screamed through the tears that were pushing their way down my face. "You were supposed to help her, to help me! You lied! You are all liars!" I stood up, spewing venomous words as quickly as I could.

By then I was sobbing. All the emotions that had built up over the years came spilling out; the floodgates had swung open. Officer Sinclair got up and put one arm around me and then the other one. She was almost restraining me in an effort to comfort me. I fought it initially, but then I gave in, letting myself sob on her shoulder, my arms hanging limp by my sides.

I remember appreciating what Officer Sinclair did. I was thankful that she did the hard thing — telling me the truth and then approaching me, not knowing how I would react to her. It was more than I could say for Gina, who continued to sit on the couch, unmoving, almost frozen in place, scared to say or do anything. The person who was supposed to be trained in these matters, who was supposed to deal with this stuff in a professional but caring way, was too scared of me and my screwed-up life to do anything in the situation. I pulled away from Officer Sinclair and wiped my face as the tears continued to fall.

"Are you able to sit back down and have a discussion?" she asked me kindly. I didn't respond, but I sat back down.

Gina broke her silence. "Summer, I can't begin to even comprehend how you are feeling. I'm not going to pretend that I understand. Your emotions are valid." *No shit.* "Let's start by answering any questions you have," she said, her hands neatly folded in her lap. I stared at both of the women for a long time, unmoving.

"Now what?" I said, my voice coming out raspy and tired.

Gina glanced at Officer Sinclair then started, "Well, as you are aware, we've been in the process of looking for an adoptive home for you for quite some time. A plan to go back with your mom was not likely.

On that front, things are the same. We will continue to search for an adoptive home, and in the meantime, you will continue to stay with the Brickmans." She paused and I tried to absorb the information. *Oh, Summer, no big deal, business as usual. Yes, your mom died, but she wasn't getting you back anyway, so we'll carry on.*

Now what? That's the question I asked, and technically, that's the question she answered, but I guess deep down, that's not what I meant. What I meant was how am I supposed to go on without a mother? Who was I without a living parent? Who would ever love me unconditionally now that Momma was gone? I glared at them and out of the corner of my eye, I saw Cassie looking heartbroken, standing in the entryway to the kitchen. I got up and stomped upstairs, falling into my bed with a thud. I crawled under the covers and cried myself to sleep.

CHAPTER 18

Texas - Now

"**I**T WAS THE HEAVIEST my body had ever felt," I say to Kash as we pull into a parking spot outside The Gallery Pub. I realize that this time, instead of falling into a trance of my trigger, I'm reliving it out loud to Kash. I haven't zoned out completely. I'm staying in the moment. I'm sharing my truth as it comes back to me. And when I'm done, I look over at Kash, the moon shining in his eyes, and he's looking at me with the most compassionate look I've ever seen. He's silent but he's completely present. He's been listening this entire time.

"Yeah. I know. It's a lot," I say, looking out the windshield and feeling vulnerable, trying to take the attention off me. "Anyways, I'm starving for these famous nachos. Can we go in now?" I say lightheartedly.

Kash takes my hand. "I'm sorry you had to go through that, Summer. I can't imagine what that must have been like," he says. I stare at him, feeling a little uncomfortable with this attention. I give a shy smile and thank him but quickly start unbuckling my seatbelt. I'm ready for some food and a conversation that doesn't revolve around my past. I'm also dying to ask him about his new plans.

"Let's go eat," I say, and we make our way toward the entrance.

We grab a booth in the back, away from everyone else. We make small talk while we wait to order. Once our appetizer arrives, I stare it down at it, curious if these nachos will live up to the hype. "Here goes nothing," I laugh, taking a chip from the pile, one that has all the delicious toppings, and pop it in my mouth. I groan, my eyes opening wide. I take another bite.

"Ok, you were not lying. These are the best nachos I've ever had in my entire life. Every bite! Every bite is good," I gush, and Kash smiles at me.

"Told you," he says, pride sprinkled in his words.

Now that I've got some food, I'm ready to get down to the bottom of this news I heard earlier. "So, I have to ask you something," I say. "A little bird named Silvia told me that you were making plans to leave us at Sullivan's and open your own place. Is that true?" I put it all out there, shoveling a heaping nacho in my mouth. Kash looks at me with some intrigue and a little bit of shock. He grabs a bite, and I can tell he's contemplating how to address my question.

"I have been dabbling in some goals, yes," he says with a hint of a smile.

"Are you going to spill the beans? Or will I be the only one who lays it all out on the table?" I joke.

Kash brushes crumbs off his hands. "Yes, you heard correctly. I talked to Maverick about my plans to branch out and start my own place. I haven't been happy with my day job for a while now. It pays the bills, but it's just not me. I'm so alive when I'm performing. I want to play as much as I can." When he's done sharing, he's all lit up. I can tell this is what he's passionate about. I take another bite and encourage him to keep going. "That's my goal — whether long-term or short — I haven't figured that out yet," he finishes, taking a sip of his beer.

I smile at him. "That's really amazing, Kash," I say. "Please keep me in the loop with it all. You know that none of us want you to stop playing at Sullivan's, but everyone will support you in your new venture, just like Maverick is." He looks like he has more to add, but he's holding back. I want him to know that I'm in his corner even though I'll miss his bright smile at work. "You know, Silvia had so many good things to say about you this morning at breakfast," I add. He lets his head fall back and laughs a boisterous laugh, even though I know he doesn't handle compliments that well. He's as humble as they come. Randomly, he grabs a napkin and starts jotting lines on it with a Keno pencil. ˈ

"Um, what are you doing?" I ask.

"Tic-tac-toe" he says, grinning and flashing his beautiful teeth. We sit, mindlessly playing, letting our conversation flow while we enjoy each other's company. We order dinner — a buffalo chicken sandwich and fries for me and a bacon cheeseburger with onion rings for him.

"So, what happened after?" Kash asks me out of the blue, looking deep into my eyes. My body stiffens. I know what he means but I'm taken aback at first.

"After what?" I ask, gathering my thoughts.

"After your mom died. Did people rally around you? What happened?" His questions are genuine, and I know he's not prying, that he truly cares, but I feel so exposed. I glance around nervously, and he rests his hand on top of mine. "You're safe," he says. "If you don't want to talk about it, we don't have to. I'm just giving you the opportunity to share if you feel comfortable."

There's a long moment of silence between us as I stare at my food and decide if I'm ready for this. I sigh, leaning back against the booth, contemplating what to do next. This part of my story is hard for me to put into words. That time in my life was filled with shame and embarrassment. It's challenging for me to think about those years in my adolescents when I turned into the person that everyone expected me to be. I was the kind of person who burned bridges and constantly screwed up. I was consistently gliding off the tracks.

"You know those infamous rails people speak about?" Kash gives me a single nod of his head. "Yeah, well, I went off of them."

CHAPTER 19

Kentucky - Then

I T HAD BEEN THIRTY-TWO days since my momma died. It was February, and I was just going through the motions: going to school, coming home, and spending any extra time I had with Dan and Meg. Jason and I still didn't hang out much, at least not like we'd done before, and he was always hanging out with his football buddies. We were civil to each other, but it just wasn't the same as it had once been. But I didn't care. He was giving Dan the cold shoulder because we were dating, which was ridiculous because it's not like Jason had a brotherly obligation to protect me. Also, I wasn't even his sister, and he didn't seem to pay any attention to the guys that Claire was dating, mainly Trevor at that time. Dan didn't act like he cared, probably because none of it made any sense to him either.

They were both getting ready to head off to college in a few months, and things started getting more strained between us. It seemed like Jason should have just let it go, let Dan and I do whatever we wanted to do.

He should have been thinking about himself and what was next for him, but instead, he decided to hold a grudge. Because things had become increasingly awkward with us, I was indifferent about Jason leaving for college, but I didn't want Dan to go.

Since the day my momma died, I'd felt hollow on the inside, like I had been scooped out and left to wallow there. My steps always felt heavy, I couldn't get out of bed in the morning, but I also couldn't fall asleep at night. I felt so alone. At first, everyone walked on eggshells around me, until one day, they didn't. They just went back to their normal lives. No one was checking in on me, asking me how I was doing.

The worst part was that I felt like I was expected to move on from my trauma overnight — move on from being ripped from my parents at age eleven, from losing my abusive father a year later, from watching my mom sink herself into her early grave by the time I was sixteen, and from having to pick up the pieces of whatever my life had become. In everyone else's eyes, enough time had passed. I was expected to put on a happy face. There was no space for my discomfort. Everyone made it crystal clear that it was time for me to move on.

One Friday night that month, Meg asked me to go with her to a party in another town. I really didn't want to go, but she kept begging me, and I finally thought that it might be fun. I didn't want to ask Cassie or Greg for permission because it would have caused a scene, especially if Jason wasn't going and I really didn't want him to find out about it. Being around him had become increasingly uncomfortable. So, I decided to sneak out.

I told Meg to pick me up at nine-thirty on the street behind the Brickman's house, and I would meet her there, one way or another. Claire was staying at her friend's house that night, which made my plan much easier. Before I left, I made sure I had a key to get back in because climbing down the lattice was one thing, but climbing up was another thing entirely. I didn't want to risk getting stuck outside. I got ready to head out — wearing a jean skirt, a tank top, and UGG boots. It was chilly outside, so before I left, I grabbed a zip-up hoodie and threw it on. At 9:15, I arranged my pillows under my covers to look like I was sleeping and made my escape.

Meg was waiting for me in her white 1993 Corolla on the next street over, just liked we'd planned.

I climbed in the front seat and gave her a look. "This party better be worth it. If Cassie and Greg find out I snuck out, they will for sure wipe their hands clean of me," I said, buckling my seatbelt.

"You'll be able to sneak back in just fine," Meg said, smiling mischievously, and we headed off to the party.

It took us twenty minutes to reach the destination. When we pulled up to the house, people spilled out onto the front porch surrounded by clouds of cigarette smoke. *Gross*, I thought to myself. Meg took my hand and pushed us through the crowd to the door and into the house.

The inside was exactly what I imagined — enormous and full of very nice furniture. The people who lived here were obviously rich, and they were gone for the weekend, so the kids were throwing a huge party. I had never seen so many unaccompanied minors in one place and it was slightly unsettling. The living room was hazy and crowded. Everyone held cups filled to the brim with unidentified liquids that sloshed onto the floor as they walked and danced, causing sticky puddles all over the place.

I glanced around at the scene unfolding before me. Meg was talking to a girl with long raven black hair, who she introduced as her cousin, Emily. She must be the one who told Meg about the party.

"Hi, I'm Summer," I said with a smile. Emily had been drinking — she spoke with slurred words, her arms flailing about spastically as she spoke, and her balance was off kilter. She had this euphoric look about her, as if she believed that this party was the most amazing place she'd ever been in her whole life.

"My boyfriend started a fight with me this afternoon, and he can go screw himself," Emily said with a laugh, followed by a hiccup. "Because I am having the time of my life," she added, raising her voice so that everyone around her heard then hollered and cheered, mimicking her excitement. I looked at her, intrigued, wondering if the liquid in her cup was some sort of magic potion that made her not care about the conflict in her life. If so, maybe I needed to try some of that potion. I looked around to see if I could find something to drink but didn't see anything.

"I'll be back," I said to Meg as I headed toward the kitchen to find something to fill a cup with. I'd never had alcohol before, and, truthfully, up until then, the thought of it repulsed me and reminded me of my father. But that night, watching and listening to Emily celebrate in spite of her pitfalls made me curious. She had, unknowingly, dangled the temptation in front of me just within reach. It made me wonder if I could numb my pain somehow. So, like Eve and the apple, I bit.

I found hundreds of red plastic cups in the kitchen. Most had already been used, and some were tipped over, resting on the spilled contents of what was once inside them, but I finally found a clean one. I had lots of choices of which type of alcohol I wanted to try first. There was a huge keg, many half-empty bottles of liquor, a few bottles of champagne, and copious containers of juice and soda. I picked up a bottle of clear liquid and inspected it. Vodka, it said on the label. I poured a tiny bit into my cup and smelled it. My eyes squinted, and I pulled my head back.

"Put some of this in there," I heard someone say behind me, and I turned to see a tall kid with hair long enough to put in a ponytail. He handed me a bottle of ginger ale. "It will make it taste better," he added, flashing me a smile. I thanked him as I took the ginger ale from his hands, wondering if anything could make vodka taste better. It didn't go unnoticed by me that this guy was good-looking. I poured some ginger ale into the cup with the vodka and gave it another smell. Much better. I took a sip. The taste wasn't bad, but the mixture burned going down and the aftertaste lingered. I tried to control my disgusted face as much as I could. Laughing, the guy took the ginger ale bottle from the table and poured a little more into my cup. "Now try it," he said. I did, and this time, it was much more bearable. I could almost instantly feel my cheeks getting warm and my head beginning to tingle.

"Thanks," I offered.

"Zack," he said, outstretching his hand for a shake.

I offered mine. "Summer."

He smiled. "I like that name."

I jokingly rolled my eyes in exaggeration. "Everyone says that," I responded, taking another sip from my cup.

"Sorry. I hate that name?" Zack said it like a question, and we both gave a little laugh.

By then, I had taken roughly four sips and I knew something was happening inside but instead of stopping there, it suddenly made sense to me that I should pour myself some more. So, I took the two bottles and filled my cup so I'd have something to carry around with me.

"Want to sit outside?" Zack asked.

"Sure."

I following him out the kitchen door and onto a patio that was lit up with warm lights, overlooking a huge in-ground pool.

We sat on a bench, me with my red cup filled to the brim and Zack with his bottle of beer that I had yet to see him take a sip of.

"Are you just pretending to drink that?" I asked him, motioning toward the mostly full bottle.

"Kinda," he replied. "I drove my car here, and I want to leave soon, so I have this but I'm just taking tiny sips," he added with a shrug.

"That's very responsible of you," I said, taking a big sip from my cup. "My friend drove here. I should probably check to make sure that she is also being responsible." I let out a laugh, getting up from the bench.

I headed back into the house and started making the rounds to try and find Meg. I turned around to see that Zack had followed me inside, and we made small talk as we walked through the huge house.

"So where are you from? I know you don't go to St. Michael's. That's where most of these people go. But I've never seen you at school."

I shook my head. "No, I definitely don't belong here," I said with a chuckle. "I go to Northwest High."

"Oh, that's a good school."

I gave him a questioning look. "What are you, like, forty or something?" I asked, gently making fun of him. "First the responsibility, and now you're giving your opinion of school reputations?" My tone was humorous.

Zack kicked his head back and laughed. "Yeah, I guess you're right. Sorry, let me ask something more interesting." He looked like he was trying to think of something really good to ask. But instead, what came out pissed me off.

"Does your mom know you're here, or did you sneak out?" he asked, bouncing his eyebrows, assuming this was an enticing question. The alcohol was really beginning to get to my head, and I felt like I was starting to float through the air. I put the cup down and looked up at Zack, a smirk on my face.

"Well, my mom is dead. She died last month, all alone under a highway overpass." The silence between us was deafening. "Oh, wait. Maybe you mean my foster mom. No, she doesn't know I'm here, and if she finds out, I'll probably find myself living under a highway overpass as well." My words came out slurred and jumbled but I felt free. When would people stop asking about families? What business was it of theirs to ask these kinds of questions?

"Oh, shit. I'm so sorry to have brought something up that was so painful," Zack said, just like a typical forty-year-old. I studied his face. It was kind of chiseled, and his blue eyes were so light they almost looked fake. I stared at him for a second, and then, before I could talk myself out of it, I stood on my tiptoes and kissed him. At first, he was shocked, but then he wrapped his arms around me and continued what I'd started.

I clearly wasn't thinking. I wasn't thinking about the consequences or about Dan. All I was thinking about was how I'd drank that disgusting liquid to help me forget my pain, and how it hadn't worked. There was no escaping my past, my trauma. At every turn, I was still reminded. It hit me then that I would always be triggered by something or someone, and the desperation to escape that reality began to take over.

Suddenly, I heard a familiar voice and there was Meg, standing beside me and Zack, cheering excitedly. She pulled out her Polaroid and snapped three pictures before I realized what she was doing, and I quickly pulled away from Zack. I gave her a friendly shove. And then I realized — Meg was drunk.

"What the hell, Meg? You need to drive us home," I yelled at her.

"Oh, relax." Her words were slurred together. "I'm not drinking anymore. I will be fine soon." But I wasn't convinced. She looked and sounded worse than me, and I wasn't in good shape.

Meg began stumbling to the door. "Look, I'll show you," she said, attempting to steady her steps. Zack and I hurried after her. She made it to her car and opened up the driver's side door. I wasn't buying that she was ok to drive, and I definitely wasn't getting in the car with her.

Zack stopped her from getting in the car. "I'll drive you guys home. But I have to tell my buddies that I'll be back for them in a bit. Don't move. I'll be right back," he said as he started walking backward toward the house then turned and jogged the rest of the way.

"You're an idiot," I spit out at her. She looked at me, annoyed. "I'm not mad that you got drunk. I'm mad that you got drunk and then insisted that you could still drive me home." I was starting to sober up fast now, and I was so thankful that this random guy *who I made out with* was going to take us home.

We climbed into Zack's car. As he drove, I stared out the window, replaying the night's events in my head. We dropped Meg off first, and then Zack drove me to the Brickman's. He pulled over a bit before we reached the house so they wouldn't see the lights. As I reached for the door, he asked me for my number, but even though I'd made the first move with him, I wasn't interested in seeing him again. I was feeling incredibly guilty about kissing Zack when I was seeing Dan. But I would worry about how to deal with that in the morning.

I said goodbye to Zack, quietly shut the car door, and made my way into the house without a hitch. I tiptoed up the stairs and into my room without waking anyone. After I changed into my pajamas, I climbed into bed and took a deep breath. I couldn't exactly pinpoint how I felt, but it wasn't how I thought I'd feel after a night out like that. I should have felt full of life, high on the memory of the experience and the fun I'd had, and excited about what I'd gotten away with. But instead, I felt a heavy sense of dread that I just couldn't shake. Eventually, I fell into a restless sleep.

———

When I woke up the next morning, my computer screen was blinking with instant messages. I climbed out of bed and walked to my desk.

Meg: *Summer. Dude. Wake up. My mom is bullshit. Can you ask Dan if he can take me to get my car?*

Dan: *Good morning, beautiful. Message me when you get up.*

My stomach lurched and my heart ached for Dan and what I had done the night before. I decided I was going to pretend it'd never happened. It wasn't like Meg would remember. And I'd planned to pretend that I didn't remember much either.

Me to Meg: *Hi, yeah I'm awake. I'll ask him.*

Me to Dan: *good morning :)*

Me to Dan: *Meg left her car at this house we were at last night. Can you bring us to pick it up?*

Dan: *? uhhhh sure. Where is it?*

Me to Dan: *We went to a party at her cousin's friend's house.*

Dan: *Ok yeah. What time?*

Me to Meg: *What time do you want to go?*

Meg: *ASAP*

Me to Dan: ASAP

Dan: *I'll be there in about thirty minutes.*

Me to Meg: *Me and Dan will pick up in about thirty minutes.*

Meg: *omg girl. THANK YOU*

I got dressed quickly and headed downstairs. Cassie had some muffins out on the counter with a note. *Greg and I went to run some errands and grab Claire. Be home later. Enjoy a muffin!*

I grabbed a blueberry muffin and poured a glass of milk. I sat at the table and ate alone in silence for a bit, wondering where Jason was. Around nine-thirty, Dan knocked on the door. I cleaned up my crumbs, put my glass in the sink, and headed to the door. I gave Dan a hug and let him hold me for a second.

"So, you guys must have had fun last night," he said with a smile.

My eyebrows went up. "Yeah, I guess you could say that," I casually responded, getting in the car. We pulled away from the curb and headed toward Meg's house.

"So, it was a good night?" Dan asked me, digging for more details.

"Mm-hmm," I responded with a smile. Regretting what I'd done, I didn't want to talk about the evening at all. Flashbacks of the dumb thing I did kept popping into my head and making me physically shudder as if I was trying to shake them away.

"How was your night?" I asked him, attempting to change the subject.

He shrugged. "Not too interesting. I went to Jake's after basketball, and we played video games for way too long." He chuckled under his breath. "How are you doing, Summer? Are you feeling ok about everything that's been going on the last few months?" Dan shifted the conversation, asking me this with the utmost sincerity. He had been there for me for many years, and I considered his friendship to be a lifeline. At first, I didn't answer his question. I just looked out the window. How *was* I doing? I didn't even know. It felt like I was entering a phase of destruction, I could feel it brewing inside — my desperate desire to bury all the trauma that kept building and building. Thoughts about the future were beginning to nag at me, and not having an idea of where I was heading was unsettling, to say the least.

"I'm fine," I finally responded. A lie that would frequent my mouth. Dan put his hand on my knee. He wanted to reassure me, let me know he was there for me. I appreciated the gesture, but nothing helped, and I'd accepted that long ago.

When we arrived at Meg's house, Dan had barely put the car in park before she ran out the door toward us. She looked disheveled, in the same sweatshirt she'd worn the night before, her hair a mess, and her makeup still smeared on her face, mascara running under her eyes. I looked back at her with wide eyes when she got in.

She rolled her eyes at me. "Enough with the third degree, Summer."

"I didn't say anything," I snapped back defensively.

"Your face did." Her words were ringing with agitation as she took her gaze out the window.

"Are you ok?" I asked her nicely. She just nodded. I didn't know why she was acting mad at me. I didn't do anything.

"My mom is pissed I left my car." Meg stared out the window. I got the impression she was directing this comment and her annoyance toward me.

"Well, would you rather I have let you drive home and possibly end up killing yourself?" I asked her, with a tone that was elevated. She just rolled her eyes again. She had nothing else to say.

When we got to the house, we found Meg's car parked a few houses down, just where we'd left it. "Thanks, Dan," she said as she opened the door. "See you later, guys. Not for a while, of course, because I'm grounded." She said it with an epic eye roll as she slammed the door. We rolled down our window and said bye to her as she walked away, heading to her car. I watched her go and wondered how long she was going to stay mad at me.

"I'm proud of you," Dan said, watching her get into the car. "You did the right thing. It's always better to have someone be mad at you and still be alive than the other way around." He pulled away from the curb. I nodded but I wasn't so sure he was right.

"Want to get takeout from the diner and eat it at the Brickman's?" I asked, suddenly starving.

"Sure," Dan agreed. On the way home, we stopped at Sophie's Diner and ordered eggs, pancakes, bacon, and hashbrowns to share and waited at the little counter, sitting on squeaky stools. We talked about high school and college and other mindless stuff until our food was ready. We walked out and got in the car, and it immediately filled with the delicious smells of our meal. My stomach began to growl.

Soon enough, we pulled up to the Brickman's. I got out of the car, carrying two of the takeout containers, and Dan took the others. I waited for him at the front of the car so we could walk up the walkway together, but he stopped and did a double take in the backseat.

"What the hell...?" I heard him mumble under his breath.

"What's up?" I asked, unenthused by the stalling. He put his containers on top of the car and opened the back door. Impatiently, I tapped my foot and looked down the street at nothing in particular. When I looked back at Dan, my heart sank as he stood there holding a Polaroid. I couldn't see it for sure, but I knew what he was looking at. My grip tightened on the containers of food, and I held my breath.

"Are you kidding me, Summer?" he yelled. "What the fuck is this?" He was angry, losing control, and I just stood there frozen, no words would come out, my eyes were unblinking. "After all I've done for you and then you go to a party and make out with this loser and God knows what else?" Spit shot out of his mouth and his cheeks were turning red from anger.

"I...I..." I stuttered, completely lost for words. I didn't have an excuse. What I did was stupid, and I knew that, and having him find out this way was not ideal. "I was drinking. I was trying to forget. I was trying not to feel. I wanted to have a night where my problems didn't consume me." My voice caught in my throat and tears formed behind my eyes.

"Well, I guess now you have a whole new set of problems," Dan deadpanned.

"I guess I do," I said sadly, locking eyes with him. I wanted him to see that I was hurting, that I was sorry, that I regretted it as soon as it had happened. But whatever words I chose to say next would just be excuses.

Dan shook his head and looked away from me, down the street. "So, what's the story?" he asked, giving me a chance to make it right.

Once when I was little, I dropped a glass in the kitchen. I watched it shatter right before my eyes. I gasped and held my breath as I quickly scampered to the ground to begin cleaning up the mess, cutting my finger on the shards of my careless mistake. Dad barreled into the kitchen, having heard the sound of the glass slipping from my grip and meeting its fate on the floor. *What's your problem, Summer?* he had yelled, his face reddening at my expense. *What's your excuse this time?* His words spewed like venom. I stammered, scared of what was to come next. I had no excuse. I was careless. I was useless. I was incapable of simple things. *I'm sorry*, I whispered. *It was all my fault.*

"There is no story," I responded to Dan, my tail between my legs. "When we got there, Meg walked away from me, and I didn't know anyone. Everyone was drinking, and they looked so happy, so carefree. I thought that if I filled a cup and drank from it, I would feel that way too. Only, I just felt fuzzy." I looked down at the ground. I sat on the curb, put the food next to me, and put my head in my hands. Dan sat next to me, but he didn't console me. That would be wrong. I was the one who messed up.

"You know, you can't always blame every bad decision you make on stuff that happened to you, Summer." His words held a hint of compassion.

I whipped my head up from my hands. "Oh, really, Dan? That coming from you, who's had a perfect life handed to you on a silver platter? You, who has never been beaten, never been hungry, never been neglected? You're going to tell me how to react to life? I don't even have a family! You have no idea what it's like to be me every day. You have every right to be mad at me for what I did. I hurt you. But you have no place to tell me how to respond to shit." I said the last part through gritted teeth as I looked directly at him. He didn't say anything for a long minute.

"I can't do this, Summer." He sounded defeated. "I can't keep picking up the pieces to just have them fall out of my hands again and again." He got up from the ground, walked to his car, and got in. He sped off so quickly that I didn't even have time to process it.

I stood there on the curb alone, and just like all the other times, it was all my fault.

CHAPTER 20

Texas - Now

"**O**H MAN, SUMMER. DID you ever catch a break?" Kash asks me.

"To be fair, I made out with a stranger, and it was caught on camera."

"But it's so much more than that."

I look at him thoughtfully. No one has ever said that to me. No one ever seems to notice the pain. "Yeah, well, I couldn't hang on to anything back then," I say, glancing around the restaurant. "The next day, I found out that Meg left that picture there on purpose. It didn't just fall out of her sweatshirt pocket, so my social circle was basically whittled down to no one in one weekend." I take a deep breath, fiddling with my napkin.

Kash cringes. "Well, what you did, I wouldn't define that as 'going off the rails'."

I look up at him. "Oh, that was just the start of it."

I fidget in my seat, hesitating, then decide to keep going. "Pretty soon after that, the rumors started flying that I was a slut. I didn't try to dismiss the rumors, and I didn't do things to make them true either, but I went along with them and let people believe they were accurate. I started drinking and with my new reputation, I started getting invitations to go out, even though I didn't have any real friends. One night, Claire begged to go out with me, so I let her and then I pressured her to drink. It wasn't very hard to convince her to do it, but still, if I hadn't done that, she wouldn't have passed out in the car. When we got dropped off after the party, I had to drag her into the house, and we made so much noise that Cassie and Greg came running down the stairs to find us in complete disarray. I had nothing to lose, so I took the brunt of the punishment. They got so mad at me and said they expected me to be a role model, even though I was only nine months older than her." My words hold a hint of disgust. I suddenly feel like I've gone too far, shared too much. "Kash, I don't want you to know these things about me. It's ugly, and I'm ashamed of the things that I did back then. I don't want to associate with the person that I was."

Kash shakes his head. "You were a child. A child without guidance, without love, without a sense of belonging. I know what Dan said to you really hit home, but he was wrong. You didn't have a single person in your life, ever, who taught you how to cope, who showed you that they cared. That wasn't your fault." I stare at him. Did he just say what I think he said? *It wasn't my fault.*

Kash Holden. Where have you been my whole life?

I take a bite of my sandwich and grab a fry. I lean back against the back of the booth. "I know you're right. I have been learning that over the last two years since I found Janie, my therapist. She has helped me learn that, yes, sometimes I did bad things, but also, entirely separate of those things or completely related, depending on how you look at it, I was unloved at a time in a person's life when that is what they need most. It's the one thing a child needs to thrive, and I didn't have it. I can accept that part now. But I'm still in pain...every day."

Kash takes a bite of his burger but doesn't take his eyes off me. "You're doing well, Summer. You told me that you know what you need to heal and feel better. I know it must be hard, but knowing your goal for healing must be half the battle, no?" he asks me. I nod. I do feel better recently, having a plan and working toward healing.

"That year, I also stole Greg's car one night. I took it to a party. I didn't drink but someone put a dent in the driver's side door when they got in their car. Cassie and Greg were waiting in the kitchen when I got home. They were pissed, understandably. Cassie called me a selfish little bitch. I wore that title like a badge, along with the one that said I was a slut. Everyone around me was deciding who I was but I had no idea. I assumed they must all be right. What did I know?" I take a sip of my drink and hold it in my mouth for a second, letting the ice melt. Kash's face holds no judgment whatsoever. He wasn't there though, not when I was *that* Summer. He only knows me now, and this Summer is not the same. I'm more *me* now. Maybe not exactly where I want to be but better than where I started.

I don't share any more with Kash but there was a lot that happened during my junior year that I have squirreled away in my memory. The events of that year snowballed into a decade, or longer, of self-destruction. Sitting here in this pub, I scramble to recall the details, and I'm struggling to place them. Janie has pulled repressed memories from me before, but I'm not interested in doing that now. Sometimes, what's hidden is meant to stay there. I find myself grateful for my mind protecting me in this way.

"Ok, I'm done with the memory talk," I say with a laugh. "How's work going?"

Kash rolls his eyes. "Can I say that I hate it?" He laughs, but I know he's serious.

"If that's how work is going, then yes, you can say that."

"Yeah, I hate it." He laces his fingers behind his head, leaning back against the booth.

"Then I'm really glad you are pursuing your dream of opening your own piano bar!" I say excitedly.

"Absolutely," he responds. "I'm actually going to look at a place that's for rent soon," he adds, his eyes lighting up.

There it is. The thing he was holding back. But why?

"That's great!" I offer, taking another sip of my drink and flagging the waitress down to order another round for both of us.

"It's in Santa Monica."

Thats's why.

My breath stops.

California?

Did he just say he's going to look at a bar in California?

He reads the response on my face. "I know. It's crazy, right? But my gut is telling me to at least go check it out." Kash lets out a breath like he's been holding it for a year. I can't label what I'm feeling. Am I sad? Am I shocked? Am I just overwhelmed with thoughts of California? I'm unsure, but I know that it's important to support my friend, so that's what I do.

"Wow! Santa Monica? Are you serious? That's crazy!" *Ok, Summer, rein it in.* I take a steading breath.

Kash smiles at me. "It's not set in stone in the slightest. I'm just looking at my options. But I know I can't work in finance anymore. This is what I want to do with my life. I want a quiet existence, doing what lights me up." I look at Kash. He looks so content. Listening to him talk about this dream causes me to warm up inside.

I smile at him genuinely. "Go for it."

Kash slaps his palm on the table. "Right?" he ponders, looking for more encouragement from me.

I nod. "Yes. And I want a play-by-play of everything that's going on." I give him a look, asking for a promise.

"Of course. Thanks, Summer. Your support means a lot." I lean over the table and grab his hands in mine. I want what makes him happy, even if it takes him away from his life here and from me. At this moment, I realize that Kash and I have become extremely close over the last year, closer than I had even realized before. He is like family to me.

We finish our dinner and sit, sipping our drinks and talking for hours. My cheeks hurt from smiling so much. It's a sensation that's so foreign to me. I rub my jaw lightly in awe. Joy is brewing deep down. I can feel it — just sitting there enjoying time with a great person. It is something to note. I feel at peace.

———

In the car, on the way home, we start talking about Farrah and Joey's wedding. The countdown is on. It's only two weeks away. "I can't wait to dance!" Kash says, laughing.

Junior year, Dan invited me to his prom, and I was apprehensive but thrilled by the idea of it. Cassie took me to get a dress — it was midnight blue with diamonds at the top and I felt beautiful in it. But I will never forget the pitiful look she gave me when I came out of the dressing room — like I was some sort of dressed up insect. *You look so different,* she said with a hint of arrogance. That was her idea of a compliment, I had assumed. I let her words slide off my back and allowed myself to savor how beautiful I felt, looking at myself in the Filene's dressing room mirror. I couldn't even imagine going to an event like prom, but I was certainly looking forward to it.

But I never got to go.

I ruined my chance the night I made out with Zack. I watched as my world fell apart, and my first and my *only* opportunity to experience that rite of passage plummeted into nothingness.

I smile at Kash. "I have never danced on a dance floor before." I share this tidbit of information and feel Kash glance over at me from the driver's side. Thankfully, he doesn't act shocked.

"We are going to change that, two weeks from today. Meet me there, or be square," he says.

I laugh. "That's cheesy."

He shrugs. "You want to stargaze?" Kash asks me as we drive past the park by the river.

"Sure."

He pulls over and parks along the water. He gets out and heads to the bed of the truck, grabbing a blanket. As I get out, he motions for me to follow him over to the grass, where he lays out the blanket.

"Let's count," he says as he's lying down. I stare at him and quickly follow his lead, lying next to him on the blanket.

"Let's just look. I don't want to count right now," I whisper, looking up at the stars. The expanse of velvet black sprinkled with little specks of light ignites something in me, like it always does. It's like looking at a familiar picture you've walked by a hundred times, but then one day, you glance at it, and it's almost like you see it for the first time.

My eyes find the brightest star right away, and I think of my momma. After she died, I used to pretend that was her when I'd go up on the roof at the Brickman's. I would talk to that one bright star and hope that wherever she was, she could hear me.

"Isn't it weird that the stars are always the same, no matter when you look at them?" I ask, not taking my eyes off the sky. Kash doesn't answer right away. "These are the same stars I looked at when I was younger. That one right there," I continue, pointing at the brightest one, "I used to pretend it was my momma."

Kash looks over at me and then back up at the sky. "I used to believe it was my dad," he whispers. The skin on my arms tickles with goosebumps. So, Kash has a connection to the stars too. We probably talked and cried to the same stars at the same time while we were growing up and experiencing our own trauma.

"So, the stars are special to you, too, then?" I ask. He nods but doesn't say anything as I gently rest my hand on top of his.

I can feel my breath moving in a steady rhythm, my heart beating along with it, calm and at ease. A shooting star flashes across the sky, and we both gasp. I make a wish, but I already physically feel it coming true — the pieces of my heart are being mended back together.

CHAPTER 21

Texas - Now

FARRAH AND JOEY'S WEDDING

"**W**ELL, THIS IS A first," Maverick says as he tapes the sign to the inside of the bar's window.

Sullivan's will be closed this Friday, Saturday, and Sunday for a special wedding in the Sullivan's family.

We will reopen Monday at 2 p.m.

I can't imagine the hit Maverick will take financially. I know I'm taking one for not working at all this week. But he seems excited. Maverick offered to drive me and Silvia up to the lake where the wedding is being held. The rest of the staff will meet up at the hotel tonight for the rehearsal dinner. Kash is on a flight back from California as we speak, and he is heading straight there from the airport. I talked to him on FaceTime a lot while he was there the last few days. He showed me around the empty bar that he was looking to rent. He turned his camera around to show me the view out the windows: I saw the Pacific Ocean, the pier of

Santa Monica, the ferris wheel, the crowds dressed casually and soaking up the sun. Every time we talked, Kash looked elated, as if his dreams were sliding into place. Though I'm looking forward to hearing all of the details of his trip and what will come out of it, there is part of me that is dreading it. I know my progress and healing needs to be centered around me, and not being dependent on another person, but I have never had friends or family before, and my Sullivan's family is everything to me. Kash has become such a close friend and I think I'm allowed to fear losing a best friend.

As we drive to the lake, I begin to doze off to the sounds of Maverick and Silvia bickering about the routes we should take. I float in and out of consciousness for an hour, hearing snippets of voices and sounds — Silvia's laugh and Mav humming along to the music and tapping on the steering wheel to the beat.

About an hour and a half later, we arrive at the lodge. I look around and take in the surroundings. This is the perfect place for Farrah to get married. It suits her well — simple and beautiful. The lodge rests steps from the edge of the lake, and out in front of it, on the lawn, there are rustic wooden chairs, some around campfires, some at tables, some facing the lake, all complete with pillows and blankets. The trees are wound with tiny twinkle lights that aren't on yet, and I can't wait to see what it looks like out here once darkness falls. Over to the left is an arch, simply decorated with eucalyptus and blush-colored flowers. Sprawled out in front of the arch are roughly forty chairs set up for tomorrow's ceremony. I imagine Farrah standing there tomorrow marrying Joey and I smile to myself.

I'm pulled from my thoughts by Farrah, who comes bounding out of the lodge. "Hi, guys!" she yells and gives us each a hug. Joey is trailing behind her, beaming. They are both glowing, and I love seeing this unfolding right in front of my eyes. When you've had minimal, if any, experiences witnessing love, it's breathtaking when you do finally see it. I watch them, memorizing every look, every touch. I store these images away — something to remind myself of possibilities for the future.

"How was the ride up?" Joey asks us.

"Well, I slept the whole way, so it was great for me," I say with a smile.

Mav chuckles. "It was fine. No traffic at all," he says, popping a piece of gum in his mouth.

"We would have been here faster if we took my route," says Silvia, jokingly punching Mav in the arm. We all laugh.

"I'm so glad you're here! Go get settled in. Appetizers and dinner will start at six. We will all meet in the lobby, but everything will be taking place right here," Farrah says, gazing out over the quaint little set-up. "Wear something cozy and comfortable tonight. I want everyone to just feel like they're at home." Farrah is practically bouncing out of her shoes with excitement.

We all head into the lodge to check in. I make my way to my room, which is next to Silvia's. It's small and cozy with a view looking out over the lake. The bed is plush and white, and I want to crawl in and sink into the fibers, but I don't. I put my bag down next to the bed and sit in the chair by the window, looking out at the lake. I take a sip from my water bottle and enjoy the silence while I let my mind wander. I used to hate the silence because my wandering mind is good at inviting in intrusive thoughts. I tend to rely on the TV to keep the intrusion at bay, but I know that I need to work on that and I am. Here, the silence isn't scary, though. It's peaceful. I see the lake water sloshing against the shore from the wake of a passing boat. I practice what Janie has taught me — focus on what I see and label it, and if my mind wanders, bring it back.

Water.

Boats.

Sun casting light on all of it.

Kash.

Kash! I see him outside looking around with his bag on his shoulder. His hair is in a bun, and he looks tan from being out in the California sun for a few days. He looks tired from traveling. I am so happy to see him that I run out of the room and greet him outside. He smiles at me and opens his arms for a hug as I run into him. I squeeze him as tight as I can, and he does the same. "Hey, Summer!" he says into my hair.

"Hey," I say with my eyes closed. "How was your flight?" I ask, pulling away.

"It was fine. We left a bit later than we were supposed to because we had to switch planes once we were all boarded, but I made it so it's all good," he fills me in, starting to walk toward the lobby entrance. "This place is awesome."

"It really is amazing." I look back over my shoulder at the water again.

Kash's room is down the hall from mine. I walk him to his door and then head back to mine so he can rest for a bit before we all meet for the evening festivities. I pull out an outfit I want to wear and lay it on the bed — dark jeans and a knit sweater that falls off the shoulder, both are from Old Navy. I take a shower and let my hair air-dry and plop down on the bed in the lodge bathrobe. I go to pick up the remote but decide to leave it where it is and grab the book that I brought with me instead. I decide that's a better use of my time.

At five-thirty, there's a gentle knock on my door and I wake with a start. I didn't realize I had fallen asleep. *Shoot,* I think to myself because I still need to get ready. "One second," I say groggily as I head to the door, tightening the robe strap around my waist. I look out the peephole and see Silvia. I open the door to see her looking polished and ready then I look down at myself. "Sorry, I'll be quick! I fell asleep," I announce apologetically.

"You have time, hunny. I just came to see if you wanted to go sit outside and get a glass of wine before everyone gathered."

I smile at her. "I won't be long," I say. "Go on out and I'll meet you in ten minutes."

"Ok, dear. See you in a few," Silvia says as she turns and begins making her way down the hall. I get ready fast, pulling on my clothes, braiding my hair and doing a quick, one-layer mascara job. *I'll spend more time on my appearance tomorrow,* I think to myself as I rush out the door to meet Silvia.

She's sitting in a chair facing the water. There's a glass of white wine on the armrest for herself and a glass of red for me on the chair next to her. I sit down and put the soft blanket over my knees, cuddling up as I notice the temperature has started to cool off a little bit this evening. "Thanks for this," I say, picking up my glass and holding it up to clink with hers.

"Not a problem, dear," Silvia says, tapping my glass then taking a sip of her wine. "This is a lovely place for a wedding, don't you think?"

"It sure is," I respond, looking out at the water, taking in all the beauty.

"I'm not much into the marriage thing but I do think Farrah and Joey are happy and I'm glad for them," Silvia says. I look over at her, wondering where her opinions of marriage came from, and it's like she read my mind. "Yeah, old single Silvia," she continues with a laugh. "Did I ever tell you that I was engaged once?" I shake my head no. "Yup. I was twenty-four. My fiancé was twenty-eight. He traveled a lot and had a wandering eye, as they say." She nods a few times and pauses, taking another sip of her wine. "I caught him in the bathroom with a waitress at our rehearsal dinner. Can you believe that? Our rehearsal dinner! We were going to be married the next day." She shakes her head in disgust. My mouth has fallen agape listening to Silvia tell me this story about her life.

"Oh my God, Silvia, that is terrible," I say sympathetically.

"Yeah, I never found marriage to have a point after that." Her voice is distant as she gazes at the water. She shrugs her shoulders. "Maybe that wasn't the right thing for me to do. Maybe I missed out on things because of that attitude. But what can ya do?" She takes another sip of wine, but this one seems to have the purpose of stifling a tear.

I put my hand over hers, trying to reassure her. "I don't think you missed things," I offer. "I think you just took a different path, one that led you to things you would have missed otherwise. I think that's what life is about, right? We constantly come to forks in the road, and we have to go one way or the other. We'll never know what was down the path we didn't take, and I think I'm starting to believe that that's ok."

Silvia smiles at me without showing her teeth, her eyes wet with emotion.

"And I can tell you one thing, Silvia, I am so grateful that our paths led us to meet each other." I give her a warm smile and get up to offer her a hug.

"Oh, dear, you are so sweet," she says, hugging me back. "And I feel the same about you, love." She takes my face in her hands and looks at me with love in her eyes.

The rehearsal dinner guests begin slipping out of the lodge and onto the lawn. Silvia wipes her tears, and we pick up our wine glasses and walk up to meet them. I see Farrah's mom, who I've met before, and go over to say hello. She introduces me to Joey's mom and aunt. I meet the few cousins that Farrah has here but really that's it for her family. She told me she'd just have a small number of family members attending the wedding and she was right. The rehearsal dinner consists of five people from Joey and Farrah's family plus the Sullivan's crew — Farrah's chosen family. The setup on the grass consists of two large wooden circular tables topped with greenery and minimalist bouquets, candles, and simple place settings. I look at the lights strung on all the trees, and I'm enamored with the softness they spread over the whole space. It is truly magical.

We sit around the tables and enjoy each other's company, the air filled with the sounds of clinking silverware, laughter, and the crickets lingering around us. I feel warm on the inside and I'm wrapped in a sense of comfort and peace. This is something noticeable because it's not a feeling I get often. I look over at Farrah and smile. She is grinning ear to ear and Joey has his arm around her, gently rubbing her shoulder. Everything I see fills me with joy, and I take a second to silently express gratitude for all that is happening in this moment. I take a deep breath and allow myself to be completely present.

After dinner, Joey stands up and announces that we are moving into the lounge to do karaoke. Some people hoot and cheer, and others roll their eyes in good fun. Me? I'm indifferent. I won't participate, but I will cheer for everyone who's brave enough to do it. We all shuffle into the lodge, drinks in hand, and begin to fill in the seats around the small dance floor where a karaoke machine is set up. The lights are dim, and the group begins to discuss who is going first.

Farrah and her cousin, Cate, run to grab the microphones as they call the first song. They choose "Waterfalls" by TLC. We all sing along with them and cheer when they're done. I'm super impressed with their skills.

Kash comes over and sits next to me, handing me another glass of red wine. "Thanks." I smile at him. "What song are you going to sing?" It's not really fair, he's pretty much a professional at this. I can't wait to hear what he's going to sing. He smiles, looking over at Joey, who's grabbing the microphone from Farrah. The happy couple is singing a country duet.

"I'm not sure. Silas was supposed to be here, but he can't make it until tomorrow. I would have sung something with him." He shrugs his shoulders.

"You can do it by yourself, you know? You are a musician," I say, teasing him and giving him a big smile. He just looks at me. My mind is a little fuzzy from all the wine and the good vibes throughout the night, but this look on Kash's face scares me. "What?" I ask.

"Will you do a song with me?" he asks with a sparkle in his eye.

I gawk at his request. "Me?"

"What? I've heard you sing to yourself while wrapping silverware at the bar. You can carry a tune, you know," he says this with assurance, but I'm not buying it. "Come on," he says, grabbing my hand. "You want to write songs. At some point you will have to sing them." My stomach lurches at the thought of what he just said. I always assumed someone else would do that part for me.

I look around nervously. What is this feeling I'm experiencing? Is it excitement? Is it dread? It's definitely some type of fear, but I can't pinpoint it as all negative. "Um, what would we sing?" I ask, quietly.

He beams at me, knowing he's making progress. "Let's do 'Picture' by Sheryl Crow and Kid Rock." He sounds determined.

I furrow my brows. "Seriously?" I ask. "What made you think of that one?"

"I heard you sing it to yourself once at the bar. It was beautiful."

My cheeks warm, and I look down at my hands. "Ok, fine," I say. I chug the last of my wine, trying to give myself some extra courage. So far, the songs have all been loud, and the singers have been laughing and yelling. This song seems like it's going to take the mood down and that concerns me. My heart is beating fast and I'm starting to feel a little sweaty. But I follow Kash up to the machine anyway, and he tells the person running it what we are going to sing next.

My hands are shaking as I reach out for the microphone that's being handed to me. Kash winks in my direction.

"Ready?" he asks with a grin on his face.

I nod once but I'm not really ready. This is not something I could ever be ready for. I hear Farrah screaming my name and people clapping as the music starts. Kash's part is first; I watch him in awe as he sings the first verse. He's such a natural, he makes it look so easy. As my part comes up, I'm torn between curling up in a ball on the floor or running out of the room. But neither is an option — I face my fears and start to sing.

I start my part of the chorus and look up from the prompter to see shocked faces. Farrah has her hands on her face, and she looks like she's crying through a smile. Kash and I sing our combined parts, and before

I know it, it's over. He hugs me, picking me up off the ground and swinging me around.

"That was amazing" he gushes in my ear. "I'm so proud of you. I know that was scary but man, look what you did for yourself. You did something scary. You were brave." He's holding my shoulders and looking right into my soul. I choke out a laugh that's mixed with tears and emotion, and then I give him another big hug. My heart is beating way too fast, but what I am feeling right now is brand new, and I never want it to go away.

Farrah runs up to me on the dance floor and squeals. "Are you kidding me? Why didn't you tell me you could sing like that?" she asks, half annoyed, half elated.

I shrug and laugh. "I don't know."

But I do know.

Growing up, I went through life practically invisible. No one saw me for who I was, for what I was desperately trying to become — someone worthy of being seen. Coach Riker would encourage me to reach for my potential on the volleyball court. *I see your light underneath, Summer,* she would say. *But you have to dig it out. You have to show them,* she would emphasize, pointing at the other team, passion ignited in her words. *Show them who you are.* Her words would echo inside of me, but I never believed her. Because really, the only people I wanted to prove myself to couldn't be bothered to come and watch me. So, I hid behind my walls and never allowed myself to reach any potential that may have been there. I didn't believe in myself. I couldn't.

I give the microphone back to the guy and head back to the table with Kash. "I need water," I say, and we decide to head out to the bar for a breather and some hydration. Kash has not stopped smiling and neither have I, once I got over the shock. We stand at the bar, waiting to order and he reaches over and gives my shoulder a gentle shake while biting his lip, as if he's stifling his excitement.

"That was amazing, Summer, for so many reasons. I wish I could show you how you looked while you were singing." He shakes his head and orders two waters.

"I feel high," I say, and he laughs.

"I'm sure you do! Do you want to take these waters outside and sit by a fire? I want to tell you about my trip." I nod but, deep down, I don't want to talk about that right now.

We head out to the lawn and find some chairs. I take a blanket off the chair and prop the pillow up, giving me a little back support. I sit down and wrap the blanket around myself and sit down, facing the fire.

Kash sits next to me and wastes no time. "So, honestly, Summer, what did you think of the space when I Facetimed you? Did you think it was cool? Worth it?" he asks, waiting for and expecting my honest opinion. Though I want to lie and tell him that it isn't good enough for him, *or that it's too far away,* I tell him the truth because he deserves that.

"It's perfect," I say. "You looked so happy and excited every time I talked to you." I stop for a second and stare at the fire, afraid that if I look at him, I'll cry. "I remember you telling me that night at Caliente's that you would drop everything and go to California if you could. This must feel right. No?" I ask, taking my gaze from the fire, back to him.

"I paid the first and last month's rent on the place, Summer," he whispers the words like he's afraid to say them. "I worked with a bank while I was there. I'm going to get a business loan once I'm out there, and I have savings from my finance job that I hope will keep me afloat while

I get started. I know it's a leap, but I need this. I really do." He stops and waits for me to say something.

"What? Why didn't you tell me that?" I ask him, shocked that he had all this planned already.

"I wanted your opinion, but I needed to tell you in person. I don't know what I would have done if you hadn't agreed with me, but I wanted to know how you felt," he says, looking at the fire. I knew this was coming, and as his friend, I'm so happy for him, but I feel a lump forming in my throat and a tear falls from each of my eyes. I quickly wipe them away.

"What's the matter?" Kash asks softly, sitting up in his chair and putting a hand on my knee.

I shake my head. "I'm sorry," I say, attempting to shake off the sadness. "I'm so happy for you that I could burst but I'm going to miss you so much," I add, my voice hitching at the end.

Kash looks at me with sad eyes. "I know. I'm going to miss you, and everyone and my life here. It's my only hesitation. But I'm being pulled. I need to do this for myself." He is so sure of this that there's nothing else to do but congratulate him. I stand up, letting the blanket fall to the ground, and step closer to him to offer a hug. He stands and embraces me.

"I'm so proud of you," I say into his shirt, wetting it with fresh tears.

"And I'm so proud of you," he whispers into my hair. We embrace for a moment then he pulls away, "Shall we head back in?" he asks.

I nod. "So, what are you going to call it?" I ask as we walk toward the lodge door.

"Two WhisKEYS," he says proudly. "Get it? Like..."

I cut him off. "Yes, I get it," I laugh. "Piano keys." I smile big at him. "Thanks for including me in watching your dreams come true."

"Well, they haven't come true just yet. I gotta make something of this first."

"And you will," I say, wrapping my arm around him, and I know there is truth in my words.

The next morning, I wake to a cloudless sky, the sun pouring in through the curtain I forgot to shut last night. I climb out of bed and use the mini coffee machine to make myself a quick cup of coffee. As I wait for it to brew, I stretch, trying to wake up. Once it's ready, I sip it, looking out onto the lawn where lodge employees are busy putting the finishing touches on the little wedding venue.

It's eight-thirty a.m. and the wedding doesn't start until two o'clock. Since I've got some free time, I think about what I want to do this morning. I decide that a walk along the water's edge sounds relaxing, giving me some time to soak in the beauty of this place.

The woman at the front desk yesterday told me there are some beautiful trails. I decide to try and walk for an hour before having a late breakfast and then I can enjoy a leisurely time getting ready for the festivities. Taking the last sip of my coffee, I walk to the closet to look at my dress, inspecting it for any stains, wrinkles, or any other issue, but thankfully, it looks great. I spent a lot of money on it when I was out shopping with Farrah a few weeks ago — money I definitely should have allocated to other things, but such is life. It's a champagne color, fitted, knee-length, and it accentuates my curves. It's strapless, which I usually hate, but when I tried it on, it seemed like it had good wiring to stay in place. I brought a shawl in a similar shade that has a shimmer to it, in case it gets chilly tonight, which I'm thinking it will, given the temperature last night. I put my gold strappy shoes underneath the dress, leaving everything together, so I can easily get dressed later. I shut the closet door and walk to my luggage then change into leggings and a sweatshirt and grab a water bottle from the table to head out for my walk.

For the last year and a half, since I moved to Texas, walking has been very healing for me. It gives me time to decompress and process some of my emotions. Sometimes I get angry thinking of things from my past, and I walk faster. Other times, I think of things that make me sad, and my body is forced to breathe deeply to steady the tears. No matter what, after I'm done, I always feel stronger and that's been a game changer for me.

Out on the lawn, I head down to the right, approaching the lake. The view in that direction seems better — beautiful trees lining the shore, a mist hovering over the water. I start walking down the trail, and my mind immediately starts to wander, and I let it. I don't pull it back. I go back in my memory to the most painful event in my adolescence, a memory that was repressed for years, one I only recently recalled with the help of Janie. Once I recalled it, there was a part of me that wished I never had, but now I'm realizing that I was never really healing with that memory still tucked away. I'm learning that I only started healing once I began to face my demons.

Pain, the emotional kind, is tricky. For my whole life, I've ached so much from the things that were done to me, how I reacted to those things, and how those experiences shaped me. I carried all that pain and regret around with me, weighing on my shoulders, crushing my heart, day in and day out. When I started to get better, there was a lightness that I began to feel that I had never experienced prior. I've made a lot of progress, but there have still been times over the last eighteen months that I've slid back into depression when I started to feel the pain taking over. It became physical, debilitating even. I learned this is normal for people who have experienced significant trauma. My whole life, I never knew it as that — trauma. I just knew it as my life. I didn't know anything different.

I pick up my pace and shudder away the memory. Sometimes, it makes me sad, sometimes it makes me angry, and today, I feel the anger, and I use that to my advantage. I start a light jog and try to take even breaths to keep up my pace and work through it. I've recalled this memory, I've talked about it with Janie, and I've weaved in and out of my feelings surrounding it, but acceptance just hasn't come yet. I'm not sure I'll ever get there. Janie asked if I forgave the Brickman's for what happened, and the answer is an easy *no*. Maybe that's why I haven't reached acceptance, because I can't forgive.

An hour has passed by the time I make my way back to the lodge, feeling breathless and light. Exercise always leaves me feeling immensely better, that rush of endorphins cleansing my soul. I head to my room and towel off the sweat I worked up before heading back out to the breakfast buffet. I notice I've worked up a little bit of an appetite, so I grab some yogurt, a plate of fruit, and a blueberry muffin that looks delicious and homemade. I fill a mug of coffee and sit alone at a table by the window to watch the water while I eat. I sip my coffee slowly, savoring the flavor and the warmth. I think about the wedding, and I start getting excited about the festivities. I look at my phone and see that it's already eleven. I don't see anyone I know in the buffet room, so I finish up and head back to my room. I sit in the chair by the window and decide to read a little.

It's one-thirty, only a half-hour before the wedding, when I slip my shoes on, ready to head out the door. I'm meeting the rest of the Sullivan's family in Kash's room for a few minutes before the ceremony. Before heading out the door, I sneak a look in the full-length mirror, and it surprises me. I can't remember ever being this dressed up. My dress looks amazing, and the shoes are just the perfect touch. I put on a full face of makeup for the first time in months, and my hair is half up, the rest falling down my back in loose curls that I was able to achieve with a curling iron, instead of my usual braids or buns. I smile at myself and grab my clutch before walking out the door and down the hall.

Kash's door is propped ajar with the door stopper. I push it all the way open and see everyone gathered, chatting and sipping seltzers and beers.

"Summer! Oh my Lord, dear!" Silvia says, rushing over to me. "Look at you!" she exclaims, holding my shoulders at arm's length. "You look so full of life!" I give her a questioning look and think about what she said. *Full of life.* Do I usually look like life is sucked out of me? I don't have to ask her; I know the answer. I do. But here I am, little by little, getting my life back.

Kash walks over to me, and our eyes meet; his widen as he eyes my dress. He gives me a big hug, and I linger in his embrace for an extra moment. "You look amazing" he says, with less enthusiasm than Silvia, but his words inch their way under my skin and give me instant goosebumps.

I smile back at him. He's in a navy suit that fits him perfectly, and his hair is fixed away from his face which is unusual for him. His dark eyes are on clear display. "And you look dashing yourself."

"Thanks," he replies with a little laugh. "Want a Truly? I have your favorite flavor — mango," he says, reaching into the cooler.

"Sure, thanks." I take the can that he opened for me and enjoy a cold sip. We look out the window at the ceremony space, all set up and ready to go.

"It's going to be a fun night," Kash says, his hand in his pocket. I nod, and I believe it, too. We make small talk for a few more minutes, him talking about the great music last night and me sharing about my morning jog around the lake. As everyone finishes their drinks, we head out to the lawn together and take our seats.

I'm sitting in an aisle seat with Kash sitting to my right. Joey is standing up at the arch, looking like he can't wait to get started. He doesn't look nervous; he looks like he's in love and ready to get married. There's pretty music playing in the breeze. I enjoy the moment of anticipation; the sun finally came out from behind the morning clouds, and it beams down on us as we wait, warming my face.

Just a few minutes later, I hear the music that Farrah's walking down the aisle to, and I whip my head back to see her coming out of the lodge. She looks radiant. Her dress is satin and looks like it's painted onto her skin. Her hair is pinned up in loose curls, glistening in the sun. She walks arm in arm with her mom, who is smiling and crying at the same time. They stop at the back row of seats, and we all stand up. My cheeks hurt from holding such a large smile for so long now, but I keep it on my face as she approaches me.

As she walks, I look down and notice that her foot is about to wrap around the bottom of her dress, no doubt tripping her. I gasp and want to yell her name, but I don't have enough time. It's too late. Before I know it, Farrah trips over her dress in the most dramatic and drawn-out way possible. In an attempt to catch herself from the fall, she flails about and ends up going down to the ground in a heap. Her mom gasps and stumbles too, falling by Farrah's feet.

Shocked, I turn to look at Kash, who has his hands covering his mouth. I look back at Farrah, who, to my complete and utter surprise, is laughing so hard she's shaking, no noise escaping her gaping mouth. Joey abandons his place at the arch and runs down to help her up, and they are both laughing hysterically. Then, I lose it. I begin to laugh so hard at the absurdity of all of this, and how fast it happened, the memory of Farrah's shocked face as she stumbled and fell to the ground in her wedding dress. Tears are streaming down my face and my ribs start to hurt.

After they gain their composure, Joey slowly helps Farrah up from the ground, and she takes a minute to catch her breath and steady herself. When they finally begin making their way back down the aisle, the whole crowd cheers and laughs as Joey and her mom bookend Farrah the rest of the way.

When they finally reach the arch, we all sit down, and the officiant makes a little joke about the ordeal and everyone chuckles. But not me, I'm not just chuckling. I can't control my laughter, and my body shakes as I try to hold it in. My stomach hurts, my eyes burn, and I gasp as I try to breathe. I slowly blow a breath out but it's shaky, and I don't trust myself to not make a scene. I look up at the sky, trying to rein in my laughter, and put my hand on my stomach to settle it while I concentrate on just taking in air. I glance over at Kash, who is looking at me with a mischievous face, like he's holding in laughter, too, which doesn't help me. I hear a tiny squeak escape my mouth, and I grab Kash's water bottle from under his seat and take a sip. That helps. I focus hard on the water going down my throat, anything to get my mind off what just happened.

Kash leans down to my ear. "You did it," he whispers. I look at him, confused. "You laughed so hard, your stomach hurts."

———

The rest of the ceremony is a blur to me. As I sit there, I feel like I'm outside of my body, as if I'm watching from above, seeing myself let go of all my pain and allowing myself to truly laugh. I told Kash weeks ago that this would be a sign that I was healing — when I could actually laugh that hard. It may seem like a small thing to someone else, but to me, it's not. To me, it's everything. The fact that I can see progress gives me more hope than I've felt in a while.

As the ceremony ends, we all clap when Joey and Farrah make their way back down the aisle. Farrah jokingly gestures like she's going to fall, and I completely lose it all over again. I can't breathe. I grab Kash's arm, and he starts to laugh again too. Why had no one ever told me how good this would feel?

The cocktail hour is a blast. Farrah and Joey already took their wedding pictures before the ceremony, so they are with us, hanging out and celebrating. We're reliving the ceremony; Farrah can't stop talking about her fall. I admire her positivity, I always have. As we mingle, I try all the passed appetizers, and everything is delicious. My favorite is the lobster risotto balls — I eat two. It's so nice to enjoy fancy food and drinks with everyone. Usually, we are the ones waiting on our guests at the bar. It's a welcome change.

Kash orders a glass of wine for me toward the end of the hour, and we head to our table. Farrah sat all of the Sullivan's family together. Kash sits next to me on one side, and Whitney is on the other. Our table is filled with all the people I love most, and it's not lost on me how special this evening is. For a minute, I wish that it could always stay just like it is at this very moment. But I know that can't happen. I'm very aware of what's coming. We are all evolving, me probably most of all. But right now, at this table, we are all together. I savor it with everything I have.

I'm in the middle of chatting with Whitney when I see a hand in my line of vision. It's Kash. I glance up at him and see the lights from the tent reflecting in his eyes.

"I'm sorry, Whitney, can I steal Summer for a moment?"

She smiles at him and shifts her gaze to me, raising her eyebrows. "Absolutely."

I allow Kash to guide me to the dance floor and as I take a step onto the glossy, laminate wood pattern, my stomach begins to crawl with nerves. I'm sure that my lack of dance experience will embarass me, but Kash doesn't allow me time to overthink. He spins me around and gently pulls me into his chest. We sway to the beat of the music, Kash leading me effortlessly. "I didn't want you to be square," he says, his eyes smiling as he looks down at me.

I chuckle and rest my forehead on his chest. I can't find the words to explain my gratitude, so I remain quiet. However, inside I am fully aware that dancing on a dance floor for the first time was worth waiting for.

———

The next morning, after all the festivities are over and we've packed up, I drive back to the city with Kash. I'm feeling heavy and sad that the weekend is over. I've looked forward to it for so long, and I haven't had that much fun in a long time, maybe ever. Kash reminds me that time doesn't stand still, that just like bad things end, so do the good things, but that's life. "Be excited for your next great thing, your next great laugh," he says, looking over at me. I smile back. I know he's right, but when you grow up lonely, alone, and missing out on good times, you have a sort of scarcity mentality. You try to hold on so tight to those moments as they come so they don't slip through your fingers like sand, never to be again.

We drive along the highway talking about anything and everything when a song comes on the radio. I gasp loudly, sucking in air, unable to release it.

"What's the matter?" Kash asks.

"This song. It reminds me of something really bad that happened to me." As I say this, I am very aware that I, again, haven't slipped into a triggered daze like I usually do. I'm here, in Kash's car, telling him about my experience.

"Do you want to talk about it?" he asks me.

Do I? Is this my chance to tell someone other than Janie about the night I became homeless? Do I want to share this now? I look out the window. I work really hard to stay present as I start telling Kash about the worst thing that ever happened to me while the song plays softly in the background.

CHAPTER 22

Kentucky – Then

I TAPPED MY FINGER on the frame of the window in the front seat of Jason's car and quietly sang along to the lyrics of "How to Save a Life" by The Fray. We were heading to a party at his friend, Jake's house. All the seniors from last year were home from college for spring break. Jason was still home and he was commuting to a school in the area. He planned to transfer the following year to a school out of state. Over the last year, Jason and I had grown closer again. I was a senior, and I'd climbed, if only slightly, out of the hole I'd gotten myself into during my junior year.

In the fall, I played volleyball, and during the winter, the Brickmans included me in their holiday activities. I had a job at a grocery store in town with Claire. We shared a car, if you could even call it that. After we went to driver's ed together, Greg and Cassie gave Claire a car that they sometimes let me use. But "sharing" the car and working at the same place meant it was easy for me to always have a way to get to work.

Claire and I were still just acquaintances who lived in the same house. She had really tried to be my friend for a long time, but it wasn't mutual. Overtime, I felt like she was looking down on me from up on her high horse, and it made me dislike her. Even though I didn't care to be Claire's friend, I was glad that Jason and I had connected again. Since he wasn't in high school with us anymore and was doing his own thing a lot, I think he felt safe letting me in again, which I appreciated. He was the only one in that family who made me feel like I was human.

As the song played, it made me think of the *Grey's Anatomy* episode I had watched that week. That show was such a good distraction for me. The drama and the horror that unfolded every week made me think I had some things I could be thankful for. I was healthy. I didn't have to try to save patients who had weird, scary illnesses. I didn't have a budding romance that was ruining my life. The rest of the family refused to watch it with me. I think they were too sheltered and watching it made them think of dark things they didn't want to imagine. I used to think about how nice it must be to know no darkness in your life, except for the foster child you let stay with you for a bit, while trying to do a good deed. The foster child who came but never left. I guess that was the only horror they had to deal with back then.

"What's up? You look bummed out," Jason said, looking over at me as I glanced out the window, breaking me from my thoughts.

"No, I'm fine. Just thinking." He reached over and put his hand on my thigh, a little too high up, and squeezed it gently. I jerked my head in his direction and pulled my leg away. It made me uncomfortable. He'd never done that before. Surprisingly, my reaction didn't alarm him. He pulled his hand away absentmindedly and whistled to the tune. By the time the song ended, we were at Jake's house, and Jason's gesture had left me uneasy.

I got out of the car and pulled at my jean skirt and adjusted my T-shirt before heading toward the door, trailing behind Jason. I realized that I would be seeing Dan for the first time in a while and that made me tense.

We walked into the house, and into a loud and boisterous atmosphere. People were all over the place — sitting and standing on the stairs, lining the hallways, sitting on the furniture. Smoke thickened the air, and beer cans and red Solo cups were strewn about the room. The house was jam-packed; I had never seen this many people there before. Usually, when I'd come over to Jake's house years ago, there would be a few of us in the basement hanging out — but nothing like this. I groaned to myself, wishing that I was in my bed, under the covers and reading a book.

Jake stumbled over to us and handed both of us a cup filled to the brim with what looked like some sort of melted candy. I was a little apprehensive about this concoction.

"Jungle juice!" Jake yelled. I decided to give it a try, so I took a sip. It was sweet and cold and tasted nothing like alcohol. When I was older, I learned that meant you shouldn't drink much of the stuff that didn't taste like it had any alcohol in it. That stuff was always dangerous. But I didn't know that back then. I took a few long swigs of the drink and walked away from Jake and Jason, looking to see if any graduated volleyball players had shown up.

A few hours later, after several more cups of the special drink, I was dizzy and had the sensation of floating. My brain felt disconnected from my body — the result of way too much jungle juice. I spotted Jason talking to Dan, and he looked completely wasted.

Great.

I was going to have to find another ride home. I rolled my eyes to myself as Dan walked away from Jason and headed over to me. As we made eye contact, I tensed up on the inside. I was definitely not in any position to talk to him, but I had no choice. There was no escaping.

"Hey, Summer," Dan said with a soft smile. I smiled back at him but didn't say anything, taking another sip.

Bad idea.

"How's school?" I asked, looking over his shoulder, not really wanting to engage with him. He had barely spoken to me since we broke up the year before. I wasn't interested in the judgment and the pity. *Poor Summer, always fucking up her life and leaving herself lonely and abandoned.* I held my last sip in my mouth and lifted up my cup, indicating I needed a refill, my attempt to get out of the conversation. Without waiting for a response from Dan, I waded through the crowd and headed over to the bowl of the pink liquid. He followed me. I took the ladle and scooped enough into my cup that it sloshed over the side.

"It's fine," he said, offering nothing of substance. "So, how's senior year been going?" I wasn't sure if he was all of a sudden interested in me again or if he was just making small talk.

"It's fine," I responded. "I'll be out soon and on to other things. Not sure what yet." I shrugged my shoulders. "How's Clemson?" I asked, not looking at him.

"It's good. Remember? You already asked me that," he said with a smile plastered across his face. I gave him a disparaging look and he sighed.

"It's great. I like it there," he answered then abruptly changed the subject. "Look, Summer. I feel bad about what happened between us. I hate what I said to you."

I looked at him and narrowed my eyes. I didn't understand why he was apologizing to me. After all, I was the one who had messed up. Yes, he did say some things he had no right to say, but he was mad, and I understood that. I had accepted it and moved on. I didn't want to talk about it anymore.

"I don't feel well," I said, shamefully, but the juice was running through me, and I was feeling like I was going to lose the contents of my stomach soon.

"Let me help you to Jake's room so you can rest a bit," Dan said, nodding his head toward the stairs. *I know how to get to Jake's room*, I thought. *He used to be my friend too.* But I let him guide me up there anyway, leading me slowly up the stairs.

Once we were in Jake's room, Dan pulled a blanket off of the desk chair. I lay on top of the bed, and Dan gently covered me with the blanket.

"I'll come back up before I leave to get you and take you and Jason home. He's wasted," he said, tucking me in. I nodded my head slowly, and my eyes fluttered. I squeezed them shut, trying to stop the spinning.

I heard Dan turn off the light and shut the door; the muffled sounds of people talking in the hallway were the last thing I heard as I drifted in and out of sleep.

I didn't know how much time had passed when I woke to a noise that I thought was the door opening. I opened my eyes, but they wouldn't stay open, so I just let them flutter shut again.

"Summer?" I could hear Jason's voice as he gently shook my shoulders. I couldn't bring myself to move much so I just continued to lay there, my back toward the door. My eyes fluttered as I tried to force them open and focus on what Jason was saying.

"Hi," I said, my mouth thick and the room still spinning. The bed lurched as I felt Jason take a seat on the edge. My eyes were so heavy that they shut again. Jason began to rub my back, but not in the brotherly, friendly way he should have been.

Something didn't feel right.

My eyes shot open, my heart began to race, and my body tensed. Jason started mumbling something about being attracted to me, and I rolled onto my back and looked at him with concern. I was starting to wake up fast.

"What are you talking about?" I asked him, hoping that he was just kidding.

"Come on, Summer. We aren't actually related. You're going to be leaving soon. I'm going to Arizona next year. Let's just have a little fun tonight." His gaze scared me, and I suddenly began to feel very sober. I sat up and quickly backed myself up against the headboard, trying to create as much space between us as possible. He inched closer to me as he leaned in to kiss me, but I jerked my head away and pushed his chest back with some force.

"Stop, Jason. You are out of your mind," I said sternly, mixed with a little bit of fear. A look fell across his face that I couldn't quite place, and I immediately had flashbacks of other times when Jason had looked at me with a similar gaze, times when I had just brushed it off as nothing.

"Oh, please. You know you want it too. I'm the only person you like hanging out with so it's kind of obvious you want me. Besides, everyone knows you're a slut."

His words cut me, deep, and I felt like my heart and soul were bleeding out onto the bed. Until that moment, I had considered him to be one of the only people who ever really understood me and let me be me, and it was all unraveling.

As his words sank in, I panicked. I had to get out of there. I got up from the bed, but he grabbed me and forced me onto my back. I tried to scream, but only a little yell came out before he forcefully covered my mouth with his hands. He forced himself on top of me, putting all his weight on me, pinning me down, and I couldn't move my arms or legs. He'd taken his hands off my mouth, but I was panicking and starting to cry, too scared to even scream out. And who would even hear me? Everyone was downstairs caught up in their own dramas, drunk and having a great time. No one had any idea I was upstairs, trying to fight for my dignity, to save myself from being lost and broken.

Five, four, three, two, one...

The sun begins to set behind the horizon, where water meets the sky. I watch the colors — pink, orange, and a shade of beautiful purple. I am mesmerized by the magic in front of me that seems utterly too good to be true because it is, but I don't allow myself to leave this alternate reality. Not yet. My toes reach the water, and I jump as the tide wraps my ankles in an embrace that soothes me. I bend down and put my hands in, burying them under the smooth sand. I back up from the water, watching my footprints disappear as if I was never even there in the first place. Because I wasn't. I'm not in this serene place that I long to be.

Where am I?

Right. I wasn't at the ocean.

I shook awake from the illusion, and there I was, in Jake's bedroom, on his bed, Jason peeling himself away from me.

He got up, pulling up his pants, the look on his face turning my stomach into waves of nausea that felt as if they would never settle. He put himself together, as if he had done nothing wrong, and I didn't move. I just stared up at the ceiling as a single tear slid down the side of my left cheek. I didn't wipe it away. I couldn't. I was frozen, hollowed out. I looked back over at him with just my eyes, the rest of me unmoving. He was facing me as he tied his shoes. I looked him in the eye, and somewhere deep inside, I found the strength to say something.

"I hate you, you fucking asshole. I'm going to tell your parents as soon as I get home." I was angry, and it came out forcefully, but I was also scared to death and began to cry at the end. My weakness was all he could see.

He scoffed. "When you get *home*? Where is your home, Summer? You are not part of our family. You've been living there so long that everyone feels sorry for you and just lets you stay because you have nowhere else to go. Everyone in MY family is going to breathe a sigh of relief when you finally leave next year." He tied his other shoe. "And go ahead, tell my parents. They won't believe you. No one will believe you. You have already ruined any possibility of that with all the shit you've pulled over the years." He stood up and began to walk toward the door. "Get up. We're leaving."

As he walked out the door, leaving it open behind him, I scrambled up and slammed it shut. I fixed my clothes and took a ragged breath, my limbs shaking uncontrollably. I wiped the tears off my face and tamed my hair. I slipped out of the bedroom and down the stairs, straight out the front door, avoiding eye contact with everyone.

I ran out to the street and started walking in the direction of the Brickman's house, trying to stay close to the houses so Jason wouldn't see me if he started driving around looking for me.

I didn't have far to walk. Jake lived a few blocks away, and when I got home, I unlocked the door with shaky hands and quietly walked up the stairs, heading directly to my room.

Fearing I'd wake Claire, I went straight to the window and climbed out on the roof, where I sat and cried for hours. I cried years' worth of tears that my body could no longer harbor. My chest, my throat, my head, they physically hurt. My whole body ached.

When the tears were all dried up, I devised a plan. I would keep to myself for the rest of the school year. I would save up every penny I could, and as soon as I graduated, I would get my own apartment and figure out what was next.

I'd already had countless setbacks in life, and I'd gotten through them. I was still fighting. I just needed to get to graduation, and I could start over. I pulled my weak body up off the shingles and crawled back in the window and into the bedroom and buried myself under my covers. I lay there and stared out the window until the sun started to come up, never falling asleep for even one second.

I knew it was morning because of the sunlight streaming into the room, but I didn't want to get up and face what was waiting for me downstairs. I lingered in bed until ten o'clock; then I finally forced myself to get up.

I looked in the mirror and was out of sorts from all the crying, so I smoothed out my hair and used a makeup remover wipe to smooth out my face, which was splotchy, puffy, and smeared with remnants of mascara and eyeliner. I pulled a clean sweatshirt over my tank top and left the leggings on that I'd slept in. I took a deep breath to gather my courage, opened the door, and walked down the stairs.

I was startled when I walked into the living room to see Cassie, Greg, and...Gina? Why was Gina there? It was Saturday morning. What the hell was going on? No one died because there was no one left for me to lose. My parents were both already long gone.

Cassie and Greg sat on the love seat, Cassie's face ashen and pointed. She wouldn't look at me. Gina was on the couch. "What are you doing here?" I asked, without emotion.

"Come sit, Summer," Greg said as he motioned to the chair, trying to exude some kindness that his wife was unable to muster. I sat down on the chair and put one foot on the ottoman. I tried to seem nonchalant, but I was so nervous — my insides, a mix of butterflies and jelly, mushing all around.

"So," Gina began, but Cassie cut her off.

"What she's trying to get to, Summer, is that Jason told us what you did last night," she said with disgust. I whipped my head from Gina to Cassie.

"What?" I spat.

"Oh, don't play dumb, Summer. We know all your tricks. He told us that you got drunk last night, *again*, and you came on to him." Cassie's voice began to rise an octave, and she looked at me with disgust. "How could you behave like this after all we have done for you?" she asked me, her voice shaking. "He is like your *brother.*"

I opened my mouth to protest but no words came out. What was the point? Jason was right. No one would believe me. They were just counting down the minutes until I was gone. I got up and began to storm upstairs.

"Sit back down, young lady," Cassie said through gritted teeth.

I sat.

Gina spoke up. "Summer, we are going to be moving you into a group home for the remainder of the school year. The Brickmans are ending their foster care license and we currently do not have an open home for you to move to. When one opens up, we will be able to place you into a foster home until graduation. Technically, you have aged out, since you are eighteen, but since you're still in high school, the department is going to support you through this." Gina finished, looking relieved. *How thoughtful of them*, I thought to myself, *helping the orphan while she finishes high school.*

I looked over at Greg, and his face looked like his heart was breaking. I didn't know if it was guilt, remorse, or genuine sadness for me, but that look was not enough to soothe me. Cassie ruined any sort of comfort I received from Greg. She looked cold, and she couldn't even look at me. If only she knew the truth — that her precious son, the one who she was so focused on protecting — had raped me, ridiculed me, and reminded me of the truth I was always hiding from, that no one wanted me.

I glared into Gina's eyes, waiting for her to tell me what to do.

"Summer, do you want me to help you pack your things?" she asked me with sorrow in her voice. I shook my head and looked over at the Brickmans. I forced them into discomfort as I stared at them until a tear fell down my cheek. Greg looked away, uncomfortable and unsure what to do next, while Cassie continued to glare, not backing down. I got up and walked away with my head down, carrying my heavy legs up the steps to my room. I couldn't go to a group home. I wouldn't.

I packed my black duffle bag with some clothes, as much as I could fit. I put in a second pair of shoes, and my purse that had five dollars in it, all I had to show from my job at the grocery store since I hadn't started saving. I wasn't going to go with Gina. There would be no group home for me.

I crawled out onto the roof and hid between the house and the garage so that if anyone looked out the window, they wouldn't see me. My plan was to hide until they came looking for me and realized I was gone. When they left the house to try to find me, I would climb down and take off. To where? I had no idea, but I was leaving. It was time for me to stop waiting for everyone to accept me and love me.

I took one last look around the room that I'd lived in since I was eleven. I wasn't sad. I was angry. In all that time, I couldn't get one person to see that I was worthy. No one grew to love me while I lived under that roof. Like Jason said, everyone was just counting down the seconds until I was gone. I was giving them a gift by leaving. I crawled out onto the roof and carefully held my bag against me so that it wouldn't fall.

And then I waited.

It seemed like I was out there forever, waiting for Gina's car to pull away, but then I finally heard voices in the bedroom.

I held my breath.

"She's not in here," Gina said in a panic. There was more muffled conversation, but I couldn't make it all out from where I was crouched. I heard Greg say something about the window being open and me getting out, and then it shut. I could no longer hear what was being said inside.

I waited, unmoving, until a few minutes later, Gina, Cassie, and Greg left in their cars. They all sped off, probably in an attempt to find me. But I chose to imagine that they were just going about their day, unconcerned. It made it easier for me to just walk away.

Everyone was gone. I didn't have to climb down from the roof. I could go back in through the window, walk through the house, and walk out through the front door, and so that's what I did.

I walked through the house slowly, my bag slung over my shoulder. I looked closely at the pictures on the walls of the staircase; none of them were of me. The pictures on the mantel in the living room also held no proof that I lived there for seven years.

I ran my fingers over my backpack that was hanging on the little knob where it had always hung since I was eleven years old. How heartbreaking for a child to look back on her adolescence and realize that no roots had formed, there was no place to call home, but I felt no sadness as I prepared to walk out of that house for good. I felt hollow and empty, and because of that, I never looked back.

In the kitchen, I grabbed some snacks from the pantry and slipped them into my bag. I had to get out soon if I wanted to be sure I wouldn't be seen. I started off down the street, walking away from the house and into the unknown.

By five o'clock, I was starving and realized I hadn't eaten anything substantial all day. Earlier, I bought a bottle of water, thinking I would drink it slowly and refill it as needed. I had already eaten the few snacks I had packed from the house. I only had three dollars left and I needed to eat something. I'd walked all the way into town and headed to the Kroger to see if I could find something cheap to eat.

I was glad I wasn't going into the grocery store I worked at. I didn't want to be seen by any of my coworkers, especially Claire who was working an early shift that day. I wandered around the store, looking for a bargain.

There wasn't much. I didn't have enough money for anything that would satiate me. Desperate, I grabbed a box of crackers and looked at them, remembering a time when I did this same thing — I ran away and used all my remaining money to buy crackers. Those would have to do, although they wouldn't fill me up for long. I'd have to deal with that issue later. I walked up to the front of the store, keeping my head down and trying not to make eye contact with anyone.

As I placed the crackers on the belt in the checkout line, the cashier tried to make eye contact. "Hi, how are you?" she asked with a saccharine smile.

Me? I'm subpar, or maybe horrible, depending on who you ask. My foster brother raped me and when I threatened to tell, he beat me to it and told his parents I made a move on him and after six and a half years, I was kicked out of my "home," and since I was aged out of foster care, I am now homeless and bought these crackers with the only money I have to my name. When I leave here, I have to find a safe place to sleep for the night. Thanks for asking.

That's what I wanted to say. But I couldn't. So instead, I lied, putting on a fake smile, pretending everything was normal. "I'm good, thanks. You?" I shifted my gaze from the conveyer belt to my shaking fingers, completely aware of how exhausted I must have looked.

Why do we always say "good" no matter what the truth actually is? Even if you're falling apart at the seams, you're expected to say "good." I'd rather not exchange a single word, especially that day when the word *good* mocked me, my day, and every day I had before that. Even the good days were just a ruse into false hope.

I walked out of the grocery store, holding my sorry box of crackers and what was left of my pride, which was almost nonexistent. I looked around the parking lot, trying to decide which direction I should head. I knew I didn't want to go back toward the house, but I wasn't sure where anything else was. So, I just started walking as the sun began to set. I wished I had a plan.

Three hours later, I was sitting on a park bench in the next town over, my bag next to me and my knees pulled up against my chest as the darkness enveloped me. I looked up at the sky and found the brightest star, like I always did. "Momma, why did you leave me here all alone?" I asked aloud, into the chilly night air. No one was there to hear me, much less answer. I was alone. I let my head hang, resting my chin on my knees, and allowed the tears to fall freely.

Eventually, I fell asleep with my bag as my pillow, having no idea how I was going to get out of the mess I was in.

CHAPTER 23

Texas - Now

By the time I'm done telling him about that awful night, we are already back in the city, parked outside my apartment. I look over at Kash. He is leaning against his door and listening to me with his whole body, his eyebrows furrowed and his mouth set in gentle frown, as if he's feeling everything I told him. He doesn't say anything, and I feel the need to fill the silence. "Yeah. It's a lot." I sigh and look out my window.

"Summer..." He doesn't know what to say to me.

I turn back to him and give him a weak smile. "You don't have to say anything," I tell him. "It was a long time ago." I'm doing that thing I do, where I negate the awfulness that happened to me, downplaying my feelings, to make other people comfortable.

"But it still affects you," he says, putting his hand on my leg, not like Jason did, but like a caring friend.

I nod once. "Yes, but I don't want it to anymore. You are the first person I've ever told this story to, besides my therapist, and do you know that I feel better right now? The weight of the embarrassment, the weight of the pain, the weight of the abandonment I felt has been on my back since I was eighteen years old. I think I released some of it today, sharing this with you. And I'm sorry to put that on you. Please don't carry it for me. Just let it go. Just be my friend. No pity, no feeling sorry for me, please." I start talking fast, fearing I've unleashed too much at once.

Without responding, Kash gets out of the truck and walks around to my side. He opens the door and gently pulls me out, wrapping me in a big hug that I allow myself to melt into. "I will carry whatever you need me to, Summer," he whispers in my ear. I close my eyes and let myself just be, stress melting away from me as we embrace, and I realize what he's offering. Just like Farrah did, he's offering to take on my burdens and help me carry the load.

After a few moments, I pull away from our embrace and look up at Kash.

"Thank you," I whisper.

"You're welcome," he whispers back. "But no need to thank me."

I nod, giving him a genuine smile. I take a deep breath, turning to grab my stuff out of the back of the truck. Kash takes it from me and offers to carry it up to my apartment. We walk up the steps and I unlock the door. I'm suddenly exhausted from the weekend and drained from sharing my story, and I crave crawling onto my couch and pulling a blanket over myself to drift off into a deep sleep.

Kash tells me he is going home to get settled in from his trip and the wedding since he hasn't been home in a week. Even though I'm exhausted and worn out, I hate to see him go.

"I'm going to take a nap right there," I say, pointing to my couch.

He smiles at me. "I think you should work on writing that song of yours later," he says. "I think you'll find a lot of inspiration after today." He winks at me and turns to leave. "I'll text you later. We can get lunch or something soon."

I walk him to the door. "Sounds perfect," I say, smiling, as I open the door and he walks out. I watch him walk away and then shut the door. I look toward the couch, wanting that nap, and then decide against it. I'm suddenly feeling a little more energetic and I think Kash is right — I think I might actually have some good inspiration now. I grab my notebook.

Sitting down at my table, I open up to the page where I jotted down some poetry, or lyrics, the other day:

The stars know my secrets
The stars are my keepers
They hold no judgment
With them I am whole.

I scratch out the whole thing and start over.

When you left me I bore the weight
Of the whole world on my shoulders.
The emptiness and sorrow was my fate
They said "no one will ever hold her."
Glancing up at the darkened sky
I feel so fragile and small
No one will know the reasons why
Except the stars I come to call.
The little girl I used to be
Is hiding in there still
Too scared to look, to scared to see
To be brave, she'll try, she will.

Glancing up at the darkened sky
I feel so fragile and small
No one will know the reasons why
Except the stars I come to call.

I stare at the words on the paper and watch as a tear smudges some of the letters and I dab it dry. I feel better, letting it all out — to Kash, to myself.

I read through the lyrics again and put them to a tune and sing it. My insides feel ignited with hope, drive, passion. I lean back in the chair and release some tension I've been holding in my neck.

I deserve a rest. I've experienced a lot of healing this weekend, and that's always exhausting. Good but exhausting. I close my notebook and head to the couch, feeling accomplished and invigorated and not one bit guilty for napping after the weekend I've just had. I lie on the couch, snuggle under the blanket, and I fall asleep — for once, without the TV on.

I'm thrilled about my shift tonight at work. I haven't been at Sullivan's since the Monday before the wedding, and I am desperate for money and also ready to get some routine back in my life. I've spent the last two days cleaning, doing laundry, grocery shopping, and writing. It's been great to catch up on my chores and also have some time to process my feelings, but I can't wait to be back, and I especially can't wait to see Farrah. They didn't take a honeymoon since they just went on a vacation a little over a month ago, but they did spend a few days alone at the lodge after the wedding. But she's back, and tonight we are all on shift together.

When I get to the bar, Silvia is already there, which is very unlike her. "You're early!" I greet her with a hug.

She rolls her eyes at me playfully. "Well, I'm sick of you people making me look bad," she jokes, laughing that great laugh of hers. She is wrapping silverware, preparing for tonight, and I pull a chair up next to her so I can help.

"Thanks, dear," she says, and I smile.

"Of course!" I grab a handful of forks and a stack of napkins and start rolling them.

"Is Kash playing tonight?" she asks me.

I shake my head. "No, he's off but Silas is playing, I guess with someone else." I shrug my shoulders.

I had been preparing for this all day — seeing Silas playing with someone other than Kash. It will be sad, but I guess I have to get used to it because that's what it will be like from here on out once Kash moves. The reality of the change sinks its way into my heart again and makes it heavy, but I try to keep it at bay, shake it off. I don't want to be sad tonight.

"Kash will be coming by to visit later on, though," I say. Silvia nods and we keep rolling our silverware then start with our other opening duty tasks.

As everyone starts to arrive for the night, we reminisce about the wedding weekend and how beautiful everything was. Of course, there's lots of commentary about Farrah's fall and subsequent hysterical laughter.

Maverick is predicting a busy night because of all the days we were closed, even though it's only Tuesday. We all prepare for a crowd, working together to set up the tables and chairs. Everyone pitches in to prepare the fruit for the bar and helps make sure the glasses are ready. It's always a team effort at this place, and I truly love that.

As the evening hits full swing, we realize that Maverick predicted right. Farrah and I are swamped at the bar starting at nine o'clock, and two servers have to come to assist us. Silas is on stage playing with someone named Frankie, who I think has performed here before, but I can't really place him. They start playing a song everyone loves, so the bar crowd melts away for a bit, and Farrah and I breathe a sigh of relief. But it's not much of a break. At about ten-thirty, I look up to see Kash smiling, his finger raised in the air, like he's calling me over to place an order.

"Can I help you, sir?" I flirt.

Flirt?

Did I just do that?

"Yeah, what's good?" he asks, beaming.

"Vodka soda with extra lime," I say, knowing it's his favorite.

"I'll take it," he says as he grabs a seat at the bar to wait for his drink. When it's ready, I pass the tumbler over, free of charge of course, but he puts a ten in the tip jar and I mouth *thank you* to him.

"I'll come chat with you later," he says as he walks over to the stage and climbs up onto it during the break between songs. Kash joins Silas on his bench for a minute, and when the break is over, he plays the next song with him. I look around and see that everyone in the bar is watching the performance, unable to take their eyes off them. *What are we going to do without that duo?* I wonder quietly as I watch from behind the bar, completely in awe.

"Did Kash tell you the news?" Farrah asks, coming to stand beside me. I nod without taking my eyes off them. She puts her arm around me, but she doesn't say anything, and I appreciate that she doesn't. She knows

I'm sad, but she doesn't understand the ins and outs of my feelings because even I don't really understand them. I just know that I am going to miss him terribly.

The night wraps up without a hitch. The place clears out at a reasonable hour, since it is Tuesday, and Farrah and I count our tips — we did pretty well. Everyone works to clean up, even Kash, and I admire his devotion to us. He winks at me with a sideways smile as he pushes the broom through the dining room. The gesture warms me inside.

"Can I walk you home?" Kash asks me, stacking a chair on a table.

"Sure." I smile at him as I continue to clean up. He continues sweeping and I wipe down the bar one last time. Before long, Sullivan's looks ready for tomorrow, and we all gather by the door to say goodbye. We hug, high five, share some laughs, and then head out in all different directions. Kash and I turn toward my apartment.

We only get a few steps away from the bar when Kash lays the news on me.

"Two weeks." He says this with a heaviness that's palpable, his hands in his pockets. He says it like that, I assume, because he knows I'm going to be sad. But I know he's thrilled, and I don't want to take away from his excitement. But two weeks? That's all the time I have left with Kash in the same city? The thought of it sends dread running down my spine.

"I know it's quick," he adds. "But my lease on my new place is starting soon, and I can't afford to have two apartments."

I turn my head to smile at him. "This is amazing, Kash," I say, and I mean it. My dread is my own problem. I know that and I put it aside so I can be there for him. I can't hold him back because I don't want him to leave. He has every right to pursue his dream. He looks forward and I can see that he's smiling. He looks at ease, happy.

"Can I cook dinner for you next week at my house?" he asks me.

"Of course. I would love that!"

Before I know it, we are outside of my apartment, and we stop, Kash lingering, one foot on the first step like he always does.

"So, I wrote some verses. I'm not sure how much I like them, but I think I have a melody for it too," I say as I look up at him.

"Oh! That's so exciting, Summer! Can I hear it?" he asks me, hopeful.

"Now?" I didn't really expect that reaction, although I'm not sure why. He was the one who encouraged me to start working on my song-writing so of course he's going to want to hear them.

"Why not?" he shrugs with a smile.

As I contemplate it for a moment, I can't come up with a reason not to. I'm not all that tired, and I'm on borrowed time with him, so we head upstairs into my apartment.

I head into the kitchen and boil some water for tea, something I always do when I get home after a late shift. I offer Kash some, and he accepts.

While the tea is steeping, I leave him in the living room, sitting on the couch, and I walk into my room and pull my notebook out of the drawer in my bedside table. I sit on my bed for a minute and look at the cover, nervous about sharing my lyrics with Kash. He's an actual musician with real talent. These are words from my soul. I don't know if I want them out in the universe just yet.

When I take too long in my room, Kash knocks on the door while opening it and enters, joining me on the edge of the bed.

"It's in there?" he asks, motioning to my notebook. I nod and push it over toward him. He flips it open to where my words are written, sprawled across the page. He reads them silently and then looks at me.

"Wow, will you sing it for me the way you imagined it?" I shake my head with finality. There is no way I am singing this to him. He puts his hand on my shoulder, reassuring me to give it a try. "I want to hear it, so I can learn the sound, and then I'll figure out how to play it on the piano."

Why does he have to be so thoughtful? And why does he have to leave me?

Since he's convinced me, I give it a go. I quietly sing the words for him as he beams. He starts to sing along with me with the same tune, looking down at the words for guidance since he obviously hasn't memorized them yet like I have. When we finish, I take a deep breath and smile at him, a silent thank you.

I go in the kitchen and grab our steaming mugs and carry them into my bedroom, placing them on my nightstand.

"This is very good, Summer. With music, it will be even better. Will you sing it at Sullivan's one night?"

I laugh and shake my head. "No, absolutely not."

"But isn't this what you want? Isn't this the career you want to have?" He looks at me, his eyes filled with questions.

I take some time to think about how to answer him. Finally, I say, "Yes, but it's about little steps with me. Writing these words took all of my energy. I felt good afterwards, but I need time before I can take the next step." I try not to come off as defensive, but I guess I am a little bit — protecting my heart and my soul and defending them from all the things that can tear them apart.

Kash ponders this for a moment then eventually nods. "You're right. I'm sorry. But I'll be here for you when you're ready." He reaches out to grab my hand and shakes it, a promise. He leans back against my headboard, stretching his arms above his head and yawning. "I should probably head out now," he says. I crawl up to the headboard and stretch out next to him, and he wraps his arm around my shoulder, my head falling to his chest.

"Don't go yet, please," I say with a yawn as I snuggle closer to him.

"Ok," he whispers. And that's the last thing I remember.

———

We both stir awake to the sun streaming into the room. Kash looks at his watch and jerks out of the bed. "Oh shit, I'm late for work and I have to give my notice today." He jumps out of the bed. I look at my phone and see that it's already eight. I know he will have to run all the way home and change before heading to his office because he doesn't have his car. I want to say something but I'm too stunned, sitting on my bed speechless. "What's up?" he asks me, pulling on his shoes.

I look up at him. "I..." I start and stall a little bit. "I slept through the night. I didn't wake up once." It feels as if I'm mostly talking to myself but when I look over at Kash, his smile tells me he is celebrating with me. "For the first time ever," I add with disbelief.

"Summer, you're healing," he says to me with assurance. He reaches for me, and I let him hug me. I want to be happy, joyful even. I feel rested and invigorated, for the first time in a long time, but did I only sleep because Kash was there?

"Yeah, I guess I am," I say, slightly dazed. I get off the bed and walk with him toward the door. "Have a good day at work, Kash. Oh, and good luck giving your notice," I say, pulling the door open for him.

"Thanks. I'll text you later and let you know how it goes," he says, giving me a quick hug before he runs down the stairs. I close the door and I'm left alone in my quiet apartment. I walk to the kitchen to make some coffee, and when it's ready I bring the steaming mug back into the living room where I sit on the couch, turn on the TV, pull the blanket over me, and settle in to watch Law and Order.

Throughout the rest of the day, I get a lot accomplished — laundry, a long walk and some yoga, errands. It's only noon when I realize I've fit several days' worth of chores into one morning. Is this what good sleep means? Productivity, alertness.

It feels unbelievable.

Ever since that one good night's sleep, each night has felt better than ever. I think I'm finally catching up on all the sleep I have missed out on throughout my life. I put the extra energy I have into working at Sullivan's, releasing my anxiety through exercise, writing every day, and checking things off my to-do list. Each day feels incredibly productive with this newfound energy. I feel like a whole new person, and the hope and promise that gives me is priceless.

———

The night before Kash leaves, he invites me to his apartment for dinner. It's basically empty and kind of eerie inside, only a few pieces of furniture left and some boxes he's packed up waiting at the door. He's been packing for the last week and shipping things out to his new place in California. It feels surreal, our voices reverberating off the empty walls.

"I'm sorry I couldn't have you over until now. It's just been so crazy," he says, sympathetically. "I wanted to cook something nice, but everything is all packed away now. So, Chinese takeout will have to do. I hope you like it because I already ordered it." He laughs and so do I.

"It's perfect," I say, taking a seat on his couch where the unopened Chinese food boxes are spread across the otherwise bare coffee table. He sits next to me, handing me a paper plate, and we open the containers of food — lo mein, rice, crab rangoons, and spring rolls.

My mouth waters as I scoop the contents of the boxes onto my plate. I grab some chopsticks, unwrap them, and take a huge bite of lo mein, enjoying the aroma of all the delicious food.

We eat in comfortable silence for a bit, and a few minutes later, we settle into a conversation about nothing, really, but it feels so good — just like it always feels when we're together. For a second I find myself on the verge of tears, thinking that this is our last time hanging out together. I look down at my plate, trying to stop the tears from coming, but he catches a glimpse of me and reads the look on my face.

"I know, Summer," he starts. "It's going to be hard for me too." Talking about it is only going to make the tears come faster. I swallow my bite and take a sip of my beer, taking a breath and pushing the tears away, then set down my chopsticks and put the plate on the table. I lean back against the couch, looking up at the ceiling as if the words I want to say might be floating up there for me to grab. But they aren't and my voice is trapped inside my throat, which feels like it's filled with marbles.

Kash gently squeezes my knee. "I have something for you," he says, getting up from the couch and heading into the kitchen. I sit up and take another sip of beer, desperate to choke down the lump in my throat and ward off the emotion bubbling at the surface. A moment later, he comes back into the living room carrying a pretty silver gift bag with blue tissue paper peeking out of the top. I'm puzzled, and I give him a questioning look.

"It's just a little something." He smiles, handing me the bag.

"Wow," I say, surprise evident in my voice. I take it from him, peek inside, and reach past the tissue paper for what looks like some kind of box, and I take it out. I hold it in my hands — a small box, only about twelve inches long, simple, made of maple wood with a tiny little latch. Curious, I look over at him, and he is grinning from ear to ear.

"Open it," he says softly. I can tell he's excited about this gift he picked out for me. I open the little latch and look inside, and immediately my shoulders sink, and I start to cry. I don't know if I'm happy or sad, or maybe a little of both. Because of my trauma, labeling my feelings has never been easy for me.

I reach into the box and pull out the contents — a napkin with our tic-tac-toe game on it from when we played at the pub, a program from Farrah's wedding, the Caliente's receipt from our dinner there, a Sullivan's menu. I look up at him and I can't stop it — I let out a sob that brings tears streaming out of my eyes along with it.

Kash puts his hand on my leg to reassure me. "I thought you might want to start your own memory box," he whispers. "I put some things in there for you to get started." He places his hand in the box and pulls out Farrah's wedding program. "Like, this was the time when you first laughed until your stomach hurt. I thought it was a good memory to hang on to."

I'm just staring at him. My vision is clouded, and I'm overwhelmed with gratitude. I don't even know how to respond. Finally, I take a deep breath and speak. "This is the most thoughtful gift anyone has ever given me," I say, choking on my words.

He smiles but he's not boastful. "Everyone deserves happy memories, Summer," he says, not taking his eyes off me. "This way you can savor all those new happy memories you are making." I nod once and let him embrace me, fully wrapping me up and holding me close to his chest. We sit like this for a long time, and when I finally pull away, I can see clearly.

"Kash, all my life, I have only known darkness. I think it's why I always spent, and continue to spend, so much time seeking out the stars. I think I was trying to prove to myself that there was a possibility to find light, even in the darkest of places." I share my thoughts, looking into Kash's eyes with purpose. "You are my light, Kash." I sob again. "You've helped me more than I can even describe. I've done so much work to heal myself, but without you believing in me, I wouldn't have started on the path to finding myself. And now you're leaving, and I'm so scared." I say the last part quietly as I lean back on the couch and take a deep breath. Kash leans back next to me.

"Summer, it's not me. It's you. You're right; you are doing the hard work. But you just needed connection, a connection that was deep, for you to be able to feel that light. Everyone needs connection, and you've never had it. Now that you've experienced it, you're scared to be without it. That's totally understandable. But listen, I'm always going to be here for you, no matter where I live. We will FaceTime and text all the time." He sits up and takes my hands in his. "Do you hear me?"

I nod. I believe him but I still hate it. He sits back again, our hands still intertwined, and I lean my back against his chest. We sit here together in the dim light of the only lamp left in his apartment, talking about life and the future.

"What time are we all supposed to be here tomorrow to say goodbye?" I ask when there's a lull in the conversation.

"Seven o'clock," Kash responds, yawning.

I nod, catching his yawn and echoing it. We continue talking for a bit longer, and eventually, we both fall asleep, curled up on the couch.

A knock at the door jerks us both awake and we look at each other and share a laugh. I smooth out my clothes and fix my hair. "Can we pretend I just got here?" I ask. "I really don't want Farrah to get the wrong idea."

Kash chuckles, jumping off the couch. "Sure," he says, walking toward the front door.

Everyone from Sullivan's made plans to come by his apartment and say goodbye to him this morning; I just happened to get here thirteen hours early. Kash and I step outside of his apartment to greet everyone. I'm carrying my purse and the memory box Kash gave me last night. Farrah gives me a questioning look, but I just ignore her and walk onto the grass. "I'll drive you back to your place on my way, ok?" he whispers quietly to me. I nod.

I feel like I'm floating above all of this, watching from the sky. Is this really happening? I see Silas and Kash hug each other and share words no one else can hear. They start roughhousing for a second, just like brothers would, and I see Silas grab Kash's man bun and laugh, even though there are tears in his eyes.

Now, it's Farrah's turn. She's laughing and making fun of Kash because I know it's easier to tease him than to get emotional, and I smile.

Everyone gets their turn to say their goodbyes, and when everyone's done, we all rally around him, enveloping him in a big group hug under the trees on the front lawn of his apartment. The air is cool and crisp, the breeze blows the leaves slightly and makes me shiver, the sun hasn't heated up the day yet. There's no one else outside besides us, one big group, or family really, saying goodbye to one of our own. I take a picture in my mind: I don't want to forget any of this. Even though these aren't necessarily happy memories, they are worth remembering. A goodbye not tainted with abandonment.

"You guys promise to come and visit me when things get up and running, right?" he asks everyone as we break away from our group hug. We all assure him we will definitely be there to check out his new space. I try to imagine that scenario, but I can't. Me in California? Soaking up the sun, seeing the Pacific Ocean for the first time? That seems like an impossible dream.

Everyone piles into their cars, heading home, waving and hollering as they cruise down the street, their windows open. It's just me and Kash left. I feel an overwhelming rush of sadness as the reality of what's happening fully hits me. We climb into his truck without saying a word and begin the journey to my apartment.

Sitting here silently, I take an unsteady breath and look out the window. Flashes of color fly by as we drive along, and my mind can't seem to focus on anything right now. I have so much dread that I can't begin to compartmentalize any of my feelings. I want to pinch myself, to wake up from this crazy dream, or is it a nightmare? I know that deep down I am happy for him, but right now, selfishly, I wish that this hadn't worked out. I wish Kash wasn't leaving us and heading out to California. The feeling of dread is bubbling to the surface, and my breath shifts to quick, short breaths as he pulls up to the sidewalk at my place.

Before I can stop myself, I start crying uncontrollably. I don't hold back. I couldn't if I tried.

"Summer..." Kash starts as he looks at me but then his voice trails off. He jumps out of the truck and jogs over to my side, opens my door, and he pulls me into his arms.

"Don't go," I sob. He rocks me back and forth soothingly, but it only makes it worse. Not seeing him whenever I want, not being able to make plans with him to hang out any time, it's wrecking me.

Not once, since I was nine years old, before my mom started drinking, has anyone comforted me, connected with me, or reached me like this. He's been there for me like no one else, and the amount of gratitude I feel for him is immense. But my fear of abandonment clouds my vision of reality. I've been abandoned so many times before and that trauma is real. It makes saying goodbye even harder. I know I'll see him again but that's hard to remember when the fear is all I can feel.

I remind myself that this is life. Life is messy and unpredictable. Dreams are dreamed and chased. I know, in the depths of my heart, that Kash has to leave. He has to chase his dream. The reality of his situation is promising, and I know that, but I'm still hurting. Life is complicated but it can be beautiful, and I see that now. I can see the beauty in the pain. I remind myself that Kash is not abandoning me.

I will be ok.

"You inspire me, Kash," I say when I finally catch my breath and steady my tears. "Thank you for teaching me that going after what you want is possible." My words come out through gritted teeth and tear-stained eyes as I fight with myself to control my emotions. "I don't want you to leave, but I see how important it is to follow your dreams. You've inspired me to fight for what I want too," I say as I lean against the door of the truck and put my hand to my head, trying to fend off a headache from crying so much.

"Well, Silas is going to talk to you about performing your song with him at Sullivan's. I already gave him the music that you and I came up with last week," he says with a sly smile on his face. He can see my hesitation. "Don't say no. Don't let me down." He winks at me.

I laugh at him. I know that I have to do it, for him and for myself. "Ok, fine," I sigh. "But I'm going to have to take a shot first!" I laugh again, through my tears.

"Deal," he says, taking my face in his hands and turning it toward his. "And I'll have Farrah FaceTime me because I wouldn't miss that for the world," he says quietly, sending warmth through my whole body. I pull away and blurt out, "Drive safe. Keep us all updated on your drive there and on the whole process of opening the bar. We want to be there for you," I say looking down at the sidewalk.

"Of course," he says softly.

We slowly walk over to the driver's side. He opens the door but stops before getting in. "Bye, Summer," he says, pushing a strand of hair out of my face. "Make memories and put them in that box, ok?"

I nod. "Make memories and put them in your box, too, ok?" I say, my voice catching.

He kisses the top of my head and climbs into the seat, turns the truck on and shuts his door. Rolling down the window, he leans over and speaks his final words. "Whenever you need me, call me, and we can look at the moon at the same time, and it will be like we're right here doing it together," he says, motioning toward the steps in front of my apartment.

I let out a sound that's half laugh, half sob, and I back away so he can drive off. I stand there on the sidewalk, crying, holding my precious memory box as Kash pulls away, beeping his horn, heading toward California and away from me.

It's been two weeks since Kash left, and it surprises me how well I'm doing. I have been keeping busy, working extra shifts, writing, hanging out with Farrah, having lunches with Silvia, sleeping, exercising. Kash and I have a schedule to FaceTime on Sundays, and in between, if we have something dire we need to share.

He always seems happy when we talk — happy to hear about how things are going for me, happy to be in California, happy to be doing something that fills him up. He's shown me around his apartment over FaceTime. There are still boxes everywhere, but that's to be expected since he just moved. He has shown me the bar that is starting to fill up with furniture and decor. Everything seems to be coming together for him and his new life out west. There's a longing that's settled deep inside me. It's not jealousy I feel, more of a longing for the sense of contentment Kash has now.

It's Sunday night and time for our second scheduled call. It's ten o'clock in the evening here in Texas and eight in California. I'm sitting on the steps outside my apartment, holding my phone, waiting for Kash to call, and looking up at the sky — the same old stars and the same old moon. I start counting the stars while I wait for the familiar vibration of an incoming call.

10:01. There it is — incoming FaceTime from Kash Holden.

Accept.

"Hey, Summer!" he says with enthusiasm. I smile at him, big, because I can't hide the excitement of seeing his face. "How are things going?" he asks with a huge grin on his face.

"Good. I have been keeping busy. You'd be so proud!" I laugh.

He laughs too. "Busy doing what? Writing songs I hope," he says, and it seems like he's looking over his phone at something.

"Yes, that, and other things," I say, glancing up at the stars.

"Are you looking at what I'm looking at?" he asks me.

I smile at him. "The brightest star," I say, taking a deep breath. The comfort and ease that comes over me when I'm talking to Kash does not go unnoticed.

"Me too," he says, and I can tell he's looking out into the abyss like I am. I lean back against the concrete step and hold my phone above my face but continue looking up at the dark sky.

"Let's look at the moon right now, together," I suggest, remembering the words he said to me before he left. There's a comfortable silence for a moment.

"It almost looks like if someone were walking on it right now, we'd be able to see them," Kash says.

He's right. The fullness of the moon makes it seem like we could reach up and grab it, and even though we are over 1,000 miles away from each other, it makes it feel like we are right next to one another. I reach my hand up and cover the moon with my thumb. I close one of my eyes and then open it again. I watch the moon appear and disappear with each blink.

"How have you been?" I ask.

"So busy," he starts. "Some days I just can't believe that I actually did this, and I'm so stoked. And then other days, I feel like I'm drowning in tasks that I need to complete." Kash looks at me and waits for a response, but I just smile, waiting for him to continue because I can tell he has more to say.

"I'm going to be opening in four weeks," he says with a grin. "FOUR WEEKS!"

"What? That's so soon!" I say, shocked. "Are you going to be ready that quickly?"

"Yeah, financially I was giving myself another two months to get ready, but things seem to be moving quickly. I've hit some bumps in the road the last few weeks, but I got my liquor license yesterday, the furniture and decor are done, and my loan has been set for weeks. It just feels right."

"Wow, it's really happening." I smile, pausing briefly. "I'm so proud of you."

"Thanks, I know, and I appreciate it a lot."

"Two WhisKEYS is going to be great." I'm still smiling but tears have begun to dampen my eyes. I can't pinpoint where the tears are coming from, or what emotion evoked them, but I know it's a good feeling. Pride. Love. Excitement.

"Thanks, Summer. Your support means everything to me," he says.

We fall into sweet, comfortable silence — quiet stargazing, just like we did when we were physically together.

"So, what happened after that night you slept on the bench in the park?" Kash asks, breaking the silence.

I look back at him, taking my eyes off the sky, a little taken aback by the question. I don't say anything right away. I have to think about how to respond.

"Well," I say, dragging out the word, "I spent twelve years drifting from shelter to shelter. I dabbled in drugs. I couldn't hold a job. People stole from me when I had nothing to give. I made friends with people who would only do me wrong because I could never tell the difference between good and evil. I hit bottom...rock bottom. I remember the day when I'd had enough; I sort of woke up. I told myself that I couldn't keep going down any further, and I began to crawl out of the hole I had fallen into. That's when I left Kentucky and came to Texas with an offer I couldn't pass up. And that's when I met you, and Farrah, and my therapist, Janie. That's when I followed Farrah into Sullivan's and was blessed with the job I so desperately needed. It's been almost two years, and here I am, trying to make sure that those days of wandering and being lost are truly behind me."

I stop talking and look right into the screen, right into Kash's eyes, looking for some disgust, some shock, or some judgment because it wasn't that long ago that I was someone else entirely. But of course, I see nothing of the sort when I look at him. I only see warmth and compassion.

"Do you want to tell me about it? If you do, I'm here. I want to know all of you, Summer. I want you to trust me, if this is something you find helpful to share with me. Or not. We can always just leave it at that." He says it without pressure, and I appreciate that. I look at him intently, trying to decide what to do next.

"Ok," I say. "I'll tell you about it. But first, I am going up to my apartment. Hang on just a minute." I get up from the steps and jog up the staircase, skipping every other step. I get into my apartment, kick off my shoes, and head straight to the couch and plop down.

For a second, I think about what I'm about to do — share my story with Kash, again, without having had a triggering episode when he asked me about it. I know he asked out of care and concern for me, and I'm proud of myself for displaying the courage to share this. I owe it to myself, *to let someone in* — completely and wholly.

"That morning after I left the Brickman's, waking up on a park bench, I felt like I was in hell. I had no idea what I was doing, but going back to the Brickman's to let Gina take me God knows where seemed like worse torture than toughing it out on my own. So, I knew right away that I wasn't going back. I wandered around aimlessly that day until I found a women's shelter on the south side of town, my old neighborhood. The people there tried to help me, but I wasn't ready to be saved. I was hurt and sad. I was angry and hostile. Eventually, Gina put out a missing person's report for me, and the shelter had to provide my information to the Social Services department. I told them I didn't want the department's help and refused any support they were willing to give me. They gave me my birth certificate and some other documents I didn't know what to do with, and they washed their hands of me, and I, them."

I stop for a second and look at Kash, instead of looking aimlessly around my apartment. I can see that he's made his way back into his apartment too, and he's looking at me with intent, listening to my every word. And so, I keep going.

CHAPTER 24

Kentucky - Then

MY EYES BEGAN TO flutter awake to the sound of cups being dropped into the sink. I blinked multiple times to try and adjust to the light. I sat up on the couch and looked around. Everything looked so much sadder in the daylight — empty beer cans tipped over on the dirty coffee table, stains on the filthy carpet. I looked at the couch I had lain my head on all night and winced. It was faded and smelled of mildew. I got up and grabbed my sweatshirt from the floor and slipped it over my head, walking over to the small window that looked out onto the street. The glass was dirty, and I could barely see out. Bugs, long dead, filled the chipped windowpane.

"Mornin', Summer," I heard Piper say from the kitchen sink, her voice raspy from drinking and lack of sleep. I turned my head from the window toward her and gave her a weak smile.

"You look like shit," she said through a pitiful laugh.

"Thanks," I muttered, taking a seat on the dingy, metal chair at the small circular kitchen table. I ran my hands through my tangled hair and used the only elastic I owned to put the greasy strands into a bun.

Piper, my friend I'd met at the last shelter I was at, was letting me crash at her new place. She'd moved there just a few months prior and offered for me to stay there because I was getting hit on by the night staff manager and I needed to get out of the shelter. When he was harassing me, I'd yelled at him, causing a scene, and I knew it was better for me to just leave. I had been living there for two years already, after having been at a women's shelter for two years before that. It was time for me to move on. So, there I was, sleeping on Piper's disgusting couch.

I had no money, and my first task was to find a job. I got up from the table and grabbed my bag from the floor next to the couch. I double-checked all the documents I had to my name. I was going to need those if I was going to apply for anything.

"I'm going to Benji's tonight. Do you want to come?" Piper asked me, leaning against the kitchen counter.

I sighed, mostly to myself. I didn't want to go to Piper's new boyfriend's place, but I also didn't want to be there, alone, in her apartment.

"Yeah, maybe." I shrugged, knowing full well that I would go with her.

She smiled her big, toothy grin at me. Piper was one of those people who would have been unstoppable had she not been born on the south side, like me, and had not been pimped out by her mother's boyfriend starting when she was twelve years old. She was beautiful and full of life. But there was darkness behind her eyes that sometimes scared me. Sometimes I thought her darkness matched mine and because of the shadows from my past, there I was, homeless again, finding refuge on her couch. But at least we'd bonded over our troubles.

"What are you doing today?" Piper asked, turning to the sink, her back to me, haphazardly cleaning the cups that were used the night before.

"Job hunting," I said with a sigh.

"Oh, good luck," she turned and said with an eye roll. "It's rough out there. If you want me to talk to my new boss, let me know."

"No thanks," I balked. "Can you picture me as a stripper?"

She smirked. "Ha. No. But there are people who just bartend," she added, and it gave me pause.

"But I have never been a bartender."

"Miles will train you quick," Piper responded, flicking her hand at me like it was no big deal.

"Ok. Yeah. Give your boss my name, and I'll check in with him this week." I grabbed some jeans and a shirt out of my bag and headed to the bathroom to change. My plan was to hit all the grocery stores, pharmacies, and gas stations within walking distance. I didn't have much faith that anyone would hire me, but I didn't need that much money to get by at the time, so I hung on to the desperation with everything that I had.

After walking around for hours and going into as many places as I could, I moseyed back to Piper's, deflated and feeling sorry for myself. Every place I walked in either gave me a sad look and told me they weren't hiring, contrary to the sign on the doors, or out of pity, they offered me an application to fill out and said they would keep it on file. At those places, I stayed and filled the application out to leave with them because I was desperate for a shot at anything.

When I got back to Piper's I went into the bathroom and looked in the mirror and saw what those people had seen. I hadn't realized how gaunt I looked, dirty and unpolished. I was used to it by now, but to a potential employer, I must have seemed unkept and unreliable. I decided that I'd go to Benji's with Piper and then go to work with her the next night to meet Miles and try my luck there.

When I walked into the club the next night, my problem was exhaustion. Sleeping on a couch every night and being unable to fall asleep until all the noise around me dissipated was proving difficult for my liveliness. I felt more like I was eighty years old rather than twenty-two.

"Wake up, girl," Piper said, hip checking me as we walked in the door.

"If you could spare some of your energy for me, that would be cool."

She smirked and began waving to everyone she knew inside. I nervously looked around, taking in the surroundings. Everything was so dark — the lighting and the furniture. The music playing in the background wasn't what I'd expect for such an establishment, but it was early and there weren't any patrons there yet, just employees — dancers, bartenders, and security guards talking amongst themselves.

"Miles! Hey, this is my friend, Summer," Piper said, pushing me in front of her. I shook hands with Miles and gave him an awkward smile.

"Hi," I said before quickly pulling my hand away and looking around the place again.

"Hey," he responded with a questioning look, probably wondering what I was doing there before the place opened.

"She needs a job," Piper said. "But not dancing. She doesn't want to do that." She winked at me, and I looked back at Miles.

"Um, yeah. If you have anything else I could do, that would be cool." I cringed inwardly at my lack of confidence.

He stared at me for a few beats, looking me up and down. My shoulders sank for a second as I pulled inward, uncomfortable with the attention. But then I quickly straightened up, not wanting to seem incapable.

"Yeah, sure," Miles said, beginning to turn toward the bar, waving me on to follow him. "I could use some help with miscellaneous stuff," he added gruffly. "Tonight can be your trial run. If it works out, we can do some paperwork after we close," he said as he wiped up some water from the counter. I nodded but realized he wasn't looking at me.

"Um. Awesome. Thank you," I said, stumbling over my words. "What would you like me to do?"

"Uh, let's see. You can run dirty glasses and plates from the bar to the kitchen, load the dishwasher out here, grab the bartenders things they need from the back, clear tables, that kind of thing," Miles shrugged. I nodded again, making a mental note of the list of things I would be doing. "Maybe, eventually, I can train you to bartend. But no promises. Let's see how tonight goes." Miles walked off into the back, and I was left standing there with a giddy Piper. I looked around again. This job was honestly better than working at a grocery store or pharmacy, so I gave myself a silent pep talk and prepared myself to work hard.

"Yay!" Piper squealed. "I have to go get ready, but I'll see you later." With that, she was off, and I sat there awkwardly waiting for something to happen so I could prep or clean something. Anything to make myself feel useful.

An hour later, at ten o'clock, the doors to the club opened and people from the street began streaming in. I had straightened all the tables and chairs only to have them all rustled and jostled as people piled in and took seats. I took a deep breath, smoothed out my long hair, and walked behind the bar to see if any bartenders needed anything. Miles hadn't introduced me to anyone, so I got some looks, but after a while, I was asked to run around and do random things for people. It felt like grunt work, but if I did a good job that night, at least this would turn into a steady income for me and a way to get out of Piper's apartment and into my own place. So, I put my all into the night.

By two in the morning, I was exhausted, and I'm sure I looked like hell. Piper came sauntering out of the back, looking fresh-faced and well rested, and I just couldn't understand how.

"Good job, Summer," Miles said, wiping the counter I'd already cleaned three times. "I'll give you four nights a week, ten dollars an hour, under the table. Deal?"

I smiled at him. "Thank you."

"Alright, so I expect you here every Tuesday, Wednesday, Thursday, and Friday night. Nine p.m. to 3 a.m.," Miles said.

For a second, I contemplated these hours and my ability to manage them, but my sleep schedule would just have to adjust to match Piper's. I could do that.

"Sounds good," I responded and shook his hand.

As Piper and I walked down the street, away from the club, she rambled on and on about the night and how excited she was for us to work together. She seemed like she was ready to get to Benji's and continue to party while I, on the other hand, was desperate for sleep.

"How are you so wired right now," I asked through a yawn.

She laughed. "Cocaine."

"Are you serious?" I asked her, stopping in the middle of the sidewalk and grabbing her arm.

"Yeah, all the girls do it. How else do you think we could survive these hours and still have a social life?" she asked me, smirking. "You can come in the back with me next shift and have some, if you want." She shrugged nonchalantly, as if it was no big deal.

"No thanks," I said, starting to walk again. I had never done drugs before, never even thought about it, and I wasn't about to start then.

"I'm going to Benji's. I'll stay there tonight, and you go in my bed and sleep," Piper said. The thought of this was making me long to crawl under the covers and sleep for hours.

"Thank you, Piper."

We continued to talk about our night as we walked, and a few blocks later, we parted and went our separate ways — me toward her apartment and her toward Benji's. I barely remember getting there, climbing into her bed, and falling asleep, but I did notice how good it felt to sleep in a bed again.

By the end of my first week at the club, I was equally satisfied to have cash in my hand, while being sluggish to the point of barely functioning. On Friday night, my last shift of the week, I walked in with Piper and asked her if I could go in the back with her. I needed something to keep me going. She looked at me questioningly.

"Are you sure?" she asked, and I appreciated the care she seemed to have, knowing how adamant I was against it earlier in the week. But how bad could it be? Piper was doing great. I just needed something to help me get through my shifts, so I followed her to the back.

When we reached the dressing rooms, there were six other girls mingling with one another. I looked around and smiled at them.

"Ladies, this is Summer. She works in the front now, and she is going to join us for a hit," Piper said, putting her stuff away in her locker. The girls smiled at me and went about their business. They were all talking about their days, pretty normal stuff, while one of the girls with blonde hair laid out the materials. She set up eight lines of the fine, white powder on the table, one for each of us. I began to get nervous. I had no idea what I was doing and didn't want to embarrass myself. Piper caught on and put her hand on my back, trying to calm me down.

"Just watch me, and then you can do what I do," she said.

The girls took turns leaning over the table to use an object to snort a line into their noses. They didn't flinch and kept carrying on with their conversations as if they had just taken a sip of champagne, not ingested hard drugs. For a moment, I second-guessed my decision to do it, but then again, they made it look so simple that I felt stupid not doing it, especially being as tired as I was. I knelt down on the floor, and Piper joined me. She walked me through what to do, and before I knew it, it was all over, I had done it. My nose burned a bit, and my eyes began to water.

"Don't worry. It won't burn for too long. And it will get easier," Piper encouraged me. I gave her a weak smile while rubbing my nostril and the water from my eyes.

"Ready for the night?" she asked, beaming.

"Ready as I'll ever be," I responded, getting up off the floor.

Much to my dismay, cocaine became my lifesaver. It gave me the energy I needed to keep working at the club. Soon after I started working there, Miles taught me how to bartend; simple drinks first and then we moved on to more complicated, specialty drinks the club offered. On the nights we worked, Piper and I would be out until the sun came up and then we'd sleep most of the day. It wasn't healthy but I felt good. It was great having a job after I'd gone so long without one.

I was making good money once I started bartending, and after two months, I'd saved up enough to move off Piper's couch and into my own place. Being able to move into my own apartment for the first time felt euphoric. After all I'd been through, I finally felt accomplished, like I could take care of myself. My apartment was a ground floor studio with bars on the window. It wasn't much, but it was within walking distance of the club, and it was clean, a big plus. I furnished it with second-hand furniture and decor from Goodwill.

On my walks home from work, I would pick flowers and put them in little glasses on my small coffee table, trying to brighten the place up. My life had become pretty unrecognizable — staying out until sunrise, doing drugs to stay awake — but I looked at the flowers as some sort of symbol that I was more than this reckless person I'd become; that deep down, I was still a good person: warm and capable, deserving of happiness and joy.

But the flowers always died. And every time, I felt like part of me died along with them. I became restless and lonely again. Tuesday through Friday, I was a part zombie, part hyperactive bartender. Saturday through Monday, I nursed myself back from the dead, sleeping too many restless hours and spending too much time wallowing in self-pity.

I had been bartending for three months when I went to Piper with a new problem: I'd found myself struggling to sleep after months of consistent cocaine use. I tried not taking it for a few weeks, hoping that I would be able to push through at work and then crash as soon as I got home, then head back to work the next day rested and rejuvenated. But my attempt failed. Just like most nights in my adolescence, my sleep was wretched and filled with stress. I'd lay awake at night afraid of the things I saw in my dreams and equally terrified of the thoughts running through my head when I was awake.

It was a Friday night, my last shift of the week, and I couldn't fathom getting through the shift and cleaning up. I'd started taking coke again with Piper and the other dancers before my shifts. That night, though, I confided in Piper that I couldn't sleep at all and asked her how she managed. How was she getting any sleep doing cocaine?

"Oh, hunny, I'll give you some pills. Take half of one when you get home. You'll sleep like a baby," she said, checking herself out in the mirror.

"Pills?" I asked her, unsure.

"Yeah, I have some in my locker." She walked over to her locker, pulled out a baggie from her purse, and handed me a couple. "Put a few in your purse now," she said. "So, you'll have them when you need them."

I hesitantly took them from her. I was uncomfortable thinking about what I might be getting myself into. But also, I was desperate.

"What are these?" I asked, looking down at the pills, my eyes wide.

She looked at me like I was a little girl.

"It's Vicodin," she said, her tone hushed.

I held the pills in my hand, my eyes darting from them to Piper. I knew I should give them back to her. The voice in my head telling me that was adamant. But unfortunately, there was another voice that whispered that I hadn't had a proper night's sleep in months. It reminded me that I was slowly sinking into a shell of a human and that all I needed was a good night's sleep. That voice was telling me that I had nothing to lose; I had no one to let down. There was no one to worry about but me, just like it had been for the last six years, since I was sixteen and my momma died.

It was a dark place to be — a place where I had no future to look forward to and a past that needed forgetting. I took the pills, put them in my bag, and promised myself that I would only take them for a few nights, four, to be exact. I would cut the two pills she gave me in half and use them for four nights. I wouldn't ask her for any more after that. I just needed a few nights of good sleep. *And to forget that I was alone in the world.*

I made it through my shift thanks to my coke high, and it was three-thirty in the morning when I got back to my apartment. Eli, one of the security guards, drove me home. Ever since Serenity, one of the dancers, was mugged a few weeks prior, Miles stopped letting any of the girls walk home from the club after our shifts. It was a little bit degrading since I didn't have a car and always had to rely on someone to bring me home. Sometimes it was Eli; other times, it was Leo, another guard. Sometimes it was Benji. When Eli dropped me at my place, I thanked him and headed inside.

I sat at my measly kitchen table and played with one of the pills Piper gave me, placing it back and forth from one hand to the other. My eyes were burning as my high was wearing off, and my body begged for sleep. I went back and forth for a few seconds, trying to decide if I should take a pill or not, before I grabbed a knife, cut one in half, and swallowed it dry. I felt it get stuck in my throat. I got up from the table and walked to the kitchen sink, turning on the water and putting my head under the faucet to help it down. I walked into the bathroom and brushed my teeth, looking at myself in the mirror. My eyes had dark circles underneath them, and my complexion was pale. I watched as tears wet my eyes. I didn't know the person I was looking at, but had I ever?

I walked to my bed and crawled under the covers. I thought about the negative feelings I had about sleep. I thought about my inability to sleep and how it was dragging me down, deeper into that black hole. Soon, my mind became cloudy, my muscles felt like they were melting into my worn-out mattress. I didn't want to enjoy this feeling, but not feeling pain was something I'd longed for since I was eleven years old, or even younger. Had I finally captured it? Did I solve all my problems that night? I thought maybe I had, and I felt too relaxed for it to scare me, like it should have, as it does now, looking back on it. Slowly, I felt myself slip into oblivion. There I was, falling farther and farther down toward the bottom, rock bottom.

My eyes blinked awake to see light on the other side of my eyelids. I looked at my clock. It was two in the afternoon. I'd slept ten hours straight. I hadn't woken up at all; I hadn't tossed and turned like I had every other night before that. But the feeling I had wasn't a rested one. I sat up in bed and looked around, and for a few minutes, my vision was slow to process the things I saw in my room. I thought I'd feel like I was ready to face the day, having slept so long, but all I wanted to do was go back to sleep. I thought maybe it was because I was overly tired and that once I caught up, I would feel normal again. I didn't have to go to work, so I got out of bed and walked to the kitchen table, swallowed the other half of the pill, and plopped back down on my bed. It didn't take long; soon I was slipping back into sweet oblivion.

When I woke up again, it was nine o'clock on Sunday morning. Woah.

I'd slept all the way through Saturday afternoon, evening, and night. I pulled the covers off and put my feet on the floor, giving myself a second to reacquaint my body. I walked slowly to the kitchenette and filled a glass with water from the tap. I drank it down fast, giving my body what it was screaming for. I sat at the table, trying to determine how I felt. After about ten minutes, I concluded that I was rested. I had a lingering headache that I blamed on my lack of hydration and spent all morning sipping water. I had two more nights off work to eat some good food, go to bed at a reasonable hour, and try to get myself into a better sleep routine.

On Tuesday, I was back at work, having taken the last of the pills Piper had given me. I had getting a ton of sleep. I had hoped that, after basically sleeping through Saturday, I could save the last pill for my next work night, but when Sunday night rolled around, I couldn't settle into rest. My mind was racing with countless what-if, what-now, and what-then scenarios. So, I took the last one, which meant that every night since Piper gave them to me, I had a pill. Tuesday morning, I let myself sleep in so that I hopefully wouldn't need coke before my shift. And as I walked into the club at nine that night, I felt like I might be able to make it.

"Hey, Piper, can I talk to you for a sec?" I asked her as she was getting ready for the night.

"Sure, what's up, hunny?" she responded.

I walked over closer to her and whispered so only she could hear." I need some more Vicodin," I said sheepishly. "When I took the ones you gave me, I was able to sleep for the first time in years."

Piper gave me a concerned look but didn't take long to respond. "Ok, I'll give you four more tonight, but if you need more after that, you'll have to pay Benji for them. They're expensive, you know." She said this lightly, not accusatory.

I nodded desperately, and she walked over to her locker and pulled out her little bag. She gave me four more, and I zipped them into the inside pocket of my clutch. I held it close to me, like a prized possession, and then quickly shoved it into my locker and walked out of the dressing room alongside Piper and a few of the other girls.

It was almost opening time, and I felt awake but also at ease knowing that I had a way to fall asleep later and that I wouldn't be wading through painful memories and self-loathing, unable to sleep. There was rest in my future, and that was a great feeling. It made the lack of coke more manageable.

As ten o'clock rolled around and the first patrons started making their way past Eli and into the main room, I took a deep breath and gave myself a silent pep talk: work, make money, get out of there. I didn't feel energetic like I usually did when I took coke, but I was present and I didn't feel like I was slogging through mud, so I took that as a win. The night started off like all the others before it, uneventful and routine. Another bartender, Sasha, and I worked the main bar by ourselves because Tuesdays were our least busy nights. We joked around a bit, rang the bell when we got a big tip, and danced around to the thumping music.

About an hour into the night, I was wiping down a section of the bar where a group of four had just left and another group was clambering to get their spots. I sprayed and wiped, not looking up until I had it just right. I didn't pay much attention to them as they sat down. As I slid a few drink menus on the bar, I looked up to greet the new patrons, sucking in air that became lodged in my throat, giving me the sensation of choking.

Jason.

Jason Brickman.

"Well, hello there, Summer," he said, looking at me like an animal sizing up its prey.

I didn't say anything. I couldn't. I just stared at him, frozen. He waved his hand in front of my face, trying to get my attention, and snap me out of my trance. I moved my eyes to the stool next to him where Jake was taking a seat.

"Dude, Summer, is that you?" he laughed as he pushed himself closer to the bar.

I was still speechless. I couldn't get a grip on the reality that was staring me in the face. Was this really happening?

"I haven't seen you since that night at my house," Jake rattled on. "The night you hit on Jason." He let out the most obnoxious laugh, slapping Jason on the back. Jason joined in on the laugh like it was the funniest joke he had ever heard — at my expense.

"Can I get you something?" I asked, my eyes narrowed to slits.

"Two Bud Lights," Jake said.

I walked over to the cooler and pulled two out, twisting the caps off and placing the glass bottles, rather aggressively, in front of them. I took their cash and started to walk to the register when Jason asked me how I was doing.

How was I doing?

How could he even ask that? What I wanted to say, what I should have said, was that he ruined whatever was left of my life four years ago. Any potential I was grasping at during my senior year was ripped right out from under me when he raped me and told everyone it was me who initiated it. And Jake made it clear that the lie was not forgotten. Jason came out the rich boy who got his way, and me? I got what everyone expected of me — a life of screw-ups, scraping by, and living in pain, but not the physical kind of pain, the kind that deteriorates your insides and sucks you dry.

"Great," I responded, not looking at him and keeping myself busy behind the bar, taking someone else's order.

"What have you been up to?" he asked, slurring his words.

Oh, you know. Living in shelters and doing drugs to stay awake and get some sleep.

"Working," I said.

"Aren't you going to ask how I am?" he asked with a smirk.

I stared at him through narrowed eyes. I didn't give a shit about how he was. He had to know that.

"Well, I'm great," he said, beaming, and I knew he was going to keep going. "I got a job downtown after graduation last year. I'm working in accounting at my dad's office." He leaned back on his stool, and I stared at him, resenting the fact that for the rest of his life, things would continue to be handed to him on a silver platter and that was just how the world worked. "I make great money and got a condo in the city." He was boasting, and I couldn't figure out why he felt the need to belittle me. I did nothing to him.

"Cool," I said, walking away to help another patron. I took some orders and put tips in the bucket, trying my best to ignore Jason and Jake. Eventually, Jake flagged me down for another round. I looked to Sasha, hoping she was available to serve them instead of me, but she was in the middle of mixing four drinks. I took a deep breath and walked back over to them.

"Another one," Jake said, holding up his bottle. I looked at him with disgust. "Please?" he added rudely.

I grabbed two more Bud Lights, put the bottles in front of them, and grabbed their cash.

"It's all set," Jason said with arrogance "I don't need the change." I looked down. He had handed me a fifty-dollar bill for a ten-dollar check. I gave him a questioning look but walked away, shaking my head, not wanting to engage with them for more than I'd already had to. I put the change in the bucket.

"Aren't you going to ring the bell? That has to be the best tip you ever got," Jason said, laughing in Jake's direction. I reached up and rang the bell, glaring at them.

"What's your problem, Summer?" Jake asked me. "We haven't seen you in four years, and you're being an asshole," he added. "We were good friends at one point."

Until we weren't.

He said that as if my behavior was ruining his night, which was ridiculous.

I stared at them and debated if I was going to continue to ignore them as best I could, or if I was going to unleash all the words I'd held inside for all these years, words I wished I'd said to everyone who'd wronged me while I grew up.

"I'm the asshole?" I asked, laughing, but not because it was funny, laughing because it was asinine. "I lived in this kid's house with him for almost seven years. He was like my brother. When I had no one, he was there for me." I stopped for a second and gauged their faces. Both of them stared at me, waiting for more. "Until he raped me and blamed it on me." My words hung in the air like pixels, hovering between us. I stared at them and waited for any kind of response.

Jake looked at Jason, unsure of what to say. Jason stared at me with hate in his eyes.

"Summer, you're just looking to blame someone for what happened to you and why you ended up here, doing this," he said, gesturing around the club, "instead of what you could have been doing had you not fucked up so many times."

I couldn't believe he could just deny everything he'd done with such ease.

He continued, as if he hadn't said enough. "And here you are, back where you started. You know when you'll get out of the south side, Summer?" he asked, not expecting me to answer. "When pigs fucking fly." He got up from his stool and motioned for Jake to follow him. They sauntered out of the club without looking back, and I was left standing there behind the bar unable to move.

Deep down I felt the truth in his words. When people speak hard truths to you, it's paralyzing. Dad told me it would be a cold day in hell when I could outsmart him. He was right; I never could. Sarah Tate said my mom would get me back when pigs flew. And she was right. Momma could never get her shit together and then death found her, and it was too late. I knew Jason was right, too. He had to be. Even when I took a few steps forward, I always stumbled back five. I was drowning, and that simple, overused phrase caused me to tumble further and further down into darkness.

I didn't know how much time had passed when I finally found the wherewithal to move my legs. But eventually, I made my way over to

Sasha and told her I had to go to the bathroom. I ran back to the dressing room, threw myself on the couch, and hung my head in my hands. I cried for a long time. Tears spilled out of my eyes, leaving dark spots on my jeans, as I let out all my emotions.

After what felt like hours of crying, I was all out of tears, and I got up and practically stumbled to the mirror to look at myself. I was blotchy and swollen, my face red from all the tears, so I splashed some water on it and dried it off. I took my ponytail out and redid it, smoothing down the lumps. I sucked a long, slow breath into my cheeks and blew it out, unsteadily. I felt heavy, like my head was filled with bricks, a headache slowly starting to creep its way in. I began to walk toward the door but as I walked past my locker, I did a double take, remembering the pills that sat inside, waiting for me. I walked over and opened the door, took my purse out and unzipped it, reaching in to take one pill out. Without giving it a second thought, I popped the whole thing in my mouth and swallowed it. I walked to the sink and assisted it down with some water.

As I walked into the hallway and out to the bar, I knew that what I had just done was not very smart. Was I letting myself become dependent on these pills? Was I using them to numb my pain? I felt as if I'd just opened a door that would prove nearly impossible to close. But I'm not sure I really cared.

After that night, I slipped into an addiction. Vicodin no longer just aided me in falling asleep; those little pills also numbed me. After Jason and Jake left the club that night, and I swallowed that pill, I didn't feel anything. I floated around the rest of the night and didn't care about how my world was crashing down around me. And then, every minute of every day, I longed for that numbness. My tips were used to pay my rent and to buy pills. I stopped buying much food — I basically only ate leftovers from the bar at the end of each shift. The only food I bought was cereal and crackers because I needed most of my money for my new saving grace.

For about a year, I continued to fall down that hole. Eventually, I was no longer productive at work. I was consistently running late, breaking glasses, and calling in sick. While Miles tried to be patient with me, I started to burn bridges with him. I had been working there for eighteen months when he let me go and washed his hands of me. I had pretty much severed ties with Piper because I was isolating myself from everyone. I wasn't fun anymore. I didn't go out. I was just holed up in my apartment most of the time, hiding and praying that I would never run out of my drugs. I was so obsessed with getting my next fix. So, Piper, too, washed her hands of me for the most part. It took her a while to let go of me completely because Benji still needed my money, but she kept me at arm's length. And then, she cut me off when I had no more money left to feed my addiction.

Two months after being fired, I was evicted from my apartment, and there I was again, back on the streets, looking for shelter. I had packed all my clothes into my black duffle bag and put whatever money and pills I had left in the bag, zipped safely into the inside pockets. I left my furniture and walked away without looking back. There was no point in being sad about what I was leaving behind. I had learned that the hard way, after leaving so many times before.

I spent the next five years losing myself in the south side. I slept on benches and open shelter beds. I ate at soup kitchens and went hungry one too many nights. I had stopped doing drugs because I couldn't get my hands on any.

I was completely alone, disappointed in myself for allowing my past to define me. I wanted to feel good. I wanted to be whole. I wanted to be someone I could be proud of. But I had no one in my corner; I never had and coming to that realization only made things worse. What was the point? I couldn't figure it out. So, I wandered, lost and starved for more than just nutrition. I ached for someone to just see me.

About six months after my twenty-eighth birthday, I woke up in a strange bed under a crisp white sheet, an overhead fluorescent bulb flooding the room with bright white light. I had several IVs in my arm and the steady sound of beeping surrounded me.

"Oh, good. You're awake." The voice was coming from my right. I whipped my head around to see...a nurse?

"Where am I?" I asked, pulling myself up to a seated position, my heart beating rapidly.

"You're at Silver City Hospital," the nurse replied, approaching my bed.

"Why?" I asked, trying to calm my panic.

"I'll get the doctor," she said, closing my chart. "He will explain to you what is going on. Ok?" Her voice was calm and assuring.

I looked at her with wide eyes, suddenly feeling entirely insecure.

A few minutes later, a tall man in a white doctor coat with salt and pepper hair that was cut close on the sides, walked into my room with what seemed like compassion radiating off of him. What news was he coming to deliver to me? My nerves rattled.

"Hi, Summer, I'm Dr. Wright," he said, looking down at my chart. "You were found in a park down the street. You were having a seizure." He looked at me soothingly and then wheeled over a stool and perched himself at the side of my bed. I found myself at a loss. I had no words. A seizure? Was he sure? I had never had a seizure before.

"Do you do drugs recreationally, Summer?" he asked me, seemingly without judgment.

"I haven't done drugs...Vicodin. I haven't done Vicodin in, like, five years," I said, barely above a whisper, feeling completely ashamed as the visions of how my life had played out danced around in my head.

Dr. Wright looked at me softly. "Sometimes if a person is withdrawing, they can have seizures but we didn't find any drugs in your system."

"Then why did this happen to me?" My voice, shaky and unsure, faded off as I waited for clarification.

"Your seisure seems to have been caused by malnutrition and severe dehydration."

I nodded one time, looking forward, away from him. What was I supposed to say to that?

"Your vitals are stabilizing, and you should be ready for discharge in a few days," Dr. Wright told me. "Do you have somewhere to go, Summer?"

I looked over at him and shook my head, letting it fall. It was true. I had absolutely nowhere to go. I had no one to call.

"There's a program at a facility down the road," Dr. Wright informed me. "They could help you pro bono if you're willing." He placed his right ankle over his opposite knee and settled in to stare at me. I knew he meant well but I was feeling self-conscious and unable to make sense of what he was saying.

"What kind of facility is it?" I asked.

"Rehab mostly. But they do a lot more than just that. Not everyone there has had addiction problems. They work with people who suffer from all types of mental health issues. They work with a lot of people who don't have a support system or adequate funds. It's a nonprofit and I think you could really benefit from it, if you are in the right headspace to make a change in your life."

I looked straight ahead, and after a few breaths, I turned toward Dr. Wright and nodded my head, my eyes clouded with fresh tears. He gave me a kind smile and began to get up from his stool. He wrote something down on my chart. "I will have someone from the clinic come over this afternoon and meet with you and give you the information," he said, heading toward the door. "I will be back to check on you in a bit." With that, he was out of the room, and I was alone sitting with this new reality.

I couldn't believe that this was really my life. I had let myself become homeless, wandering through life with no vision, no path.

Me. That was my identity.

But I had bigger plans for myself, I always had. Unfortunately, I had no idea how I would ever reach them. I had already proven that I wasn't trustworthy when it came to facing my past. Triggers would send me into a tailspin that I couldn't ever escape. They set me back. I lay back on the bed and looked up at the ceiling, memorizing the spots and watermarks. I stayed that way until Dr. Wright came back in, along with a woman who wasn't a nurse.

"How are you feeling, Summer," Dr. Wright asked me sincerely.

"I'm ok," I responded, propping myself up.

"This is Kayla Shaw. She is from Champlain House, the place I was telling you about earlier." Dr. Wright sat down in one of the guest chairs as he introduced Kayla.

"It's nice to meet you," she greeted me warmly.

I smiled at her but was lost for words.

"As Dr. Wright mentioned, I'm the director at Champlain House, but I'm also a counselor."

I looked into her eyes, searching to see her soul, to see if I could trust her. There was something in her eyes that seemed kind, and I decided that was a good enough reason for me to let her in, if only slightly.

"Nice to meet you," I said softly.

"It's a pleasure to meet you, as well," she said, and it seemed like she meant it. "Can I tell you a little bit about what our program entails?" I nodded and she began.

I tried as best I could to focus on all the words, she was telling me, and I thought I got most of it. Ultimately, I agreed to go there with her after I was discharged. A car would pick me up to transport me to the facility, which was two miles away. I would be staying there for at least three months, more if needed, but not less. Dr. Wright and Kayla kept trying to assure me that the three months would go by fast, as if I had somewhere else I needed to be, someone waiting for me. I just nodded in agreement with what they said and settled into the realization that this was what I was doing. But in all honesty, it was a relief. I was glad to have shelter for a significant amount of time. I was glad to have food every day. This would give me stability for a little bit. Maybe I could get my head back on my shoulders.

"But what about the cost? I know these types of programs are astronomical," I said.

Dr. Wright and Kayla exchanged glances, and it made me feel uneasy, like I was some sort of charity case.

"Our program runs off the tuition from our paying patients as well as donations from multiple sources," Kayla informed me.

I nodded, looking between both of them.

"I'm consenting," I said, knowing that was what they were waiting for me to say.

They both smiled at me, and for the first time in years, I felt a sense of peace, like I was safe and cared for even though I was still sitting in the hospital bed, and I had no memory of how I got there.

I didn't know it then, but that was my first step toward finding myself — a journey I continue to travel, even to this day.

Just under a week later, after Dr. Wright was pleased enough with my test results, I was sitting on my new bed with clean yellow sheets in my new temporary home. I pulled my knees up to my chest and looked around. It was so quiet, I could almost hear the blood rushing through my ears, my heart pumping in my chest.

Kayla had taken me to my new room when I arrived at the facility. She gave me a tour after I dropped my one bag in my room. I saw the grounds — the lush gardens full of plants and flowers, the dining room with round tables for eating at, the recreation room that offered a reading area and ping-pong table, and a sitting room with a fireplace and comfortable couches.

After the tour, I headed back to my room to gather myself. I just sat on the bed in silence, contemplating the last five years of my life. The images that floated through my mind were cloudy and tainted, my brain's attempt to protect me. The last clear memory I had was watching Jake and Jason walk out of my life for the second time. The years that followed were filled with sorrow, self loathing, and a kind of loneliness that was indescribable.

I looked around my neat little room at Champlain House and couldn't visualize my future, but for the first time in a long time, I could see clearly. That had to mean something. I slid off the bed and padded softly around the space. I was expecting my room to be cold and impersonal, much like a motel. But it was warm and inviting, like a bedroom. Delicate cream curtains hung by the windows that overlooked the gardens below and the walls, a light purple, seemed to wrap me in a hug. The bed was made with a lush comforter and soft pillows, inviting me to crawl in and sleep, but I relented.

I walked around the room, slowly, taking in every corner, every crevice. I lifted my arm up to touch a beautiful painting of a pond that hung by the door. It was clean, looking freshly dusted, unlike the rooms in the shelters I had stayed in previously. I leaned against the door, my palms touching the cool surface, and closed my eyes. I pulled air into my lungs and held it there before blowing it out slowly, calming myself. Though the room, the whole place, was foreign to me, much like every place I had laid my head in recent years, I felt a sense of belonging deep down—like I was where I was supposed to be.

I was pulled from my thoughts when an announcement came over an intercom system, startling me. Dinner was ready and everyone was invited to go to the dining room. I was relieved because I was famished, my body felt weak and unable to function. I needed a hot meal and some good nourishment. I peeled myself from my thoughts, slipped on the facility slippers they gave me, and made my way out into the hall and down the stairs to the communal dining room. I trudged down the hall; I was not in any shape to be meeting people and socializing, certainly not people who were in a similar situation to me. But I was hungry, so, I put one foot in front of the other until I made it downstairs.

The room was filling up with people, men and women, young and old. I looked around, my arms crossed protectively over my chest. I found an empty seat at one of the tables and took it.

"Hi, I'm Amber," said a woman who looked like she was a bit older than me, offering her hand. She had dyed her hair purple and had wide green eyes. She was frail and tiny, but her kind smile warmed me.

"Hi," I said meekly, "Summer." I put out my hand to shake hers.

"I haven't seen you around," she said.

"I just got here today," I responded, fidgeting with my silverware, a little anxious to talk.

"Ah, well, welcome. You'll like it here," Amber said, looking around at the crowd of people. "When I got here, I was in a bad place." She stopped to laugh. "I guess we all are when we get here, right?"

I smiled and raised my eyebrows, hoping that was enough of a response to appease her. As the room continued to fill up, others joined our table and introduced themselves — I met Bob, Kathleen, Amelia, and someone whose name was actually Junior. I was pleasant to these new acquaintances, but I wasn't going to open up to them. I certainly wasn't ready for that. I enjoyed my dinner, though. The staff served us ham, buttered green beans, and delicious mashed potatoes. We even got a dessert — strawberry shortcake. I was impressed with the service and the food.

That night, I went to bed full, not full enough to put me to sleep but full enough to lay in my bed comfortably, dreaming of what was ahead. I was getting excited about the possibilities of this place. I had my first meeting with a counselor the following day, and I hoped it would be

Kayla, but I wasn't in any position to make requests. I was staying there for free after all. I put my hands behind my head and looked up at the ceiling, pretending it was covered with stars, and I began to count myself to sleep.

I woke up to find a small piece of paper that had been slid under my door earlier that morning. It was a summons to my counseling session — in the Rose Room, room 103, at nine o'clock. Since it was only seven forty-five, I still had some time to get ready and get breakfast before heading to my session. I got dressed and walked to the dining room to check out my options for breakfast. They had a continental breakfast, so I grabbed a bagel and a cup of coffee and took them outside to eat in the gardens — partly because I didn't want to talk to anyone and partly because it was so peaceful and serene.

When it was time for my counseling session, I walked into the Rose Room to meet my counselor. No one was there yet so I got to look around for a minute, taking in all the decorations. Everything was light and calming. There were flowers in a vase on the coffee table, comfortable-looking furniture, and a bookshelf filled with what seemed to be self-help books. I took a seat on the cozy couch, and a moment later, Kayla walked in with a pleasant smile and a notebook.

Kayla's voice warmed me. "Good morning, Summer."

"Hi, Kayla," I said, letting out a breath I didn't realize I was holding in. I was grateful that she was assigned to me, a familiar face.

We exchanged a bit of small talk, presumably in an effort to make me comfortable, and then she jumped right into some heavy stuff.

"Tell me a little bit about yourself, Summer. How did you find yourself in a hospital bed unaware of what had happened?"

I suddenly felt very exposed, as if I was sitting there naked. I looked at her, but no words were forming. I didn't know what to say. By that point in my life, my childhood and adolescent memories would sometimes come flying back to me at random moments, but I'd blocked a lot of them out, petrified of where the flashbacks would steal me away to.

"Where are your parents, Summer? Or any family members?" she asked me, trying to get me to talk.

I couldn't do it. I stood up from my place on the couch and ran out of the room and back upstairs to my quiet space. I walked into my room, shut the door, and leaned my back against it, closing my eyes. My breath came in and out in heavy, painful bursts. Tears streamed down my face. I knew I was expected to give it my all, to try and heal, but it was all too much, too fast. I slid down the door and sat on the floor, dropping my head in my hands, and I had zero energy left to get up and walk over to the bed. I just sat there.

A few moments later, there was a gentle knock on my door. "Summer, it's me, Kayla. Don't open the door. I just wanted to let you know that you're safe here. When you're ready, I will be here to listen. Take your time. And get some rest."

As she spoke, I held my breath, tears drying on my face. I didn't respond, I couldn't, but I heard her loud and clear. I wished that I could open up my voice and say something, anything to respond to her, but it wasn't in the cards for me then, not yet.

I would describe Champlain House as a therapy sanctuary. In the hospital, Kayla told me that it was somewhat of a rehabilitation center, but she said it was much more than that. I saw firsthand what she meant. There were people living there who had attempted suicide, people who had experienced immense trauma and abuse. If you had endured suffering of any kind, that facility was for you.

There were all kinds of activities for us to participate in if we wanted — art, pottery, and gardening. There was a journaling room and a swimming pool with water aerobics classes. The individual and group therapy sessions allowed me to begin to visualize a life beyond my past, and that's exactly what I needed at that time. I had been so caught up in what had ruined me that I couldn't see anything beyond that.

Over the next month, I slowly came out of my shell, not completely, but I loosened up a bit. Amber became my closest friend at the facility, but I also had a few other acquaintances. Todd was a man in his fifties who had lost his son in Iraq, after losing his wife in a car crash one year prior. He was so wrapped up in grief that he lost himself to heroin and was trying to find the light again. My heart ached for him, as his heart probably would have ached for me, if I had ever gotten around to opening up and sharing my story. Sierra looked like she was younger than me. She had a fresh face, dyed black hair, and a septum piercing. She liked to skateboard around the property, and she had a meek smile that she only allowed herself to show every once in a while. I never really found out what her story was — she was closed off, like me, but I found her to be kind.

When I was at Champlain House, I realized that darkness didn't have to be hateful. This idea was reinforced in all the people I met there, most of whom had been through some pretty dark stuff, just like me. I was reminded that even though someone had a difficult past, it didn't mean they would automatically succumb to a life of negative hostility.

Growing up, everyone in my past had always painted me as *bad,* as a person who made the wrong choices, said the wrong things, and made the wrong kinds of faces. But inside, I felt different than that. I always just felt sad, broken in all the places that didn't seem fixable. I just needed someone to see the inside of me, see me for who I actually was, and not a product of my situation.

I started to open up a little in my sessions with Kayla, but never fully. I never named names, and I always beat around the bush.

I was in foster care.

My parents died.

I don't have anyone.

That was the most I could seem to offer. She always looked at me with compassion, and I wondered if those looks would have been looks of pity had she known the truth, all details in between the lines. I never ventured into the depths of my nightmares with her. Because to me, they weren't actually nightmares, they were real, and they were painful. I wasn't ready for that, and I certainly didn't want any pity.

In my third month at Champlain House, Kayla suggested something to me that never had seemed possible. "So, Summer, I have been thinking," she said to me as our session was wrapping up. I looked at her, curious. "Have you ever considered relocating?"

Relocating? How could I possibly do that with no money, no high school diploma, never mind a college degree? I had no connections, nothing. I shook my head at her. Her dreams for me were bigger than my own.

"If you could go anywhere, move anywhere you wanted, where would it be?" she asked me.

"California," I said, glancing out the window.

She nodded at me and gave me a small smile. "Why California?"

"Because when I was little and I needed to...escape, I would imagine I was at the shore, putting my feet in the breaking waves, my toes buried in the sand. As I got older, I pictured that beach and that place as California," I responded honestly. Kayla looked at me as if she realized she was getting somewhere. "I saw pictures of the Pacific Ocean in school, and it seemed so peaceful to me."

"I see," she said softly. "Have you ever seen the ocean?"

I shook my head again and a lump formed in my throat. I felt like I never would.

"Well, we don't have a facility in California, but we do have one in Austin, Texas. It's called the Champlain Bridge. It's more of an outpatient facility. They have a few beds for emergencies but mostly they do counseling sessions, support groups, dinners, that kind of thing." Kayla gave me a moment to ponder what she just told me. Leaving Kentucky seemed impossible, but the way she laid everything out made it seem like it was something I could do. But how?

"I can't."

"But why, Summer? What's holding you back?" she asked gently.

"I don't have a car, or a job, or even experience for that matter. I have been living in shelters for almost my whole adult life. No one would trust me enough to hire me."

"You've worked in a grocery store, no? And you've been a bartender. That is experience," Kayla informed me. "And we have services both here and in our Austin facility that can help you while you get things in place for yourself." She looked at me, hopeful that I would make this leap. "People here want to see you succeed, Summer. You survived a lot of trauma but now it's your chance to *thrive*." She leaned forward and put her hand on my knee.

My heart was beating faster than I ever remembered it beating, and I realized I had been holding my breath again. I let it out in one burst, and with it came a small squeaking sound as I tried to hold in the emotions that were tangling around inside.

"It's not TOO far from the ocean," Kayla added, a tear forming in her own eyes. With that, I sobbed. My shoulders slumped and I leaned my head over my knees, shaking as I cried. I knew then that I was going to go. I had to. I was going to leave Kentucky behind me and never look back. I didn't know what I might gain but I knew I had absolutely nothing to lose. I came to the realization that day that the people there at the Champlain House wanted to help me. They wanted to do it without gain but instead, out of the goodness of their hearts. They weren't boastful, like my foster parents, or taking advantage of me, like Jason. They saw my pain and my flaws, and they didn't let it define me. They embraced me and were committed to helping me get somewhere else, anywhere but there, which is exactly where I needed to be. I smiled through a sob and with it came a small laugh.

"Your time here is almost over. I told you when you arrived that you would have the opportunity to stay longer if you needed to and that offer still stands." She held my gaze and looked so proud of me. "But I don't think you need it, Summer. You need to go and find yourself. You're ready and I believe in you."

I got up from the couch and let Kayla hug me.

"Thank you," I whispered into her shoulder.

It's true what they say, sometimes having someone else believe in you is precisely what you need to start believing in yourself.

———

Three weeks later, I was on a bus heading to Austin. It was going to take roughly twenty-four hours for the whole trip, including a bus switch, but what was another day when I had been in limbo for almost thirty years. I rested my head on the glass window and watched the mirage of trees flying by in swirls of greens and browns.

As a parting gift, Kayla gave me a journal and I spent most of the bus ride writing in it. I jotted down some poetry and thoughts as they came to me, like I did when I lived at the Brickman's. Amelia and Sierra had given me some books but reading seemed to be making me car sick so I left them in my bag and figured I would read them at some point.

As we traveled the road, I couldn't pinpoint the feelings I was having. I figured I should be nervous, but I wasn't feeling nervous. I associated nervousness with the feeling of my dad's footsteps, heavy on the floor, as he searched for me in my hiding spots. Or the feeling I had in the pit of my stomach when Sarah Tate asked me to pack a bag, that I would be leaving my home and my momma. Even though I didn't know at the time I'd never be returning home, I was nervous, and I think it was just my intuition. I also associated nervousness with the thought of seeing Jason walk into my life again, like he did a few years ago.

But now, I wasn't nervous. How could I be? With every passing mile, every new state we entered, I was putting more space between me and everything that ever made me feel uneasy.

Was I excited? Was that what the feeling was? I didn't know. But I knew that it felt hopeful, and I never wanted to let that go. I was being given an opportunity to start over and it was up to me to take advantage of it.

I arrived in Austin on a Thursday afternoon. There wasn't a cloud in the sky, and the air was thick with humidity. I left the bus station and found the cab they had arranged for me. I took it to Champlain Bridge, where I would be meeting the director who would go over the next steps.

Kayla said that they would set me up with an apartment and pay my rent for a few months while I searched for a job and got settled in. She assured me that the staff there would be my lifeline while I figured out what was next. I trusted her because I had no other choice. Looking back on that time, I realize that I put a lot of faith in their hands, but I'm glad I did.

The cab pulled into a parking lot, and I noticed a beautiful large building with lots of character — arches, alternating levels, and stained glass windows. I couldn't wait to see the inside. I climbed out of the cab and thanked the driver as he drove off. Standing there, staring up at the building, I held my old duffle bag in my hand and took a steadying breath before making my way into the building. Inside, it was warm and inviting, just like the Champlain House.

"Hi, you must be Summer," I heard a voice approaching from my right. As I turned to the voice, I put my duffle bag down and reached out to shake the hand of a tall woman standing in front of me. She had blonde hair mixed with some gray, and it was pulled into a loose, low bun. She looked comfortable and approachable in jeans and a crew-cut sweatshirt. "I'm Ginny," she said, smiling from ear to ear, showing me her extremely white teeth.

"It's nice to meet you," I said softly, shifting on my feet.

"Come on into my office," she said, turning and guiding me down the short hallway. I grabbed my duffle bag and followed along, looking at all the pictures displayed on the wall. Her office was spacious and neat, and I took a seat in the chair across from her desk.

"We have been expecting you, and we are so glad you are here. Kayla said you are very ready for this new chapter." She continued to smile at me.

I nodded. "Yes, I don't think I have ever been more ready." I let out a soft laugh.

"Well, that is perfect," Ginny beamed. "You will be staying here in one of our rooms for a few days until your apartment is ready. I hope that's ok." I nodded vigorously. What did I care? I was thankful for all of it. "During these next few days, you will meet with the staff and participate in a support group session. Tomorrow is a dinner session. You'll get to meet some great people, and I think you'll enjoy it. You will also be introduced to your counselor and have a session with her before you move into your apartment. Your counselor is," she flipped through her paperwork briefly. "Oh, yes, Janie. Her name is Janie Sears, and she is wonderful. I think it will be a smooth transition for you from Kayla." She finished, interlocking her fingers on her desk.

"Thank you. Thank you for everything," I said meekly, feeling extremely humbled.

"Oh, dear, it is our pleasure," she said with such assurance that I actually believed her, one hundred percent. "Is there anything you are dying to see in Texas?" she asked, gathering up her paperwork into a neat pile.

"The ocean," I said without hesitation, a huge grin on my face.

Ginny smiled at me. "It's a bit of a drive, several hours to Galveston, but we can make that happen. We would have to spend the night there. We have a fund for things like this, though," she said, smiling. "How about tomorrow, after our group session and dinner, we make plans with some other guests to make a trip down with you?" She looked at me for approval of the tentative plan. I nodded happily.

When we were finished, Ginny offered to show me to my next and hopefully final, temporary room so we headed down the hall. As we walked in, I noticed the window was open and the white curtains were flowing in the breeze. They reminded me of how the curtains in Claire's room billowed in the wind, and I had to swallow the lump in my throat and try to calm the trigger that was threatening to take me down. I took my eyes off the windows and looked around, trying to focus on something else. I noticed how cozy the room was, very much like the one at Champlain House. The walls were light yellow, looking freshly painted. The bed was large and plush with a white comforter and several fluffy pillows. A chair sat by the window and looked out into the backyard, full of trees and shrubs. There was even a tiny bathroom inside the room, which was an upgrade from the one I had to share at Champlain House. I pinched myself. I knew I was lucky to have this opportunity, and I found myself thanking God that I'd had a seizure in a Louisville park that day because it had led me here, to my journey of healing and finding myself. I smirked at the irony.

The group session was not what I expected. It was different from the ones I'd participated in before, in a very good way. There were six guests, and Ginny and two counselors, Janie and Grant. We didn't sit in a circle on plastic chairs as I had predicted. Instead, we sat at a circular dining table in comfortable chairs. We sipped mugs of tea or coffee, and the other guests filled everyone in on their week — trials and peaks, ups and downs.

Ginny introduced me to the group but thankfully didn't force me to speak, which I appreciated. I wasn't ready yet. Janie and Grant offered supportive insight and tips throughout the session. There was laughter, knee rubs, tissues passed. I looked around the table constantly, wanting to pinch myself again. Is this where my life had really taken me over a three-month period? I felt incredibly grateful to be surrounded by this amount of support.

"I was thinking we could take a field trip!" Ginny exclaimed, clasping her hands at her chest.

I sat up straighter. Everyone looked at her and then at each other, wondering what she meant. I could tell that they had never taken a field trip before.

"What do you mean?" Grant asked, accompanied by a thunderous laugh.

"Well, Summer has informed me that she really would like to get to the ocean. She is from Kentucky and hasn't seen the Gulf before."

I appreciated that she didn't tell the whole truth. I looked around the table to witness the reaction of the others in the group, people who I realized then that I hadn't remembered their names from our introductions.

"So, what are we doing?" one of the people at the table asked inquisitively.

"Well, I was thinking we could take the van down to Galveston tomorrow, and whoever is interested can come along," Ginny said, beaming.

A mumbling erupted amongst the group. There was definitely excitement in the air.

"I'm in," said a small woman with auburn hair to my left.

"Me, too," two others said in unison.

"Well, then, it's settled," Ginny said. "We can meet out in the lobby. How about nine o'clock? Does that work for everyone? I booked a few motel rooms in the area. It will be smart to spend the night, with the long drive and all." Everyone agreed on the details.

It was settled. I was going to the ocean like it was no big deal, like the visions of my dreams weren't being laid out in front of me in real life. My insides felt light, as if I was floating off the ground. As I walked back to my room and fell into bed, I worried I'd be too excited to sleep. But although my sleep was restless, it was speckled with bright dreams and flashes of joy, and I woke up feeling alive and ready for the day, the sun streaming in through the wild, white curtains.

As we loaded in the van, I noticed it smelled of worn leather with a hint of vanilla. I took a breath from my nose, memorizing the scent, as I took a seat in the back by the left window. I buckled my seat belt and settled in for the ride, my nerves on edge and a feeling in my stomach that I couldn't place. The radio played softly through the speakers, and I listened to the low murmurs of the voices in the car, but I wasn't ready to participate in the conversations.

Ginny drove the van and Janie was beside her in the passenger seat. Grant and a guest with jet-black hair sat in the second row, and I shared the third row with two others. I vowed that I would know their names by the time we got home from the trip. The guy sitting next to me was slight, with dark hair and a pointed nose. He seemed shy but kind. Next to him was a girl who looked about my age with long braided auburn hair, freckles sprinkling her nose. I wondered to myself what their stories were and if they were similar to mine. But I wasn't ready to ask. My gaze turned back to the window and the passing landscape where it stayed until hours passed and I started to see the terrain change — trees started to disappear, transforming into low-lying brush surrounded by intermittent mounds of sand. I sensed we were approaching our destination.

A few minutes later, I started to see blue outside the window on the other side of the median. I sat up straight and fast, leaning forward as far as I could. I grabbed hold of the seat in front of me, my breath suspended.

There it was — the ocean. I wanted to jump out of the moving vehicle and run the rest of the way. Thankfully, just a few minutes later, Ginny pulled into a sandy parking lot. Gulls flew overhead and shrubs lined the lot and blew in the gentle breeze. She turned the van off, and I looked at the two people sitting next to me with anticipation. I hoped they would get out quickly. Otherwise, I might have had to run them over on my way out.

Once I was out of the van and standing on the concrete parking lot, I looked down at my feet. Sand was blowing across the asphalt like tiny little diamonds. I had never seen anything so mesmerizing. All around me, I could hear the voices of everyone talking about things that didn't seem important. Here we were, at the ocean. But this wasn't a life-changing event for them like it was for me. They weren't experiencing their haven, their safe place, in real life for the first time, like I was. I walked away from them without a word, toward the water that seemed to be calling my name.

I stood there, halfway between the parking lot and the water's edge and froze. My hair blew in the breeze, just like I had imagined it would when I was a child. I looked up at the sky and closed my eyes, trying to grasp the smell: to label it, find recognition, and hold the memory deep inside me. It was briny — something that seemed familiar, which wasn't possible because I'd never come close to the sea in my life. I sat down right where I was, unable to go any further yet. My head fell to my knees, and I began to sob uncontrollably. I cried for the old me, the little girl who was lost and abandoned, the one who always needed to escape but never actually could. I saw her right then, for the first time since I left her back in my childhood home. I wrapped my arms around my legs and squeezed, desperate to give her a hug, to soothe her, to tell her it was going to be ok someday.

After a few minutes, I peeled my head up from my knees and stared at the waves crashing right in front of me, only steps away. I was scared to get closer, afraid of the emotion that was erupting inside me. I felt raw and exposed, standing there in the middle of the beach, surrounded by tons of people but feeling completely alone. I felt a shadow approaching on my left and I looked up to see Freckles coming to sit by me.

"Hi," she said softly. "I knew you needed a minute, but I figured now you might need a friend. Is it ok that I join you?"

I looked at her blankly, but I nodded. "I used to pretend I was at the ocean when bad things would happen to me as a child. But I have never seen it before in real life. It's all a little overwhelming." I surprised myself by opening up. "I'm afraid to get any closer."

She looked out onto the ocean and nodded understandingly.

"Well, I can go with you, if you want," she said without force.

I looked at her again, this time with intent. "Yes, please," I whispered.

We stood up from our spots and faced each other, brushing the sand off our legs.

"I'm Farrah," she said, reaching out her hand to me.

"Summer." I smiled at her, taking her hand in mine.

We slowly made our way to the ocean, where I put my feet in the salty water for the first time in my life. I felt the tide rushing in and looping around my ankles then pulling away again, the tops of my feet getting buried in the wet sand. I laughed out loud, the sadness sucked out into the horizon where the water met the sky. My first step into the ocean, with Farrah by my side, was another small step toward leaving the past behind me and moving on with my life.

CHAPTER 25

Texas - Now

"AND THEN, FARRAH TOLD me about Sullivan's on the way back to the facility. She told me to go in with her the next day to meet Maverick," I say to Kash, who is still hanging on my every word, an hour and a half later. "I saw you that night, coming in to get ready for your set," I add. "But we didn't meet until —"

Kash cuts me off. "Two weeks later when you started."

"Yeah. You and Silas were up the first night I worked. I couldn't believe the energy. I couldn't believe I had nailed that job."

Kash looks at me through the screen, and I blush. I have been talking for over an hour about the darkest parts of me, and I'm slightly overwhelmed by the fact that I've bared it all.

"Summer..." Kash starts but trails off. I'm not sure I want to know what words are going to come next. "You are the strongest person I have ever met."

I shake my head as my eyes gloss over. There's that word again: strong. A word that still does not seem synonymous with me.

"Yes, you are, Summer," he insists. "You inspire me. You have been through so much and are still kind and generous, you see the good in people. Now I want you to see the best in yourself."

Kash sees the best in me still, and it warms me inside. Even now, knowing the whole truth, he is making sure that I know my worth. I let out a slow, cleansing breath, mostly to control the tears and stop them in their tracks. I'm having trouble finding words to respond.

I look around my little apartment. Though I love it here, for a while, I have felt stuck, like I was given this opportunity and this cozy apartment but that was all I could make of myself. I've felt like I'm never going to get any further from where I am now. And I have resented myself for not being able to do that on my own. But talking to Kash tonight about all the things that led to where I am now, it seems to be a little clearer.

I am more than the sum of my past.

"Thanks for being a great friend, Kash," I say and mean it with my whole being.

"Thanks for sharing your story. You deserve to not fight this alone," he says kindly.

Let people in. Check.

I maneuver my body around and sit up fully on the couch, holding my phone and propping it up on my bent knees.

"So, your bar is going great?" I ask, changing the subject abruptly.

Kash laughs. "Yes, I'm on my way to opening," he says, beaming.

I smile back.

"What are your next moves, Summer? Are you ready to sing your song at Sullivan's with Silas?"

My eyes grow wide. Even talking about it gives me butterflies. "Yes," I respond, more like a child than a grown woman, my eyes rolling.

"Ok, so, Silas and I thought maybe next month," he says nonchalantly.

"Oh, so you two are just planning this behind my back?" I joke.

"I guess you could say that." He laughs, rather pleased with himself.

I shake my head at him with a hint of a smile.

"Ok, so let me know the date, and I'll be there," I say through a yawn.

"Time for bed, sleepyhead."

"Yes, please." I stretch one arm above my head and stand up from the couch. I head toward the bathroom, turning off the lamp as I walk. "I'll text you tomorrow."

"Sounds good. Sleep well," he says, and we hang up.

I look at myself in the bathroom mirror while I brush my teeth. Peace is settling inside, and I can't quite grasp it, but I know I feel better. The toothbrush hangs from my mouth as I take the warped and wrinkled Post-it off the bathroom mirror. I read it one more time and crumple it up, tossing it in the trash. I don't need the reminder anymore.

A week after sharing with Kash about what it looked like when I was at rock bottom, Farrah and I meet for brunch at Alessia's. Farrah is relaxing in our booth when I walk through the door, ringing the tiny bell overhead. She waves me down.

"Hey," she says, spinning the tiny napkin her water was sitting on around with her finger. She's smiling but she looks off.

"Hey," I respond, falling into the booth opposite her. "What's up?" I ask, taking off my jacket and pushing it to the end of the booth.

Farrah looks like she's holding her breath. I give her a confused look and she puts her hands over her mouth. For a second, I grow nervous but then I notice that her eyes are smiling.

"What is going on?" I ask with a laugh.

She slams her hands onto the table. "I'm pregnant!" The words come out in an avalanche of excitement, and I gasp in what seems like all the air around me.

"What? Are you serious?" I squeal. I get up from the booth and pull her out of hers, wrapping her in my arms and squeezing her as tight as I can.

She starts to shake in my arms, tears streaming down her face as her emotions come tumbling out. We sit down again, and I pull her hands into mine.

"This is amazing, Farrah!" I say, my heart warming, joy for her filling me up.

"Yea, we were very shocked. It was always the plan but definitely not yet!" she shrugs her shoulders. "But such is life!"

I settle my back against the booth and think about that word.

Life.

It always seemed like a journey that wasn't worth the pain, and here I am feeling things I have never felt before — excitement, joy, anticipation. *I could have missed this*; I think to myself. I could have kept myself closed off from everyone, forever, had I not chosen to be uncomfortable over the last two years.

I think back to the day I met Farrah and what she gave me — a sense of belonging. She showed me that life has peaks and valleys, but without one, the other doesn't matter. I met Farrah when she was on the upswing of a downward spiral. Joey had checked her into Champlain Bridge when he was too scared to walk alone beside her on her rocky path. He needed help. But he loved her enough to push her to be better. She didn't do it alone, and neither did I. I had help that I resented at first but have now grown to appreciate immensely. I grew up not trusting anyone to be there for me because no one ever was. And in turn, asking for and accepting help was impossible. Until now.

"We're having a baby!" I yell, through happy tears.

"You're going to be an auntie!" Farrah adds.

An auntie. I never had one and I don't know how to be one, but I am going to love that baby with everything in me. That baby will never be without love.

"I'm so happy for you, Farrah," I say. "You and Joey are going to be the best parents."

"Thanks, Summer."

Barb comes over to celebrate with us and brings us mimosa mocktails — orange juice with sparkling water in cute champagne flutes. We all toast to the new life growing inside Farrah, and I give a silent cheer for the new life I'm creating for myself.

After Barb leaves us, I ask Farrah about her plans for work.

She shrugs, "For now, I'm just going to continue working until it feels right to take a break."

I nod. "That's a good plan," I offer. "Who else knows?"

"Just you!" She laughs. "Oh, well, and Barb too," she adds, looking over at her. "We are telling my mom tonight at dinner, and everyone else will have to wait a bit. I'm still so early — only six weeks."

I cross an X over my heart, winking at her. "Secrets safe with me."

We finish up our food and drinks, sharing little things here and there — talking about the bar, Whitney's new girlfriend, Maverick's new waitress, and anything else that comes to mind. It's easy being with Farrah, and when we walk out a little bit later, I feel light on my feet. The air outside is crisp, and the streets are bustling with weekend activity.

Farrah and I stroll down the street, arm in arm, with nowhere to go. We stop for tea at a new shop at the end of my street, and eventually we part ways with a big hug, heading back to our own apartments.

I stroll down the street, slowly, in no sort of rush — Austin on my mind. I think about the last two years and the growth I have experienced here in this city. It settles deep in my bones that I am alive and am not just surviving anymore. The ache that once weighed heavy on my chest has dissipated, and my breaths, once ragged and painful, are now controlled and cleansing. I remind myself that I still have work to do, but the thoughts are without judgment. They are filled with hope.

I walk past a coffee shop that I remember sitting in when I first arrived in Austin. I look in the window, and the memory comes flooding back. I had sat right there on that bar stool looking out onto the unfamiliar street, my hand shaking as it brought the coffee cup to my mouth. I was so unsure about what was ahead, but as I sat there, my hair a mess and my clothes unkempt, I slipped my right hand into my hoodie pocket and felt the tiniest pieces of earth, speckles of sand, that had made their way into my clothing the day before. I remember smiling to myself when a wave of light washed over me, and I recalled the tide carrying away my nightmares out into the horizon. I sat on that barstool, smiling as I looked out into the busy street and letting myself believe I had found a home where I could heal. That day, on that stool, I let myself trust for the first time in my life that I was worthy of joy.

After that wonderful memory, I continue walking down the street, my back a little straighter. I remember it hasn't been an easy road to get to where I am now, but each step is proof that the direction I am going is the one I am meant to be heading in.

I walk into my apartment and make myself some more tea before I grab my notebook from my bedside table. I sit on the couch and open to my song lyrics. I start putting the words in song form, testing the sounds as they come from my lips. It feels strange, and I'm not sure if I like it, but I keep going. I keep warming up my voice, playing with different sounds.

I text Silas:

Hey, want to get together soon and run through some music? Kash said he talked to you about that.

It doesn't take long for him to respond.

Hey! Yeah, that would be sweet. I'm free this afternoon before I have to get to Sullivan's. Are you working tonight?

Yeah, we can go in together after we sort through this.

Sounds good. I'll be over in an hour or two. Sound good?

Sounds great. See ya.

I play around a bit more with the words, trying to think of them as lyrics so they come off more poetic and a little smoother, but my insecurities are nagging at me. I get up from my spot on the couch and pace around the living room, attempting to ease my nerves and allow my creativity to take over. I plop back on the couch with my mug of tea, which has now grown cold. I decide not to pick up the lyrics again until Silas comes by with fresh eyes.

I text Kash:

Silas is coming over to work on the song!

A few minutes later, he responds.

Amazing! I can't wait to hear about it. Call me tonight?

I'm working but I can call after if you're up for a late call.

Always.

I turn the TV on and wait for Silas.

Silas shows up at two, and I'm jerked awake from a cat nap by his patterned knock. I scramble up from the couch and let him in.

"Hey, thanks for coming. Come on in," I say, opening the door for him and gesturing him inside.

"No, thank you for including me. This is going to be so fun!" His excitement surprises me, and it also ignites a little excitement in me too. He walks past me, holding his keyboard.

We head to the couch and sit, getting right down to business. I show him my handwritten words...*lyrics*. He looks at them, reading them intently, and I watch as a knot grows in my stomach. It's like watching someone get a glimpse into my innermost thoughts and wondering what they will say about it. I bite my lip. I take a deep breath in and let out a slow exhale as I wait for him to say something, anything.

"This is awesome, Summer," he looks up from the notebook, his smile telling me he's being truthful. I know how to read people like that. "Kash gave me some ideas for music, and now that I'm reading the lyrics, I see he was right on the money."

I smile shyly, slightly uncomfortable with the attention but also moved at how much time and effort Kash has invested into this.

"So, what do we do first?" I ask.

"Ok, I'm just going to play some notes on my keyboard. I'll put the lyrics in as I go and figure out a melody," he says, setting up his equipment. "Once I figure out what works with the sound, you will sing them, and we will see what we need to tweak. You give me all your input, too, Summer. It's your song."

A chill runs down my back and goosebumps cover every inch of my arms.

Your song.

My song.

I'm really doing this. I am really going to stand up on stage and sing all by myself. I suddenly feel excited. The thought of doing this isn't suffocating me. I can do it. I know I can.

Silas and I work on the song for hours. I learn that his eyebrows furrow when he's concentrating, and he slams his palms into surfaces when he celebrates something. The amount of effort he is putting into my song proves to me just how much he cares. His kindness and friendship are greatly appreciated. I smile as I watch him, feeling perplexed at how I got so lucky to be here in this moment, working on a song that I wrote. The experience is uplifting, hopeful even.

We make infinite changes to the melodies and the intro, but eventually, it feels perfect. We work right up until it's time to head to Sullivan's.

"What do you think?" Silas asks me, packing up his equipment.

I beam at him, showing all my feelings, and he smiles back at me.

"I'm actually really looking forward to this, if you can believe it," I say.

"I know you are kind of shy, Summer, but we can practice a few times a week until next month, and you will be able to do it in your sleep," he says, giving me a high five.

"Deal," I say. "Let me change quickly, and we can head out. Did you drive here?"

"Yeah, you can jump in with me," he answers, and I head off to my room to change into my work outfit — flared jeans, a black V neck shirt with the Sullivan's logo, and my black sneakers. I take a look at my hair in the mirror and decide to braid it in the car on the way over, so I grab an elastic as I walk to the living room.

"Alright, I'm ready," I say, turning off the lights and opening the front door. Silas and I walk down the steps and jump in his car, and once we head down the road, I pull out my phone to text Kash.

I think it's going to be great :)

As soon as I send it, I see the three dots come up on the screen.

Me too

And with that, I'm ready for the night.

CHAPTER 26

Texas – Now, 4 Weeks Later

SUMMER'S SONG

I can't stop moving my body as I brush my teeth in front of the mirror in my bathroom. My nerves are elevated to maximum capacity. I'm nervous, terrified, thrilled — all at once. I talked to Kash on the phone earlier today because I needed some encouragement. I needed him to tell me how much he believed in me. And, of course, he did. As I stand here in my bathroom almost ready to leave, I can't help but feel a pang of sadness that he's not going to be here to watch me do this. Farrah's working tonight and they set it all up so she can FaceTime him, so he'll be able to see the whole thing. It helps a little because I know I will perform better knowing he's watching because I won't want to let him down. His pride in me is palpable, and it's a driving force for me.

I take one last look in the mirror and inhale as much air as I possibly can. My hair is up in a high ponytail, the back of it hanging over my shoulder, curled slightly at the ends. I'm wearing dark skinny jeans and a black shirt Farrah bought me for this very occasion. It's not me at all, sparkly and kind of loud, but she told me that was the point. I'm stepping out of my shell tonight and have to look the part. I'm going to wear black heels but not until I get there. I want them for the song but not for anything else. My makeup is heavy compared to what I normally wear, but that part I can deal with. The lights on that stage are as bright as anything. No need to worry about anyone being able to see the pimple that formed last night.

I've got a few minutes before I have to leave so I go into my room, grab my notebook and flip through it to the page with the lyrics. The original page is marked up with notes from Silas, and I read through them. Over the last few weeks, he has helped me master this song and knowing he will be up there with me is comforting.

I sit on my bed for a few minutes, staring out the window. I start to think about what I'm about to do. I have no idea why I am doing this or what will come from it, but I feel like I'm about to pop out of a cocoon. I'm a ball of nerves — my muscles are twitching, and my leg is bouncing. I need to get out of my apartment and go to Sullivan's so I can be surrounded by the familiar noise of my friends while I wait to take the stage. I grab a bag and put my heels and wallet in it. I find my flip-flops in my closet and slip them on before heading out the door.

I walk into Sullivan's at 4:10 p.m. and see a painted sign hanging from the bar that reads *Go Summer!* I smile to myself, and when everyone turns to see who walked in the door, they all stampede me, wrapping me in their embrace.

"Thanks, guys!" I say. "I'm freaking out!"

"Oh, dear, you are going to do fabulous. We are all here for you," Silvia says, rubbing my arm.

"We can't wait!" Maverick says. "Do you want a drink; something to calm your nerves?"

"Not right now, thanks," I respond as Farrah hands me a glass of water with a wink.

"Thanks. This I could use. My mouth is so dry from nerves," I say and take a long drink of the cold water. I look up and see that they are all standing around me, staring with smiles.

"What, guys? I haven't even done anything yet," I say, uncomfortable with the attention.

"I know, sweetie, but we love you. I consider you like a daughter. We all feel that way, like family, so let us love you," Silvia says.

Family. That's something I never thought I would hear.

I nod and let my head fall, afraid tears will come and wreck my make-up. I take another sip of water to slow it down.

"You all *are* my family," I say, my voice wavering. "I have never had a family, and you all have been the best things to ever walk into my life," I stop there, afraid I'll start crying if I go any further, but I let them hug me again, and I feel the love. With them by my side, I have nothing to be afraid of, I know that now.

I help everyone set up for the night even though they keep yelling at me not to. I'm afraid of idle hands, though. I want to keep moving, keep my mind busy. Less time to think about what's to come.

"Why don't we just go in the back, and you can warm up your voice," Silas offers.

"Sure," I say with a sigh and follow him to the back room.

"How do you feel," he asks me as he tinkers with the piano in the back.

"I feel good. Anxious. But good," I say. "Part of me is ready and wants it to be over and done with, and the other part of me hopes that time stands still so I don't have to do it at all."

"That's the best way to be, Summer," Silas encourages me. "You need to have some nerves or else you won't be prepared, and you and I have prepared. You are ready."

I smile at him, and we begin to warm up.

I head out into the main room an hour later, and Maverick is getting ready to open the doors. It's five-thirty, and in two hours, I will be standing on that stage singing a song I wrote. I wipe my sweaty hands on my jeans and walk on shaky legs to the bar to talk to Farrah.

"Hi! I'm bouncing all over the place, girl," she says, wiping down some water on the counter.

I raise my eyebrows, my stomach flipping again. She gives me a hug. I feel my phone vibrating in my back pocket. I pull it out and glance at the screen. It's Kash calling.

"Hey," I say.

"Hey, I just wanted to call and wish you good luck! I'm sitting outside my apartment. It's quiet and serene. The perfect atmosphere for me to watch you later."

"Really? It sounds kind of loud there." I laugh as I continue to wipe the sweat from my hands onto my jeans.

"Oh, yeah, there are some people walking on the sidewalk below, but I'll go inside if I need to," he assures me.

I smile and take a shaky breath. The nerves are making me feel sick, and I can't wait for them to pass, hopefully before I go out there, but I'm not counting on it.

"Go outside for a second," he says to me.

Curious as to why he wants me to go outside, I head to the door and step out onto the sidewalk.

"Ok, I'm outside," I say, looking up and down the street, wondering if maybe he's going to pop into my line of vision.

"Ok, good. Look up."

The stars. He's not here, but the stars are. I look up and feel myself relax a bit.

"I'm looking," I say, barely above a whisper.

"Me too."

There's a comfortable silence between us for a few minutes while we both look at the sky, together, but apart.

"You got this, Summer."

"Thank you so much. I'll talk to you after, ok? Thank you so much for calling. It means a lot to me," I say, and I really mean it. We say our goodbyes and hang up. I slide my phone back into my pocket and shake out my arms in an effort to calm down even more, to let go of some of my nervous energy. I head back inside and straight to the bar to find Farrah again.

"Girl, take a breath," she says calmly, gently grabbing my shoulders.

"Seriously, do you know how many breaths I have taken today? Deep ones! And lots of them. There is no calming this feeling."

"Just think, in a little bit, it will be all over and that might make you sad. Try and enjoy it," Farrah says, and I think about her words.

"You're right," I say and let out a closed mouth scream, and she joins me.

I head to the back and change into my heels, and for the next hour, I keep myself busy by talking with Maverick and Silvia, greeting patrons at the door, and going over the lyrics in my head. As it gets closer to showtime, I actually start to calm down a little, as if the pressure was in the waiting.

The lights in the bar have dimmed, and the ambience is soft and inviting — the warm tea lights on the tables, twinkling lights hanging around dark mahogany wood throughout. It gives me peace as I prepare to go up there and face my fears.

I look over at Farrah, who is on her phone behind the bar, her finger in her opposite ear to block out the background noise so she can hear the caller. She looks concerned, and for a moment, I get worried. I think of Joey; I think of her baby. But then she throws her head back and laughs, and my shoulders relax. I still find it weird for her to be on her phone at work. She never does that.

I look up at the clock — 7:27 p.m. I have about thirty minutes before Silas and his new partner, Keenan, take their first break, and then after that, Silas and I will start off the second set together.

"Thank you, beautiful people!" Silas yells. "It's time for a break from us, but when we get back, I have a special guest coming up to sing her very own song, and you don't want to miss it. Get your drinks filled and get back to your seats." He jumps down from the elevated stage where the microphone and pianos sit. He walks over to where I stand by the bar. But the bar starts to get crowded with people getting up from their tables, so I walk away toward Silas and meet him in the middle of the room. He takes a sip from his water bottle and pushes a tiny braid out of his sweaty face.

"I'm pumped," he says, out of breath but beaming.

I give him an uneasy smile, and he hugs me. I look over his shoulder while he squeezes me, and my mind plays a trick on me — I could swear that I see Kash. He's right there, walking, or more like running, into Sullivan's. But it can't be. I must be going crazy. I pull away from Silas and move to the side, looking at the guy I thought was Kash, who now has his back to me, talking to Maverick. Is it Kash? The person has dark hair like him, a bun on top of his head, and...an arm full of tattoos.

"Kash?" I say quietly, mostly to myself, but Silas hears me and turns to look in the direction I am facing. The mystery person turns around and scans the bar, looking for someone, and I realize it's him. It really is him. And he's looking for...me.

Silas starts saying something to me, but I'm running. Kash sees me and begins smiling ear to ear, swiftly making his way to me. I jump up into his arms with force, finding it difficult to determine if this is real. But I feel him. He is here holding me close to him as I laugh into his chest. It really is him. He swings me around and when I'm standing on solid ground again, I look up at him, touching his face, making sure I'm not dreaming.

"It's really me," he says through a laugh, sensing my doubt.

"What the hell? What are you doing here?" I ask, out of breath.

"Are you kidding? I would not miss this for the world. FaceTime wasn't going to cut it." His words are warm and spread like honey through my body.

He takes my face in his hands as my eyes fill with tears. "No, no, don't cry," he says. "You're my best friend. This was always the plan. I was afraid to let you down if something fell through at the last minute, so I wanted it to be a surprise." He smiles. My cheeks puff with air, and I let it out slowly. I hug him again.

"Thank you," I say, but it comes out as a whisper because that's all I can muster.

"Go get ready. Silas is waiting for you," he says, nodding over in Silas's direction. I look over at him, and he's waiting for me by the stage with a huge smile on his face.

"Ok, I'm going," I say. "Wish me luck."

He shakes his head. "You don't need it."

I walk over to Silas, my legs feeling a little stronger than they were when I woke up this morning and even when I first arrived here at Sullivan's this evening.

"You ready?" Silas asks, giving me a single nod of his head.

"As ready as I'll ever be," I tell him, following him up to the entrance of the stage, waiting there while he climbs up and goes to the center of the stage.

Silas grabs the microphone from the stand. "Ladies and gents, we are back for set two!" Everyone claps. "I would like you to give a warm welcome to my very good friend and Sullivan's very own, Summer James!"

The cheers echo around me. The sensation is unsettling but also invigorating. I walk up the steps to the stage and make my way to the microphone, lowering it to my level as Silas walks to the piano.

"Thank you, Silas," I say, looking back at him, and he gives me a thumbs up.

"Thank you, everyone." I speak into the microphone, waiting for a lull in the applause. "I wrote this song you're about to hear. It means a lot to me. The lyrics came from some hard things I've gone through in my life." I look up to see Kash sitting right in front, smiling at me. I take another deep breath, trying to steady my nerves. "But what I have learned during the last two years is that I just needed some friends who loved me." I quickly make eye contact with all my people and then I glance back at

Silas and give him a nod. With that, the music starts to play, and I know there is no going back now.

Farrah was right — the performance is over before I even realize it's officially begun. I stand there in awe, gripping the mic stand, half laughing, half crying. I'm frozen, not wanting to leave the stage. The patrons are clapping generously, but the Sullivan's staff, my family, are standing and screaming.

I've spent my whole life wishing time away, praying that moments would end so I could find reprieve. But now I'm standing here trying to stop time and remain in this moment for as long as possible. I'm desperate to memorize every sound, every smell. Knowing that it's possible to feel this way makes me long for it to happen again and again. My tears are blurring my vision, my thoughts are clouding my senses, muffling the sounds around me. I'm wrapped up in my own euphoric thoughts, a strange feeling radiating through my bones.

I wipe my eyes and my senses come back into focus. It's loud. So loud. I turn to Silas, who is standing up next to his piano clapping. I run to him and give him a big hug.

"Thank you for everything," I say into his sweaty shirt.

"Don't thank me; that was all you, my friend," he winks at me. "I gotta play again. Go see everyone. They're waiting for you." He motions his head to the stairs, and I run down them as fast as I can. Everyone's abandoned their posts and are waiting to greet me when I get off the stage. Farrah, J.J., and Whitney are beaming at me, Silvia is crying, and Kash looks so proud he could bust. They give me a group hug, and at this moment, I know I am loved by them. This must be what home feels like.

It's one-thirty in the morning, and Sullivan's has cleared out, except for the staff. We're all sitting around the bar, and everything is cleaned up, ready for tomorrow.

We are celebrating — J.J. brought out some appetizers and two bottles of champagne. I know what I did isn't really that big of a deal, but the way they have cheered me on and supported me through this experience warms my heart. I am filled with immense gratitude for each and every person in this room.

"Your voice is angelic, dear," Silvia says, handing me a glass of champagne, tears in her eyes.

"Seriously, can you NOT keep secrets like that again?" Farrah laughs. "When you sang at our rehearsal dinner, I was shocked. I had no idea you could sing like that!"

"Thanks, everyone," I say, taking a sip from my flute. "I am so lucky to have ended up here in Austin. I've grown so much since leaving everything behind in Kentucky and arriving here that sometimes I don't even know who I am anymore." Everyone is looking at me intently. "But I like who I am becoming, so again, thank you from the bottom of my heart."

Kash holds up his glass to toast. "To Summer," he cheers, and we all clink glasses and take a sip. Farrah puts her glass down a tad too early, and Silas catches on.

"Not drinking tonight, Farrah? Rough night last night?" he says, jokingly. Farrah's eyes grow wide. She looks at me, and I can tell she doesn't want to steal my thunder, so I give her an assuring nod.

"Um," she begins. "Well, Sullivan's is going to have a new family member," she says, waiting to see everyone's reaction.

They all look at each other, confused for a minute, and then it dawns on them what she's saying. Excitedly, they break out in congratulatory hugs and high fives. I watch as voices mount on top of one another. I take mental notes, again, for the second time tonight, grasping onto this moment as best I can — to remember Farrah sharing this wonderful news with the people I love the most, the people I love more than I have ever loved anyone, the people who deserve my love in return.

When we finally wrap up the night and begin to clear out, it's two-thirty.

"Can I walk you home?" Kash asks.

"Of course," I say. "Where are you staying?"

"The motel on Venus Street," he says. "I'll grab an Uber from your apartment."

I nod with a smile, and we start heading down the street toward my building.

We make it to my apartment in no time, talking about Kash's flight and his new apartment, my sessions with Silas, and Farrah's news. When we approach the steps in front of my place, it feels surreal, like old times. Kash sits down on the second to last step, and I join him, leaning back. We find ourselves looking at the stars, and we're silent for a moment.

"Come with me," he says.

I look over at him, confused.

"Where?" I ask, not sure if he means to brunch tomorrow before he leaves, or what.

"To California," he states with finality.

"For vacation?" I ask. "When?"

"No, Summer, for good."

I sit up abruptly, facing him.

"What are you talking about?" I ask, nervous laughter mixing in with my words.

He looks up at the sky briefly.

"I'm talking about your life, Summer." He sounds so passionate, and I know that he's serious.

"Um, I can't. My life is here. My work...Farrah..." I say, suddenly unsure, my voice trailing off.

"Yes, this is your home, and we all are your family, but it's ok to fly from the nest."

I lean forward, placing my head on my knees, looking at him.

He continues. "Farrah is going to have a baby soon and, most likely, will not be working at Sullivan's anymore. Her life is going to be changing drastically. You have dreams to do more, Summer, and you proved to yourself tonight that you are more than capable of doing hard things." I don't know what to say. "You have dreamed of California. Will you at least think about it? Don't let everyone else evolve around you while you allow yourself to stay stuck."

His words hit me in the gut, and I suddenly feel defensive.

"Kash, I have worked so hard over the last few years to evolve, and I have grown so much. Don't you see that?" I ask, hurt in my voice.

He stands up and reaches out for my hands. He helps me up and holds me in an embrace. He whispers into my ear, "Summer, I have never seen someone change so much right before my eyes. Of course, I see it; I have always seen you. I have always been cheering you on. But sometimes, I think you don't believe that good things can happen to you. I'm offering this leap to you as your friend who sees your potential."

I squeeze my arms tightly around him, feeling overly emotional. I pull away, then sit back down, patting the spot next to me for him to join me. I look up again at the sky and instinctively start counting to myself.

"I see your lips counting," Kash says. "Are you anxious about everything I said?"

I shake my head. "No, I'm just thinking."

Out of the corner of my eye, I see him nod.

California. Move there? Leave Texas and this family I have created? To do what? Bartend? It all seems so ludicrous.

As if reading my mind, Kash starts to reassure me. "You could stay in my office until you got your own place. You could stay as long as you wanted, and I could get a bed in there. It's not big, but it's something, and you wouldn't be alone. I can walk to the water, that's how close I am to the ocean. You would love it. There are palm trees everywhere, and it's constantly sunny, I guess like here, but it feels different." He's rambling a bit, but I find it endearing. "And you can work with me, if you want. I hired a few people already. They don't compare to our crew here though." He motions his head in the direction of Sullivan's. "But I think it's going to be great."

I stare at him with wide eyes. This is crazy.

"We could perform together. We can do covers and songs that you write. You can try them out at the bar and then pitch them, like you always wanted."

His words are spinning dreams in my mind that are wildly colorful but also feel equally unattainable. I can't just up and leave Austin. Can I?

Kash looks at his watch. "Look, it's three-thirty. I'm getting a rental car in the morning and driving down to Waco to see my mom for a few days, and then I'm flying out on Wednesday. It's late, so I really should get going. But I want you to seriously consider this, Summer. Please, will you just think about it?"

"Yes," I whisper. "I promise to think about it."

Kash takes out his phone to get an Uber. "Good. That's all I ask." He flashes me his smile, and I rest my head on his shoulder, silently hoping the Uber takes its time. Another moment I just don't want to end.

"But it's crazy, right?" I ask Silvia.

We are sitting at an outdoor cafe in the city. The sun is blaring down on me, and I adjust myself so I'm under the umbrella as sweat forms on the crown of my head. It's been a month since Kash asked me to move to California.

"My Lord, dear, take a breath. You're all hot and bothered," Silvia says, her Southern accent prominent.

"Well, it's sweltering," I retaliate, fanning myself with the paper menu.

"No, you're just all in a tizzy," Silvia bats her hand in my direction to fan me as she takes a sip of her water.

"I need a drink," I say, looking around for the waitress. "And you still haven't answered my question. It's crazy, right?" I ask, looking her directly in the eyes.

"Can I please have a glass of rosé?" I ask the waitress as she comes over. "And a glass of chardonnay for my friend." I order for Silvia without even asking. Words are just spilling out of my mouth, my nerves rattling.

Silvia puts her elbows on the table, resting her chin on her clasped hands. "Summer, what do you want?"

I stare at her for a moment. I'm finding it difficult to find the words to describe how I'm feeling inside my extremely mixed-up mind. I put my head in my arms on the table.

"I don't know what to do," I say, my voice muffling into my sweaty arm.

"I think you do, doll. I really think you know what you want." Silvia is adamant. I look up from my pitiful position and groan as the waitress sets our wine glasses in front of us.

"I want to go, but it feels impulsive."

"Impulsive or whimsical?" Silvia asks me, and I ponder that thought.

"Whimsical?" I look at her, my eyebrows furrowed.

"You have spent almost two years struggling to find yourself, Summer. You are crawling out of that as we speak, right in front of my eyes. And now an opportunity has presented itself. And, by the way, that's what this is, an opportunity, not an impulsive, crazy idea." She gives me a motherly look. "This is not a hard decision, Summer. Go to California. Live your life."

Tears well up in my eyes, and I gently wipe them away with my napkin. I take a sip from my glass.

"But I can't leave you guys. I can't leave the only family I have ever known. I just can't. I wouldn't be where I am if it weren't for all of you," I say sadly.

"Kash is a part of that family, too, Summer. And do you think we'd be showing you love if we made you stay here with us for the rest of your life?" She gives me a look that makes me feel a bit silly. "Families let each other fly, Summer. And you need to soar. You need to experience life and do something that ignites your soul. I want that for you. We all want that for you."

I nod. Though I am frightened and unsure, I know she is right.

"What did Farrah say when you told her?" she asks me.

I cringe. "I haven't told her yet. You're the first person I told."

Silvia nods understandably.

"I'm meeting her tomorrow for lunch before our shift. I'm going to really think about this tonight, and then I'll talk to her about it tomorrow."

"I think you should make your decision first. Make the decision *you* want before you tell anyone else. It's not about what anyone else feels or thinks. Everyone is going to support you, you know that. But make this about you, Summer. Because with support also comes sadness. Farrah, Maverick, all of us really, we are going to be sad to see you go, but you cannot let that shape your decision. It has to be what you want."

I reach across the table and grab Silvia's hand. "Thank you." I mouth the words, but no sound comes out.

———

After lunch, I walk home, taking the long way, walking slowly and taking everything in — kids eating ice cream cones while globs of it melt down their forearms, couples holding hands, people laughing. Everything looks crisp and brand new, like I'm seeing it for the first time — the leaves on the trees, the color of the sky, and the way the buildings seem to touch the clouds. Do I want to leave this place? The place that brought me back to life.

I stop by the park and find an empty bench by the lake and take a seat. I glance out at the water, watching the ripples move rhythmically in a steady beat. The truth is, I don't want to leave. I'm not looking to run from Texas like I wanted to run from Kentucky. Over the last few weeks, I've felt confused about making this decision because I'm not trying to escape. But Kash is right. While everyone around me finds their way and takes different paths, having babies and getting married, I don't want to find myself stuck, latching onto something just because it was the first good thing I ever had. There is more out there for me, and I'm starting to realize that.

I close my eyes. I can see my childhood home, and I'm grasping for something, anything, that brings joy from these memories, but nothing comes. I see anger, tears. I see pain, so much pain. I think of Autumn Sinclaire, her kind eyes and gentle voice. It wasn't her fault that I got taken away from my momma. It wasn't her fault that she had to break the news to me that my momma had died. I wish I could thank her for not making me feel like everyone else did, like I was a character in an after-school special.

Thoughts of the Brickmans begin to rush my mind. I'm not sure that I have even come to terms with the fact that I spent my formative years in a home that despised me and looked down on me. What started as a way for them to "pay it forward" turned into a chore they regretted. I was left to deal with the repercussions of how both my birth parents and my foster parents treated me, and though I was strong, no one thought to *really* check in on me, the child going through hell. And because of that, I fell into the darkest hole imaginable.

I think about the younger me, who would look up in the stands during my volleyball games and see a swarm of faces and colors but never see anyone who was there to cheer me on, not unless obligation reared its ugly head. Guilt will do that to people.

Silvia is right. I am actively coming into the light with each passing day. I shouldn't be holding myself back. I look down at my knee, bouncing, a nervous habit. I put my hand on it to steady it and take a deep breath.

I'm going, I think to myself. I'm going to California to start a new chapter. I pull out my phone and FaceTime Kash.

"Hey! Where are you?" he asks, smiling at me through the screen.

"Hi! Oh, I'm sitting at the park. I just had lunch with Silvia and decided to take a long walk home and ended up here." I take my eyes off the phone and look out at the water again.

"What's up?" Kash asks.

I look back at him and my insides feel like they have been shaken up and spilled out.

"I'm going to come to California, Kash."

"What?! Are you serious? That's amazing!"

I laugh along with his excitement. "I have been thinking about it ever since you asked. I talked about it with Silvia today and just now, sitting here by myself, it's all I can think about, it's the only thing on my mind. I know it's the right choice, and I want to say thank you for offering me this chance."

"Summer, please don't thank me. Just accept this as a path you choose to take. Opportunities get offered in life, and it's up to you whether you take them or not."

I nod. "So, I guess I'm getting on a plane for the first time in my life," I say lightheartedly.

"I guess you are! When do you think you would plan on making the move?"

I shrug. "I don't know. It's not like I have much to move. I'll probably send a few boxes and then travel with a carry-on and that's it. I'll want to give Maverick some time to hire someone else, of course." I finish my sentence, and I'm filled with dread when I think about telling Maverick, and everyone else for that matter.

"What's the matter?" Kash asks me, reading my face.

"I don't want to disappoint Mav," I say. "Is he going to be mad at me?"

"No, Summer. He will probably be sad, but he will want what's best for you. Just like he did with me."

"Yeah, that's what Silvia said, but I still feel weird."

He looks at me softly. "It's ok. Do you want to go over what to say together?"

"No, let me talk to Farrah first. We're having lunch tomorrow before our shift. I'll tell Maverick at some point tomorrow night." I smile, but it feels forced.

"You weren't put on this earth to make everyone else comfortable, Summer. It's time you put yourself first, unapologetically."

"Ok. I'm trying."

Kash smiles at me. "And you're doing great."

I get up from the bench and start walking in the direction of my apartment, holding my phone out in front of my face.

"I gotta go, Kash. Talk later?"

"Sounds good," he says, getting up from wherever he was sitting.

We hang up, and I keep heading in the direction of my place. *What am I doing?* I think to myself. Is this really happening? Am I really going to move to California? It seems insane, but at the same time, it feels like the right thing to do.

When I get into my apartment, I look around at the quiet, serene space I created here. When I was surrounded by darkness, I made it bright, a place to cheer myself up. I finally have a few hanging plants that I kept alive, and that was more telling of my growth than anything, really. I think about my first apartment in Kentucky; the ground floor studio where everything I brought in there died, including my spirit. I hadn't realized until now how much this apartment has given me — independence, security, rejuvenation. Everything has always felt so serene here in this little apartment; even in darkness, there was light here. Just like the stars in the sky. This place has given me all that it can, though, and now it's time for me to leave my home, my nest, and fly.

I decide to spend the entire rest of the day and evening here in my apartment. I make a cup of coffee using my Keurig and grab my notebook. I jot some thoughts down — poetic and melodious as I am feeling very reflective as of late, as my life begins to change right before my eyes. And for once, it feels hopeful and joyous.

I curl up on my couch and read a little of the novel that has been sitting on my coffee table for some time, and eventually, I get up and make myself a small dinner of spaghetti and meatballs. I sit down with a glass of Cabernet and find something to watch on Netflix. I'm noticing how comfortable I am being alone right now and it's interesting because usually I'm restless, anxious, and unsettled.

At ten-thirty, my eyelids are growing heavy. I turn off the TV, fold up my blanket, and head to my bed. I crawl in and pull the covers all the way to my chin, resting my head on the pillow. I sleep heavily all night long and I wake up feeling rested. I remember the news I have to break today, and I'm nervous about it but I am content with my decision, glad I'm taking Kash and Silvia's advice about deciding what's best for me and not anyone else.

At the diner, I take a seat in a corner booth. I'm fidgeting with my hands while I wait for Farrah to arrive. I order a cup of coffee, and when the waitress brings it over, I fill it with a container of creamer and hold the mug in my hands to keep them steady.

Farrah.

How am I going to leave her? I suddenly start to think back to the day I met her. Flashes of memories flicker in my mind. I saw her from across the dining room at Champlain Bridge, her auburn hair and freckles catching my eye. I was drawn to her light and her smile, and I remember feeling like I wasn't alone in my battle, in my need for help. If she was there, then she must have needed guidance and support, just like me. But her positive energy gave me immense hope from the second I saw her — hope that there was life on the other side of the mess I'd been in.

When she introduced herself to me a few days later at the beach, I knew our souls were meant to meet. When you grow up learning that everyone will let you down, you take special care when deciding which people have the privilege of seeing the real you. I knew right away that Farrah was one of those people. The friendship she has given me has played an important part in me becoming a stronger version of myself.

I see Farrah walk in. As she comes over to the table, a smile on her face, I see a tiny bump poking underneath her shirt, and instantly, I feel calm. I get up to greet her — embracing her for much longer than necessary, but I need her to know I love her with all my being. Farrah Pine — the sister I never had.

We both settle into the booth opposite each other. "How are you feeling?" I ask her, as she takes her bag off her shoulder and puts it beside her. She fixes her ponytail and smiles at me.

"Pretty good!" she exclaims. "I still throw up once a day when I first wake up. But it's not that bad." She takes a deep breath and leans back on the booth. "How are you?"

"Good," I answer too quickly, and she gives me a sideways look but then lets it go. "I had lunch with Silvia yesterday," I say, taking a sip of my coffee. The waitress comes over and fills a mug for Farrah then takes our orders. When the waitress walks away, Farrah starts to say something, but I cut her off. I need to get this over with.

"I need to tell you something," I say. I try not to make it sound like it's bad news, but she gives me a worried look.

"What's up?" she asks, concern in her voice.

"Well..." Suddenly, the words I had planned have sprung from my head, and I'm at a loss for how to begin. "I'm moving." I stop there and wait for a reaction.

"Like to a new apartment? How come? You love that place!"

"No, I'm moving to...California."

She doesn't say anything, but her eyes quickly fill with tears and her throat bobs with an enunciated swallow. "What?" she mutters in a whisper.

"Kash offered me a chance to work at his bar and perform my songs on a regular basis with him. And I'm hoping to transition to other open mic nights, and I really hope to be able to pitch my songs to record companies or artists." She's hanging on to my every word. I stop and wait for her reaction.

She nods a few times and picks up her napkin to wipe her face. "I'm sorry I'm crying," she begins. "I don't want you to think I'm not supporting you. I'm just shocked. Ever since I met you, you have been my person, and I never thought you would leave." She pauses and takes a sip of water as the waitress delivers our meals. "But now that I think of it, that isn't a fair assumption to make about you, Summer."

"What do you mean?"

She shrugs her shoulders. "I don't know. I just thought maybe that you had found your place here in Texas. I thought that being away from Kentucky and having friends here would mean that I would always have you right here with me. But you are not done finding yourself, Summer. You have been a light in my life, and you don't even realize how much you shine. I'm so glad you've found the courage to do what's best for YOU. Even if it means you're leaving me." Her voice hitches at the end, and the tears flow faster from her eyes. I join her on the other side of the table and wrap my arm around her shoulder. I begin to cry too.

"I have been dreading telling you, Farrah. I didn't want you to be mad at me. I didn't want to feel like you weren't cheering me on. I was so fearful of that."

"Well, if I did that, what kind of friend would I be?"

I laugh. "Silvia said the same thing!"

"What? You told Silvia before me?" she accuses, laughing.

"I wanted to talk it through with her before I made a decision. I didn't want to tell you if I wasn't even sure."

"It's ok, Summer. I'm just joking." She rests her head on my shoulder. "So, little Junie is going to have an aunt who she sees on FaceTime...every day. I can live with this." She seems to be reassuring herself more than me.

"Junie?" I say. "Do you know it's a girl?" I ask, my voice rising.

"Yes!" she yells. "And I wanted to name her something after you, so we picked June." She's smiling ear to ear.

"Are you serious?" I ask, my voice sticking in my throat.

"I'm very serious. I have never been more sure of anything in my life."

We hug each other and stay like that for a while, our burgers and fries growing cold on the table.

———

It's four o'clock, and I'm making my way through the doors of Sullivan's when I notice that the main room is dark, which is strange. This is usually where we gather before a shift. I look in the kitchen, and no one is there either, so I head back to the front of the restaurant and into the small room to the right of the front door, where we sometimes have private functions. I push the door open, and to my complete surprise, everyone is there, holding signs that say, "We Love You Summer" and "We Will Miss You" and "Don't Forget About Us." *What the hell*, I think to myself. *How do they know?* Everyone's cheering and clapping, then a few of them set down their signs and walk up to me to give me hugs.

"What are you all doing?" I ask, completely confused.

"Farrah called us all this afternoon," J.J. states. "She knew you didn't want to tell us, so she told us. It's hard to break this kind of news sometimes, so we're trying to make it easier for you."

I look around at everyone, shocked. I see Maverick, standing back from the crowd and leaning against the window, his arms crossed over his chest but there's a sweet smile on his face so I instantly calm. I go over to him and hug him.

"I was planning on talking to you tonight, right now actually. I wasn't looking forward to it. J.J. is right; I was extremely worried, but I was going to do it. Are you disappointed in me?" I ask, desperate for him to say no.

"Absolutely not," he says, and I can tell he means it. "Summer, the thought of you leaving and Kash being gone and Farrah probably taking some significant time off sucks. It all sucks. But that's life. I don't love you because you are a dependable employee. I love you because of who you are."

I squeeze him as tight as I can then pull away, turning to the group.

"Thank you all, seriously. I'm beyond grateful that you all support me and love me the way you do." I take a deep breath and suddenly feel sad. This has been my home for two years, and leaving is so bittersweet. "Any chance you all want to move to California with me?" I ask everyone, half joking, half completely serious. They laugh, and we all join in on a huge group hug.

"Alright, alright, I have a business to run. Everyone, go get ready for the night," Maverick says, shooing us out of the function room. We all head back into the main room and go to our stations to start getting ready for the night. I head to the bar with Farrah, and once we get behind the counter, I look at her lovingly.

"You," I say with a smile.

"What?" she asks sweetly.

"Thank you. That was really kind of you."

"It's what best friends are for," she says with a wink. She starts cutting up a container of limes, and I grab the lemons and begin cutting those up. We chat like always, small talk with some bigger topics mixed in there — babies and big moves — but it's all so comfortable. It's all so perfect. I look out onto the floor to see everyone hustling around while Silas is setting up his equipment, and I can't believe I was nervous about coming to work tonight. Now that the hard part is over, I have no idea how I ever even assumed that these people would make me feel anything but loved. I feel my phone buzz in my back pocket, and I take it out. It's Kash.

How was it?

It was so good! Farrah told everyone ahead of time and when I came in, they were all hiding in the function room and they surprised me with signs and stuff.

WOW! That's perfect!

Yeah - how lucky am I?

:) Have a great night at work. We can talk tomorrow about the next steps. Yeah?

Sounds good. Have a good night. :)

The night is perfect. Silas and Keenan bring in a huge crowd, and Farrah and I make good money. We are all riding the high of an epic night at Sullivan's as we clean up and chat amongst ourselves. It's not lost on me that this will be one of my last nights working here, so I take the time to memorize every part of the room, every fault in the walls, every light, the smells, and the sounds. I never want to forget this place, and I don't think I ever could.

While preparing for my move to California, I noticed this ache inside of me, like something was unfinished, and I eventually made the decision to face my past. That's how I now find myself back in Kentucky. I went back and forth about it for a while, but in the end, I knew I had to do it. I had to come back here and confront the nightmares that constantly tore me down for all those years. I had to come and show my younger self that I had moved on, I had risen above my past. That version of myself is still tangled in a web of pain, and I need to release her from that.

When I told Farrah my plan, she offered to come with me, but I knew I had to do this on my own. I have to save myself. No one else can do this for me. Joey offered me his truck for the drive, and I was thankful not to have to take the bus.

The drive to Louisville took two days. I drove most of the day on Saturday and spent the night in Memphis, then drove the rest of the way on Sunday. When I got here, I checked into a motel near my old high school.

It's Monday morning now, and as I sit here on the edge of the motel bed, I can feel my old self sitting here with me. A tear slides down my cheek. I can't help but feel like I abandoned her here. But back then, I didn't know how to comfort her, how to help her heal. But I'm doing that now.

I glance at the clock. It's 8:02 a.m. As I get up from the bed, it squeals from the release of weight. I take a breath and head out the door and straight toward Joey's truck. It's time to go see Momma.

The wind whips my hair around as I stare down at the measly gravestone. Her name, her date of birth, and her date of death are all it states, etched into the stone in plain, bland letters. It's all she leaves behind on this earth. Once a daughter, then a wife and a mother but no one besides me will ever know that. This is where she rests, turning to dust beneath my feet. I look up at the sky and wonder if that's where she is now. Is she at peace? Does she see me? Is she proud?

I once blamed myself for my circumstances. Everything always felt like it was my fault. No matter who I was around, my problems and the negative feelings of those around me seemed to stem simply from my existence. For far too long I put the blame on myself for everything that happened to Momma. But it wasn't my fault. I know that now. She wasn't strong enough to face her demons, and I once believed that I, too, would suffer that same fate. But I didn't. I didn't allow myself to succumb to the cards I was dealt. I always thought I was waiting to be given a new hand, but it was me who had to put things into motion. I had to take control.

"I forgive you," I whisper, remembering how I once screamed at her after she was gone, wherever she was, wondering why she left me. But I know now that if she was still here, alive in this city, then I probably would be, too, and I'd rather be anywhere but here.

I place my hand on her gravestone and stay like that for some time. I stay until I know I'll be ok if I never come back here again. This is my final goodbye.

I walk to Joey's truck, climb in, and slam the door, looking one final time at the place where Momma rests.

"Good-bye, Momma," I say as I shift the truck into drive and pull away from the grassy edge.

I drive through town, passing by all the places where my ghosts still wander — the club where I worked, my first apartment, my high school. I sit at a red light, waiting to turn right toward the motel. But then suddenly something takes over, and I flip the blinker to turn left, just as the light turns green, and I take the turn...left, toward the Brickman's.

My breathing picks up a bit as I get closer, driving past the larger houses and landscaped lawns of my old neighborhood. This wasn't my plan, and I have no idea what is going to happen when I pull up to the house where I lived for so many years. Soon, I find myself pulling up to the big white house with flower boxes in the window. I park against the curb, the same spot where Sarah Tate first parked when she brought me to this hell, the trash bag full of my possessions in my lap.

Coming here to Kentucky wasn't about seeing them. It was about releasing my pain and forgiving my Momma. But now that I'm here, I've come to realize that this is actually the only way to move on. Every part of my soul that was broken before I got here was shattered to pieces in this house. I look up at the roof over the garage and a lump builds inside my throat. I picture myself up there, night after night, the rough shingles under my palms as I counted and talked to the stars. It's been twelve years since I last sat up there, hiding from Cassie, Greg, and Gina. I see the lattice where I climbed down time and time again, now with a fresh coat of paint.

My eyes slide down the garage to the driveway where two cars are parked — a white Mercedes and a black SUV, much like the cars that were parked there years ago.

They're home.

My mind begins to jumble as my heart races, my breath comes in short, shallow bursts. I grip the steering wheel, taking my gaze straight ahead of me, away from the house. I take a deep breath to calm my nerves. I turn the car off and open the door. I step out of the truck on shaky legs, and, with no plan, I make my way up the familiar walkway, climb the front steps, and stand on the porch, ready to ring the doorbell.

I have no idea what I'm doing, but I do know that *this* is what I need, what the younger me deserves — to prove to these people who broke me and shattered my spirit that I put myself back together, all by myself. I lift my arm and ring the doorbell as my ears fill with white noise. This feeling inside is something I can't identify because it's new, it's foreign.

And then it happens: the door swings open as if it's in slow motion. There she is, Cassie Brickman, standing in front of me with a look of utter shock on her face.

"Summer?" she utters, a nervous laugh escaping her mouth. "What are you doing here?" She looks over my shoulder, up and down the street.

My eyes narrow but no words form. What *am* I doing? What am I going to say?

"Greg!" Cassie yells over her shoulder. She seems a bit frightened, as if the person she had assumed that I would become, is standing here in front of her instead of the person I actually turned out to be. The person I have always been, but she refused to see.

Greg comes and stands beside her, the same look of surprise painted across his face. They both look the same, just slightly aged.

"Summer...is that really you?" he states, dumbfounded.

I continue to stare at them, my face cold and unforgiving.

"Do you want to come in?" Greg asks, opening the door wider, giving me a clear view of the stairs, the ones that lead up to the room where I used to sleep. The stairs where I sat and eavesdropped on all the conversations that no one wanted me to hear. The hooks where Jason, Claire, and I hung our backpacks and coats after school still rest on the wall. I feel the strongest sense of repulsion I have ever felt.

I nod and allow them to usher me into the house.

"I'll put some tea on," Cassie says, walking swiftly to the kitchen, discomfort sprinkled in her voice, as Greg and I follow behind.

We sit down at the table. It's different from the one they used to have but it's in the same spot and it *feels* exactly the same.

"So, Summer, what have you been up to? It's been so long," Greg asks, seeming unsure of what to say. It's like they both are looking at a ghost, the ghost of a girl they assumed was dead and gone.

"It *has* been a long time," I say looking at each of them. "I have been up to...a lot, I guess you could say." I force a smile.

"Jason said he saw a few years back...at a strip club or some place?" Cassie cringes, seemingly uncomfortable.

Typical Jason, leaving out the whole truth to paint a picture that only benefits him.

I nod once. "I was a bartender at a club, and yes, Jason came in one night."

"I was hoping he got your number or something, so we could check in on you," Greg says.

Lies. If they wanted to see me, they could have shown up there to check on me. But they never did. It was better for them to have me on that side of town, where they always assumed I would end up damaged and broken. And I'm glad they never came to see me. I can't even imagine what I would have done or said.

"You were wrong about me," I say, my voice hushed.

They exchange uncomfortable glances with one another before looking back at me.

"Summer, we..." Greg begins, but I cut him off, putting both my hands up to stop him before he can go any further. I am not interested in their excuses.

"No, I would like to say something first." My expression strengthens as I look Greg in the eyes, then Cassie. "I was a child when I moved in with you. I was just a little girl." My voice isn't strong yet, but I feel it building. "Do you know what you did to me? For years, you wrecked my spirit.

My confidence was non-existent when I lived with you. Did you even realize what you were doing?" I don't wait for a response. "You called me a guest up until the day you kicked me out. A guest. Even though you were basically in charge of raising me during my formative years. You were basically my parents. Parents who only attended a few of my sporting events in all the years I lived here, parents who treated me like a third-string child and sent me away to stay with strangers so they could have a break from me even though I never did anything wrong. I was just a sad and broken kid. I only wanted you to love me. But you couldn't do that, not even a little bit." I look at them. They look hurt. But I know it's just guilt. "I was here, in this house with you for SEVEN years. And then you kicked me out, and I was homeless. *Homeless.* Let that sink in. I was homeless because your son, who I loved like a brother, raped me." I take a deep breath, holding back the tears.

Cassie flinches at my words, and I let the weight of the truth sink in.

"Why didn't you say something, Summer?" she asks, so quietly, her voice barely audible.

I smirk, but it's not in vain. I can't believe she had the nerve to ask me that.

"You wouldn't have believed me. That's what Jason told me that night, and I knew he was right." I take a breath. "Telling you the truth would have landed me in the same situation I ended up in. It didn't matter what I said that day. Your hatred toward me was palpable." Neither of them says anything back to me, their mouths slightly agape as if they want to talk but don't know what to say.

I continue. "I was weak when I left here. I suffered because I never had a single person in my corner for my entire life. I wasn't taught the skills I needed to be emotionally sound, to take care of myself. Thanks to you, I failed out there in the world," I say, looking over toward the front door. "But I saved myself. I did it without you, without anyone. I didn't think I would ever be ok, thanks to you. But I am. I found people who love me and care about me, who have helped me figure out how to believe in myself. I'm a songwriter, and I'm moving to California to chase the dreams you never thought I was even capable of visualizing." They continue to stare at me. Farrah and Kash spring to my mind, and it reminds me that this house and who I was here is no longer my truth. "I came to Kentucky to visit Momma. I thought that's what I needed to move on with my life. I never planned on coming here. But once I arrived, it all became crystal clear. It was YOU who I needed to face. I'm just here to say I made it, against all odds. I did it."

I take a deep breath, and my insides feel lighter. I hadn't realized that since leaving here, I'd spent my years tortured by the image these people had of me. I had lived here for so long, but they never really saw me. They just saw the me they thought I was. And that affected my whole life, even long after I'd left. Showing them the real me, the one they could have loved, makes me feel better. It's as if, suddenly, after bearing my soul, their image of me no longer defines me anymore, not even the me who once lived here. I've left it all out here on their table and I don't have to carry this around anymore.

The teapot whistles loudly, and I get up, heading toward the door, uninterested in having tea with these people, or hearing what they have to say. It no longer matters to me anymore.

"Summer, wait," Greg says, trailing behind me. I walk straight out their front door and all the way to the truck, then I open the door and crawl in the cab. He grabs the door before it closes. "Wait," he says, exasperated. "I always believed in you, Summer. I knew that what Jason

said happened at the end wasn't true. I knew you didn't come on to him."
He says these words thinking they will make it better.

I smirk. "Well, it's a little late for that, isn't it?" I glare at him, my face stoic and strong. "But I forgive you. I forgive all of you. I can say that now and mean it." I smile at him, but the expression is for me, knowing that forgiveness leads to *acceptance*, something I never thought was within reach. I slam the door and pull away, leaving them forever in my past. I head away from the neighborhood, toward my future, toward my dreams.

I have been back in Austin for a few days and have spent most of my time packing. I'm standing in my room, looking around at the progress. I call Kash. I put him on speakerphone and leave the phone on my bed while I continue to go through my things.

"What are you up to?" he asks.

"Oh, just looking through my closet for things I can donate or get rid of. I'm not bringing everything with me. I need to purge a little," I say, tossing a shirt into my "take" pile on the floor.

"That's productive," he says. "So, what are you thinking about in terms of when you're leaving?"

"Hmm. I think in a few weeks. Farrah and I got a lot of money in tips last night. I'm using that for my flight," I say. "She is coming over tonight to help me book my ticket since I have never been on an airline website before in my life," I admit, somewhat embarrassed.

"Oh, good. That will make it easier."

"I'm going to ship three boxes to your apartment tomorrow, ok?"

"No problem! I'll put them in the office when they arrive."

"Great, thanks."

"What are you doing with all of your furniture and stuff?" he asks curiously.

"Silvia is taking my bed frame and dresser, Farrah is taking my couch and living room chair, and my kitchen table, if you can even call it that, is going in the dumpster downstairs. And honestly," I say looking around, "that's about all there is."

"Easy enough," Kash says. "It really seems like you have everything figured out. This is really exciting."

"It is," I respond, but when it comes out, it sounds like I'm unsure.

"What's the matter?" he asks.

I sit down on my bed and feel a sudden rush of emotion that I can only describe as feeling overwhelmed.

"Nothing's wrong," I state. "But I'm still riddled with anxiety when I really think about what I'm doing. It still doesn't seem possible. It feels like I'm going to wake up tomorrow or the next day and everything is going to be as it was. And then part of me wonders if it would even bother me if tomorrow was the same, if I woke up and it was all a dream. Then I second-guess my decision."

I start to babble, and Kash stops me. "Summer, whatever your decision is now, last week, tomorrow, whatever decision you make is going to be ok. What do you want?"

"I want to go to California," I say. "But I feel so mixed up inside. Is this normal?"

Kash lets out a little chuckle. "Yes, it's normal. They are just feelings, and you're working through them, second-guessing. When I went to college, do you know how many times I changed my mind before I decided on where I was going? I won't let you answer. Just know that it was...a lot. It drove me crazy thinking about the what-ifs and the unknowns. But now, looking back on it, I know that it was all necessary. I had to get all my thoughts and feelings organized so I could make a decision that was right for me. At least it was right for me at the time. But where I am now is a pleasant space, and I couldn't be happier. Where are you going to find joy in the coming years? Where do you see yourself?"

"With you," I say, and I immediately change the wording, realizing that what I said sounded slightly like I was confessing my love to him, which I'm not. "In California, working with you at Two WhisKEYS and following my dreams," I finish.

"Then let's make it happen."

After a little more discussion, we hang up, and I plop down on my bed and take a deep breath. I stare into my closet and notice something sticking out from under a box in the corner. I don't pay it much mind, but I get up to figure out where it's going to end up in my packing frenzy.

I pull out the box and then reach back to grab the black object that was underneath it. It's a duffle bag, tattered and worn. I sit down on the floor and gently feel the fabric between my fingers. The only bag I had when I left the Brickman's sits here in my hands. It was the only bag I owned until I moved here to Austin. My insides feel jumbled, and my limbs are weak. I frantically unzip it. There isn't much inside — a receipt, some old candy wrappers — but zipped in the side pocket I find my old copy of *The Lion, the Witch and the Wardrobe*. I hold it in my hands, my breath suspended. I flip through the pages and hold the sweet book up to my chest. Mrs. Harper's face comes into my mind, and I smile. A childhood memory that fills me with joy. I allow a few tears to fall as I lean against the bed, hugging the book close to me.

I feel pride in my younger self, remembering the ways I taught myself to cope, to survive, to escape. In no way was it fair, but I did survive. I made it out of the darkest of places and realize this is something to be proud of. I get up from the floor, still clutching the book, and walk into the living room where my different piles are heaped on the floor. I open up a big plastic container that's ready to be shipped and pull out my memory box from Kash. I lift the lid gently as I smile to myself and place the book inside for safekeeping. Little Summer deserves this memento to be cherished and kept safe. I walk back to my room and grab the duffle bag, tossing it into the pile designated "trash."

———

I sit on the couch in Janie's office, my right leg crossed over my left. My posture is strong, my breaths flow in and out with ease.

"You look calm, Summer," Janie says, through a bright smile.

I beam back at her. "I feel calm. Or at least calmer." I slide my hands under my thighs and take my gaze out the window. I'm smiling but I feel tears coming.

"What are you thinking right now?" Janie asks. "Are you nervous about the next part? Are you worried about what comes after you leave Austin?"

I shrug my shoulders and look back at her. "I can't really pinpoint what the feeling is, actually," I say with utter honesty because I have no idea. Am I happy? Yes. Am I nervous? Of course. Scared of the unknown? Most definitely. I'm feeling all of these emotions equally.

"That's very normal, Summer." Janie looks at me with care. "You are leaving the only place you've ever felt safe. That is bound to bring up some feelings of uneasiness."

I nod at her again, not sure what to say. "I think I depend on you a lot, Janie. I think I'm scared because I won't have you to talk to anymore." A tear sneaks out.

"Summer, we can do telehealth appointments. That is always an option. We do not have to end our work together."

I smile at her and grab a tissue from the small table next to me and wipe my eyes. I cover my face with my hands and nod, letting her know that I would like to do that. Going to California knowing that I can still connect with Janie makes me feel a lot better.

"How are you doing with your mantra?" she asks.

I let out a small laugh. "I threw it away a while ago," I admit.

She smiles at me. "I don't mean the physical proof of your mantra," she laughs. "I mean how are you doing with believing it?"

"Oh, yeah. Well, I threw it away because I felt like I didn't need the reminder anymore. I feel like I believe it as much as I possibly could."

"I'm proud of you, Summer. I hope you feel the same."

"I do," I say with strength in my voice. "Thank you so very much for helping me find myself again. I didn't think it was possible, but I know now that I just needed to do the work and face healing head-on."

"You have climbed a very steep hill to get out of the place you were when I first met you. You will still need to work at it, maybe forever, but you are more than capable."

I know she is right, and it feels amazing to see the truth in what she's saying. I end my last session with Janie knowing that even though we will be states away, I can still count on her. It's a gift I will not take for granted.

CHAPTER 27

Texas - Now

GOODBYES

"So, I hope you all are planning to come visit soon. Mav, you can shut the bar down again. No big deal, right?" I say, making a joke, even though my heart is breaking.

Maverick rolls his eyes. "No financial problems at all," he says sarcastically, pulling me in for a hug.

"And Farrah, I want to be on FaceTime, propped up somewhere, so I can see Junie being born. And that's an order," I say, trying to muster a laugh. Farrah sobs and pulls me into her arms.

I move over to Silvia. "Who is going to call me 'dear' and help me make decisions?" I ask her, looking lovingly into her eyes.

"Oh, dear, don't make me cry. Call me every Sunday, you hear?" she says.

I take Silas' cheeks in my hands. "You." I smile at him. "Thanks for helping me become a butterfly," I say, winking at him. He pulls me into a hug, lifting me off the ground.

"I'm going to miss you more than you know," he whispers into my hair. He places me back down on the ground and taps my nose before crossing his arms across his chest, flashing a big smile.

"Maverick, thanks for taking a chance on me. When I met you, I had nothing, and you believed in me. I can't find words to thank you for what you gave me," I say, hugging him again.

"It was the easiest decision I have ever made, Summer. I love you, girl."

"Tell J.J. and Whitney I love them," I say, swallowing back my tears and suppressing the lump that has formed in my throat. Everyone nods, wiping away their own tears.

My Uber has been patiently waiting on the curb outside my apartment for ten minutes. I pick up my bags and make my way over to the car and ask the driver to pop the trunk. Maverick grabs my bags from me and loads them in the car. I get in and shut the door, quickly rolling down the window. I buckle and let my arm hang out.

"I love you all," I say as the driver pulls away. I wave to everyone, my family, until they are completely out of sight. Then I take a deep breath and watch the city pass me by. I say a silent "thank you" to this place that found me and saved me when I thought being saved was for other people, not for me.

───────

The airport overwhelms me because I've never experienced anything like it before. Thankfully, people help me figure out where I need to go, and I use my judgment for the rest. I get through security with no issues, minus the awkwardness I feel because it's very obvious that everyone around knows exactly what they are doing except for me.

I make a pit stop in the bathroom then find a snack stand where I get water and some hummus with carrots to munch on while I wait for my flight. Before I check out, I stroll through the store and decide to grab some things for the plane — more snacks, some candy, a magazine, and a book. After I pay, I continue toward my gate. The gate is full of people waiting, but I find an empty seat and take it.

I've got a bit of time before we start boarding, and I tap my nail on the top of my carry-on in a sing-song pattern. Am I nervous? No. I don't think so. Not anymore. I want to believe that where I am going is where I am meant to be, but, after all I have been through in my life, I still feel like there isn't a place where I truly belong. But I'm getting there. Slowly but surely, my wings are expanding, and I am falling in love...with me. I was raised believing I would never amount to anything, that I wasn't worthy. I was unwanted and unloved. But none of that is reality. I finally know that.

I look at the travelers around me. Some sit alone with headphones in their ears, books in their laps, nodding off. Some have young children who are running and jumping, getting their energy out before the long flight. These parents have wearied, tired faces that are filled with love.

I slow my bouncing knee. "You're ok," I whisper to myself. I fiddle with a loose piece of my hair that has fallen out of my thick braid. I tuck it behind my ear and take a deep breath. They call my boarding group, so I stand up and head to the line at the gate. A little girl is in front of me; she's six, maybe seven, and is holding her dad's hand.

"I love your backpack," I say to her, admiring the colorful rainbows and intricate unicorns displayed on the outside.

"Thank you!" she says. "Would you like a sticker?"

"Sure." I reach out my hand for her to give me one.

"Well, which one do you want?" she wonders out loud.

"You pick," I say. She thinks for a minute then places a sweet little barn cat on my hand. I smile at her dad.

"Do you want to tell her your tradition?" he asks his little girl.

She beams. "Every time I go see Mimi, I put a sticker on the outside of the plane as we get on. Dad says I'm leaving my mark on the world."

I smile with wonder at this little duo, father and daughter, a little team. I feel so blessed to have crossed paths with them, a vision of a life that passed me by. "Wow, that is quite the adventure your stickers go on," I muse.

The line inches forward. Father and daughter check in, then I hand the flight attendant my boarding pass, and we silently make our way down the walkway to the plane. Everyone slowly makes their way on the aircraft, greeting the pilot and the flight attendants as they get on.

"Ok, what's it going to be, Luna?" the father asks his little one as we inch our way toward the plane.

"This one," she says with confidence, placing her sticker on the outside of the plane. I smile to myself and absentmindedly look around as I wait my turn to step over the threshold. I glance at the sticker. Pink and small.

A pig.

Something warms deep inside me, embers reigniting, lighting my soul and releasing my wings. *I am finally free.*

THE BEGINNING

Thank You

It's challenging to put into words the gratitude I feel toward everyone who has guided me along this journey toward bringing this book to publication. What I once thought was impossible, has turned into a dream come true. I wouldn't have been able to accomplish this dream without the support that these lovely individuals gave me.

To anyone who has texted, called, or messaged in any type of way to cheer me on during this process, I appreciate you and I remember each and every message.

To my editor, Erin, what can I say? This book would be on the struggle bus without you! Your honest feedback helped me learn so much about the process of writing a novel. You deserve an infinite amount of credit for taking on the task of working with someone with zero experience. Thank you for your knowledge, expertise, and the care you put into assisting me get this book out into the universe. I am forever grateful.

To my cover artist, Christy — you heard my gasp when I saw your first draft of the cover but you missed my reaction to the final draft and it was a gasp times a million. You captured my vision absolutely perfectly. Thank you for helping me bring Summer's story to life. You are amazing.

Dorna, thank you. I know you are going to see your name here and cry and I wish I could see it! Your constant push for me to "write that book" became an inner voice of mine which led me to this publication. I know you want me to write a memoir but this will have to do for now! Thank you from the bottom of my heart, for encouraging me to do what I have always wanted to do.

Kayla, my cheerleader. Thank you for reading along as I wrote the first draft. Your comments and excitement for me were what kept me going. Your love for Summer was evident from the beginning. You helped bring her to life by feeling everything she felt and hating everyone who wronged her. Thanks for being there, exactly how I needed you, during this process.

My beta readers – Kayla, Angela, Meg, Iris, Rita, and Valerie, you are the real MVPs! The time we spent pulling my first draft apart is sacred to me. I enjoyed our journey together and I absolutely love that your voices are sprinkled throughout this story. I hope you love the final draft. Thank you for your time and your effort in seeing things that were needed that I may have been blind to. I am so thankful for you.

Thank you to my ARC readers for taking the time to read my little book (even though I sent you the unedited version!) Your time is valuable and I am grateful you gave some of yours to me!

Dr. Cole, I'm almost certain that had I not started working with you in September 2022, there would be no book. You gave me my life back. There would be no early morning writing sessions if you did not give me the tools I needed to heal my body from the inside out. My energy, my sleep, my soul, they all are better because of you. Thank you.

Diane, I miss you. I am so glad you got to read a draft before you were called to Heaven. You were so proud of me and I thank you for always telling me and making me know for certain that I was worthy of this. I'm at ease knowing that you are with me, cheering me on.

Mom, when I was little you told me that I think faster than I write. I have never forgotten that and while writing Summer's story I made sure to outline and organize when my ideas were flowing faster than I could get them on paper. Thanks for always asking if I added more to the book so you could jump on and read the additions. You have always called me a writer and now look! I'm a real one! You have always believed that I could write a book. I hope you are proud. I love you.

Dad, ever since I was young you have always been my biggest fan. You were always so proud of everything I did. I didn't necessarily inherit your calm, cool and collected demeanor, but I like to think that I channeled you through this process, taking it in stride and enjoying it. Thank for all you do for me. I love you.

Yaz, without you there would be no book. Last summer you asked me what I would be if I wasn't a teacher and I told you I would be a writer. You told me it wasn't too late for me to write a book. You were right and now because of your words, your mom followed her dreams. Thank you for always asking how many pages and how many words I had as I was writing. Thank you for being the best son I could ever ask for. I hope you follow every one of your dreams.

My girls, Meadow and Londyn, this is all for you. I hope you know you can do hard things. You both are strong, smart, and silly. Thanks for making me laugh, and giving me the best hugs. You are the lights of my life.

ML, thanks for encouraging me even though we constantly have a million things going on. Your fast and creative wit brought Two WhisKEYS to life. Writing this book was like having a second full time job. You don't know how much it means to me that you allowed me to find myself again through this process. I love you so so much.

Thank you to everyone who reads When Pigs Fly — for giving a girl with a dream, a chance to go after it. <3

About the Author

Krissy Lanier was born and raised in Massachusetts. She lives there with her husband, Matt, and three children. They have a dog named Memphis, a cat named Joey (after Joey Tribiani), and a gecko named Echo. Krissy has been teaching kindergarten for 11 years and recently was inspired to go after her dream of being a writer. *When Pigs Fly* is her first novel.

When she's not teaching and writing, Krissy can be found at the beach with her family or with her nose stuck in a book. She is passionate about spreading awareness about foster care and Type 1 Diabetes, which she has had since childhood. Want to follow along with her journey toward book number two? You can find her on Instagram @krissylanier_writes.

Made in the USA
Thornton, CO
11/30/23 10:48:26

25c2beec-6831-4d78-9e23-bc0d7aa198c4R01